ODE

ODE

The Scion of
Nerikan

RICHARD SWEITZER

Richard G. Sweitzer III

ISBN: 979-8-9865578-1-6 (softcover)
ISBN: 979-8-9865578-2-3 (eBook)
Library of Congress control number: 2022923474

Cover art by Patrick Brazier
Map art by Chaim Holtjer

Second Printing, 2023

www.RichardSweitzer.com

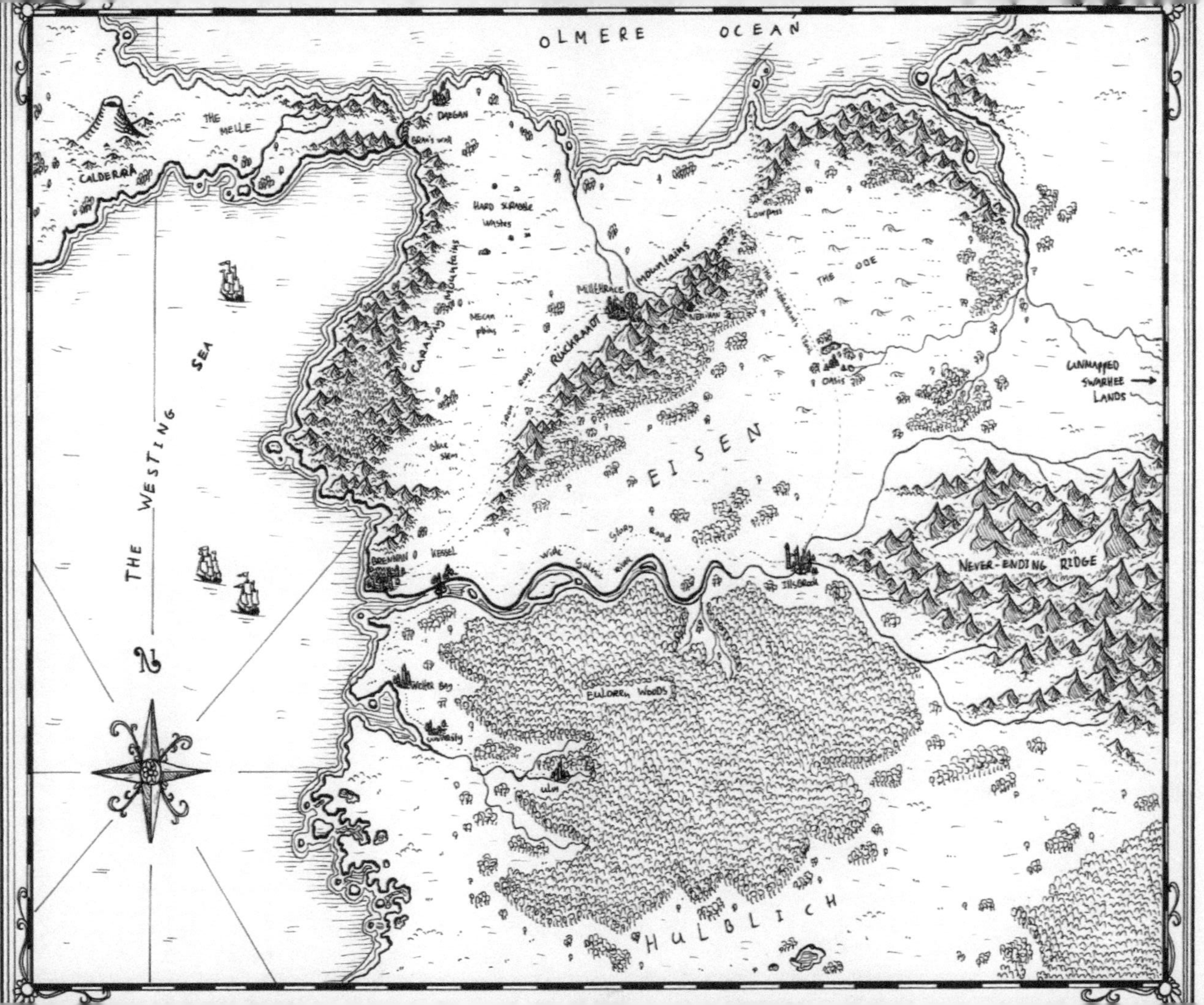

OLMERE OCEAN
THE MELLE
CALDERRA
DARGAN
BRAN'S WOE
HARD SCRABBLE WASHES
CARAWAY MOUNTAINS
NECRA PLAINS
MILLRACE MOUNTAINS
RUCKRAMDT
MELHAM
LOWPASS
THE ODE
EISEN
UNMAPPED SWARHEE LANDS
THE WESTING SEA
JANA ROAD
BLUE STEM
SLOWG ROAD
WIDE SWAIM
BRENNAN
KESSEL
TILLBROOK
NEVER-ENDING RIDGE
WEIR BAY
EULORRA WOODS
UNIVERSITY
ULM
HULBLICH
N

Contents

An Agreeable Ham

He had almost not run. As shadows stalked him in the dark forest, he had nearly stood his ground and welcomed his fate. He was caught, surrounded, and a hundred leagues away from any hope of rescue. He had lost a foolish game and he accepted that. He did not fear the certainty of death. He was far too wise and lettered to believe in life eternal. No, the inevitability of death did not rattle his spine one facet.

But dying sure did.

The thought of being torn apart at the soft corners by a pack of wild beasts offended him so much, that for the first time in forty summers Edwin the Observer climbed a tree. He climbed through darkness. He climbed through fear. He climbed while shouting erudite curses over his shoulder. It was midnight in Ma'alabrad Forest, and as devilish hounds howled at the old man, the old man howled back.

"Callow shadow-beasts!" he shouted, his aged muscles kicking himself to safety. "Be proud of your elderly capture!" He could not see what type of creatures had chased him through the woods. And even if he could, animal science was one of the few subjects he had not mastered. In fact the only animals he remembered from University were the bothersome library cats who would leap onto his writing paper and then drop to their sides as if suddenly struck with a bout of ennui.

"To hell with you all!" he cried.

He performed a miraculous chin-up and barked a triumphant laugh. He had climbed to twice his height, which was not very far, yet far enough to be proud. He was struggling up even higher when a sandal slipped from his toes. He dropped to his backside and hugged the trunk as hungry shadows tore at the fallen sandal.

"It's just a damned shoe, you fools!"

Safe now and settled in, he grasped his suddenly bare foot and rubbed his soft soles. He had been searching the dark woods for shelter when he had happened upon the hell-hounds pacing ahead. They were just ghosts then, soundless shadows in the night; and they must have sniffed his magnolia-rubbed skin.

He lifted a woven sack from his neck and hung it on a jagged spur. Within the bag were the travel-needs of any gentleman of Ulm: Some books, magnolia oil, a lump of dry cheese, a charcoal pencil, and a five-honor promissory note from his eldest aunt, signed in a script very much like his own. Also in the bag were little things of unknown value he had picked up along the way; otherwise useless trinkets and curiosities that he had found likeable and just had to have. Not within the bag were any tools rationally geared towards survival.

He pulled his uncle's travel cloak tightly around himself, shivering in the cool night. Not one star pushed through the black forest's canopy. The veil was full dark, like dreamless sleep. Dreamless indeed, he thought, for this evening would allow no slumber.

Soon the dark predators ceased pacing the leaf-strewn floor and the forest fell dead-silent. Yet a hollow reverb trembled the air like inside University's Great Rotunda at nightfall. He found himself looking over his shoulders at echoes, much like he had done while walking alone at University.

Even at his advanced age of fifty-five, Edwin had not finalized his Historian's degree—though not for lack of effort. It was simply his need to observe the world had always pulled him away. He had a keen, almost uncanny, awareness of knowing just when and where great moments would happen. It was an urge inside of him compelling him forward to a select spot at a special time. Thus over the years he had witnessed the most significant events in this land's making.

No, not this land, he thought. This dark land sat much farther north than he had ever been drawn. Rarely had he left the cultured southern mainland of Hulblich for these northern wilds of Eisen. Eisen, land of illicit and illiterate brutes, more apt to dispute an ale house tab than debate the subtleties of a well-polished ode. Workers lived here, artless and unsophisticated, save for their brutish skills in bending iron and cutting stone. In the cities of Eisen, vocation trumped education, which to Edwin—who had never broken a sweat in labor—was sinful.

It was here in these northern lands that Edwin's mind—and quite literally his gaze—had been drawn. For the past few weeks at the family home in Ulm, his mornings would find him staring beyond his pork sausage and buttered bread to the white-topped peaks on the northern horizon, wondering what siren called to him from beyond the great dividing river. His aunts would comment on the light in his eyes as he peered dreamily beyond, and then rap their knuckles on the long table snapping him back to health. He had blinked away this trance as often as he could, knowing full well that in the end, his will would fail. For when the urge to observe took over, Edwin ultimately could not resist. Which was why his ragged behind now sat in a hardwood so far north of University.

He moaned and the beasts howled their reply.

"Quiet, damn you! Leave a gentleman to his thoughts!" he snapped.

The shadowed creatures were like the first-year youth at school, leaping and running and chittering all day and night, never giving a true scholar his much-needed peace.

A cool breeze passed over. He pulled up his brown hood and waited in the chilled darkness, hugging the trunk and trying not to fall asleep. After a time longer than he had ever spent in unforgivable discomfort, bright rays of morning light finally worked their way into the deep Ma'alabrad Forest. He looked below and finally saw clearly. Four black beasts padded the ground as they circled his tree. They were bearlike in size, though as wolves they prowled, hunter-like, predatory. They stood paw to shoulder as tall as Edwin, with withers broader and hair coarser than he had ever seen. Thick ropes of muscle strung down their necks and held aloft wide skulls of the size one would expect on the fabled elefant. Bold white canines curled up and out of their jaws at jagged imperfect angles, and their snouts were tipped with a distinct porcine bluntness. They were a faerie tale amalgam of forest creatures, wolf and boar stretched over the frame of a bear. They stalked, howling and whining for their own morning sausage just out of reach.

These creatures did not belong here, he thought. Not in these woods, not in this land, not in this world. Something was wrong in Eisen.

Edwin assumed he was either the first to discover such creatures, or simply the latest in a long line of encounters that left no witnesses. For these huge beasts appeared to be machined by the heavens for one purpose, the quick and easy fragmentation of soft-bodied interlopers. And none were as soft as he.

Very well, he decided, but his life would not end like a starving desert nomad. He dug in his sack for his jute-wrapped cheese. It had been the only food stuff he had been able to smuggle out of his aunt's pantry before being chased away by the cook's mate. He chewed off a blue-green corner and spat it at the wolf-boars. They pounced on the morsel, muzzles knocking and forepaws clawing. Then they howled for more.

"Oh please," he called out, as if addressing a hostile beggar. "You will get your meat soon enough. Patience!"

Jittery locals had cautioned him about entering the so-called haunted forest. He had scoffed at their naive fears and strolled into the woods alone, on principle. Eisen-folk would not dare search after him, nor would his aunts or uncle send out hunters with wet-nosed hounds. It would have to be a close colleague or a friend who marked Edwin's absence. Of which, he had none.

There would be no rescue, he realized and seemed to accept his fate rationally, as any good University man would. His end would come in this old-growth forest. Ironwood, he thought, recognizing the tall twisted trunks with haphazard branches and wide bulky feet. They stood chaotically like an army of confounded ogres frozen in sunlight, creeping brown vines tangling their roots. Beautiful, in their own grim way, and dense beyond measure. He shifted his rump and chanced a look over his shoulder.

The northeast run of the great Rückraadt Mountains rose up tall behind him. Their snow-capped peaks were a north-south divider of Eisen. Yet this grand range was quickly dismissed for the vision jutting out of the ground nearby. A granite spire like a great grey dagger grew out of the mucky bed and stretched to the tree-tops just a short sprint away. Wild black vines covered much of the stone steeple in a natural camouflage. And within the vines and hewn into the granite stood two massive iron gates, black and menacing. Gates to the underworld. Atop the gates hung two iron falchions, crossed at the blades and each sized taller than a man.

Edwin dropped his cheese.

"Were you not going to inform me of this?" he yelled down to the beasts. A wolf-boar leapt high up the trunk and swiped at Edwin's robes. He pulled back, nearly jarring himself into a freefall. "Pig-dogs are what you are!" he shouted and squeezed the trunk.

And so he sat, observing the weighty gates to the underground and wondering what lay behind them and below. Treasure? Shelter? A king's tomb like they build in the east? He would most likely never know. Hunger returned and boredom overtook him, and still the beasts remained. Morning turned to midday, midday to evening, and evening again became black midnight. His empty gut pulled at his ribs aching for bread, his tongue grew dry with thirst, and his raw backside became nearly numb with pain. He decided then, in that darkest hour, that by morning, should the dogs remain, he would cease resisting his inescapable fate and let himself fall to the snapping jaws below.

Hours later a luminous fog wormed its way through the sylvan necropolis and orange sunlight crawled over the horizon. Edwin forced his jittery legs to standing. He slipped off his cloak, folding it gently, and then hung it over the spur with his sack. He hoped someone some-day would find his bag and claim the little things he left behind.

The hounds howled as Edwin stood perched above them.

"Be still, beasts. It will all be over soon," he said to the dogs. "But if there truly is a machinist behind our universal clockwork, I beg him to have you choke on my bones."

He toed the edge of the branch. The ground suddenly shifted, shuddering his tree and sending him sideways into the trunk. The wolf-boars had felt it too, and they stood alertly, sniffing the wind. Another rumble. He joggled on the branch as the rippling tremble grew like approaching thunder. Then a clang. The spire, he thought, and spun around. The gateway to the underground shuddered and clanged as if a great stampede charged it from behind.

Years earlier he had observed a demonstration at University of a substance called black powder. This acrid grain had been poured into a chiseled cavity on a great boulder and was set aflame by a jittery proc-tor. The ensuing eruption split the stone, and both rattled and thrilled all who watched. He thought of that now as the massive black gates ex-ploded open, establishing in Edwin a new standard for stupendousness.

A twisted iron hinge whizzed past his head and knifed itself deep into the tall tree. A black gate—taller and wider than any door Edwin had ever heaved open—cart-wheeled high above, gracefully as if in disregard of its own mass. The iron bird ceased its inaugural flight and slammed down on top of a wolf-boar, crushing it flat. The other gate, half-hinged, pinned itself open against the spire. One man-sized falchion had flown beyond Edwin, burying itself in the debris-stained ground, while the other black sword still hung firmly on the stone.

In the dusty fallout of the shattered gates, a creature greater than all the wolf-boars combined emerged huffing the forest air. Like a legged leviathan it appeared, released not from the ocean depths, but a dark and stony nether. Wide scarred feet stood below stout legs, rugged pedestals for its top-heavy frame. Rusted iron shackles with dangling chains banded its ankles and wrists, and rattled the ground with each deep inhale. Meaty thighs narrowed to a slender waist, only to widen manifold at the hairless chest and shoulders that made up the bulk of the creature. Its arms were unnaturally long with thick knuckles hanging just off the ground. And its face, Edwin noted, stunned beyond belief, was a sublime manlike visage, both terrifying and divine.

Moments earlier Edwin had pleaded to the heavenly architect. He had not expected a personal reply.

It stood as tall as Edwin had climbed, and scanned the woods chaotically like a horse in a burning barn. Edwin knew that look. This monstrous and naked ogre, despite its ungodly size, was afraid. It searched the forest, as if searching for direction, a hint of where to go, then its eyes found the Observer. It flinched at the sight of the small man.

Edwin, already stunned, was dumbfounded by this reaction.

Sunlight cut through the trees and lit up the monster's face. It winced and covered its eyes reflexively, rusty chains banging against its chest. Slowly its hands fell away and yellow light shone upon its pale skin. Tears pooled in its lids and confusion melted away as it welcomed the warming light. It held out its arms and respired deeply in the sunbeam like a freshly emerged butterfly drying its wings.

Then it ran.

It ran forward into the light, stamping through debris and trampling a wolf-boar. The feral dog died with a whimper. Another wolf snapped at his arm and shook its great skull side to side, tearing at the flesh. The man-beast hoisted the dog and snapped its neck, tossing it aside as he ran. The final pack member had prowled ahead. It was the largest of the dogs and moved with a cunning awareness. Fearlessly it stood before the ogre, shoulders raised and forepaws spread wide in the dirt. It managed an impressive taunting roar before the long-armed creature lashed the dangling chain from its wrist and decapitated it. The giant was already beyond the wolf as its headless torso collapsed. Then the man-beast loped away into the deep forest, shaking the ground with every heavy step.

As it tromped into the woods it revealed the scars, a collage of fleshy white knots that mottled its back and thighs, scabs upon scars upon deeper older scars. A fleshy script that spoke of endless torture.

Edwin stood stunned in the tree long after the creature fled. This was different, a new kind of observation. After a long personal debate, he slid awkwardly to the forest floor and rubbed his sore backside. A tiny war had erupted and ended in an instant right below him. Strange wolf-boars were dead and a shattered gate lay about the haunted forest. Edwin was alive, and a faerie tale creature had been unleashed unto this world.

"This must be recorded," he said, as he walked the grounds casually now, shuffling his feet through the ankle-deep debris. He clasped his hands behind his back as he observed the dead dogs. He thought long and hard on the beasts, picking apart in his mind which pieces were wolf, which were boar, and which were something else altogether; and wondering from where they had come. Then the scholar gathered his sack and built a fire.

Sitting at the flames, he opened his pack and removed a leather-bound he had borrowed from University. Elaborate hand-colored plates lined the first couple pages. He flipped ahead to the title page.

An Historie Complete
Observation, Dictum, and Didactic
On the Knowable World
In Seven Volumes
Studied and Scribed
By
Scholar M. S. Chacko

"An history *incomplete*," Edwin snuffed. "Until now."

He pulled the makeshift charcoal pencil from his tote. Then within the wide margins of the text he wrote down the events of the day. When he had used up all the white spaces, he turned the book and scribbled deep within the folds, turning pages and scribbling over text of a world that had suddenly changed.

In his journal, one strange word kept flowing out of his script: Ner-ikan. It was the name of a mythical underground. An infernal prison for the unholy, and the refuge of devilish monsters. He looked again at the open gateway. There had been no sound or movement from the deep burrow since the creature had broken free, but a rotten vapor crept out of the hole. He had thought the lost prison of Nerikan was only something of faerie tales, but as he wrote on the page, "It has been found."

This is it, he thought proudly. This is the story that needs to be told, and the observation that will finally grant him a title. A new history for the land of Eisen, as told by Edwin!

Hours later, the last thing the junior historian wrote in the borrowed book was of his pleasant surprise that the shoulder portion of a wolf-boar makes a rather agreeable ham. Pleased with himself, Edwin the Observer nibbled on a shoulder bone and wondered rather casually where that creature had been off to.

2

The Silver Honor

D eep underground where the hidden mechanisms of a clock-worked city clacked and clanged, a young girl floated on her back in swirling waters. Everyone in Eisen knew about this city built upon a river, its fast flowing waters powering the countless gears and levers above. But only Olen Marine had sniffed out this pool room with its own crashing waterfall. The twelve year old was supposed to be cleaning with her sisters, but she had once again found chores impossible to do while an entire underworld demanded exploring. She kicked an arc of water high into the room.

The city was Millthrace, and she floated far below the boardwalk of the wealthy borough known as Uptown. Girls like her were not welcome upriver, but she was not *in* Uptown, she was *underneath* it. Sunlight poked through the slats of the boardwalk high above and muted footsteps echoed below as rich folk meandered above in hoof-heeled shoes, with no particular place to go and in no great hurry to get there. She pulled herself along, her arms slow churning waterwheels, also in no great hurry to be anywhere but here.

City engineers called this dark underside the Escapement. Olen wasn't sure what that word meant, but it seemed to make sense because it was both a basement and an escape. She and everyone else just called it the Scape.

She swam to a ladder-like iron pylon that rose to the boardwalk and pulled herself onto the first riser. She stood on the wooden plank that spanned the pylon's legs. The iron was gritty with red rust that coated her palms. Her mother would want her to be clean, so she splashed her hands in the pool. She dove back into the swirling pond, kicking and pulling herself along before letting the waters wash her back to the pylon. She had told her sisters about the room with the waterfall, but it had not mattered. Even Clara, always eager for a little mischief, refused to enter the Scape. She had believed the rumors of the ghouls that haunted the sewers, waiting for wayward young to enter their dark burrow. All Olen had ever seen down here were rats, and all you have to do to them is kick them aside. Rats learn pretty quickly in the Scape.

She pulled herself back onto the riser and climbed higher this time, diving right back in. The water smacked her forehead, and she surfaced quickly, rubbing her scalp. Higher, she thought playfully, and climbed up to the third riser in the dark chamber.

The room was a forgotten vault. A derelict of bad construction. She had discovered it three weeks earlier after exploring a recently repaired brick sewer she had named Big Boy. The back wall of the room was the blasted face of the Rückraadt Mountains with the waterfall and an occasional wayward trout flowing over the top. It was also the back end of Uptown, the borough highest up the mountain. Atop the waterfall there was a gap between the boardwalk and the cliff. Iron waterwheel fins churned in the stream casting spray below. To her left and right stood mortar and stone walls, windowless, and forever drenched and covered in greenish brown lichen. The shorter fourth wall behind her was not a wall at all, but a series of tunnels flowing downriver, including the only one she could pass through without crouching: Big Boy.

She stood on the edge of the pylon and dared herself to dive. Three levels high. She had never jumped in from this height before, and her forehead still stung from the last dive. She was halfway to the ceiling and much too high. She could be knocked silly and drift senselessly into the drains, tumbling through the Millthrace sewers, either a floater or bungplug. Bungplugs were the unlucky folk who not only fell through one of the many chutes and wells above, but whose bloated corpses stopped-up a narrow drain, backing up the river. The people of Millthrace had no regard for bungplugs who flooded their shops and homes with sewer water. *No one mourns a bungplug*, the Lowtowners said. She would rather be a floater. Floaters simply passed right through the Scape until their lifeless bodies flowed out by the Barrens of Lowtown like drowned rats. She imagined her father finding her, and falling to his knees—

"Dammit!" a man shouted above the boardwalk, halting her morbid daydream and sending her wobbling on the beam. Chance swears from above meant one thing only: an Uptowner had dropped something through the uneven boardwalk and into her world. An *offering to the Mechanic*, as they said. The louder the swear, the more valuable the offering. And that was a rather loud swear. A quick glint and a tiny splash. It had dropped right into the plunge pool below the falls.

Standing higher than she had ever been before, the small girl curled her toes over the edge. "Sorry Mom. Sorry Dad," she said, and dove straight into the falling waters.

Olen's forehead slapped the water, lightning flashing in her eyes. The crashing falls thrust her straight to the silty bottom as she twisted and fought the current. She reached blindly through the sludge, frantically sweeping her palms over the mud, hoping for any unusual touch, water continually crashing over her. She had to find it on the first try or it would be lost forever, whatever it was. A rupture of air escaped her lips and the falls again pushed her against the silt. She kicked aside and palmed the muddy base, fighting the urge to inhale. Needles tapped her temples. Her ears were bass drums pounding. Her lungs quivered and ached. She had to give up. As she turned to rise, her hand skimmed a small object. She clasped it tight and shot to the surface.

She burst out of the water, sucking in breaths. Fresh blood pounded in her temples, and her eyeballs ached. Quivering muscles fought to keep her afloat as she coughed and spat. Dizziness faded and her senses returned. She shook her fist in the stream, washing away silt. The object was flat and round, heavy for its size. Like a coin. Her most prized possessions were the items clumsy people above had let fall into her world. Some she had found just lying on the ground, like a lady's hair pin and some small tools. Others she had retrieved from the shallow waters, like a rusted barrel key and a carved ivory button. But beyond all of that, her greatest treasures were the three copper pennies she had scoured out of the dark sewers of the vast underground Scape. She pulled her hand out of the water and opened it. It was indeed a coin, but it was not a copper.

"Silver!" she cried out and slipped back under, swallowing a mouthful.

She kicked back to the surface and paddled herself to shore, keeping her open palm out of the wash. A silver honor, she thought, and despite her severely-patched clothes laying on a dry stone, she believed herself to be wealthy. She stood on the shore and shook off the water, then she ran to a large stone that had been blasted away from the mountainside. In a nook below the granite boulder she brushed away the sand and pulled out a palm-sized tin box. Here were some of the few objects she had collected in the streets, and the random offerings that had fallen from above. She dumped them out and set aside the three copper pennies. She placed the large silver coin next to them and marveled at it. It was freshly stamped and shone brightly. The coppers alone would get one a couple rides on the Skywheel and a bag of red rock candy, but this was a silver honor! Second only to the gold manor as the greatest coin in Eisen. She had no idea the coin's actual worth, but she knew it was great.

She held it up again. The honor glinted in the checkered sunlight. In her mind she was already telling the story to her parents. They would marvel at how high she had climbed, how deeply she had dove, and the great wealth she had won. She titled the story "The Silver Honor" and added it to the pile of adventures she would tell them someday. When she found them. She kissed the coin, and placed it and everything else in the tin.

She dressed on the sandy shore, but her mind kept returning to her tin box. Those three coppers had sat unused for too long. They seemed small now, unimportant next to the silver. They were expendable. Spendable. She popped back open the tin and dug out the pennies. She had never purchased anything with money before. Children like Olen got things via more creative means. But she had coins to spare now, and she knew just what her first purchase would be. She stuffed them in her pocket and ran back into the Big Boy sewer, kicking aside a wet rat.

Olen wore a patched brown skirt with a much-abused white apron at her hips. A tight black vest was tied crisscross over a faded white top. She had rolled her shirt sleeves up to her shoulders, uncovering coffee-colored arms. Her skin was most eager to darken in spring, and least willing to lighten in the cloudy winter. While many of Millthrace avoided this change by donning wide-brimmed hats and long sleeved shirts, even on the warmest noons of summer, Olen bared her face, neck, and arms; welcoming the sunlight even as the autumn breezes turned cool. She clomped through the sewers in black boots two sizes too large, her raven braids flopping as she went.

This red brick tunnel she had named Worm because of its slimy walls. She raced ahead through the darkness of Worm, keeping her hands and elbows tucked in. A vibration, as large stone slabs slid unseen overhead, told her she was nearing the granary, one of the busiest parts of the city. The arced roof of Worm lay damaged and open here. She leapt to the brick overhang and climbed out of Worm and onto the damp soil. She dashed across the ground, leaping over rough stones and a crude flotsam bridge. She jumped into the sewer dubbed Quickwater and dropped onto her backside. One long joyous shout later and the tube elbowed. She seized netting hanging over the side and pulled herself out. From here she stepped into the rancid brown-water tube she despised, and had given a name she dare not say out loud. She covered her nose, stepping widely as she travelled down the chute.

She came upon a wide beam of light from above. It was a vent up to the Midtown section of the city. She paused just out of sight as baritone voices rumbled on about city politics. As the voices faded away she leapt up high, grabbing an iron railing and scurrying to the top. Then Olen Marine pulled herself out of the dark sewers and into the sunny and populous streets of Millthrace.

3

A Gift of Mutton

Millthrace buzzed, or better yet it hummed. A gentle drone from the great geared city reverberated through Olen's heavy boots. It was a soft whirring heartbeat that comforted the locals and disturbed the sleep of newcomers. Within the city, bearded tradesmen sat on splintered crates in the open-air borough, smoking pipes and squaring deals with a handshake. Children squealed as they chased chickens across the boardwalk and fancy handmen shouted for commoners to step aside as Uptowners in brightly-dyed suits and gowns passed through. This part of the city was busy, loud, and to Olen, one of the few good things about living here.

Along with the crowds came the unrelenting movement of a city of water-worked machineries. Large iron and wood wheels rolled into the sky, hauling sacks, or grinding grain; creaking and rattling a regular slow rhythm. Buoyant vegetables floated to market down rickety water chutes, bumping and churning their way like playful children. A crackle-faced trader shook on a deal and hooked an iron claw over a thick-roped crate. He kicked an oaken pole jutting out of the boardwalk, and a sluice fell open. Water surged through the channel, splashing against a finned wheel. Hidden gears cranked away, hauling rope and crate to an upper level storage room. A shirtless boy hung out of an open shutter. He hooked the crate and pulled it in, stowing it away in a storage attic that Olen just had to explore later some night. This was Lowtown, the business sector of Millthrace. It was the district farthest down river, and the poorest.

In the Barrens of Lowtown, where the boardwalk gave way to dusty strips of open land, young women and girls—orphans—knelt on the shore of a stream washing and mending clothes, scrubbing pots, and talking freely—punctuating their speech with giggles whenever one of the working boys passed through. An older heavyset woman in a faded red skirt and white top walked the shore watching over them, helping when needed. And when traders from beyond the city wandered over, this guardian in red slid smoothly between hunter and prey, deflecting the men back towards the square.

The public square for traveling tradesmen sat in the center of Lowtown, and in the middle of that square was the Well. The Well was a large brick-lined hole in the boardwalk that opened above the deepest part of the Oiskonn River. Had tourists stopped for more than a moment in Lowtown, this would have made for an impressive view. But visitors to Millthrace quickly passed through Lowtown on their way to the nicer districts upriver. So instead, young boys with long cane poles dropped hooked lines into the dark waters, hoping to snag a fat trout that could quickly be sold to hungry workmen for a hack—a copper penny sheared in two. But, as usual in the browned waters of Lowtown, the fish were not biting.

Beyond all the commerce and commotion stood a tall barricade. Towering tree trunks planed smooth were bound and cemented to an impervious looming barrier. And here in Lowtown also stood the one huge gate into the city and out to the world.

Olen leapt off her perch upon a fountain and tramped down the long stairway to Lowtown clutching the three coppers in her fist. A throng of colorfully dressed travelers had paused on the steps to admire the Skywheel, a towering water-powered spectacle those with coppers to spare could ride to get an eagle's view of the city. She bundled through their midst, ducking under arms and passing through the circle of wealthy gawkers, keeping on to the Lowtown square. She brushed against a man, and he shouted, rousing armored guards that stood nearby. They clutched their spears and straightened as the man patted his vest. He pulled his coin purse from his breast pocket and exhaled.

"No need to worry, men," he said as the guards relaxed. "This town may have its rats, but apparently not all are thieves."

She leapt down the last few stairs and kept on, unoffended. She had been called worse during her years in Millthrace, and she had spoken worse herself. Besides, it was the tiny dagger on his hip that she had really been after. She slid the bent little knife into her apron as she hurried into the crowd.

She checked the bob as she raced by the Well. The bob was a cork pole in a latticed shaft that hung down to the river. Lines and numbers were etched all up and down the shaft, marking high and low points of the water. All people ever really talked about in Lowtown was the level of the bob, and the certain doom it meant. If there had been no rain for weeks and the bob was low, the fear would be the mills shutting down. And when the winter snows melted in spring and the bob floated too high, the worry would be flooding in the market. The bob so troubled the townsfolks' minds, she claimed it was the reason there were never any children in Millthrace named Robert. The bob looked good today, she thought, not really knowing the difference.

She poked her finger through the lattice and patted the bob, watching it bounce as if giving her an approving nod. She nodded back and pushed on to the square.

An array of carts were lined up past the Well in the market square, and she ran straight over to the apples.

"Olen Marine!" an angry voice called out, stopping Olen in her boots.

An older woman stomped across the square, clutching the front of her hem in balled fists. Her worn-out red skirt was faded almost as much as her red hair. It was Mistress Haggart, the woman from the river and master of the Ward, a home in the Barrens where parentless children lived. Olen lived there also, but that would change once she found her parents. Haggart may have had skin dirtier than most of her wards, but she acted like a perfect lady, except when one of her girls was in trouble.

"Olen Marine!" Haggart said again, bursting through the leather-clad tradesmen like the star of a stage show. "Sloughing off on a day when we actually have work! There are chores at the river, and Schmid's wife came about looking for youth to muck the horse stalls. That's nearly half a copper gone! Do you expect your sisters to do all of the work while you reap the rewards at dinnertime?"

She always referred to the girls at the Ward as sisters, though Olen could not imagine a worse family. The younger girls were fine; they were too young to know better. But the older girls, the ones who had long since passed over that innocent age where their cuteness alone may have found them a home, they were the worst. They were trapped in the Ward for a few more years, and knowing that made them wretched. The anger Mistress Haggart showed right now was nothing compared to what the other girls would show her later. Yet even as she berated her, Miss Haggart gently tugged at Olen's vest, setting the laces, and brushing her hands over her shoulders rolling her sleeves down her arms.

"I'm sorry, Mistress," Olen said. "I promise I'll work harder."

"*Harder* is a degree we can aspire for. You will work, period! And why is your hair wet?" Haggart asked, picking at Olen's shiny black braids. "Don't tell me you fell into the Well again?"

"I never *fell* into the Well," she insisted. "I told you I was *thrown* in. But no, this time I just...dove in."

"Dove into the river?" Haggart said, smelling the braid and wincing. "And yet when I *ask* you to take a bath you refuse."

They held for a moment, and despite their best efforts, they both cracked a smile. Haggart shook away her grin. "Regardless, swimming and wasting the day isn't worth two coppers in this world."

Olen grinned widely at that old remark.

"What are you smiling at, child?"

She opened her fist and showed the three coins; intimate wealth to this Lowtown duo. Haggart glanced sideways to the guards on the corner, then rolled her rough but warm hand over Olen's, closing the coins inside. She leaned in and whispered harshly.

"You haven't been thieving, have you?"

"Of course not!"

"Picking pockets?"

"I wouldn't even know how," she said innocently, while smoothing out her apron.

"Let me guess, you found them?" Haggart asked.

"In the river," she replied.

"In the river," Mistress Haggart repeated, nodding slowly. She took a couple deep breaths, still nodding. Whenever Haggart spoke to her, she always seemed to be having a silent debate with herself. Finally Haggart straightened her spine, and checked the guards who were now looking her way. "Well then, you stick to that story, *found in the river,* you understand?"

"I understand," Olen said, "Because it's the truth." She found it strange that she so often got away with mischief, only to be questioned and doubted while innocent.

"The truth seems to vary with you, dear," Haggart said. "Now back to your sisters."

The old woman turned, and Olen said, "Of course Mistress, but first, the Ox-man brought in a cart this morning. He brought something special." She held two of the coppers out to Haggart, who turned back as if tempted by the devil. "A cart full of apples!"

Haggart pondered that news dreamily, as if savoring a remembrance of long ago. She asked, "Green or red?"

"The reddest!" Olen said, beaming.

"You're a curious child, Olen Marine," Haggart said, before letting her own wry smile slip across her face. "And I'm glad you're mine!"

Mistress Haggart snatched the two copper pennies and turned away as she said in her most demanding voice, "Don't let the other girls see you, and as soon as you're done...pots!"

"Yes Mistress," Olen chimed and danced in thick boots over to the apple cart.

Olen sat back on storage crates in the heart of the city eating the crunchy sweet apple, its juices rolling down her chin. She had only ever had baked apples before, overripe and desperate for a dash of cinnamon. But this apple was as cool and fresh as drinking from Quickwater chute. No need to rush, she thought as she chewed away. She had untied her braids and fanned out her hair to dry in the afternoon sun. Her sleeves were once again up over her shoulders, soaking up the warmth. She liked Haggart. She was hard at times but reasonable. And when she finally sneaks away from the Ward, she might actually miss Ol' Haggart. She curled her tongue and spit a black seed high into the air. It landed on a rambling tradesman who looked at the sky only to see a passing eagle.

And still Millthrace buzzed. Traders haggled and gossiped in brutal accents, animals for feast or function bleated and *mrrrred*, and shirtless suntanned boys dangled hooks in the Well on lines too thick to fool a trout. Olen lay back on the crates nibbling away at the apple core, happy and hale but feeling nowhere near home.

A guard perched high above the city's main gate called down to someone outside the walls. Olen tossed the core to a thankful goat and sat up. The gates to Millthrace only opened twice a day, once in the morning to let out the tradesmen, and once again at night as the farmers, barterers, and travelers headed back in to safety. Each opening gave her a glimpse of the world outside. *Raiders* was always the fear beyond the gates, but no one could explain to her just who or what exactly Raiders were.

Samantha, with that pink and white scar down her cheek, was the only person she knew of who had ever even seen a Raider horde and lived. And despite what Olen thought were subtle advances, Samantha had always refused but the barest details. That was until one bright day at the river when she spoke of her escape.

"When everyone was running away, I got confused and ran right at them," she had said, touching her scar. "I think that confused them too because I pushed right through the horde. There were so many of them, and my parents were already...gone. But I pushed right through. And then I was all alone, but I could still hear the screaming." Then she had looked to Olen as if she was supposed to say something, but Olen had not known what to say. At that moment Olen had decided to not ask her any more about Raiders.

It was only midday now, but the high guard turned back to the city and signaled the operator below, who quibbled before reluctantly heaving a large pole across its axle. Olen climbed atop a stack of crates to see over heads. Somewhere below the boardwalk a sluice opened and river water surged through, setting an iron-finned wheel in motion. The top portion of the wheel arced above the boardwalk as sleepily it rolled its iron plates. Chains buckled and jerked, and pulled themselves taught between the wheel and the immense front gate. Unable to resist the waters of the mighty Oiskonn River, the gate began its ascent. It climbed steadily if slowly, like a great mouth yawning, until the guard signaled again. The operator closed the floodgate and the door hung open. It was her first ever image of the outside world at midday. Brightly colored birds, as in Uptown, flitted from tree to tree. And unlike the browns of Lowtown, everything outside was green. It was an image of the world that awaited her once she finally left the Ward.

An aged man stood outside, judging the gate-mouth fearfully. Iron-bound tree trunks hung above, giant fangs precariously held in place by water. The sluice-master kicked a plate over the cone-like holes in the ground and swept his arm, yelling at the man to pass through. The grey-haired traveler, balding and wrapped in brown robes, quickly ducked under the gate and scurried into the city. Once past the hanging teeth, his gait evened, and he took on an air of importance, despite the fact that he wore only one sandal. The operator pulled back the plate and slapped again at the large pole. River water fed back out of the sluice, lowering, and then dropping the gate with a heavy thud.

The traveler approached the gatesman and tipped him generously for the rare midday passage. By the operator's face it was probably enough to buy the entire apple cart. But before that could happen, she wanted one more. She dug into her pocket and pulled out the pilfered dagger. It was thin and quite bent, but it was metal so it still had value. Gerta had once whispered to her that the first rule of pilfering was to sell or trade away your goods as soon as possible. "It doesn't matter if you trade up or down," she had said, "as long as you get rid of it, and fast!" Olen figured this useless letter opener must be worth an apple or two. She sauntered over to the cart, in no great hurry to return to the Ward. Mistress Haggart had her pennies for the day. Pot washing would have to wait.

***

Edwin the Observer addressed two city guards just beyond a cesspool the locals nastily called the Well. In Ulm they kept their sewer pits hidden, thank you very much. One soldier listened halfheartedly as Edwin demanded to be taken to the mayor's office. The other guard sat on a netted crate gnawing like a dog on a thick hunk of jerked mutton. Edwin said that if the mayor was not available then he must speak to an army general at once. The officer replied that he did not respond to demands from tradesmen.

"I am no common trader!" he shot back and straightened his dusty robes. "I am an Historian from University!"

This finally sparked some interest from the guardsmen as one leapt to his feet in delight. Perhaps this land was not as crude as Edwin had thought.

"A traveling historian!" the guard exclaimed as he tossed his half-gnawed jerky behind the crates. "We haven't had a good storyteller here in ages. What tales do you bring the mayor-general? Will there be singing?"

"I am no minstrel!" Edwin proclaimed, as a distant memory resurfaced. "I do not prance around in leggings for a fool's delight. I am an Historian. I write the histories of this great land."

At Ulm, at University, even Welter Bay, such an introduction would have been met with brisk handshakes and invitations to dinner and drinks. The guardsmen stared gape-mouthed as if pondering a grand theorem. Frustrated, Edwin insisted, "I am an educated fellow!"

As they argued, another guard approached from the Midtown stairs.

He was a head taller than the rest, and of a lanky but densely solid build. Though younger than the others, this soldier bore armor festooned with blue crests, the markings of a higher ranking sergeant. The blond-haired sergeant could not have had more than twenty-five years behind him, yet he carried himself with the casual confidence Edwin had only seen in the most tenured of professors. As he neared the small group, the two guards straightened to attention. Edwin continued to insist.

"Now I must see the mayor on a pressing issue."

"And what issue would a tinker have with the mayor-general?" the sergeant asked. His tone was sour yet familiar, for it was a tenor Edwin himself had used often with inferiors. "Someone short-change you for fixing their pots?" the sergeant asked.

The children playing and fishing in the square had quietly moved away at first sight of the sergeant, and the traders paused in their dealings, turning away as if trying not to be seen. It was as if the Chancellor had sauntered through the University gardens, his mere presence quieting the doctorates and scattering the philosophers.

"I am not a tinker," Edwin said, struggling to retain a noble posture under the young sergeant's fierce glare. He told them he was neither a storyteller nor a trader, instead he was an Historian with important news for this city's leaders regarding a threat from Ma'alabrad Forest.

The two soldiers scoffed at those words, but their leader leaned in close. He warned Edwin to be careful what he said next, for there were many merchants in this square that would not like their customers scared away by ghost stories. "Even I and my men would not be able to stop a mass that size."

"I understand and appreciate your concern, Sir Knight," Edwin said, shrinking.

"City-Sergeant Koertig," the armored man growled.

"Sir Sergeant Koertig," Edwin continued nervously. He had met folk like Koertig before. At University they were the finest children of the wealthiest families. They had won some holy game of lots, being gifted with not only wealth and status but strong bodies and beautiful faces. He had at first resisted these young men and women as they flexed their prepotency in his face, but he had quickly learned that these were not people to be played with, and that sometimes it was wisest to defer.

He assured Sergeant Koertig that he brought no ghost tales, but perhaps something more frightening. "I have witnessed a jailbreak of sorts, deep within Ma'alabrad Forest. The lost and fabled Nerikan Prison has revealed itself and its great doors no longer hold. It is giving up its prisoners as we speak!"

This changed the man. Koertig, no longer smug, stiffened and straightened his back. He snatched Edwin by the front of his robes and thrust him to his guards. "Take him to the hall," he said. "I will get the mayor. But I don't want any more talk in the streets of this madness."

The two guards hauled Edwin away, but Sergeant Koertig stayed back, staring at the front gate of Millthrace as if struck by an all-consuming remembrance. Edwin observed the stoic sergeant as he was pulled backwards up the large staircase to Midtown.

***

Olen had ducked behind the crates as the guards argued with the old man. She had seen Koertig coming down from Midtown as she traded the dagger and knew it was always best not to be seen—she did not need to be tossed into the Well again. She sat on the ground with her back to the crates as a gift of dried mutton fell out of the sky and landed in her lap. No child of the Ward would shy away from half-eaten meat, so into her shirt it went. The men argued something about a storyteller coming to town, which she hoped was true.

The tone of the men had changed as Sergeant Koertig took over. Alas, the balding man was not a storyteller after all, but some sort of educator. She thought this a wise time to slip away, but then the old man spoke of Nerikan Prison and she froze. She had heard of Nerikan, every child who was told faerie stories had. It was home to demons and witches and monsters that tossed lightning from their fingertips. It was all just stories to scare the kids, but on certain nights when storms roared overhead and strange winds moaned through cracked windows, and when children lay alone in beds with no parents to comfort them, it was easy to believe.

She squatted behind the crates and remembered the time she had asked her eldest sister Philippa about Nerikan. She had asked, if the *bad* magic users came from Nerikan, then where did the *good* magic users come from? And Philippa had answered in no uncertain terms, that there were no good magic users.

"They're all from Nerikan," Philippa had said. "And in Nerikan they'll return."

Even back then Olen had not quite believed Nerikan actually existed, but to hear adults talk about it as a real place was more frightening than the faerie stories themselves. *They're all from Nerikan*, she thought, *and in Nerikan they'll return.* Once Koertig finally turned and left the Square, Olen hurried to the safety of the Ward, not wanting to think any more about that haunted prison.

4

The Black Painted Jar

Olen abandoned the wooden streets of Lowtown for the hard packed dirt of the Barrens and the Ward. Haggart's home stood like an old swayback mare. The roof buckled in the middle from a collapsed rafter and both ends threatened to fold in. She often wondered what would happen if it crumbled while she was asleep in her bed. Two floors of windows—many cracked, some boarded over—spread out from the central entrance. An old army dispensary, the Ward had once held the finest soldiers within its bold white walls. Now most of that paint had chipped away leaving a half-peeled frame of grey flat-boards and wrong-sized lath patches. It would never be home for her, but for now, it was a good enough shelter. She pushed open the double doors and walked in.

She entered the empty lobby and thought the same thing she always did, "This is it. My last night here. Tomorrow I'll be gone." It was like she was trying to convince herself to stop dreaming and just go. But even as she said it, she knew she would be back again the next day. Back with her "sisters" back with Miss Haggart, and back to dreaming.

A circular iron chandelier hung from the buckled ceiling, practically pulling the roof in. The candles rounding the great wheel were never lit, as its rusty drop-chain had long since fused to the pulley, leaving the chandelier forever out of reach. It swayed menacingly above a wide stairway that led up to the bedroom halls. To one side, a room for the youngest girls like Olen, and to the other, the more sparsely populated hall for the older girls. An uncommon silence sat in the foyer air as none of the girls were about. The scent of warm broth was in the air. Dinner was ready, and after sloughing off her chores, Olen had to face her sisters.

She walked past the parlor and slid open the only pocket door that still moved, its metal wheel screeching in its groove. Were her eyes not so sharp, she would have thought she had walked in upon an Uptown meeting of Eisen's finest ladies. Nine young girls and one adult sat poised around two long tables, their hands folded in their laps and their elbows at their sides. Candles of conflicting size, shape, and waxen hue ran the length of each table, painting a healthy yellow glow onto the young ladies' faces. Carved-horn cups and hardwood bowls, warped and rippled from years of use, sat before each child. The girls were all silent and nodded slowly as servers ladled soup into their bowls and placed small bread rolls on their plates. Only one head craned up to look at Olen, then quickly pulled back.

These were not Eisen's finest ladies. These girls still wore the dirty work clothes they had worn at the riverside. Their hands and faces were clean, but their hair was matted in clumps and their clothes were patched and worn. These were the girls that Eisen had abandoned and Millthrace abhorred. They were the parentless children of the Ward, and they were supposedly Olen's sisters. Mistress Haggart sat at the head of the first table.

Olen slowly walked around their backs, the wooden floor creaking louder than the Lowtown boardwalk. Low murmurs growled deep in the throats of girls who had toiled all day. One young girl, blissfully unaware, gave a vibrant wave. It was little Maggie, the youngest of the sisters and certainly everyone's secret favorite, even Haggart's. She had a permanent smile and uncontrollable blonde hair. Her straw-like locks always looked like they had just survived a wind storm. She curled her index finger at Olen, a secret wave only they shared. But when no one else welcomed Olen, Maggie's finger slowed, and her hand fell to her lap. Olen returned a couple quick finger curls and took her seat. Mistress Haggart simply looked ahead as the servers moved about the room, her head cocked with an air of queenly serenity. The servers—the lucky ones who avoided river duty this day—gave soup and bread to the latecomer, evoking gasps. Haggart rapped the table with her knuckles but said nothing. The girls all sat up and waited.

When the last server left for the kitchen, Mistress Haggart began.

"A lady," she said, in a precise diction she only used at the table, "waits quietly for her meal to be served. She is neither over-anxious to be fed like a starving hog, nor disappointed at the meal given her."

Philippa Cree, the oldest girl and the one who sat at the head of the second table, spoke up. Her wide muscular frame made her too big for the hand-me-downs the other girls wore, so Haggart had given her a woodsman's tunic she had acquired years earlier. It was dark brown with soft white trim, which Philippa had hopelessly tried to garnish. The girls joked behind her back that she had strayed from the pageant wagon. Her hair was canary yellow, though one hardly knew it as she kept it tightly wound in a circular braid atop her head. She spoke to Haggart while pointing at Olen, "But Mistress, it's not the food. It's this gadabout motherless child."

Olen kicked back her chair and stood up, "I am no orphan!"

Philippa stood also, meeting the challenge, "You are a sneaking, thieving, and loafing motherless mouse!"

"Ladies!" Haggart cut in, and lowered the girls to their seats with a soft gesture. "None of you are motherless. Remember that. Nor are you without your sisters. You are part of the largest family in the city, and for that you are lucky."

Even if that were true, Olen would hardly call herself lucky.

Haggart continued, "But if you are to learn manners, then Philippa, you must remember that only the Mistress chooses who dines at her table. And while I depend on you for so much in this home, you are not the Mistress."

Philippa was not the Mistress, and it was unlikely there was a home anywhere in Millthrace that she would ever head. She had passed the common age of adoption, and now could only wait out the last two years until emancipation. And if the rude comments the boys said behind her back echoed what most men felt, then it was unlikely Philippa would ever find a husband of her own. She had started sitting in with the midwives at night so she would have a career when she was old enough. That made for long hours, little sleep, and an irritable disposition.

"And Miss Marine," Haggart continued, "is certain to make good on her chores by cleaning up the kitchen after dinner. Isn't that right, Olen?"

Olen nodded reluctantly.

Haggart nodded to the group, and they turned to their meal. The girls ate silently, though occasional tips on manners from the Mistress broke the silence. "Head up, Samantha. Don't hover over the bowl like an inmate," she would say, quoting from some unknown standard on etiquette. "Skim from the top of the bowl, dear Maggie. No need to clank your silver at the bottom with every scoop." Of course the girls had no silver, only dry wooden spoons that dragged roughly at the corners of their mouths. The meal continued at the Ward as the girls in rags sat like proper ladies and ate their bread and soup.

At the end of dinner Mistress Haggart said she had a surprise. "As I'm sure you ladies heard, this morning one of the ox-men brought in an apple cart. Well, you should know our sister Olen had a bit of luck today."

Maggie turned to Olen, who winked at the little girl. Maggie tried to wink back, but blinked both eyes.

"She had stumbled upon some mislaid coins," Haggart said, and more than one girl puffed air between pursed lips, disbelieving the coins were mislaid. Even Gerta smirked. *No apples for you,* Olen thought. Haggart told them Olen had donated the coins to the Ward, and that she had been so impressed with the sister's generosity that she had added a few more from the emergency fund as well. "And after a little bartering with the apple merchant..." she said, and clapped her hands together twice. The servers came out of the kitchen carrying three trays of apple tarts.

The girls chirped and awed as the servers circled the room, forgetting or forgiving Olen for her offense. Marta, with her perfect white teeth, smiled and patted Olen on the back, while others, like the shy but lady-like Ellery thanked the Mistress. Many acted like girls instead of proper ladies, but this time Haggart did not correct them. The servers placed warm pastries on all of the plates.

"Be sure to save some for yourselves," Haggart reminded the servers. They nodded and smiled before returning to the pantry.

The girls around the table eagerly waited for Mistress Haggart's approval. "Oh, just dive," she said. And they did, pouncing at their plates like hungry children should. Marta tossed the steaming tart from hand to hand, blowing on her burning fingers. Maggie took a big bite, unaffected by the heat. Ellery chose to spoon the dessert into her mouth, but no proper training could hide the hunger in her eyes. Even Mistress Haggart leaned over the table and scraped the bottom of the plate, her etiquette trumped by delight.

Among the flurry of scooping hands and turning heads, it was a stillness that caught Olen's eye. Philippa Cree stared her down from the head of the table, her apple tart untouched. Olen held the larger girl's stare. Philippa discreetly pointed to Olen then back at herself. She mouthed the word "orphans" and bit into her dessert.

Olen laid awake that night in a bedroom hall that looked and smelled like an attic. The ceiling and walls were bare wood that appeared to be slapped together with as much care as an old shipping crate. Her small bed was just one of nine cots that lined the walls. The slow rhythm of sleeping breaths echoed off the high-roofed hall.

She did not fear Philippa, but she was glad the older sister slept in the other hall. Olen was not an orphan as Philippa claimed. Not a motherless-child. She just knew it. And yet the Mistress and her sisters kept treating her as one. They wanted her to give up hope like the others and join this so-called family.

There was a bubble around her these days, unseen by all. It was a bubble that stiffened whenever Haggart smiled and touched her hair. A bubble that thickened and cut off all sound whenever another child called her "sister". This magic bubble was part of what remained of her parent's love, and it fought off all who tried to claim her.

She had been just a baby when they had lost her. What little she knew of them came from Haggart, who had never even met them herself. But they were facts she constantly rolled through her head. They were from Kessel, a city far to the south. They were travelers. They had named her. That was all. But that was enough for her to find them, for she was tired of waiting. And there was something else, a secret she kept from everyone. It was because of this secret Olen just knew her parents must still be alive...

Excited voices chattered outside her window. She pulled her chin onto her cot's iron railing and saw the Square below. Most of the tall wooden row buildings were dark and shuttered, and thick clouds had rolled over the moon. Sluices were dry and the mills silent, but in the Scape wheels still churned, waiting for gears to re-engage. A large group of Midtowners came down the wide stairway carrying fire in glass lamps. Five city-soldiers led the crowd, and amongst them, a cluster of well-dressed men hurried along. They were politicians and wealthy business owners from Uptown. The entire group followed a balding man wrapped in brown robes who spoke dramatically, gesturing often. It was the educator Olen had seen earlier in the day, the man who had spoken of Nerikan. He appeared to have found some new sandals. One from the crowd rushed ahead and opened the door to the tavern. They filed into the pub and pulled the door shut. It was story time at the Eagle and Trout.

Olen lay back in bed, staring at the angled wooden ceiling and thick wooden beams that crossed above. Iron springs stretched and coiled as a sister turned to her side. Philippa had said all magic users—good and bad—came from Nerikan. She had also said that into Nerikan they would return. If that were so, then Olen must hear this old man's story, however frightening.

If it's meant to be, she thought and peeled off her blanket. She wore a thin faded slip that had been handed down through the generations. She pulled the covers back over herself and a familiar tremor rippled through her frame. It was like a wave of bugs rushing up her skin. But unlike bugs, this did not disgust her. When she looked again, she was dressed in black. *I guess it's meant to be.*

She sat up and looked over her outfit. The tight arms were long and soft against her skin. A hood rested against the back of her neck. She now wore slacks, snug and form-fitting, something the Mistress would never have allowed. Her shoes were also soft and black, more like a sturdy slipper, and perfectly sized. She thought not one whit about her enchanted attire, only about getting outside.

She eased herself over the whining bed springs and set her feet soundlessly onto the floor. The doorway was at the far end of the room, down a hall lined with cots.

"Where are you going?" a muffled voice asked dreamily from the next cot. A sleep-filled eye peered out of a large moth hole in a blanket. Olen slid the blanket off the little girl's head, and Maggie sat up, half-dazed, mostly asleep. Her yellow hair angled like broken straw and her golden eyebrows arched high desperately trying to hold open her heavy lids. She did not seem to notice Olen's dark outfit. The little girl clutched a large glass jar against her chest with both arms. It was painted black on the inside.

"That's a curious doll," Olen whispered, while glancing at the other cots.

"It's not a doll," Maggie said mid-yawn. "It's for catching fireflies."

Olen slid the jar out of her hands and set it on the floor. She eased the girl back onto her cot and pulled her blanket up to her chest. Maggie's eyes fluttered shut. Olen pulled her own blanket off her bed and slid it over Maggie also, tucking her in. The tiny blonde child slept for a breath and then opened her eyes wide as if frightened. She reached over the cot and pulled the jar back to her chest, hugging it protectively.

"It's all black," Olen whispered, resetting the blankets and combing her fingers through the little girl's hair. "How am I supposed to see your fireflies?"

"You're not supposed to see them," Maggie murmured as she pulled her knees up to her chest and her eyes fell shut again. "That's why I have to catch them..."

Olen drew her fingers across Maggie's brow until the youngest child's breathing joined the rhythm of the others. She kissed her forehead and felt the warmth on her brow. Even at six years, Maggie still smelled like a baby, fresh and warm and clean. Haggart had once called that the smell of innocence.

Olen backed away and spied the doorway at the end of the hall. In her young career of mischief, she had already learned some important tricks. For example, sneaking. The first night she had snuck out it was with Marta. They had been so cautious it had taken them till dawn just to ease down the stairway. She knew better now. The instinct may be to walk slow and steady, but the trick was to not be timid

Be bold, she thought.

She raised her heels off the floor and ran silently on her toes, past her sleeping sisters, down the hall, and out of the room.

She eased the door shut behind herself and stood atop the staircase, a shadow in the dark hall. A light flickered inside the parlor doors below and soft voices drifted out. Mistress Haggart was entertaining a guest. Perhaps another aging mid-town gent, unwed and trying to convince Haggart he only seeks a "helper" for around the house. *Take Philippa*, she thought, *if you dare.*

She crept down the warped wooden stairs to the main floor, stepping closest to the railing, knowing stairs only creaked in the middle. Baked apple and cinnamon lingered in the air and candlelight danced her shadow on the walls. She could not get out the front door without passing the parlor, but she knew another way. At the bottom of the stairs, she ducked around the thick railing and scurried down another staircase, this one made of concrete and stone. At the bottom she pushed open a cold wooden door and entered the basement.

Faint moonlight trickled in from the few high windows that

remained. Wooden planks covered the rest. It was a cluttered storage room, a chamber of junk that would never be disposed of without someone offering a copper hack. Iron bed frames, rusted and bent, lay angled against the stone wall awaiting a desperate smithy. A three-legged chair sat askew in a corner, the fourth leg lying crossways in its moldy seat. A carpenter with an extra wedge-penny might surely trade for such a simple project. Wooden railings from absent stairways, wheels, gears, and cracked crates of all sizes littered the damp basement floor.

In the darkest corner of the basement lay a heavy slab of wood bound by iron straps, a hatchway to the sewers, and the doorway that had begun her exploration of the Escapement. Above the slab hung a hook on a chain. She pulled the trapdoor's iron O-ring and heaved it open, but the damp ring slipped from her fingers and slammed shut. A tremor rumbled through the Ward, and Olen sat motionless for many heartbeats waiting for any sounds upstairs. When none came, she again hoisted open the hatch, and this time heaved it far enough to catch the hanging hook. Stale air blew in from the open pit as she stuck her head in the hole. Below the basement ran a small and open finger of the Oiskonn River. It may have been a garbage chute for the nurses of old, but for Olen, it was a gateway to freedom. She splashed down in the shallow stream and jumped to the thin shore. Then she ran upstream to the Well.

5

⚮

An Historian Entertains
the Pub

It was not the first tavern Edwin had ever been in, but the Eagle and Trout was by far the largest. The barrel-shaped pub and hostelry was the most popular evening stop in all of Millthrace. The sturdy wooden hall stood three floors above the boardwalk, with rumors of a vast fourth floor hidden below. Thickly lacquered dark cherry wood lined the inner walls, railings, and all the tables; and a grand fireplace of grey stone stood menacingly against the far wall. The ground floor of the arena-like pub was the main floor for drinking, dining, and dancing. Above circled the wide balconies of the second floor with sleeping rooms which travelers rented by the night. High above that hung the shadowy terrace of the third floor where only the privileged few were allowed. And below it all, again the mythical fourth floor which Edwin learned was not to be talked about. There were taverns in Ulm, but not like this. In Ulm the taverns were quaint abodes where one sipped instead of gulped.

He worked his way past grabbing arms and filthy shouting mouths, every man wanting to hear his tale first hand. He felt like a celebrity, this lone visitor from Hulblich. Musky workmen and powdered businessmen alike clumsily passed tankards of ale, carelessly splashing each other, while somewhere in the crowd revelers jangled bells and beat wooden spoons against tin pans. It was like the famed University parties he had so often heard of. Dead things rotated over orange coals, smelling hardly better than they ever did alive. *My fortune for a warm bisque*, he thought as a bearded drunk backed into him.

"Mind your tankard!" Edwin shouted, patting down his wet robe. The hairy sot stumbled away, not hearing.

Women cackled in the upper balcony while peering over the darkly stained rails, waving handkerchiefs to familiar faces across the expanse. The wealthier Uptown men who had paid a premium for the gallery view angled and shouldered their way closer to the ladies.

Edwin pressed through to a makeshift dais at the back of the tavern. The mayor and his guards had saved him a space. As Edwin climbed the three steps, the crowd hushed.

"He's just a storyteller!" a soused lowbrow called out, scratching the fleas in his scalp and drawing laughs.

Edwin turned on the frothy crowd. "I am no such thing," he scowled, straightening his robes. "I am an Historian, an educated fellow."

Again they chortled and jeered and clanked their tankards.

A fully inebriated woman, whom the crowd all knew as Miss Egg, held up her cup and called up to Edwin, "Tell us a story, love!" She wore an old woman's nightcoat and a limp cap. Smoke and ale had aged her beyond her years, and only four canines remained of her devilish smile. She was as filthy as the beggars he had met on the road, but at the Eagle and Trout, she was as if a beloved mascot. The brutes roared.

Mayor-General Janus Brynn stood next to Edwin and raised his hands, quieting the room. Brynn was a small-framed man with a grand personality. The Brynn name, he had learned, was well-known amongst the northern people of Eisen. Each of the major cities had seen their own Brynn pass through the ranks of government over the past hundreds of years. This Brynn himself was the ancestor of another Mayor Brynn who had served the city of Daegan generations ago and had overseen the mending of a vast rupture in Bran's Wall, and was even related to Zem Brynn who had built the bridge at Kessel that had joined wild Eisen to the cultured southern mainland of Hulblich.

Brynn held the unique title of mayor-general. He oversaw the city government and attended to all civic duties, while also heading the strong Millthracian army, though he had been quick to declare this was neither a dictatorship nor a military state. He was simply a man with the knowledge and skills to head both branches of rule, and was granted the titles by near-unanimous vote. He seemed almost embarrassed of the honor. Brynn had been offered many a tankard this evening and politely refused them all. Edwin genuinely liked the man.

He addressed the crowd.

"Gentlemen," Mayor Brynn began, in a smooth but commanding voice that took Edwin back to the lecture halls. Full black hair sat above dark soft eyes. He wore a daily-trimmed mustache and short beard just on his chin. Unadorned robes of dark purple hung regally off his shoulders. "City-guards and shopkeepers, traveling tradesmen and landowners, mechanics and laborers, all those who keep this great city spinning." Groups shouted hurrahs and drained their cups as their occupations were named.

Such a talent, Edwin thought, to be able to master such a crowd with just the tenor of his words.

Brynn continued, "I have heard this man's story first hand, face to face. He has confirmed in exacting detail the rumors of Nerikan that have so quickly spread." Brynn added in a more somber tone, "And like all storytellers, I found his tale fantastical, inflammatory, and un-believable."

It was as if quarrymen had set off a blast as the barroom exploded, nearly tearing the roof off the Eagle and Trout. Ale splashed and hur-rahs turned again to laughter—a biting merriment at Edwin's expense. The old Observer fell back as if kicked in the chest, betrayed by the wise mayor. Brynn raised his hands and again quelled the drunken crowd.

"I say I found his *tale* unbelievable," he continued, and gave Edwin an approving nod, "but I found the *man* to be honest, intelligent, and a gentleman of conduct."

Edwin swelled. Not an overripe fool, not a wayward hermit or mind-wandering pedantic, but an honest, intelligent, gentleman of conduct! He stared deeply into the mayor's sagacious eyes and felt himself being read, observed, and for once in his life...understood. In that moment he thought of Brynn as a friend and knew how easily this man must have come to rule.

"But fantastic beasts?" a groundling tailor called out, a measuring string slung over his neck, and an array of needles and pins running down his lapel. "And an ogre? These were faerie tales even before my grandfather's day. How can that be?"

The mayor-general began to speak, but Edwin cut him off. Brynn stepped back a pace without a hint of offense.

"At *University*," Edwin began proudly, "I studied the history of our beloved domains, but I also studied the *literature* of our ancestors. Simply a pastime for me, or so I thought. In these stories I had read myths of the land. These fantasies spoke of magical people. Men who could race across the span of Eisen in a day! Women who spoke aloud the secrets in our hearts! And others who could perform feats that sent the faithless kneeling. Aurlings they were called. I too believed these to be nothing more than faerie tales to excite lesser minds—"

"Tell us the stories!" a boorish voice yelled out, and was seconded by the crowd.

"I am not here to tell stories!" Edwin demanded. "But I have seen them. I have seen the man, the ogre as you call him, bigger than your tallest man, and many times as strong. I have seen the creatures in the woods, wolves and boars twisted into awful stalking beasts. In the old stories they called these mixed creatures *scions*. We thought them to be myths, we must now accept those old stories to be true as they were written."

The crowd rumbled again and demanded to hear from the mayor. Mayor Brynn stepped forward and raised his hands to silence the crowd. "It does concern me about this ogre," he said. "Wolves and boars, scions as you call them, I trust to the sharp arrows and sharper aim of our fine hunters. But this man-beast, should he exist, must be captured."

An Uptowner in hosiery and a wide shouldered top called down from the balcony, asking why they should trust this wanderer from afar. "Shouldn't we demand proof?" he asked, appearing uncomfortable even so high above the filthy horde.

"We have your proof!" a harsh voice called out from behind the crowd. Inebriated townspeople spun awkwardly as City-Sergeant Koertig strode in the doorway wearing full body armor. His breastplate gleamed in the firelight as he stood a full head above the rest. He carried himself like a war-hardened general though his face revealed just a few years of adulthood. The soldier passed through the mass of men as if walking through stalks of corn. A regiment of city-guards, similarly dressed followed, their long spears reaching high into the room. The last four guards lugged in a makeshift stretcher fashioned out of horse blankets and two long spikes. Atop it sat a great rounded object wrapped in blood-crusted burlap. It was larger than the tavern's biggest boiling pot. Koertig ordered a table cleared and with a heave the four guards lifted the mass on to the slab. Even Edwin looked on most curiously, not sure what to expect.

"You demand proof of your mayor?" Koertig asked. "Here is your proof."

He ripped off the burlap, revealing the large black head of a wolf-boar scion.

The crowd gasped and hollered. Some even screamed. One young lady, lost in the crowd, blurted a vulgarity that mortified Edwin. The braver men and women approached the long-dead scion and tugged at its jutting canines and pulled at its fur, testing its genuineness. After a few moments of jostling about, the crowd turned back to Edwin.

"Quite impressive," Edwin said, a bit unsure of himself. "I have been here but a day, yet my journey took nearly a sevennight. How did you travel so far, so fast?"

Koertig gave his answer to the mayor. He explained that they had encountered the swift Daegan cavalry just north of the city. They had been returning from Ma'alabrad and had confirmed Edwin's claims.

"Apparently our guest has been telling his story to anyone who would listen."

"Yes," Edwin said nervously, "Well it had been difficult to find an attentive ear." The mayor seemed bothered by this news, Edwin noted before continuing. "Now let me tell you about the creature that killed it."

He had his rapt audience again, and thought perhaps he was not that different from a storyteller after all. Three levels of townspeople, and many levels of caste, listened quietly as he spoke. But as his tale unfolded, he could not help but notice one man who was not impressed. It was the head-guard Koertig, tall, blonde, and years ahead of his age. City-Sergeant Koertig sipped his tankard of ale while leaning back onto the bar. Edwin saw no wide wondering eyes from Koertig, only a stony glare. He felt the sergeant judging him, considering him, waiting for him to trip over his tale and spoil the ruse. As innocent as he was, that look convicted him of an unspoken sin as he stumbled nervously through his story.

***

Olen crawled out of the Well and slipped across the moonlit boardwalk to the Eagle and Trout. Her soft-soled shoes were silent on the wooden walk. She crouched near an open window that vented venison and ale and curling wisps of pipe smoke. Neither the ale nor the pipeweed thrilled her, but venison would be a rare treat, so she waited patiently for a plate or bowl to be thoughtlessly left near the sill.

Inside, Mayor Brynn and the old man from earlier took to the stage and spoke of books, and Aurlings, and something called scions. As she waited for him to say something interesting, the city's gatesman behind her kicked open the sluice and raised the great front gate. Soldiers on horseback rode gently into Millthrace, their hooves clicking lightly on the boarded walk. It was Koertig and his men. She dropped behind an oxcart, nearly invisible in her black garb. As the armored regiment passed her by, the soldiers dismounted soundlessly before opening the front door to the tavern. After they all had entered the Eagle and Trout, she again sidled up to the window and peered inside. Dark devil eyes stared back at her. She screamed a curse she had learned in the streets and then quickly covered her mouth. Large black orbs, shrunken and rippled like moldy plums peered at her. Saber-like teeth on a hairy black skull jutted out before her, and a thick bloody slobber oozed onto the tabletop.

A monster, she marveled and wanted to wake the entire Ward. She wanted to touch it, and she wanted to run away. It was a nightmare made flesh, and it was an arm's length away. The great beast's head sent frightening shivers down her spine, and great thrills right back up it. Nerikan was real, and this was its proof. Monsters live.

After a commotion in the tavern died down, the balding man in brown robes addressed the crowd and spoke of a giant ogre. He held his hands high above his head and stomped around the stage miming how big this creature was. She had to laugh as he acted out. They said he was an educator, but he was not like the teachers the Mid and Uptown children had to see five days a week. Those teachers were humorless, but this guy made her laugh, whether he meant to or not. He showed a stack of leather-bound folios. Even from this distance she could tell they were quite ancient and tattered.

"I must thank your mayor for allowing me into his personal library," the old man continued as the scent from the decaying wolf drifted out the window. "He maintains quite a collection of ancient documents."

She rested her arm on the oxcart tarp, and something shifted below it. She lifted up an end and peeked. "Potatoes," she sighed, and slapped down the cover.

"I have learned much from these histories," the educator continued, holding one folio, but then trading it for another. "Yet I realize now that it is the myths and faerie tales of our great-grandfathers that we must review with a critical mind. We must glean truth from ancestral fiction. Therein we will find the answers to questions such as these," he said, and gestured to the wolf-boar. He lifted a leather tome above his head, "Knowledge is what will save us!"

Olen had no interest in book-learning, she only wanted to know why her clothes rippled and changed, and where her parents were. The stench of the rotting wolf made her sick, so she ducked away from the window and sat behind the potato cart. The square was quiet again and a soft hum purred through the sleepy town. She loved the city at night, so quiet and empty. The Ward stood dark and brittle like an abandoned hall waiting to collapse. But for now, that ailing structure was her home. *All magic users were from Nerikan,* Philippa had said, *and in Nerikan they'll return.* Not if there are creatures like that scion in there, Olen thought.

At an upstairs window a tiny point of light blinked on, danced a half circle, and fizzled out. A firefly, Olen thought, and hoped Maggie had her jar ready. She reached back under the tarp, snatched two potatoes, and slinked back over to the Well.

6

A Thief in the Night

Olen tossed the potatoes up the open hatchway and pulled herself out of the Scape and back into the Ward. The dank basement air was only a mild relief from the Lowtown sewers, but they were both better than that rotting skull. She had not known wolves could grow that large. Not wolves, scions, she corrected as she closed the heavy lid. That was what waited for her outside the Millthrace walls, scions and Raiders. She could not let fear stop her from escaping this place and finding her parents. She had to be bold. She scooped up the potatoes and walked to the stairs.

A rough hand reached out of the shadows and snatched Olen's wrist. She pulled back but was no match for the strong arms of Philippa Cree. "A thief in the night!" the older sister cried out as the potatoes fell to the floor. "Is this how you earn your stay? Slinking about in black like the stray cat you are, all to thieve a couple potatoes?"

"Let me go," the smaller one twisted and fought. Sneaking out was hardly a concern, and stealing potatoes was only slightly worse, but Philippa had seen her dark clothing and if she told Haggart, that was something she would not be able to barter away with a couple pennies.

"All day your sisters bust their knuckles on river rocks, but where is Olen Marine? Is she on dinner duty? No. Is she tending the newborns?

Never! Instead, she's gladding about the sewers and thieving! You think you are better than your sisters, but you are just another orphan!"

"That's not true!" Olen cried, as Philippa dragged her to the stairs.

"Haggart has let this go on long enough," she said, wrestling with the wiry girl. "And she rewards your mischief with pastry!" She hoisted Olen up the stairway and dropped her to the foyer floor, still clutching her wrist. "If one sister is caught thieving, then the entire Ward will be looked upon suspiciously. Who then will bring us clothes to mend? Who then will offer us a real home? I should take you to Koertig myself and tell him your crimes!"

This was a common threat from Philippa, daring the disobedient girls to have her *take them to Koertig herself*. It was also something the girls giggled about in their rooms at night, because even the youngest saw this as a feeble attempt for the bigger sister to impress and fawn over the hated sergeant.

Philippa kicked aside the parlor doors with her bare foot. Haggart startled awake in her chair and jumped to her feet. One of the younger sisters, Icha, awoke from the couch.

"Mistress," Philippa said, "I've captured a black-clad rat in the sewers!"

Haggart eased Icha to her feet and sent her upstairs, saying something about not fearing her dreams. She then turned to Philippa, "Black clad? What are you talking about?"

"This!" Philippa said and jerked Olen forward by the arm. "I found this rat—" Philippa stopped cold and saw the child dangling from her grip. Olen knew Philippa's disbelieving look, and knew why. She had felt the change moments ago and could not stop it. Philippa had snatched up a girl wearing the midnight clothes of a common thief, but she was no longer in black. She wore the same old faded-white nightshirt she had worn to bed every evening for the past three years. She was barefoot, and her hair was in disarray as if she was just pulled out of bed.

Philippa stared at her, much like Olen had stared at the wolf head. Disbelief. Wonder. Fear. "How?" she asked, her confused tone a weak cousin of her normal roar. "I never let go of your wrist." For the first time she saw a helpless fragility in Philippa. She thought she had nabbed a simple thieving child, but instead held the wrist of something much more horrific. She threw down Olen's arm and backed over to Mistress Haggart. "She's a witch! A witch, a devil, or worse, I don't know. But I do know that a moment ago, I pulled this rat out of the sewers, and she was dressed neck to toe in the garb of a black prowler."

Olen pulled herself off the ground and stood up, straightening her nightshirt.

"Philippa, please," Haggart said in a warmer tone. "Must you sisters always accuse? Olen was wrong to miss work today, but she paid in kind with copper. She is not a witch," she said, and ran her fingers through Olen's tangled locks. "Would a witch have suffered so long," and she laid a hand on Philippa's shoulders, "as *all* of my girls have?" Philippa pulled away, but Haggart continued, "My girls are neither witches nor rats. They are sisters. And sisters sometimes argue and sometimes fight, but not in this home." She then spoke directly to Olen and scolded her for sneaking out at night and disrupting the home. "No more adventures, sister Olen. Tomorrow you will work the stand."

Olen fought off the urge to smile for she loved working the stand.

"Mistress, you don't understand," Philippa demanded, still staring in frightened wonder at Olen. "The stories that have been going around town! The ghosts of Nerikan! I am no longer concerned about her sneaking and thieving now that I have seen her true self."

"And I am no longer concerned with sisters who fight under my roof," she said and urged Philippa to go off to bed. She reminded the older sister she was assisting the physician at the dispensary tomorrow and she must be well rested.

Philippa ran up to the bed hall, certain to wake the three other older sisters and tell them there was a witch in their midst, and to be honest, Olen could not say that Philippa wasn't right. By morning, all twelve girls would know. They wouldn't believe Philippa of course, which was good Olen thought, because witches belong in Nerikan.

Haggart moved back over to her chair and sat, telling Olen to take her bedroom for the night. Then with a flick of her hand she sent Olen down the hall. Olen curtsied as best she could and walked away, tugging at her nightshirt and cursing herself for being so careless.

***

Philippa did not return to her cot in the older sisters' hall, but instead turned left atop the stairs and entered the room where the youngest, suddenly precious, girls slept. She cursed herself for not trusting her instincts earlier. There was something different about Olen; she had always sensed that. But she had not searched out why the child had always disturbed her so. Philippa walked past the sleeping girls, their breaths soft and even. A Nerikan witch, she thought, living amongst her sleeping sisters, the only family she had ever truly known.

A small fire ignited in her belly as she watched the helpless children sleep. It was for now just embers, but of a flame she never knew existed. For the teenaged girl who had been abandoned by her family, passed over for adoption, and disregarded by the local men; Philippa had believed her life was a mistake. The sky and stars had spun in perfect harmony since the beginning of it all, turning the seasons and cycling the fits and fervors of man, until high above far beyond anyone's reckoning, a cog cracked, a wheel slipped, and out popped Philippa Cree. Cold, alone, and accidental.

But now that rising flame. The fire grew as heavenly gears shifted back into line and moonlight shone in on Olen's empty cot. A witch lived here, and her sisters were in danger. This was why she was made strong; this was why she was left behind. This empty cot, a demon's crib, was why her sorrowful journey had led her here.

The Ward needed a protector, someone who would give her life for those she loved, and her name was Philippa Cree.

7

The Ogre

Freedom at last, he had thought as he trampled the woods. Had he spoken these words out loud they would have been but a jumble of sounds akin to the mumblings of a madman. Decades had turned slowly in his prison, centuries had crawled. And in his time of chains, the only words had been screams of torture rejoined by mad laughter.

In his mind his thoughts were structured and wise, but the words had devolved. A cheery hullo might seem a simple thing, but even a babe is not born with this skill. Such is the same for one lost to several lifetimes in dark solitude. The most basic words are forgotten, their exact utterance a false echo of a long ago sound. His words were wrong, but his thoughts were clear: He was free, at last.

He had trampled and squeezed so many in his escape, and for that he was pleased. These once proud jailors, torturous and cruel, had found out how frail their bones truly were and how powerful he had become. He had torn off heads and ripped apart limbs, delighting in the horror of mangled torsos strewn about. They had made him a monster, so then a monster he would be.

But then he had seen the sun.

He had always known he would escape his chains, it had happened before. But he had never before found the doorway to the outside. Even as he had raced up the long incline and saw dust falling through yellow beams, he still had not let himself believe this was truly an escape. But as he thrust those great gates open wide and stood in the warm heat of the closest star, he knew that he was finally free.

But then he had seen the man.

He had seen the old man in the tree and how tiny he looked. He knew his jailor had made him strong, he knew he had grown large. But until he saw that tiny man, he had not known just how huge he had grown. He searched his mind for the word, and it finally came to his thoughts: ogre. They had made him a monster. There would be nowhere in this entire world for a creature like him to hide away, nowhere he could live in peace. And that confirmed in him the plan he had crafted so many years ago, the promise he had made to himself to ensure he would never again be bound in chains. To escape the threat of eternal torture, he would travel to the fire mountain of Calderra and climb to the top. There he would look back upon a world he had once loved, but had hated him, and he would fall back into the fires and let the flames consume him. Let the world mourn this beast they had created.

But much like his words, he had also forgotten his way.

And after many days of searching for the mountains of Calderra, the ogre was lost, and the ogre was hungry.

8

Potatoes for Onions

Edwin nibbled on an oat biscuit and sipped tea. Rented rooms were hard to come by in Midtown, but he was afforded one of the finest at a minstrel's fee. One story a night and two coppers, which was all Miss Egg had asked for, and he had eagerly accepted. He requested a week's stay and was offered a discount by paying all in advance. He handed her twelve of his quickly vanishing pennies, which she shook in her palm and left abruptly for the Eagle and Trout. So the monetary fee was paid, he thought, but little did she know that the rest of his storied observations were significantly less fantastic than last night's.

He had been scratching away at his folios all night since leaving the pub and had found a new excitement in his research that he had not had at University for quite some time. To be certain, he had always loved learning, but as he aged out of his classes, he had become a joke to student and staff. Even his aunts and uncle had stopped asking about when he hoped to finish his studies and find a wife. They would merely sign another semester's note and turn back to their chatter.

He sipped his tea and continued on. He wrote in the large folio, dipping his pen frequently in the iron-gall ink. Books and letters sat around him, piled on the floor and stacked high on his desk. The books had been borrowed from Mayor Brynn, with also some children's books from the Uptown school. He searched through the records and compared notes as he etched his own words on a new sheet he had titled, *A Definitive History of Nerikan Prison*. His candle had burned down to a waxy stub just as morning sunlight topped the high rampart walls of Millthrace. The suddenly bright rays pulled his eyes off the paper and on to the front gates of the city. The gorgeous sunrise called to him! But there was work to do. He shook it off.

By comparing faerie tale to recorded history, he believed the first of the Aurlings had come the day after the world shook. He etched away at the paper:

> *Many texts speak of a great quake that shook the world. It was a convulsion that began at midday and rumbled on until twilight. University texts refer to this event as the Great Shift, as the world settled into its final form. Period writings from Eisen describe the event as the formation of the far-off fire mountain of Calderra. While rare Swarhee religious texts deliciously describe the long jolt as the shattering of a crystal veil that once shrouded our world.*

He crossed out the word *deliciously*, thought about it briefly, and then inked it back in.

> *Not long after this jolt, a speechless man had walked into the village of Odannah, shamelessly naked. He—for there had been no doubt as to his gender—was flawless in his features, and kingly and precise in his movements. He had walked through the village and witnessed the commerce of life, as if for the first time. The man stooped to observe a child, and the two looked at each other, their faces painted with the same sense of wonder. A brave lady approached the naked man and wrapped an apron around his waist before backing away quickly. He appeared to appreciate the gesture and smiled. It was at this point the guards approached the man and grabbed his arms. The man easily brushed the sentries aside. They retook their detainee, and gripped tightly at his arms. The tales told mostly of his face, and how his*

calm, nearly emotionless features fell dark. He scowled at the guards, and all in the village felt scolded as if by a parent. The man grabbed both guards by the arms and...

Edwin lifted his pen. No, no, no, he thought and peered out the bright window. This is a scholarly paper, do not drift into gore. "Yet the tale must be told," he whispered and wrote on:

How quickly the poor guards shriveled up. Their skin sunk to their bones, and their lips stretched tightly across their teeth. Even their eyes collapsed like grapes left in the sun. So swiftly the guards dried up in that creature's grip, they never had chance to scream. The creature released his hold and two dry husks of men crumbled to the ground, swaying in the afternoon breeze. Calm bewilderment returned to the creature's face, and he continued his tour of the village.

Edwin sat back and pondered the tale. He had tried his best to separate fact from fiction, history from faerie tale, but his work still seemed fantastic. Had he never seen the creature in the woods, he too would have been skeptical. University had taught him that.

More creatures had arrived over the years, much the same as this first. Yet many were different. Some arrived fully aware of their surroundings and fluent in the local tongue. Some Aurlings controlled frightful skills akin to magic, while others possessed skills not worthy of a hack-penny side-show. Yet all were magical and unique in their own way, and that scared the people of Eisen. Aurlings were strong, but the people of Eisen were resourceful. One by one, and often with the aid of proselyte Aurlings, these creatures were rounded up, cast into Nerikan Prison, and sealed away.

This ogre must be an Aurling, Edwin thought, while leafing through the pages. The stories were quite old. He checked for dates. They spanned the ages, but by his estimation the age of the Aurlings ended eight generations ago.

"Two hundred thirty years," he said aloud, and scratched the back of his head. "That would mean that *thing* wandered the halls of Nerikan for two hundred thirty years!"

He was again drawn to the sunlight cascading over the front gates and felt the urge to go out and greet the morning. He slammed the shutters closed and hefted another stack of documents onto the tabletop. There was a lifetime of information in front of him, and he was already an old man. He must work now. He continued in his fancy script:

> *The history of the Brennan ironworkers shows that it was they who were commissioned to build the Nerikan gates. The legend goes on to explain the three-ringed design on the gates as representing—*

The last word drifted off the page as he dropped the pen. His jittery hand floated up to the dark shutters and lifted a slat. He stared in wonder at the front gate to Millthrace. "Oh no," he muttered. It was that old familiar feeling. It had returned, that tug and pull that always drew him away from his schoolwork and on to his next great observation.

It had first happened when he was a young man of University and just starting to make friends. Something inside him had insisted he leave the campus and traverse the Euloren Woods. Weeks later, as he neared the eastern edge of the forest, he had come across a flower that he knew did not belong. As he observed the lone blossom, one by one its petals turned grey and fell. He later learned it was named Stargazer Lily, and it had been quite the last one.

They were not always grand journeys. Sometimes the urge merely sent him down dark halls, or across campus. But every journey always ended in an observation, no matter how cryptic.

And now the sensation had returned. It was a fanciful feeling starting low in his spine and climbing up to the base of his skull, tickling as it went. It made his heart thump, his neck tingle, and his eyes glow. It was overall a very good feeling, which he hated completely.

He could fight it no longer. Edwin the Observer was needed at the gates.

***

Olen yawned as she dragged a wooden folding stand across the boardwalk towards the gates, clacking and rattling it past drowsy traders. The otherwise silent workers pulled tarps off their carts as others hauled goods down from Midtown. She found a spot where the boards were not warped and kicked open the stand's legs. Maggie followed along carrying a tray of old bread and a tiny box of nails which had been selectively pulled from the Ward's own walls by Haggart. She sat the tray on Olen's stand and rushed back to the Ward waving goodbye over her back. None of the girls had even looked at Olen crookedly when she had left in the morning. Perhaps Philippa had not said a word after all.

Olen had not said anything either, but she had thought about it all night. She had thought out a chain of events that made perfect sense to her: Aurlings used magic. She could do this magical thing with her clothes, so she must be an Aurling. Children get pieces of themselves from their parents, so her parents must be Aurlings also. And that is why, she had thought as she had drifted off last night, her magical Aurling parents were still out there, just hiding away, waiting for that moment to come rescue her.

She placed her palms on the table and shook the cobwebs out of her head. She was tired, and her head was full of thoughts and ideas, but she also had to work, at least a little. She was barker for the day, the sister who bargained for work for the Ward. She needed to shake clear her mind for a few hours and pull in some coppers, or else it was back to river duty. She loved being the barker, though she was rarely allowed to do it due to her habit of wandering away.

Barkers worked deals for most any domestic chore. For just a hack— or wedge as the travelers called half-pennies—a tradesman could have his textiles washed and mended without ever leaving his stand. And even though Mistress Haggart would never admit it, everyone at the Ward knew barking was also a form of begging. Wealthier townspeople and politicians who had the unfortunate luck of passing through Lowtown were immediately set upon by barkers. These swarming children begged to wash already bright clean garments, pleaded to carry light loads, and offered damaged trinkets to those accustomed only to finery. These marks either passed straight through, blatantly ignoring the children or sometimes pushing them away violently. But every now and then a nobleman, embarrassed by his entourage in rags, would toss a copper penny far away, sending the kids scrambling while he escaped to Uptown. Olen had never caught one of those pennies, but she felt today may be her day. She stretched her back, cracked her knuckles, and began.

"Wash your pots!" she called out to no one in particular. "Fresh bread, just five days old!" And like birds in the breaking dawn, she had launched a chorus. "Leathers and furs," another merchant called out, still setting up his shop. "Apples," chirped another. And soon all of Lowtown were singing their wares.

Two men in stag-skins and worn-out traveling shoes carried a box down the wide Midtown staircase. Their long lean faces showed them to be father and son. A burlap tarp covered their long thin box. Hidden things intrigued Olen, and she wanted to know what was in that box. She checked the river for Haggart, then laid a towel over her stand before running up to the traders.

"What's the wares, gentlemen?" she asked pleasantly.

"Onions," the younger man said, as his father pulled him along. "Freshly dug two days ago."

They had not had onions at the Ward even longer than they had had apples.

"Fair trade?" she asked, pulling a potato out of her pocket.

She had sat awake much of the past night in Haggart's room waiting for the lights down the hall to finally die out. After what felt like hours, they had finally dimmed and Haggart closed the doors to the parlor. Olen had then scurried back down to the basement and found her potatoes right where she had dropped them.

The younger trader said to his father, "It does sound fair, Baboo, does it not?"

The old man sat the box down and snatched the potato. He examined it like a rare jewel, looking for flaws. But this gem was flawless. A caged rooster called to the morning.

"Too small," he rumbled, slapping it back into her hands.

"Two for one," she said, showing them the other potato. She had no use for these potatoes and would accept nearly any bad trade. But when the younger man stared at it as if it were steak, she knew she had them. "How many days have you been eating onion soup?"

"Baboo?" the younger asked.

The older man was beaten. He ripped back the burlap tarp and told her to drop them in. Then he grabbed a fat yellow onion and tossed it far behind her.

"Thank you!" she said, as she rushed over and cornered the rolling vegetable. "One more thing," she called back to the men. "Have either of you been to Kessel?" The father grunted and pulled his son along. They mingled into the crowd and took their place in front of the gates of Millthrace. A line of men, women, and donkey carts lined up there, waiting for the gates to open. "Guess not," she said. She sniffed her prize and thought onion soup did not sound too bad. She stuffed it into her pocket and skipped in heavy boots back over to her stand.

"Wash your pots!" she bellowed, startling an Uptowner in green leggings.

A few small barters later and the guard atop the front gates gave the signal. The gatesman below kicked the pole. It was time to open the gate. The channel flooded with water, and the large wheel spun in the plaza. Slowly the massive fangs of the Millthrace gate eased out of the ground. A cloaked man hurried past Olen, nearly knocking her to the ground. His brown robes were caked with dirt.

"Cleric!" she called out, racing after him, again abandoning her stand. Religious men always had money on them, though it took a little work to get them to share. She caught up and tugged at his cloak. "Wash and mend your clothes, cleric?"

The old man tore the brown hood off his head and exclaimed, "I am no Cleric! I am an Historian from University and I must say...the talk of the town!"

It was the educator she had seen speak at the Eagle and Trout. It was the man who had spoken of Nerikan demons. "I'm sorry," she stammered, stepping back as if he knew her secret.

"If I had a silver honor for every profession you people have accused me of, I could purchase the halls of University," he said. "Cleric!"

A regiment of six guards marched down the Midtown stairs. Sergeant Koertig was leading his group on morning rounds to ensure order at the gates. This time she did not have the chance to hide. The soldiers paused near her as the old Historian raved on.

"A problem with a trade, Storyteller?" Koertig asked dryly, looking down on them both.

"No, no problem," the robed man said, still angry. "Just abject frustration with the uneducated factions that seem to populate this bitter land."

Koertig posted his men and returned to Midtown as Olen slinked back to her stand. That could have gone a lot worse, she thought as Koertig disappeared up the stairs. The storyteller could have recognized her as a Nerikan witch and set Koertig upon her. Instead, the old man seemed to dismiss her from his thoughts and continued off to the gates.

She would have to ask book-smart Clara what *abject* and *factions* meant.

The massive gate reached the top and the exchange of goods began. A train of carts rolled out of the city, loaded with goods made in Millthrace. There were sacks of grain freshly milled, tall lumber logs cut precisely on whirling blades, and war weapons and farming tools honed sharp on revolving stones. Families moved out, riding trailers loaded with knitted finery, baked goods, and dried meats for outlying towns. Following behind were the fancy carriages with Uptown travelers heading out for business or pleasure.

When all of the city's merchants and travelers had moved out, those that had waited beyond the gates finally filtered in. This was why the Ward needed a barker, and why it was time for Olen to work. With their carts and clothes dirty from the road, these were the people from which she could always negotiate work. But as a parade of tired travelers walked and rolled by, she mostly just asked if anyone was from Kessel, as she searched their faces for dark eyes like her own.

***

Edwin still fumed at being pulled away from his dissertation. Once again that hidden urge had taken over his body—indeed his soul—and had pulled him away from his proper work. At least, he thought, as he shuffled through the plaza, this time he was only being drawn to the gates of Millthrace and not a village in a far country, because if that were so, he would have no choice but to follow the siren's call.

"Cleric," he muttered to himself, after leaving the street girl behind. He believed himself to be just the opposite of a cleric; he was a man of science and learning, not fantasy. He watched the tradesmen tramp in from the wilds beyond Millthrace. Perhaps there was a man among these common farm-folk he was supposed to meet. Maybe a rare item hidden amongst these goods he was to discover.

She had seemed frightened to see him, he thought, his mind returning to the market girl. He surmised she had not met many men of his stature while selling wares in the street. University men could be quite intimidating, especially to the unschooled.

He had shouldered his way deep into the crowd, searching faces and carts, even staring down passing cattle, hoping to feel that trigger in his bones.

Besides, he thought, the poor girl spends her days working in the square when she should be getting an education. "Damn her parents!"

Oxmen rolled their carts and a few approached him with their wares, but nobody gave him that sensation that said this was why he was here. That girl, he thought, as a tickle traveled up his spine. That poor, poor, child in the street.

Then he shook his shoulders and said aloud, "That child!"

He turned back from the gate and saw her. She held the dirty clothes of a thin travel-woman and poked her finger through a hole. They seemed to be bargaining on a price, and then shook on a deal. It's not the gate, he thought, as all of Lowtown seemed washed away in a blur and the child's focus grew ever clearer. It's the girl. He walked her way, pushing past weary tradesmen. How crowded the square had become in so short a time! He peered over shoulders. There was something about this child he needed to observe. She showed the older tradeswoman a small object, a vegetable of some kind, but the woman waved her off.

Finally pushing through, he emerged. "You there!" he shouted, and the girl spun around guiltily.

"It's not stolen," she said, stuffing the onion in her pocket.

Shouts rang out from above the main gate. The guard high in the tower called furiously to the gatesman below. Yet he was no longer like a guard, proud in his tall post. He was childlike and cowering as he tossed his helm over the side and hurried down the tall ladder. The lower gatesman, eager to get the first take on new arrivals, had strayed away from his post. He ran back to the waterwheel and offered a hand to the guard, only to be shoved aside as the officer leapt the final few feet and fled into the city. Only then did the gatesman see what others had seen beyond the gate. He kicked shut the sluice and escaped up the Midtown stairway, Lowtown be damned. Water spilled from the channel, and the massive gate began to slide back to the ground. Straggling traders hurried under the wide wooden teeth, pushing and pulling their carts just past the enormous tree trunk spikes, risking crushing death over some unseen threat from the fields. Edwin did not need to see to know what approached.

"More wolves?" the girl asked, sidling next to him.

"Worse," he said, as the last men and women rushed through the gate, screaming. The frantic traders pushed through the crowd and dashed up the staircase to Midtown. And just as the great gate of Millthrace dropped nearly to the ground, two gargantuan hands reached underneath, stopping it cold.

"The Aurling," she said, stepping forward. "It's real!"

He grabbed her shoulder and held her back. Tradesmen abandoned their oxen, carts, and indeed all of their worldly possessions. The two huge hands, each one larger than a trader's crate, squeezed tightly around the bottom of the gate and lifted. The massive door moved but slightly as the spinning waterwheel forced it down. A groaning, like the tallest tree in the forest slowly falling, came from behind the door and it moved up faintly. The forced gate pressed on its gears, slowing the waterwheel. A great strained growl groaned behind the doorway. The hands and arms pulled again, and the wheel slowed to halt. Water splashed over the sluice and flooded the square. Another great groan from behind the gate and the waterwheel began spinning backwards.

Save yourself, thought Edwin as the gears tore apart and the wheel collapsed below the boardwalk. Run away back to University. Yet still he stood fixated, not on the gate, and not on the creature beyond. Despite the chaos and terror that shook Lowtown, he felt a calm certainty in his core that he was exactly where he was supposed to be and at exactly the right time. And the reason he was here was to see this child and know that she was alive.

"You're a part of this," he said as more of a question, as traders rushed past them.

She looked up to him and said, "I hope so."

The gigantic gate rose higher, and with a heave broke open. Then with one arm holding the gate high above its head, the prisoner of Nerikan stepped into the city of Millthrace.

* * *

Philippa brushed the chairs in the parlor. The finest room at the Ward would be one of the nastiest of Midtown, or the most shameful of Uptown. The walls still held most of the paper that had been pasted on years before she had arrived. Light blue forget-me-nots trailed up each panel like tiny azure footprints. And while the chairs and settees here were as threadbare as an old horse blanket, they were brushed and washed weekly to keep them fresh and clean.

She had been met with disgruntled sighs last night when she had woken Ellery, Clara, and Lysa—the three older sisters. It wasn't so much that they had not believed her about Olen, it seemed more so that they had simply not cared. The three had turned away in their cots and slept as Philippa had laid awake wondering what she could do.

Maggie slid open the tall door and asked what she was supposed to do next.

"I helped Olen get the stand," she said. "And there's nothing at the river today, yet."

Philippa said she could either help her clean the parlor, or she could go outside until lunchtime and play with Renata and Katia. The little blonde sister was gone before she got the second name out.

She brushed and scrubbed the room, gently washing the walls. It did not feel like work, cleaning this parlor. There was something about this one beautiful place in this otherwise decrepit Ward that she loved, and even if she was sick or hobbled or tired beyond measure, she would still find the strength to keep this one thing perfect.

Between the chairs she straightened Haggart's books of verse, then noticed one was not a poetry folio. She unfolded the paper and leafed through the freshly cut pages. A suddenly familiar word stood out amongst the many tightly printed pages. *Nerikan.* She skimmed the paragraphs and saw emerge the tale of an Aurling whose buttery voice had sent men into madness and mayhem. Philippa folded back to the cover and saw that she held an old book of faerie tales. Not the kind of which were spoken in humorous jest to children. This was a book to either frighten—or warn—adults...and Haggart was studying it.

Screams shattered the quiet, and Philippa jumped, dropping the book. Out the window tradesmen raced past the Ward, with nowhere to go but the river. Philippa tore open the glass only to hear more screams. There was a vast commotion near the front gate. She called for Maggie and her sisters to come back in, and then slammed the window shut. She picked the folio off the floor and stuffed it into her apron's pouch before running out to round up her sisters.

9

⧉

Miss Egg's Marmoreal Repose

Four city guards clambered down the wide stairway and rushed past Olen, their armor clanging like washing pots. They skidded to a halt when they saw what awaited them. It was like the legendary elefant, minus the flailing snout. Crackled grey skin hung loosely over long muscles as the beast tore open shipping crates and scooped whatever it found down its wide gullet. It champed and swallowed, grunting like a mating auroch. The guards dared go no closer, and even turned to Olen and the robed man as if asking what to do.

Run away, she thought. It's not here for you. The old man was right, I'm a part of this. This Aurling creature is here for the witch, an emissary from her parents, finally come to take her home. Anywhere but Nerikan, she added. She had asked for something like this, well not exactly like this, but for years she had begged for rescue. So often on those long nights, as the evening dark held off the dawn, she had lain in bed wishing on the stars for rescue. I am here, she had repeated in her mind, sending her thoughts across the universe to her magical parents, come find me. And if you cannot come, send any enchanted creature you desire. I will trust you and follow.

That was the promise she had made, but now as the gigantic creature tore about Lowtown, she was not sure she could go anywhere with this monster.

It rose up like a rearing horse and searched the Square. The guards shrunk as it loomed above them, its long arms hanging nearly to the ground. This must be what it is like to stand before a god, she thought, awesome wonder coupled with petrifying fear.

It wore what appeared to be burlap shipping sacks, torn apart and then crudely sewn into a poncho-like top, with yellow twine binding the seams. At its low waist, more twine circled its hips as the long tunic hung down over its thighs. Even young Maggie would have stitched a finer shirt. An empty burlap sack hung off its neck on a long rope. Iron clasps bound both wrists and ankles. The right wrist dangled a chain. It whipped its rusty black chain against a crate, crushing it. Brown potatoes flew about.

The ogre moaned and kicked the potatoes away, bashing open another crate in frustration. Large orange pumpkins fell out. He seemed delighted at this and pulled the giant sack off of his shoulders. He filled the burlap sack with ripe pumpkins and moved on.

It was at this very moment that Olen's opinion of the Aurling changed. Her clenched fists relaxed and the pounding in her chest dropped to her belly, forcing out a little laugh. A creature that loved pumpkins and hated potatoes might not be something to be feared. Perhaps she would be leaving Millthrace after all, racing along behind this creature on one of Schmid's horses, following him home.

But then the creature hoisted the potato crate and launched it at the row houses near the Midtown stairs, buckling an upper floor balcony. A woman screamed inside, and a laundry line collapsed to the boardwalk, and again, Olen wasn't so sure.

The group of four guards must have regained their wits, for they finally approached him. They stepped forward slowly, spears drawn, like children challenging an ox. The giant man, undaunted by the approaching soldiers, bashed open a wide barrel. Bright yellow corn lit up the creature's eyes like sunlight. He swept a handful into his sack.

A guardsman she knew as Martz ran up from behind and launched his spear, gouging the creature just below his shoulder blade. The giant swung a backhand, swatting Martz across the yard. He landed in a heap near the sluice, clutching his ribs. Two more soldiers launched themselves at the ogre. But the giant man was ready this time. He snatched up the soldiers like a couple of dolls and held them off the ground. It was an effortless feat to this massive creature, holding these men with no greater strain than when Olen had delivered chickens to the butcher, her arms out before her, dangling the squawking birds by their yellow feet. The Nerikan beast squeezed his fists, and the men cried out as their armor buckled around their chest.

"Stop!" Olen shouted, drawing the wild man's gaze.

The storyteller that had stood beside her this whole time took one long step backwards. Then he quickly sidled over to the blacksmith's shop and tried the locked door. Defeated, he scurried away up the Midtown stairs leaving Olen, as always, alone.

"Don't do it!" she yelled at the creature. "Let them go!" There was something about him, his movements, calculated and precise, that told her he was not a wild beast, not a mindless killer. There were thoughts in his head, thoughts no different from any man or woman. It was his eyes, she realized. His eyes were ancient and wise. Despite his looks, this was no monster.

He roared and hoisted the men like a trophy catch as she moved closer, taking easy non-threatening steps, hands up. Again, his face. Just like a man's, though stretched and pulled to cover a great skull. He roared like a monster, but she knew, this was just a man. A very big man.

And she had worked with men all her short life.

She dug into her pocket.

"Trade," she said, and offered the vegetable. "Onion. Trade only," she said defiantly, and rolled it over.

He still held the guardsmen aloft while the injured Martz was pulled away from the sluice. The monster's raging had subsided and he seemed to be considering her offer, considering her. She was right, he had thoughts, he was thinking.

"That's all I've got," she said, and held up her empty palms. "One onion for two men."

Still the creature considered the little girl as the soldiers ceased crying out and their eyes fell closed.

"Please," she begged, "They're dying."

The beast looked shamefully at the men in his hands and set them down onto a pile of broken crates. One regained his breath quickly and pulled his fellow soldier away.

"Thank you," she said to the pile of muscle and skin standing before her, but he did not appear proud of himself. When the soldiers were all gone he rode heavy steps over to her. She stood stone-like as he crouched low and brought his face to hers.

"What?" she asked nervously, her head craned back. She wanted to touch his face, as if feeling some grand statue. His dark chestnut hair hung in ropes, ropes coated in oil, dust, and debris. His nose was a wide bellows, pulsing with each inhale, and his eyes—brown and wise —rolled over her slowly, steadily. He was studying her as much as she was him.

His features shifted to a certain look of disappointment, as if after studying her he had determined she was not what he had hoped. He pressed his snout against her shirt and sniffed around at her armpits. She swatted his nose, a reflex she regretted instantly. He roared at her, a thundersome blast furnace that pushed her back a step.

"I'm sorry," she said quickly, and held up her palms. "Sometimes I just react." They stood together, inhaling each other's scent. Hers was of river-water and smoke from the kitchen fire; his was musky like a leather tarp. "That man," she said, indicating the absent storyteller, "He thinks I'm the reason you are here."

The creature measured her silently as he took deep breaths.

"Did my parents send you?" she asked. "Are you here to take me home?"

He again smelled her shirt, and then jerked his head high and sniffed the air. He pounded the ground with his fists and then snatched up the onion and his sack. He tossed a dented tin cooking pot into his bag and then loped up the grand staircase to Midtown.

When he was out of sight Olen reached inside her shirt near her armpit and pulled out the jerked mutton. The butcher, she thought, and ran.

*** *

"That girl is going to get me killed," Edwin said, as he scurried away from the market square and headed to Midtown. The creature's roar faded behind the tall row buildings. "You cannot reason with beasts!" He quickly strode across the tall boardwalk, and after several frantic wrong turns finally found his rented room. "She is part of this, somehow." As he neared Miss Egg's house he fumbled through his pockets for his barrel key. The boardwalk rumbled as he found the metal piece. The rumbling grew, and he saw what he feared. The ogre was climbing up the wide staircase from Lowtown.

"He's eaten the girl, and now he wants his pudding!" he whimpered as he crowded the doorway. Nervously he jammed his key at the eyehole, but the hole jumped and bounced. The key clanked against the metal knob, knocking free of his fingers and falling between the uneven slats of the Midtown boardwalk.

"Dammit!" he called out, drawing the unwanted attention of the monster.

The ogre approached, and the aging scholar pressed his back against the wooden door. With his balled knuckles he gave a flurry of quick short raps against the door behind him. "Miss Egg," he stage-whispered, in a crying voice, "I've lost my key. Miss Egg?"

The behemoth swung his large head up to Edwin's face and poked him in the chest. "Treeee," it said in a voice that shook his innards.

"Yes," Edwin gasped, stunned the creature could speak. "Yes, so you saw me in the tree then? Very good. Carry on."

The beast sniffed the breeze and stomped away to Uptown. Across the way, movement on the rooftop caught Edwin's eye. Atop the mayor's office, Sergeant Koertig adjusted his gear as footmen strapped on his armor. He stared down at Edwin, much like he did at the Eagle and

Trout. Judging him, convicting him, and now just awaiting sentence; for what, Edwin did not know. Just then Miss Egg opened the door, and he fell back into her arms. She wore a soft cap, a thick sleeping gown, and smelled of vaporated gin.

"What's with all the bangin' then? I was dead asleep!" she growled, dropping Edwin to his backside. "A lady needs 'er nap."

He kicked the door shut as Koertig turned towards the creature.

***

When the beast had left the square, Olen knew he would lose himself in the insane labyrinth known as Midtown. It was the largest of the boroughs and the one that had changed the most over the years, with homes and rows and bridges and troughs built not according to an artist's design, but following instead the demands of the falls and flows of the Oiskonn River. Because of this, the borough of Midtown had become a maze that often confused even the locals. But she knew a quicker way.

She hurried over to the Well and leapt from crate to cart and up to the ledge. She spun around, crouching low and swung her legs into the wooden pit, dangling them in the slick-sided Well. No one was left in the Square to see an escape she had only ever made at night. She kicked blindly, searching for the hidden notch, the river rolling one very long scream below. Her boots caught the top notch, and she eased herself down the wet logs. She climbed down two more levels of log, and four of stone before jumping to the shore next to the fast moving river. Daylight beamed down from the Well and the knot-holed boardwalk, illuminating the Escapement like the sun through spotty clouds. She ran upstream, certain to pass the creature before it ever neared the Uptown butcher.

Across wet shores and in and out of brick sewers she ran towards Midtown. She had always seen the Scape as the back of a clock with its many gears and levers constantly clacking ahead. She hung one-handed from a horizontal waterwheel that swung her over a stream, then she pulled herself up a rocky crag. Makeshift bridges of driftwood and old boards spanned across the branching rivulets. She next caught a ride on a waterwheel to the next level up the mountain, and continued on in checkered light. It was a path she could follow with her eyes shut. The pounding on the boardwalk let her know she was gaining on the creature, as his wayward steps searched for a path through the Midtown labyrinth of shops, homes, and storage buildings. A long knotted rope, purloined from Haggart's cellar, dangled from the rafters leading up a cliff to Uptown. She shimmied up it without slowing. From here she leapt into the sewer Embers, then over to Worm and Big Boy, and then back into her secret chamber.

The massive wheel churned far above, sending spray and rainbows into her room. That wheel, that hole in the ceiling was her exit. She hurried over to the collapsed boulder and dug out her tin box. She grabbed the silver coin and held it up. She would need this if she truly was leaving Millthrace.

Leaving Millthrace, she realized and paused. Leaving Haggart and her sisters. Then something unexpected happened. For a moment, she was sad. A pang in her chest wanted her to say goodbye to the Ward and everyone in it. She shook the thought away and stuffed the coin in her pocket. She had wanted this for so long, she would not allow doubts now. Then she set the tin box back in the sand.

She ran into the river and waded out as far as she could. Then she swam the short distance to the tall iron and wood pylon that braced Uptown. She climbed onto the first wide beam. *Seven levels*, she thought, daring herself higher. The boardwalk rumbled and dust and debris shook loose from the floor boards. He had already found his way to the upper borough! Seven levels, then across the beam. He was nearing; he had smelled the meats curing in Uptown. She would have to cross the high beam, push past the waterfall's spray, and then leap through the opening to the outside.

She scurried up to the second level, and then the third.

Not even halfway to the top, she forced herself to the fourth riser. She held tight to the pylon, feeling a phantom swaying in the sturdy beams. The fifth level, the sixth, and she paused before the last. The iron-bound wooden risers here were damp with moss. She had always wanted an escape from the city, but she did not need to die trying to make it happen.

Bungplugs be dammed, she thought, and pulled herself to the top beam. The boardwalk hung low here, and shook from the manic townspeople racing about. She hung her head just below the boards. Standing hunched over, she held both hands to the ceiling while walking heel-to-toe across the long beam.

She stepped lightly, acrobat-like, across the wet hardwood as a strong mist sprayed her. Blinded, she wiped away the water and moved one step closer to the waterfall. The water crashed over the cliff, though through the spray she could no longer see the whirlpool stirring far below.

The churning wheel and roaring water pounded in her ears. She eased ahead slowly, feet firmly on the beam and palms tight against the ceiling. She neared the cliff edge as now water, not just mist, splashed against her. She had to push harder.

She thought of Samantha, the sister who had encountered an entire Raider horde and had simply pushed on through. Now here Olen stood confounded by spraying water, she thought, and told herself once again to be bold. She raised her heels off the beam and dashed ahead. She ran across the wet beam and leapt onto the cliff edge, rolling herself onto to the dry lip. She kicked herself through the gap and was outside of the city lying in green grass and staring at the blue sky.

A wide barrier of tall logs circled Millthrace, but rats knew of secret passages through small holes. Already to her feet and running, Olen pushed through thick green chaparral to the rampart wall and searched for a panel she had only seen from the inside. Behind a thin tree she found the small weatherboard pressed against the rampart. Hidden behind was a fissure in the bulwark. Who had made this hole she did not know, and who had poorly mended it she did not care. She pulled the panel aside and forced her thin body through the crack. With a final tight push, she was in the bright fantasy known as Uptown.

There was much less boardwalk this far up the city, and even less strife. Here many homes and stores stood upon the grass and stone of the mountain, each with its own small waterwheel churning at its side. Trees and ferns grew along short open spans of river. And colorful birds flitted from leaf to lane, unafraid of being snatched up and eaten by hungry Lowtowners. Here the air smelled naturally like the lilac perfumes Midtown ladies bathed in. And here throughout Uptown permeated a certain wealthy calm. Usually.

The creature tossed an empty barrel over the rampart walls as the screaming masses scattered. A man in a flamboyant tunic with dark leggings, the type who normally would never travel downstream without a valet, tossed his tea cup into the flowage and raced down the stairs to Midtown, scandalously hatless. Two girls, in bright flowing dresses as if ready for an autumn dance, tore at each other trying outpace the other to the shelter of home. Others cried, some fell ill and collapsed, while many more sat back in wooden chairs, smoking long pipes and watching it all unfold as if seated before the pageant wagon. And still the birds danced and flopped in the Uptown trees.

Olen ran across a grassy park and cut inside the smokehouse.

It was a squat and solid structure for fancy Uptown, made all of brick with three stone chimneys and only two small windows. Butchers and smokers may have seemed unlikely shops for this fine borough, but their product was just as precious as the jewelers and furriers. And she was certain it was their jerked mutton that had lured the creature.

Two men in bloody white aprons lay on the floor behind the counter. They held their hands over their heads and whimpered. Olen pulled her belly up onto the counter and reached behind it, snatching away a long rope of linked sausages.

"Hey!" a butcher cried, swiping meekly at Olen's hands before again covering his head as the creature roared.

She ran back outside and saw the giant tearing open balconies, looking for the smokehouse.

"Here!" she called out, holding up the sausages. For a second time the creature stilled and considered the child. "Is this what you want?" she asked. "Come and get it!" This time the beast's deliberation was brief as he pounded the ground and leapt at her.

She turned and ran, ducking back through the uneven ramparts. As she tore through the tight beams, she snagged her skirt on a splintered beam, dropping her to the ground. Her shoulders and head were out of the city, but her lower half dangled within. Then, for the first time for anyone to see, she let that ripple travel over her frame. A tingle, then a tickle down her spine, and her skirt and top tightened to a sleek body suit. She slipped free of the snag and kicked herself away as seemingly a herd of cattle crashed against the rampart walls, bowing the beams and spraying splinters. She rolled to her feet and scurried into the woods as the beast wailed and attacked the back wall of Millthrace.

The whole wall shook as a wave thundered through the ramparts. It was only a few angry punches before timber cracked like overhead thunder. Iron hinges snapped, wooden beams split, and like a gate the back wall to Millthrace fell forward. The ogre walked across the logs, dragging his gigantic sack of food, looking for the girl. She had hidden in the bushes and let her clothes recede back to rags. When both the meat and the girl were nowhere to be seen, he let out a cry not of rage but of heart-rending defeat.

Then the creature loped towards the woods seemingly unaware of all the horror and destruction he had just caused. As he neared the forest, she jumped out of the bushes.

"Wait!" she called out, startling the creature. He jerked and dropped his sack, spraying corn and pumpkins on the ground. "Sorry," she said, though she laughed as she said it.

He growled at her as he swept up his food, then he moved on into the woods.

She ran after him. "You're an Aurling," she said. He kept walking, but his gravely breaths became more and more agitated like a rabid hound readying a strike. "You escaped from Nerikan!" she insisted.

He swung his sack over her head and toppled a tree. She dove and rolled away as the tall timber crashed to the ground. He walked on, but she caught up, scurrying around just out of his reach. "Is it true? Are there others like you?" she asked, tugging on the sewn sacks he wore as a shirt. He turned, but her quick feet darted about, like a small dog annoying a bear. "Just talk to me!" she demanded, and the creature stopped and threw the sack to the ground with a thud.

Back in the city, Koertig had rounded up the city guard. The soldiers assembled at the back wall as women and older men handed them weapons.

"Here," Olen said, tossing the string of sausages at the monster's feet. She stood beside him, her head reaching only to his hips. He waited, staring at her, before finally reaching for the meat. He snatched it up and stuffed the entire rope into his mouth, chewing loudly.

"Watch this," she said. She held her arms out to her side. A wavelike blur ran down her skirt and apron, and then back up. When it passed, she was dressed in crudely sewn burlap just like the creature, though much, much smaller. "How come I can do this?" she asked.

She had hoped for a reaction, to startle him, excite him, but instead his shoulders dropped and his head fell. He was not impressed she could do magic; he was troubled, concerned. Concerned for her. She thought he would be happy to see this, not burdened with some new worry.

The cavalry pushed their horses through the crowd and set ranks atop the fallen wall. Foot-soldiers lined up behind the riders, and an impromptu militia of townspeople followed behind, carrying makeshift weapons of garden tools.

The giant man grasped her lightly in his wide hand, lifting her to the treetops. He looked between the girl and the militia, back and forth, as if debating what to do. "Take me with you," she said. "I'm not afraid."

His hands were rougher than stones, though he held her softly. The broken chain dangled from his scarred wrist and swung against his legs. Up his arms and along his entire body were white scars, as if he'd been tortured and stabbed over and over again with a fiery blacksmith's cone. She touched a rough scar on his arm and wondered at the horrors he had endured in Nerikan.

"Who are you?" she asked.

His wide head turned to the fallen gate and the men assembling there, then back to her, his eyes anything but bestial. In a slow gravelly voice he answered, "Bakku."

"Bakku," she repeated, smiling at him. He did not smile back.

Bakku looked far beyond the horizon and seemed to reach a conclusion. He took a deep inhale and let the breath fall out slowly, then he sat her on a tall branch and loped off into the woods carrying his sack of food.

"Wait!" she called out from her perch. "Do you know my parents? They're Aurlings too! Take me with you!"

Bakku rushed off into the dense forest that led to the rising mountains behind Millthrace. His heavy footsteps shook the land, and slowly drifted off like distant thunder. Olen sat high above the ground, watching her only hope for answers run away.

Bakku was a hazy blur cresting a hill deep in the forest when Koertig's army arrived under Olen's tree. She ignored their shouts to come down and watched the magical man. And just before he disappeared into the mountain fog, the great creature Bakku paused and looked back. Olen smiled.

An Unfocused Spyglass

An hour after she was pulled out of the tree, Olen sat kicking her heels on a desk in the mayor's office. A sharply sweet scent stung her. Men had smoked here in more casual times. Policies and strategies had been formed in this room, campaigns finalized with a shared pipe. A sketched map of the city hung on the wall in front of her. These people needed a map for a city she could prowl through in total darkness. It did not even show the tiny cut-through corridors and nearly invisible drop-down hatches she had ferreted out over the years. Another sketch showed the vast Millthrace Escapement. The tunnel she had named Worm was there, along with Sulphur, slow-moving deep-watered Bath, and all the others. On the map, the sewers were simply numbered.

A fair-haired clerk snatched a cluster of charters away from under her damp backside. She shrugged her shoulders not caring, she was *told* to sit here. *He looked at me*, she thought, thinking of the giant man. *He turned back and looked at me.* Men scrambled in and out of the upper-level room shouting out numbers and assumptions about things she did not understand. The great Aurling had disappeared into the mountains, but he had taken the thought of her with him.

The office door burst open, rattling plaques. Above the entrance hung a ceremonial golden saber. Yellow cords dangled from its scab-bard, and tiny words saluting Mayor-General Brynn were etched along the blade. Were it solid gold, one could purchase all of Uptown with it. Olen was certain this ceremonial blade was the closest the mayor had ever been to actual combat. A soldier stuck his head in the room and shouted a damage report. Mayor Brynn could hardly be bothered as he and his men huddled over a long table while scratching dark lines on a checkered map and circling the most vulnerable parts of the city. Sergeant Koertig thanked the man and led him out. He approached Olen.

"It spoke to you," Koertig said harshly. "What did it say?"

"Just *his* name," she answered coolly. "You may call him Bakku."

Had the streets of Millthrace not trained her to read the subtleties of expression, she would have missed the robed city-worker, Reeve was his name, who paused just a moment at that strange name and let a smile curl up one cheek. And just as quickly as that tiny grin was born it died away as he rejoined Brynn and the dire talk of a city under siege.

"I have a guard that may never walk again, two more with crushed ribs who suffer with every breath," Koertig said, as if accusing her of a crime. "The gate and back wall destroyed, leaving this city vulnerable to Raiders. Yet this beast greets you kindly, and sets you out of harm's way. Why is that?" He leaned in tight.

Why the older girls at the Ward gossiped dreamily about this man she would never understand. He was handsome in a way, she allowed, for a man twice her age. But while her sisters debated about why the young sergeant had never taken a wife, Olen knew the answer. No Mid or Uptown lady would ever suffer such biting arrogance.

"I asked you a question," Koertig said. "Why did the creature spare you?"

Olen met his glare. "I fed him," she said dryly. She once feared this man, but after chasing an ogre through Millthrace, Koertig just seemed so...small.

A clerk leapt up the narrow steps and strode into the room carrying a thin roll of papers. He announced them as adoption papers and told Koertig the mistress had not been about the Ward, but that another had helped him. He handed them to the sergeant and saluted before leaving. Koertig looked at the first page and declared her a Kessel orphan, but she had already known that. What she had not known was that these papers existed at all, or that they had sat inside the Ward all these years. Koertig turned the page.

"I see you have a benefactor in Kessel who has kept *you* fed," he said accusingly.

"Let me see," she said, swiping the papers. It was the first new evidence of her past. She had always looked outside the Ward for answers, never thinking to look within. Yet all along Haggart had hidden this from her. Koertig snatched the papers back. "Are there names?" she asked.

He folded the papers and stuffed them in his shirt, ignoring her question. "I saw you this morning, didn't I?" he asked. "You were talking to Edwin, the storyteller."

She studied Koertig, wondering what path he was treading, and how quickly she could pilfer those papers.

He told her he found it strange that a man just happened to witness a breakout at a prison that had been lost for many lifetimes. He found it even more curious that when this beast from the underworld invaded his good city, the only two people it spoke to, and indeed did not attack, were her and this same man. "And when it broke down the back wall for its escape," he said, "Who was waiting for it outside, but the same girl I caught in the plaza earlier this morning conspiring with that Historian."

"You're insane," she said, and believed it.

Koertig pounced on her, slamming his palms atop the table.

"Koertig!" Mayor Brynn demanded. "Enough!"

The two men faced each other in a standoff. The mayor spoke through clenched teeth. "Is it not clear who the threat is?" he asked. "I want that creature captured."

Koertig swatted away her tiny hand as it reached again for the papers.

The door opened. "Sir—," one of the hallway guards began but was pushed aside as a woman in a red dress burst into the room.

"Olen, my dear!" Haggart said, and swept her off the table, embracing her fully. It was a real hug, warm and deep, the kind Olen had not allowed her to give, perhaps ever. Haggart practically manhandled her pulling and squeezing, juggling her in her arms.

Olen's reaction was to awkwardly giggle. To seize up, tuck in, and squirm away from her hug. To fight off or laugh away the love Haggart showed her was only natural for a child who had so rarely been held. She dipped her shoulders and ducked her head as Haggart pelted her temples with kisses. Olen did not do this on purpose. She simply had never learned how to accept affection. This was her bubble; this was how it worked.

"Oh, they said it had stolen you away!" Haggart cried. She held Olen out by her shoulders. "I was ready to chase that thing into the mountains and snatch you back!" she said and again pulled Olen in tightly. "On my life I swear, nobody hurts my girls. On my life."

She smelled of lilacs and lye soap. She wondered if all mothers smelled that way. She disappeared into Haggart's fleshy arms and billowy dress, tumbling out of the lonely world she had known and into the safe and warm land that so many others took for granted. Just this once. She would let this happen just this once. Things were happening, the world was changing, and she would be leaving the Ward soon to be reunited with her parents. The Aurling Bakku would let them know she was here, and they would come. So just this one time, she thought, and reached her thin arms around Haggart's waist. She let her bubble fall away. And like a revelation, like a dawn, like knowledge of a new world, she no longer needed to run.

Mayor Brynn flicked a backhand towards Koertig, like brushing away dust. The soldier deferred. "Please ma'am," the mayor said. "We have much to do. Just take the girl home."

"Yes. Yes, of course," Haggart said and pulled Olen by her wrist.

Koertig stepped over to the window defeated. There he watched the townspeople below, still running about in disarray, trying to make sense of the day's events.

Olen walked out of the room and down the stairs, arm and arm with the mistress. And as they stepped outside, she thought Mistress Haggart in her red dress was the prettiest thing she had ever seen.

***

Koertig rested his palm against the window as the Lowtown rats descended. He was not wrong about the girl. He knew it in his bones. He had always been able to read people, and this was no different. He had told the mayor straight away that the wandering storyteller would bring nothing but trouble, and he had been more right than he had guessed. And now this girl, as he looked upon Midtown. She was hiding something. Simple thievery? Of course there was that. All street people thieve, it's in their blood. But this child hid more, he felt it. He thought of his father, the parent he had lost so many winters ago and the truths the aging man had told him.

"Abandon your tears, boy!" his father had said, as he saddled his pack for the long ride down the mountainside. He forced his steed to pivot with one hand pressing its flank, and the other holding its rein. He spoke in a diction raised beyond that of the other mountain men. "I'll be back before the thaw, but for now you are constrained to the protection of this home."

The younger Koertig quavered, but his father stopped him. "You are aggregate of the finest stock, and you are superior," he had said, as he slid his long sword into the scabbard hanging sidesaddle on his horse. "In time, you will become adamant and wise. It is why I chose your mother, you understand? She is supple, and I sturdy and strong; she is lettered, and I intuitive and carnal! From two parts, you shall be a greater whole. What has made me strong, will make you stronger. Not just of body," this beautiful man said, tapping his son's forehead with wide bearpaw fingers, "but of mind."

He stepped into the stirrup and with one quick motion righted himself atop his mount, a beast atop a beast. "Trust your learned perception, Son of Koertig. And your instinct!"

The mayor called in his men from the hallway, jarring Koertig from his reverie. They wanted plans to fix the gates. Koertig was no carpenter. He was the law. The old woman and her young charge exited out of the door below. She pulled the girl across the street, talking constantly. The girl danced alongside her.

But something was not right with the girl. She seemed blurry, like he was seeing her through an unfocused spyglass, while all around her the world was clear.

Men with oxen pulled carts back onto their wheels. Merchants restacked crates. Traders argued over which produce fell off their carts, and which had rolled over from another vendor. Mothers rushed through the streets calling out their children's names. And the two from the Ward continued down the street. Yet still, something about the girl did not seem right.

"That girl," Koertig asked the room, without turning from the window. "The child."

Mayor Brynn, rolling up the large map, gave an exasperated response, "What of her?"

"What was she wearing?"

The mayor sighed angrily and passed the roll on to his handler, Graeme.

He was a good mayor, but a weak soul. His term had inherited a strong army, which he immediately bound to the city. No more forays into the Mecan Plains to hunt outlaws. No more marches to Brennan and Illsbrook to sweep out the filth. It was Brynn who had thrust the ranks of city-soldier on his army to remind his men where they were most needed. Had the son of Koertig run this city, he would have—

"Rags, sir," the fair-haired clerk at the still-damp desk responded. "The girl wore patched brown and white rags."

City-Sergeant Koertig stood at once and called his men from the hall as he watched the Ward Mistress lead the little child, clearly seen now, each wearing the exact same frilly red dress.

11

True Colors

Olen let Haggart pull her along, bumping and weaving through the still-hectic crowd of Lowtown. River birds squawked overhead as Machinists in their blue-grey shirts and pants stood before the crooked front gate, describing with their hands plans for repair. Carpenters already knelt on the boardwalk hammering back into place the boards Bakku's heavy steps had shaken loose. Uptowners had also journeyed down to see the destruction. The damage to the back wall of Millthrace was much worse, but the best talk and taverns were in Lowtown. For once all the classes mingled easily and talked together about the terror that had attacked them. Bakku grew taller and more frightful with each tale.

Olen and Haggart pushed through this lively crowd and bumped straight into Philippa Cree. She stood there, a breakwater stone in a swirling sea, as waves of locals moved around her. Two armored guards appeared behind her.

"There," Philippa said, and pointed to Olen.

The guards lowered their spears at her.

"What is this!?" Haggart said, pulling Olen in tight.

Shouts rang out as more guards rushed through the dense crowds. A horn sounded in the square, and three soldiers on horseback paced

80

through the mob. They circled the two from the Ward, weapons drawn. Then pounding feet and metal clanking as more troops arrived. A wide circle of warriors, thirty at least, drew their spears and aimed them directly at Olen and Haggart. In front of them all stood Philippa, defiant, victorious.

Sergeant Koertig strode through his men and brushed past Philippa. She fell aside unoffended, perhaps even delighted by the touch. He approached Olen and lowered his spear to her face.

"Koertig!" Haggart pleaded, "The girl answered your questions. The mayor would never stand for this."

Koertig held steady as Mayor Brynn emerged from the tight band of soldiers. Brynn's look was frightened and disbelieving as he studied Olen. An oversized chest plate, tied on with loose straps, hung lopsided over his purple robes. The thin golden saber that had adorned his wall now rose uncertainly in his nervous grip.

"So the amicable mayor-general is a militant after-all!" Haggart said.

Koertig made the slightest nod towards Olen. Haggart turned, seemingly unable to understand the fuss. As she looked upon the girl she had protected, she saw the red dress and she knew.

"No, no, child," Haggart whispered, and let her hand fall away from Olen's. She looked Olen up and down. Olen sensed her tracing back through all the years she had spent housing a witch, the times she had tried to love her, the night she had let her sleep in her bed. Haggart's breaths came faster now as if a terror grew inside of her. She shook her head in disbelief and backed away, lance tips pressing against her spine.

"The Mistress didn't know," Philippa called out from behind the circle of guards. "I only found out last night." She angled her way through to the mayor. "They don't want you, Mistress. Just the witch," Philippa said, holding her hand out to Haggart. "Come away."

Philippa pulled Haggart away, hugging her tightly. They were moving out of the circle when Haggart stopped and looked beyond the crowd to the decaying old Ward. She stared at the place that Olen had never truly felt was home, and then pulled free from Philippa's arms. She lunged back into the ring of spears, darting past Koertig to

Olen. Haggart looked the child over, stone-faced and cold, then before turning away forever she spat at Olen's feet.

The crowd roared.

Olen's red dress rippled and changed back to rags as Haggart and Philippa staggered back to the Ward, arm and arm.

***

Olen's patchwork clothes were real, they always had been. It had only been in the past two years that she had found she could change them. The sisters of the Ward were to tend to their own garments as they learned how to be good workers and wives. Their dresses were to be washed on Sundays, and any tears were to be patched and mended by the wearer. Olen was not made for needlework. When she had torn the hem of her only skirt, Mistress Haggart had insisted she was old enough to learn mending. But there had been a city full of other fun things to do. So when Haggart had caught up to her later that afternoon, they had both been surprised to find that the skirt that had never left her body was already patched and hemmed.

"You're a quick study, Miss Marine!" Haggart had said proudly, confusing Olen.

The holes had all fixed themselves during the week, but on laundry day something very strange had happened. When she stripped down, the patches faded away and her skirt and top hung in rags. So as the girls at the river pulled their outfits out of the wash baskets and dipped them in the water, one small outfit always came out covered in holes. At first this was no problem, for once she slipped her clothes back on, the patches reformed, and the hems all hung straight. But then came that fated Sunday just one year ago, when she had been selected for kitchen duty, and the other sisters were charged with washing her clothes. It was Philippa Cree who had carried the heavy basket across the Barrens and joined her sisters at the river. And as the wash sisters told her later, it was Philippa who had taken the blame.

"Philippa!" Haggart had said as the strong-armed sister pulled the threadbare outfit out of the river. Strips of cloth hung off the hem, and holes opened up at the elbows and knees. "Must you be so rough with Olen's clothes? That girl worked so hard on mending them."

"But this is how it was sent," she insisted, unsure of what she was being accused of.

"If you're going to lie," Haggart said, "then you can mend them yourself."

Olen had spent that day nervously working in the kitchen, waiting for her world to fall apart. Then just before supper time, as she pulled a loaf of bread from the fire, Philippa marched straight through the kitchen and threw the clothing right in her face. She checked her outfit and found patched holes and mended seams that still held today. Her skirt was good as new, but she had made an enemy for life.

"Thank you," she said, but the older girl had already stormed out of the room.

That was how it began, she remembered now as she sat in the cage. Iron bars surrounded her, and a thick clasp chained her ankle. She sat on a pile of straw that itched more than it cushioned. From those first patches, she had learned how to change her outfit at will. Skin-tight dark clothes for sneaking at night, various garbs and armors as seen in Lowtown, and once even the fanciest of dresses as she passed through Uptown completely unnoticed. These days it was getting harder to control. If she saw something she liked, or a look that was just right, she had to fight to keep from changing. The bubble had helped her; it had kept her mind and emotions focused. But she had let the bubble burst when Haggart hugged her. The bubble was back now, and it was a cage of pure iron.

Haggart had spit at her. There was no discussion, no chance to explain. She had been disowned and cast away from the Ward without even a tear. And perhaps worse, she had been replaced in Haggart's heart by Philippa. She had been called an orphan all of her life, but for the first time she truly felt alone. She rested her chin on her knees and wrapped her arms around her shins.

Four sentries watched her cage, war machines in their heavy armor. Yet these soldiers stood not very close, perhaps a full step further away than necessary. As time went on and she shifted in her jail, that one extra step became two steps back from the Nerikan witch.

She was inside the wide barn of the Lowtown blacksmith. Gritty charcoal in the air coated her lungs. Her hands and legs had somehow picked up a greasy tar. Black chains and rods and confusing looking tools hung off the walls far away from her reach. A thick-armed man with goggles pounded his hammer against a fiery red iron rod. She sat quietly, counting the echoing hammer clangs. Her rags were gone. She wore a man's brown shirt with rolled up sleeves, a tough leather bib down past her knees, and goggles over her eyes. It was the same outfit as the blacksmith. He did not find it funny, but she was done hiding who she was.

She sat in an iron cage atop a cart with tall wooden wheels. The cage was large, but the chain on her ankle was short.

"Bang it on the red part," she yelled at the blacksmith, but he was done listening to her.

Shouts came from outside the shop. The tall carriage door slid open and more guards came in. Behind them, Koertig and his men lead the old storyteller at spear-point. The old man in brown robes, Edwin they had called him, objected furiously.

"This is absurd!" he cried, as Koertig shoved him into the room. "I am not a creature, I am an educated fellow!" Olen slid the goggles up to her forehead. Edwin saw her sitting in the iron cage and objected, "And now you've chained a poor girl from the streets? Such an innocent child! Have you all gone mad?"

"He's right," Olen said, sitting up and grasping the bars. Her goggles melted away and the heavy smock softened. A ripple ran over her body like a quick tickle and leather puffed out to rough wool. She now wore University robes just like Edwin. "We're both innocent, let us go!" She winked at the old man.

Flabbergasted, Edwin spun back to Koertig, gripping his mail, practically hugging him. He spoke quickly and softly, "I am not in league with this creature. You were right to cage her. Do what you will with this beast, but I am simply a man from University come here to study."

Koertig shoved Edwin on to his men and they forced him into the rolling jail. He cried out for mercy as his elbows banged against the black bars. Soldiers locked the cage and guards retook their positions. He called out to Koertig, begging, and offering him anything to get him out of there. Koertig paid him no mind. The Sergeant gathered his troops and left the shop, sliding shut the tall door.

"At least you're not chained," she said, wiggling her ankle at him.

Edwin plopped down in the corner farthest from her. He glowered at her, and then he hung his head in his hands, mumbling to himself. Boney fingers massaged his temples and bald crown. He popped his head back up at the young girl, glaring.

"Why did you involve me in your witchcraft?" he asked. "I don't deserve this dishonor!"

"You came to me," she said. Her robes softened to a thin white gown. "You said I was a part of this, and I don't even know what *this* is. But I think you do. Whether you realize it or not, you know something about me, and right now that's more than I know about myself." He scoffed and shook his head. "And also, you're an educator, and educators are smart." He seemed to soften at this, but still eyed her warily. Then she said, "Educate me."

***

Philippa pulled shut the parlor doors and helped Miss Haggart to her chair. Haggart sat slowly, like a woman entranced. Evening had come quickly, and a chill breeze billowed the ancient drapery. Philippa pulled shut the window and set a light shawl over Haggart's shoulders.

"The sisters are asleep," Philippa said as she lowered herself into the soft white wingchair. It was one of the very few luxuries of the Ward and usually reserved for gentlemen donors.

"They lie in their cots," Haggart finally answered. "But they are not asleep."

Most of Millthrace had seen Olen's capture, and those who had not had certainly heard of it soon after. Ellery and Lysa, two of the older girls, had been in the large crowd, and trailed Philippa and Haggart to the Barrens asking endless questions. Maggie and the younger children issued out of the Ward after seeing them all talking. After a lot of explaining and reassuring, Philippa had finally ushered the girls to their rooms, and then had taken Haggart to her parlor. Now the two sat in silence, contemplating the empty cot upstairs.

It was not a betrayal, Philippa told herself. She had not turned against one of her sisters. Nerikan demons had somehow entered her home and taken the guise of one of their own. She had merely rooted out the impostor. Anyone else would have done the same. Yet Haggart's stunned silence showed doubt in her mind. She had let the young girl get away with so much over the years, surely she could not be contemplating pardoning her latest crimes. A witch is not a child, no matter how much she may appear to be one. There could be only one reason Haggart worried so over Olen; it was something she had always assumed.

"I know you loved her," she said, the acknowledgement stinging her. "She was always special to you." It was like an admission, conceding Olen had somehow earned the one thing Philippa had desperately fought for. Some people were loved easily in this world, she knew that. She had seen it her whole life. There were the lucky few whose bodies grew within the tight borders of some territory dubbed Beautiful. They would never know what it was like to be overlooked, by men, by women, young and old. Or the peculiar and cute little scamps like Olen who garnered love, hugs, and even apple tarts as they rejected their duties and ridiculed house rules. Had she acted out in such a manner, she would have been cast into the forest years ago. "You loved what you thought was a child, but she has proven herself to be a Nerikan witch. There was no other way but to hand her to Koertig. I was only protecting this Ward."

"There was no other way," Haggart agreed, but her words fell soft and empty.

"I see you are disappointed in me," Philippa said, rising. "I just hope someday you will understand what I have done to keep my girls safe."

"I could say the very same, Philippa," Haggart said, as she slipped her warm hands into Philippa's and massaged her palms. "Olen is gone.

We did what we had to do. What I have done today, I would do any day to protect this home." She pulled the threadbare curtain from the window and looked out into the Barrens. "It is the army I fear, and this town itself. They have jailed one, and the public cheered. Cheered!" She sat back in her chair and let the curtain fall. She smiled warmly, sadly. "Olen will be fine. Don't ask me how I know, I just do. But they will be bolder next time. Next time they won't be so merciful."

Philippa sat back down in the chair. "What do you mean *next time*?"

Haggart wiped the thought away, "I mean that Koertig. You must know he has no love for the Ward."

"I saw him today stand up to save the Ward," she snapped back.

"He stood up against those different from himself. That is all," she said, and looked at the ground as if thinking about something. "You should sleep, dear. I believe we both have a long night ahead of us, tending the younger girls and calming dreams."

Philippa stood again to leave, but remained steadfast about Koertig. "When I was younger I thought the way you did about him. I found the sergeant to be arrogant and cruel. But I have learned to see his true soul. Just like how I want only the best for this Ward and my sisters, and how I will fight for that. He feels the same for all of Millthrace. If he is cold and severe at times, well then maybe that is what's needed."

Haggart rose from her chair and led Philippa out of the parlor. As she pulled the doors shut between them, she said lovingly but sternly, "Sergeant Koertig is the greatest threat to me, my Ward, and to you, dear Philippa."

***

Bakku sat among boulders of black glass far above a land he no longer knew, and a ransacked city he had never seen before. He chewed an orange vegetable as mountain winds delivered pollens and dusts and airborne oils that stirred memories if not names. He had lived in mountains long ago. Not these mountains, he was pretty sure of that, but they smelled nearly the same. He reached in the sack and pulled out another soft gourd.

Pumpkin, he thought, and tried the word aloud. It did not sound right, but it was close. He was sure it was close. Pumpkin, he thought again, thinking it sounded perfectly right in his head.

The city below was but a teardrop scar in the mountainside, with the wide river flowing right below him. He chucked the pumpkin down the hillside watching it sail forever down before making a tiny plop in the flow. He was angry at himself. Not for getting lost and forgetting his words. He was angry for feeling his will fading so quickly. When chains had still bound him and his suffering days had turned to torturous years, it had been easy to visualize himself breaking free and racing straight up the smoky treeless hills of Calderra and falling willfully within its fiery bowl. In his fantasy, his captors and all their corps would trail woefully behind, begging their pet to stop, and staring helplessly when he would not.

But he had forgotten of mountain breezes and sweet vegetables that were never meant to send one's soul soaring. Pumpkin, he thought the word again, and again said it aloud.

"Pung."

"Ghin."

That was it. That was the word. This pumpkin was the first thing he had eaten since his capture that was not wormy and rotten or otherwise spoiled. It was pumpkin, and its damp earthy flavor and wet stringy innards made him want to live.

No, he thought, and tossed another pumpkin far below. If he lived he would once again be captured, and once again he would be back in that pit chained to the wall forever. Not only him, he thought, and remembered the girl. She had magic. He did not think it was possible, but yet it was so. She too they would put in chains. He had seen it before. He had seen it so often before. He must not let himself live.

A tiny brown creature, just a puff of brown and white fur, poked out of a hole in the ground. It sniffed around the boulders on darting footsteps, racing from stone to shadow to mound of dirt. Fine whiskers twisted on its snout as it snuffled Bakku's feed bag. Then it rose onto its hind quarters and froze, as if confounded how such an abundance of goods had been delivered so high up the hillside. It turned an ear of corn in its perfectly nimble five-fingered hands and then chewed on the juicy kernels.

"Chimp," Bakku whispered, "Munk."

And there he sat much of the afternoon letting the tiny creature fill its wide cheeks with whatever food it could carry.

<h1 style="text-align:center">12</h1>

The Low Pass on the Iron Road

It was morning in Millthrace as Olen and her cage were finally hauled outside of the smithy shop. There was a menagerie of a mule-train at the hastily repaired front gate. Two bold white oxen stood at the front of the parade, followed by obedient mules, a donkey, and an uninspired cow—an iron bell clanging lazily against its neck. They pulled forward a step, snapping taut the twined ropes strung up above the massive door. Workmen checked the ropes and gears as the sun topped the rampart. The sky was clear, the air was warm, and everything smelled of baking bread.

"I don't like this," Edwin mumbled as they wheeled across the boardwalk like a carnival wagon on display.

It was her third day with this man, and he still held out hope the officers would realize they had made a mistake. She lay against the bars at the only angle that did not bruise as she chewed bread older than she had sold in the Square.

"What are they going to do, expel us from the city?" He rambled on. "All of my things are here!"

A regiment of soldiers followed alongside carrying travel packs. Two

90

other wheeled carts sat at the gate, already loaded down with supplies. She knew better. They were not just expelling the two, they were going on a journey. One way.

It's a natural thing to hate something caged, she thought, as sour frowns and heavy brows watched her go by. They said nothing, only scowled at the caged duo. Faces brightened as Mayor-General Brynn and City-Sergeant Koertig approached from Midtown.

"Sir!" Edwin pleaded to the mayor. "My books. I need my books."

Two soldiers hauled a crate over to the mayor. Brynn stood on top of it, and a crowd formed around him. She knew the faces, at least those of Lowtown. She had played with them, traded with them, and gossiped about the Uptowners with them. Of all those she saw, there were many more that were missing. Mistress Haggart and Philippa were nowhere to be seen. Absent also were streetwise Gerda, smiling Icha with her hair always hidden behind Swarhee scarves, little Leni, and all of her other sisters.

Mayor Brynn spoke, "In one day our world has changed. The faerie tales of our ancestors have proven themselves to be true. And our world has been infected by creatures, fearful and fantastic."

A Lowtown boy she had once watched at the Well looked at her like a worm.

"If we accept our ancestor's stories," Brynn continued, orating like a preacher. "We must also accept their conclusions. These *Aurlings* are creatures to be feared. They blighted our fields, altered our beasts, and corrupted our souls. We would be fools to challenge their warnings and let this world fall again into disarray. This I cannot allow."

The apple merchant hurrahed, and the crowd echoed. She wanted her pennies back.

Brynn continued, "As you know, after being lost for many ages, the gates of Nerikan Prison have again been found deep in Ma'alabrad Forest."

Edwin leaned in to his prison-mate and whispered, "Found by me, and this is my reward?" Olen's clothes rippled and changed to match

Brynn's. He jerked back to his corner and called out to the crowd, "*Found* by me, not *opened* by me!"

A guard jabbed his side with the blunt end of his spike, to the audience's delight. Even a donkey seemed to laugh.

The mayor continued, "And a dark creature has slipped his hellish Nerikan bonds and fled. We have commissioned the ironsmiths of Brennan to journey north and set their men to work. They shall once again seal the doors of Nerikan, ensuring no creature ever escape those dark halls." He waved his arm at Olen and Edwin dismissively. "You see before you the first two who are to be locked within, where the slow march of time will be their final judge."

"Absurd!" Edwin cried out. "I am not one of them! I am born and raised of these lands," he said, but the roaring crowd overwhelmed him. And then his decisive proof as he rattled the cage bars, "I went to *University!*"

"With these two gone," Brynn continued, "we can focus our efforts on the beast that terrorized our city. We will not let it flee. We will hunt it forever! And when we find it—and we shall—we will once again place it in Nerikan chains."

He nodded to Koertig, and the sergeant shouted to the farmers manning their livestock. The cattle-train lurched forward pulling the heavy rope attached to the front gate. Olen turned her back to the crowd and checked the Barrens to see if Haggart or any sisters would come running. But there were no goodbyes, only the clack clang, clack clang of the slowly rising gate.

She had guessed this. This was why she had kept her magic secret for so long. But even so, it hurt that not even one sister had come.

On a signal, the horses tied to her cage moved forward pulling her and Edwin to the Millthrace gates.

"I can't be sent to that underworld," he whimpered, as he fell help-lessly to his corner.

Cart and cage clattered over the boardwalk and through the gaping mouth. The city shrunk behind her becoming like a painting framed in the gateway's wooden border. City sounds hollowed and became distant, and even the city's hum faded away. Townsfolk swarmed the entrance as she and Edwin pulled away, and the massive gate began its slow descent. The classes mingled in the square as rich and poor, filthy and clean, crowded the gateway. As the older townspeople moved on, it was children she saw last. Little Uptown lords and ladies and dirty Lowtown scamps crouched low as the gate descended. Beyond them all she spied a familiar face. Hiding in the shadow of a broken waterwheel, little Maggie peered through the thick wooden spokes. She looked worried, frightened beyond what such a young girl deserved. Olen winked and sent a wave with her index finger, which Maggie sent back smiling. A tiny firefly circled from behind her blonde head and curled away, lost behind the falling gate.

The doorway thudded shut.

Edwin began on what she knew would be an epic rant, "Such abuse I have suffered! Not since the days of—"

"Don't," she said, staring at her lost home. "Please, for once, just be quiet."

He sat back offended, but silent.

Through midday they rode a mostly worn path moving steadily northeast keeping the mountains to their right. The outside world looked and smelled like Uptown, with its green things sprouting off rocks and trees. She fully expected to see ladies in evening gowns walk out from behind the shrubbery on their way to a fatally important dinner. Instead she saw yellow-winged darters flashing in the trees, and small brown creatures scattering to the forest edge. The outside world was a welcoming and natural land that she had foolishly been too hesitant to escape to on her own.

Two soldiers marched alongside the prisoner's carriage, moving single-file when the trees thickened and the path narrowed. Three foot soldiers, lightly dressed, towed along mules stacked high with over-stuffed burlap sacks and clanging pots. Seven more soldiers rode ahead along with Reeve, Mayor Brynn's personal clerk. Leading them through field and forest was Sergeant Koertig who rode tall and proud atop his warhorse, Tasker. It was quite the parade for a girl who hardly felt herself a threat, and an old man that begged and complained more than he intimidated. The caravan turned a sharp corner, circling past a tall granite way marker along the Iron Triangle.

Even though she had never traveled this road, she knew all about it from the traders at Millthrace. The Iron Road—or Iron Triangle, as the entire highway was called—was a hard-packed trail across the plains, and the most important road in Eisen. It led out of the Brennan ironworks, a wide and manicured highway that quickly split in two. One branch—the Iron Road proper—curled northeast to Millthrace, where cattle hauled heavy trucks overloaded with unfinished iron weapons and tools. The other branch, called Glory Road, sliced a wavy path due east. On this path, the carts were overfull with men and women, their purses bulging with hard-earned silvers, and their faces bursting with anticipation, as they rode away for a memorable stay in Illsbrook. Hardly did they ever notice the ruined and broken revelers limping back to the foundry fires of Brennan.

For many years, those two arms were all that existed of the highway. But then bold Millthracian merchants had tramped out their own dusty path southeast linking the waterwheel city to Illsbrook. They called this desperate path the Merchant's Trail, thus completing the Iron Triangle; though any branch was often merely called just the Iron Road. And while iron was a major commodity along these roads, it was the small itinerant entrepreneurs who truly thrived. It had been these merchants —forever circling the highway—that Olen had traded with so fruitfully in Lowtown. Even they would be no help to her now. Nobody would help her.

Hours later, the caravan dropped down a short hill and pulled through dense green brush. The cage rumbled over roots, jarring her and Edwin into the bars. He whimpered and cursed until the carriage exited the small oasis and was back in the open fields.

They were riding toward the Low Pass, a prairie-level break in the mountains that cut through to the eastern domain. The snow-capped peaks she had always seen peering over the Uptown ramparts had dissolved to rolling hills, and the horizon seemed spread out before her. She had always lived behind the cramped walls of the city, and even then spent her days in the tight underground. But now the prairie and sky seemed so high and wide that she felt exposed to the world—minus the cage. Compared to Millthrace, the rest of the world looked like so much unused space.

They had traveled through to the late afternoon, the clasp on her left ankle gnawing at her. She kicked off her boot and rubbed her foot. Edwin remained near the front of the cage, grasping the bars and pressing his chubby face into the gaps. He whispered promises and begged for help from any soldier whose gait drifted him near, but he got no return.

A small migrant family of four met the somber caravan. They moved slowly, tiredly, as if beaten down from the harsh Merchant's Trail. Yet the father revived upon seeing the regiment. He pulled a few small untrimmed hides off his cart and showed them to Koertig's men, even laying one over the shoulders of a foot soldier. The guard shoved the sunburned man to the ground and threw the hide into the bushes. She had seen this cruelty in Koertig, but this was a first for the other soldiers. Koertig nodded and smiled to the guard as he returned to the line. She realized this was no random regiment, these were men he had chosen. Koertig's men, hard, cruel, unyielding. The father crawled away submissively, begging his many pardons. He then pulled his wife and children behind their mule-drawn cart.

Olen gave a weak smile to the poor traders as she rolled by, but they offered none in return, looking beyond her cage as if not seeing it.

Edwin pressed against the side of his cage and called out, "You must get a message to Professors Chacko and Balhorn at University! One of their finest students is in terrible trouble!" His cart rolled past the silent family. "On my word they will gratefully pay you a handsome reward for such a brief diversion! Five, no ten silvers!"

For a man of the world, he really did not know much about life in Eisen, she thought. Fear kept one alive on the Iron Road. These people could not be bought for a handful of silvers. That reminded her of something, and she patted her chest. She still had the silver honor, though little purchase it would make in Nerikan.

A foot soldier racked Edwin's knuckles with the butt of his spear as they pulled away from the traders.

"They won't help you," Olen said dryly. "They have to protect themselves."

He plopped down and rubbed his bruised fingers. "So we are talking now?" he asked derisively, turning to his cage-mate. He had told her earlier that he had been drawn to her and he hadn't know why. Strangely, she was drawn to him too. He was like a character she had seen in the pageant wagon. He had worn a mask with an exaggerated frown and jumped around waving his arms at every little offense. Edwin was like that, and just like the performance, it was oddly charming.

"Look at you!" he said, his face reddening. "A child of devilish magic, yet you don't use it to free us of this dilemma. Or is that your plan, wait until poor Edwin is cast away into the darkness, and then rain fire down upon the soldiers, burning them black right inside their armor?"

"Can Aurlings do that?" she asked.

"Don't play with me," he sneered. "You know full well they can do that and more."

"Not me," she said. "All I can do is this." Her clothing bulged out and hardened into fine steel. Blue emblems appeared on her shoulders and chest, and a helm grew on her head. In a flash she wore Koertig's armor, only much smaller. "Or this," she said, and the metal melted away to the soft yellow linen of a flowery dress she had once seen in Uptown.

"You forgot the boot," he said dryly.

Indeed, her heavy boot had not changed. She focused on it and imagined a thin yellow sock. With a nearly audible pop, soft cloth materialized on both of her feet. She wiggled her new socks at Edwin. Then they both noticed her missing shackle. The metal clasp itself had become a sock and the links of a suddenly unattached chain sat dangling in the cage.

Edwin traded fear for scholarly inquisition. "The sock!" he whispered, as if a stifled eureka. He checked the guards. None were watching. "Take it off!"

She slipped off the sock and tossed it to him. In midair it rippled and hardened back into the clasp, clanking as it fell in his lap. The noise rattled a guard who stepped out of line and surveyed the prisoners. She and Edwin sat still and natural, casual even.

"Yes, little maiden," Edwin said cheerily, looking at the sky, "It is indeed a clear day."

The guard rattled the cage and returned to the line.

Edwin pulled open his robe and revealed the clasp, closed tightly around air. "Impressive," he said. "Can you do the bars?"

"I don't know," she said, upset with herself for not thinking of this on her own. "I'm not exactly wearing them," she concluded. "That seems to be the trick. But I'll try." She grabbed the nearest iron bar and imagined a lady's glove, a long black satiny glove that—

The cage lurched hard to the right, crashing Olen and Edwin into the same corner. He took the worst of it, banging hard against the bars. To his credit, he recovered his wits quickly and ushered her back to her side where she was supposed to be chained. They had hit a deep rut and bent the rear axle, stopping the carriage dead. The guards called out to Koertig who swung Tasker around.

Olen still sat unchained in her corner as Koertig approached. She tucked her skirt over her feet and motioned to Edwin. Understanding immediately, he tossed the clasp back over to her. In her hands it softened back into the yellow sock. She hid it in her palms.

Koertig inspected the cart. The veteran crew had come prepared. They could fix the wheel and axle, but perhaps later. It was late, and they had ridden far. He ordered his men to set camp. They would rest here for the night.

As he shouted his orders to the caravan, she slipped her odd sock back on. She pulled it over the swollen toes of her sore foot, but then had an idea. She tore off both socks and swapped them. When she slipped them back on and let her magic fade away, the heavy clasp and chain reappeared on her healthy right foot.

Impressed, Edwin gave her an appreciative nod and then noticed her left foot now bore her right-footed boot. Both prisoners spit out laughter.

Koertig grumbled something about Aurling filth, and fetched feed for his horse.

13

Bag and Blanket

The next morning the somber parade continued. They reached the Low Pass and pulled into the eastern lands. Olen played student as her cage-mate explained that Ma'alabrad Forest and the doorway to Nerikan were actually very close to Millthrace but on the far side of the mountains.

"Were we eagles, we would make the trip in one day, soaring over the snow caps," he said, seemingly accepting her company. "Thankfully the Iron Road makes for a much longer journey—," he said, as the cage shifted on the rough ground. "But a less graceful one also!"

He had taken to sitting with his back to the guards and conversing with her face to face. He had a lot of knowledge about Aurlings and scions, but nothing that could help her out of this cage. She had not been able to melt away the bars, but she thought perhaps it was because so many eyes were on her. She asked what he thought of her magic.

"It is very much like Aurling magic, but you I do not believe are Aurling." He then spoke of ancient Eisen people with a magical bearing similar to the Aurlings. *Demis* they were called. "But all I had read so far was just a mention here and there."

Similar to Aurlings, she thought, her confusion growing.

The caravan rounded a tall spire of carved granite and headed south.

"Another way marker," he said uneasily, as he craned his head back and forth trying to read etchings on the stone. He sounded out words of a foreign tongue and fell back against the cage. "We are moving quite quickly."

A vast prairie opened up to the east. They journeyed south down the flatlands east of the Rückraadt. The grasses were short and brown, a field her legs ached to run through. Harvester mice sniffed at lilting stems, and tunnel pups stood straight and motionless on hind limbs, observing the curious trespassers before scurrying underground. Let me out here, she thought, and you'll never see me again. She would happily live in this endless meadow. They rolled through the prairie as the sun passed slowly overhead. Edwin identified the birds, beasts, and stalks of life that grew colorful and tall. She spoke the names back to her teacher, and was met with a satisfied nod. How odd, she thought, that this hen-hearted wanderer, now at his most desperate hour, for the first time seemed content.

He caught her staring. "More lessons?" he asked eagerly.

"Yes, please," she said, as the caravan rolled on.

The sun fell low in the sky, another day passed. Clouds formed over the mountains while the prairie stayed clear. The train rolled up to a shallow circular stone structure just off the side of the trail. Three weather-beaten flags hung flaccid above. It was a water-well for traders on the Iron Road, maintained by the three major cities along the triangle. Koertig ordered two of his men to the well while the rest of his men set up camp.

"We're stopping," Edwin said. "One more night below the stars. If you have any more Aurling magic in you, now would be a good time to use it."

"And if your University ever taught you how to best an iron lock, I suggest you work your magic on that," she replied.

"So we sleep," he said with a smile, and laid back against the bars. She did the same, but it was full dark before sleep took her.

***

Olen was already awake when a soldier approached with spear in hand. Edwin slept nearby. He had asked her earlier if her magic let her change things besides her clothes. Well, if that spear was meant for her or Edwin, then they were all going to find out together. She thought of a quick grab, rippling spear-to-rope, a quick tug out of his hands, and then back to spear again. Stabbing this bungplug of a soldier wouldn't save her from Nerikan, but it would make her death sentence more honest. *Explain how you lost a soldier to a caged girl, Koertig.*

The soldier approached and ran his spearhead across the cage, jerking Edwin to consciousness. The old man jumped up, bumping his head. "The devil?" he said, shaking the sleep from his mind and rubbing his scalp.

The soldier laughed and reported back to the line, unaware how close he had come to ingesting his own weapon. It was morning, and time for the final push to Nerikan. Edwin pulled his cloak over himself and shivered.

"In my home, even prisoners are treated with respect," he grumbled.

"Where is your home?" she asked.

"Ulm," he sang, like a heavy bell rung. His demeanor changed quickly as he spoke of his land. "Dear Sweet Ulm. South of the Wide Galenic and past the Euloren Woods. A handsome land where the fig trees grow thick with green leaves, and the hills roll as if written in script. The land is tamed in Ulm. The worst displeasure for an Ulm man is waking to find a midnight hare has gnawed through his garden fence. It is a simple life. University is nearby, just off Welter Bay. It is there I have spent most of my years. And you, child?"

She almost answered the Ward. He had asked where she was from, and her natural reaction was to say the Ward. "Kessel," she said, wondering why that town that had dominated her thoughts for so long had so quickly become buried under thoughts of the Ward. "I'm originally from Kessel, though I don't know if my parents were from Kessel, or if they just lost me there."

"Yes, Kessel," he said. "Near Brennan. It is a small town."

She laughed, "You know where it is? I guess I just should have asked.

We could have avoided all of this," she said as the train lurched ahead. "I would have paid you a full silver honor to take me there."

"I would have required a full silver," he said arrogantly, cleaning his fingernails. "Kessel folk are not my kind."

"Hey!" she said, "I'm Kessel folk."

To his credit, he apologized kindly. "And when did you discover your...talent?" he asked, spitting fingernail dirt aside.

"Talent? I like that," she said. "Just a couple years ago. Why?"

"I don't know," he said, placing his fist on his chin. "I'm still learning."

The first sparse trees of Ma'alabrad Forest passed by the caravan. The prisoners pressed their heads against the bars to look ahead beyond the marching soldiers. The tree trunks were wider in Ma'alabrad and taller than any she was familiar with. The leaves were brownish green, and the trunks were all a lifeless grey. The trail into the woods wandered away in darkness, and the sun shone less and less down the path, like a long hallway lined with ever dimmer candles. And, she thought, this horrible forest was not their prison; this was merely the road to their prison. Soldiers pulled spikes off the trucks, and unsheathed their thin sabers.

"Any last wishes," Edwin asked.

"Yes, don't be morbid," she said, her own morbid thoughts crawling through her mind.

"I am being realistic. Many consider me an optimistic man," he said confidently, "but I fear I see no way out of this one."

"What is so bad about this place anyway?" she asked, trying to convince herself.

"You might as well ask what is so wet about the ocean, so dry about the desert. Nerikan is the denomination of all that is bad. It may not be the birthplace of evil, but it is most certainly its adopted home."

He went on to explain that it was first an iron mine with deep and twisting corridors curling far and wide under the Rückraadt Mountains. Its many paths stretched out farther than all of the roads in Eisen, its countless wide rooms forever shrouded in darkness. It was not long after the mines gave up their last cartful of ore that the deep barrow halls were acquisitioned for their new purpose. "Massive iron gates were set at the only known entrance, and one by one magical men and women were either lured or hauled in chains to the vast underground."

"Aurlings," she said, and he nodded.

The mountains faded behind the growing forest. Past those trees and over those peaks lay a city she had once called home, now already so far away. Straight through those mountains lived a group of girls she had called her sisters, and a woman who had acted as surrogate mother. How far away that life seemed already as she rode deeper into the woods. She still had not accepted this as a death sentence. In the past, she had always wormed her way out the worst trouble, or Haggart had arrived just in time to bargain for her pardon. But as the green fields faded away and shadows crept over the carriage, she began to believe that this time things were different. She could not talk her way out of this cage. And even if she could melt the bars and slink away, Koertig's men and horses would be upon her in an instant. She was stuck here, on this train to Nerikan, and no one, not Haggart, not Philippa, not any of her sisters were going to save her.

This is what she thought as Edwin droned on. Her focus drifted away from the old man to the hillside where the forest and mountain met. It was there amongst the trees that something like a shadow dropped down behind thick holly bushes.

"It would be a much more fascinating history," Edwin continued about Nerikan, "if *we* were not the next chapter."

The form moved again. Large and dark the shadow appeared, trampling heather and heath, and sheltering away behind hardwood and shrub. Too big for a man, too subtle for a beast. It trailed them, lurking, watching. A hand as big as her cot in the Ward slid through a honeysuckle bush and pulled open a peephole. *How long have you followed us, Bakku?* she thought, and smiled.

"Oh, it is nothing to smile about," Edwin said, lost in his tale. "You see, it is not just empty caves. Still today there are creatures of the underworld at play down there. Gores they call them. Scions, like the wolf-boars. Their eyes blackened by unnatural means. They see by sound. Their hollow clicks resounding off walls and feeling all that moves. We will sit in the darkness, lost to the light, and you will only know when the gores are nearing when those awful clicks rattle your ears and tap your neck. For years they survived off the wayward worms and beetles that had foolishly dug themselves into their own graves, we will not survive the gores."

"Somebody did," Olen said.

"Yes, that creature. Imagine a lifetime in darkness and chains. The daily torture and torment of those clicking fiends playing evil games with its mind. It must be like a rabid dog freed. I was there when he escaped, he is as mad as the mirror maker."

"I have never understood that phrase," she said. "But he is not mad. Angry maybe, but not mad."

She watched the tree line. The shadow leapt down a short cliff and hid poorly behind a wide tree trunk. A large sack hung over its shoulder. It was Bakku. She was certain now. Here was one who had not abandoned her. She wanted to jump and dance and cry and laugh, but she held steady as they rode into the thick Ma'alabrad woods.

***

Her sisters were different now, Philippa thought, as she sifted her rake through the horse bedding, weeding out the brown dung. It had been three years since she had worked in Mr. Schmid's stables, but the smell was the same. The sisters avoided her at the Ward now and tried to get out of doing chores with her. It was not that they were mad at her for exposing Olen, it was something else, more like fear.

"Over there, Icha," she said, as her sister arrived with a barrow of fresh wood shavings discarded from the mill. The young girl with the Swarhee head scarf set the barrow in the corner and quietly waited for instruction. "Grab the fork off the wall and help me."

They slung manure in silence, a silence uncommon to the horse stalls. Mr. Schmid often haggled over the price he paid for this service, claiming Olen and Icha spent more time talking than they ever did working. But Olen was gone now, so when Schmid's wife came around looking for help, Philippa volunteered. She wanted this change at the Ward to be a smooth one.

Icha poked through chips and dust, but never looked at her older sister, and never spoke. Yes, Philippa thought, fear. They were afraid of her, but she could not understand why.

"You will have to talk to me eventually," Philippa offered, while still raking the stalls. Still nothing from the young girl. "If you don't talk to me," she said, and motioned her fork to the pile of dung, "Then I won't share my chocolate buns."

Icha smiled at this and informed her that horse poop is not chocolate.

Philippa straightened her back and slapped her gloved palm to her forehead. "No wonder the boys don't kiss me!" she said and sent Icha laughing.

She let the good feeling remain in the air while they worked before asking about Olen.

"Are you mad at me for telling on Olen?" she asked, sweeping the last of the manure out of the stable.

Icha took a small flat scoop and flung fresh wood chips and sawdust on the bare spots of the floor. "She was my friend," she said. "I miss her."

"And she was my sister," Philippa said. "But you must understand by now, she was different."

They both scooped sawdust and chips and painted the floor a woody yellow.

"I'm different," Icha said softly.

"Your religion is different, but you are not."

"Sure I am," she said back. "Everywhere I go people say I'm different. My clothes, my hair, my skin, it's all different. And now Olen had to go away because she was different?"

How, she thought. How to convince this little girl that just because her family came from a different land, that does not mean she was a witch like Olen.

"Olen was a different kind of different," Philippa tried but knew her words fell hollow.

Too soon, she told herself. It had been too soon to talk about Olen.

She cursed herself for bringing it up, and told herself to be wiser from now on. They emptied the barrow and looked over their work. Not bad for a couple girls from the Ward, she thought, but said nothing. She put their shovels into the barrow and made to leave.

"I had a dream," Icha said, pausing before going on. "I had a dream you took me to the bad place, too."

"Nerikan? Why would I do that?"

"Because I was different. Because we all were."

"All?"

"All the sisters," Icha mumbled, on the verge of tears. "You took us all to Nerikan. And it was dark, and it smelled bad, and there were monsters."

Philippa fought off the thought, that damnable and incorrect thought that maybe she had made a mistake turning in Olen. They *were* all different, everyone at the Ward was. They were different from the Midtowners, vastly different from the Uptowners. They were even different from the travelers and traders that came through the city. They were poor orphans who didn't quite understand how families and friends and relationships worked. They were different from everyone else in the world, and they would always be that way. But even so, Olen had used magic, and for that she was unsafe.

"It was just a dream," Philippa said. "It doesn't mean anything."

"But sometimes, when I dream things..." Icha said, but refused to finish.

* * *

Olen wondered why the older soldiers, who had surely toiled for years to earn rank, took orders so shamelessly from the younger Koertig. Men nearly twice his age pounded stakes as the sergeant brushed Tasker. He was tall and bold, but his visored helm could not hide his youthful face. He ordered his men casually as the sun fell, and they submitted easily.

Night spread across Ma'alabrad. Short tents rose up around a campfire where guardsmen cooked. Olen watched sweet venison turn on a spit, knowing fair well that such precious meat would not be shared with her and Edwin. All but Koertig had stripped off their armored plates and sat around in loose shirts and trousers, talking boisterously. The city clerk Reeve sat alone from the men, eating a small portion quietly while the others passed around leathers of beer and wine.

"This is no celebration," Koertig offered unprovoked, finally pulling off his helm. "This is a somber day. We do not near the end of our task, but instead mark the beginning." He took a swig from a young soldier's cup as an owl hooed in the distance. "We would be fools to believe these were the only creatures to survive the tales." He reached to his hip and slid a small blade out of a hidden sheath. It was a thin boning knife. He looked at it as if remembering. He sliced off hunks of venison and handed them to his men. "For so long they have hidden in our world, living as one of us. They have infiltrated our universities to learn our secrets, and they have taken the form of children to influence the subtle minds of our youth."

The men rumbled at his words and gave muffled assents as they chewed. Edwin looked around the cage and then up at Olen, as if he had lost something.

"What?" she asked, also searching the dark forest for her own lost something.

"Just distracted," he whispered, and shook it off.

"They could be anywhere," Koertig continued, "secretly plotting against us, like they did so many years ago. It is not even below them to take the form of a handsome male to marry our sisters and daughters, tarnishing our bloodlines forever. This we cannot allow."

The men growled and shouted their support, but Edwin spun in the cage as if spooked, searching the deep forest behind him.

"What are you doing," she asked.

"I have this thing—don't ask me to explain," Edwin said and pointed beyond the camp, "that is telling me I really, really need to be over there."

Koertig continued, "These are just the first of many we will hunt down and cast away. Too long has our army been bound in chains, secreted behind city walls. Our mayor-general must understand we are not mere stewards of commerce. We are an army! Eisen is threatened, and we will fight for her. We must renew the old guard, and again stalk the wildest beasts," Koertig paused as if lost in thought, and then added, "Just like our fathers." A half-moon shone through a break in the clouds and lit the encampment. "The cleansing will be complete."

The men cheered and raised their flasks. Guardsmen raised their spears and swords and shook them over their heads.

"Oh dear," Edwin said to his palms.

"Just ignore him," she said and noticed how truly agitated he had become. On their journey he had calmed to the situation quite well, becoming almost complacent with his fate. But now he cowered like a frightened child huddling in a corner.

"It is not Koertig," Edwin said. "It is something else. Something is about to happen, I can feel it, something very bad."

"When?" she asked.

He clutched the cage and squeezed shut his eyes like a child flinching from a spank. Through his tightly pressed lids came the faintest dull glow.

"Now!" he cried, pulling his hood over his head.

In the forest a mule cried like a tarnished war horn's final blow. A snap like a breaking branch ended its call. A few of the more eager guardsmen leapt to their feet and slid swords out of sheaths, yet they had no direction to attack or defend. A wide black shadow flew overhead, snapping off bough and bole. It crashed into the campfire, splashing red coals into the faces and laps of dining soldiers, and then landed atop a scrambling guardsman, pinning him down. Soldiers jumped, tearing off their burning shirts and screaming for water for their scalded eyes. Men scattered as the encampment burned.

Olen's rags rippled and tightened, then darkened to pitch black cloth. She was all but invisible in the night.

"Form up! Form up!" Koertig yelled, but his panicked men ran chaotically, fleeing their own dancing shadows as a hellish orange light radiated from the scattered coals. Koertig pulled a long sword from the supply wagon and advanced on the cage.

Edwin cowered in the corner, covering his ears and crying out, "No, no, no!"

A cart crashed to their right, and soldiers who had dashed into the forest cried out. Koertig turned to the sound and raced off, pulling more men with him as he went. "We fight!" he shouted, and led the assault. Soon the encampment was empty save for the caged two, as shouts and cries came from the dark woods. She rippled her ankle and worked herself free of her chain, tossing it aside.

"Be ready," she told her cage mate, but he did not seem to hear.

A painful roar thundered through the camp, shuddering the ground. A lucky swordsman had landed a blow on Bakku. No, not luck. Koertig. Only he would have shown no fear in striking Bakku. The beast called out again, this time a cry of defiance not suffering. Two thin shadows ran past the cage and away from battle. The panicked soldiers dropped their spears, tossed their helms, and kept running.

"Cowards!" she yelled to Koertig's gutless lackeys.

Swords and spears clanged and men shouted. The beast called back and heavy thuds landed in the dark. Victorious shouts were now calls of pain and anguish as men were overwhelmed in the dark. Then the ground shook in growing waves.

He was coming.

The Aurling was coming for her.

There was no going back now. She was out of the Ward, out of Millthrace, and soon to be out of this cage. She had begged for a magical messenger for so many nights, and he was finally here to return her to her true home. She would be ready.

A child screamed.

It was Edwin.

The giant shadow burst into the clearing. It clumped barefoot over the fires and engulfed the cage. Enormous hands tore the iron prison off of the trailer. Her stomach tumbled and Edwin screamed again as they soared through the air before settling gently onto the ground. Bakku's bloody face glistened in the red firelight, and his deep iron and copper breaths blew against her. A bloody gash above his eye glowed a hollow white, and faded softly as the wound sealed itself. Gigantic fingers grasped the bars and tore them open. She slipped out of the cage.

"Go!" Bakku yelled, and turned back towards the battle.

"Go?" she shouted back. "I can't just go! You were supposed to rescue me!"

Bakku grabbed a wheel off a broken carriage and flung it into the darkness. Soldiers grunted and fell.

"Go!" he yelled again, and pointed away from battle.

She stood dumbfounded. There were already soldiers in the woods in every direction. Even those who had fled the battle would happily hunt her down and return her corpse to Koertig, begging his forgiveness. She shouted back, "We *go* together!"

The soldiers had regrouped and came through the woods. Bakku barked a frustrated roar and crouched down low next to the girl. "Up!" he growled. She scurried up his shoulder and clung to his neck. Bakku spun around and rose to his full height, whipping the girl around as he turned. She grasped at burlap, desperate not to slip off. She pulled herself to sitting on his broad shoulders and saw from an eagle's view the destroyed camp as soldiers crashed through the trees.

"Go!" she yelled to Bakku, and without hesitation he ran. He pushed through the dark woods, running straight through the heavy brush. The soldiers followed but not closely, as speed and fear were Bakku's weapons tonight. She slipped on his bloody neck, and pushed herself back up with her legs. He raced away from the campsite and up the mountainside.

A lance flew past the fleeing couple and pierced a nearby tree. Bakku spun around, nearly sending her flying. Koertig hurried after, with Reeve and another not far behind. Of all the soldiers, only Koertig showed no fear of the storybook ogre. He tore an iron-tipped spike from the hands of his fellow soldier and launched it at Olen. It flew but half a heartbeat—though a lifetime it seemed—and smashed into her chest, right over her heart.

Just days ago she had been diving for coins in a hidden pool under Millthrace, and dreaming of riding the Skywheel and eating red rock candy. Just days ago she had been in the Millthrace market trading apples and onions, and eating warm tarts. Just days ago she had a home, a mother figure, and countless sisters. And now she sat on the shoulders of a giant, lost in the woods, facing Millthrace's greatest soldier.

When he had flung the spear, her black clothes had rippled. A shell of iron had covered her chest and head. Blue emblems decorated her plate. Once again she wore Koertig's thick shell. The spear crushed the plate like an old tin tub, sending her falling backwards to the ground. She landed with a clanging thud, knocking the air out of her chest. Her armor fell away to rags.

Earlier she had heard Bakku's rage in the darkness, but now she saw it. The creature raised his long arms above his head and exploded a roar that sent boulders rolling down the mountainside. He pounced on Koertig and grasped the sergeant in his massive hands. With one horrible twist Bakku tore off Koertig's right arm at the shoulder.

"No!" she coughed out, grasping her chest with one hand and reaching out to Bakku with the other.

Koertig clasped his bloody shoulder and watched confusedly as thick blood spurted through his fingers. He dropped to a knee, still dumbstruck, seemingly disbelieving what he saw. Bakku saw she was alive and looked back to Koertig apologetically, seemingly shocked and remorseful at what he had done. He opened his wide palm and let the dead appendage fall as the sergeant fell away.

"Bakku," she said, though it hurt to speak, to breathe.

He stumbled back to her, looking often at the injured soldier guiltily. She reached up to Bakku's bloody hand. He scooped her up and grabbed his burlap sack. Then he placed her over his shoulder and ran away, sprinting uphill and dashing straight through mulberry and honeysuckle. She watched over his shoulder as he ran. She watched the forest floor as a man she had always hated, if only because he had always hated her, lay dying. Koertig had called the little girls rats and tossed them in the river when he caught them being less than perfect ladies. He had kicked them aside with his pike whenever a higher class gentleman or lady had passed close by. He had been the true terror of her younger years, this man the older sisters had found handsome, but it hurt deep inside her chest to watch his breathing fade and his head fall to its side. The rest of the guard gave up the chase and surrounded their sergeant as Reeve rushed in and fell to his knees, trying desperately to stop the bleeding.

***

Edwin cowered in his cage, his hood pulled tightly over his eyes. For a third time now he had seen the Nerikan beast, and it had gotten more frightening each time. When it had first escaped its cursed burrow, it had appeared worried and lost. Now, its face splashed with crimson beads, it was fearless and mad. It had lifted him and his cage as if they were but a child's toy and set them on the ground. And when it had torn apart the iron bars, Edwin had been certain his fate was that of the Mayden Faire hog.

The creature had stolen away poor Olen and pounded up the mountainside. The remaining soldiers had followed. But still Edwin sat in his cage, his head in his hands as he rocked back and forth, waiting for the guard to return and finish him off. He thought perhaps even the Mayden Faire hog had not suffered as he. He mumbled a song from his younger years, from before the time his aunts took over his stewardship. His voice soft and reedy, "The only way to Mayden Faire, is with a fairly maiden. And if the lass shall lay you bare, then bare you shall be—"

School boy chants, he thought derisively, and chased away the song. The truth was, he finally admitted to himself, he was still not ready to die. He understood and accepted his fate and hoped someday to be at peace with everyman's destiny, but not today. So many wasted years, he thought, studying and scribing in drafty hollow halls, turning brittle pages in ancient tomes, his clothed finger sliding over script only the learned could decipher. And when mouthing the words in some forgotten folio, and chittering with delight at some unexpected aphorism, he would then find himself most alone with no one to share in his amusement. It was this loneliness that kept him alive, this need to share his life before he could let it go.

Softly crunching coals cut off his thoughts, and he raised his head for the first time since the attack. The soldiers were gone, but a tall dark apparition sauntered through the camp, stepping carefully over still-orange embers as if pacing hallowed grounds. It was the sergeant's horse, Tasker, and it was Edwin's four-legged ferry to freedom. Distant shouts echoed deep in the woods, but the camp was quiet. Again his wits and perseverance had guided him to liberty. With a tentative step, Edwin put one foot on the ground. No one objected, so he stepped out of the cage completely.

I did it, he thought proudly, then exclaimed, "I escaped!"

Tasker reared up at this voice in the night, neighing in surprise. The great steed then turned aside, kicking his hind legs at the ground and dashing away into the woods.

Edwin stood alone in the ruined camp, just nodding his bald head. *Yes*, he thought to whoever could hear his thoughts. *Yes, indeed. Why stop torturing poor Edwin now? Have your fun, get your laughs, enjoy the show.*

He pushed away from his cage. Torn trees and abandoned gear littered the camp. A large mule lay dead. A man's legs splayed out underneath. "Heavens!" he exclaimed and backed away, bumping into the venison hind-quarter still skewered on the spit. He tore off a king-sized chunk and bit into it like a boor. Voices in the woods approached, so he quickly shuffled off in the other direction. He passed a toppled supply cart and plundered a rough blanket.

"Round up!" a voice in the dark yelled out, calling the troops.

He reached blindly into the cart's strewn goods and snatched a small bag. Then with bag and blanket and a hunk of meat, the wayward Observer scurried away into the haunted woods. He shot through the reaching black arms of shadowed trees and thought only of distant Ulm, and how he would never leave it again.

14

A Feast of Grubs

Olen rode on Bakku's shoulders all through the night. She clung to bloody burlap and stole glances at his monolithic head as he bounded over moonlit boulders and galloped across the dark mountainside. His head bobbed as he ran, his lips popping a rhythm with his breaths. Nostrils as wide as laundry chutes flared and narrowed as he chugged along on seemingly tireless muscles. And his eyes, dark brown and worried, always searching ahead for danger. He had come back for her, something no one else had ever done. And now he was taking her home to her new life. Life among the Aurlings.

A deep gash split his cheek from ear to jowl. Blood, sharp and fungal, dried over the wound. And even as she watched, the skin pinched together and sealed with puffy pink scars, days, maybe weeks earlier than expected. Aurling magic, she thought. A wound he had taken for her.

A rock wall loomed ahead of them. He grabbed the stony cliff and pulled them both up over the ledge. Here he paused and looked back over the deep Ma'alabrad Woods below. The eastern lands stretched away to darkness as grey clouds loomed over the vast valley. The only sign of man this far away from Millthrace were the black ruins of an ancient spire atop a rotting mountainside castle far across the expanse. It was a dark and unknown world to her, with vulture-like flyers circling above and darkness in every direction, but she was unafraid riding the shoulder of this giant. The stench of his blood, like rotten meat, clouded around them. It turned her stomach, but he had come back for her.

She held her palm up beside his scarred temple and splayed her fingers as he scanned the forest. Wider than her palm, his great eye searched below as if looking for soldiers in the trees. He finally turned her way, his blood-crusted cheek pressing her hand aside.

"Thank you," she said. "Sorry they hurt you."

He said nothing in return. He merely turned back towards the mountains and ran. He ran as the moon shifted above. Hours later, as the sky finally began to lighten, they at last stood above the tree line and could see far beyond the woods to the distant horizon. He turned to the southeast, moving across the mountainside, away from Nerikan and farther away from Millthrace. It was cooler this high up the mountainside and a crisp morning breeze blew against her. In spite of herself, Olen shivered. He slowed to a trot, and again turned his wide head to her.

"I'm fine," she said. "Just a chill in the air."

He looked to her thin black clothes and grunted, a meaning she understood.

"Of course!" she replied. "Why didn't I think of that?" She searched her mind for images of the Uptown ladies, ferreting out those jealous winter memories of women wrapped in sable cloaks over heavy woolen jackets. Her dark cloth rippled and thickened into wool pants and a short red-colored coat. Not quite, she thought and concentrated harder. Then as if unfurling from a roll, the coat lengthened. It flowed down her back and spilled fur-lined sleeves down her arms along with a pelt collar around her neck. She remembered the blacksmith's shop. She slipped her collar up over her face and it smoothed out to a brown leather band. Two glass circles appeared over her eyes. She now wore leather riding goggles with real glass lenses. She nodded at Bakku and hugged his neck. She stared face-first into the wind as he raced forward, her long coat trailing behind her.

Look at me Haggart, she thought as she was carried away. Look at me finally free. Thank you for taking care of me for so long, but this is who I really am, and with my family and my people is where I am supposed to be. They raced ahead, Bakku galloping smoothly like a majestic stallion, Olen clutching his neck. Look and me Haggart, she thought again, and hoped her old Mistress would be proud.

***

Edwin wandered for two mostly sleepless nights in Ma'alabrad Forest, studying the hills and trees, insisting that this bent branch or that curved trunk was somehow familiar, and perhaps a way-marker to freedom. Yet he was lost, as the sun set again. *And alone*, he was reminded by that primal part of his brain that makes rational thought a distant and forgotten friend. He was back in the realm of scion wolves, and he was once again unprepared to defend himself. Every dry leaf crackling behind him was a stalking hound, and every tickling breeze was another ghost escaped from Nerikan. This was all his scholarly intellect allowed him to ponder, when what he truly needed was rational calm.

He had long ago finished off the venison, and fresh hunger gnawed at him. The stolen blanket had helped with the chill of night, but the sack he had pilfered from the overturned cart had just been another one of creation's fine jokes played upon poor old Edwin. The heavy sack was stuffed full of silvers and pennies, a commission for Koertig's men. He had at first marveled at the possibilities, sifting his fingers through the jangling coins: Safe and comfortable travel home! A third-floor dormitory at University, away from the mocking youth! Perhaps even remuneration for his increasingly-miserly aunts...perhaps. But now as he wandered the dark woods, hungry and lost, he scoffed at the coins' impotence. He pulled out the sack and hefted it in his palm. He had not counted it all, but there were nearly forty silver honors tossed in with countless copper pennies and hacks.

He sifted through the coins, rubbing his soft thumb over the cast images. Each city minted their own honors and stamped them with images of their pride. Here was the silver profile of Mayor Brynn, backed with the finely crafted image of a waterwheel and mill. Here were Daegan honors with their proud portraits of Sig Bran and his glorious wall. Now Brennan coins and even silvers from distant Ulm.

"Useless to a starving man," he said and let tumble a handful of coins into the bushes at his feet. A startled fat hare dashed out of the undergrowth and disappeared into the woods.

Edwin dropped his shoulders and plodded forward.

He thought often of Olen and the creature that had snatched her away. No, not stolen away, he corrected himself, rescued. He was certain of that now. He should have known it the moment the creature had burst into Millthrace and all he could do was focus on the child. She had felt an instant affinity to the ogre, she had mentioned so in the cage, but he had thought that to be silliness right up unto the attack on the camp. How strange, he thought, that this little girl who had been taken away by Eisen's most nightmarish creature was most likely quite safe, while he a master of letters at University was sure to starve in these woods with nothing to eat but putrid vegetation.

He kicked the rotting leaves and something wriggled atop the soil. A fat white grub, its nest disturbed, worked its way back underground. He surveyed it somberly.

"Is this what it's come to, Edwin my dear?" a lament only those of University would appreciate and pity, "A banquet of grubs?"

The fat worm pulsated under shear skin as it wiggled into the soft soil. A vulgar reminder of how far he had wandered from whole-some Ulm.

"You were meant for fine wine and cheeses in the great halls of kings," he spoke, as if speaking a eulogy. The pale larva's bulbous tail disappeared below the dirt.

"Oh no you don't!" he called out and dove to the ground. He tore at the soil and quickly rooted out the worm. It throbbed in his palm like a slow-beating heart. He paused one last second for rescue, and when none arrived, he grimaced and stuffed the larva into his mouth. It popped on the first chew, squirting savory milk down his throat. He gave two more quick chews and swallowed. When it was down, and the ignominy behind him, he sat up and raised a curious eyebrow. "Hmm," he said, rolling his tongue over his teeth and swallowing again. "I can honestly say I have had worse meals in Illsbrook."

Edwin kicked over many more leaves and feasted.

***

Koertig saw only stars. He was moving, being moved. Quickness. Speed he could not fathom. Horses galloped, wheels turned. And stars. They observed him, judged him, as tree tops flew by.

Heat. His shoulder and neck. Burning. The stars cast fire upon him, boiling him alive. Soldiers hovered overhead, faces in shadows, tending his wounds. Tearing at him. Their words hollow murmurs, like rumors in a church hall. Echoes. Drops, on his tongue. Poison, burning. Stars in the sky beckoned him as a hand wiped his brow.

And they were not stars. It was another who observed from the distant ether. Another Koertig. Far above. Far away. Father. He had come back. Many years late, but he had come back, as his son lay dying.

Devils pressed daggers into his shoulder, their muffled speech seeping through as they dug their weapons deeper, twisting them and grinding meat. Koertig clutched tightly to his screams, only fractured breaths seeping out of the corners of his pressed lips. He would never give the devils the satisfaction.

Seemingly days passed in desperation. Seemingly eons. Dark, darker, and then just a promise of starlight.

What happened? Koertig asked, and his father answered.

You lost, the ancient voice said, and the stars dimmed.

I lost, young Koertig repeated. *I was not supposed to lose.* A fiend tightened a noose around his shoulder and pulled it tight. His body stiffened and jerked, but he would not beg for mercy. He was Koertig the strong!

The stars were unimpressed.

You lost, his father said again, the voice of flickering space. *But you are not defeated.*

I am not defeated, Koertig repeated, waxing and waning with the stars. *I am not defeated,* he thought, but his thoughts lacked conviction.

Son, you are aggregate of father and mother, and you are superior.

But Mother has gone, Koertig said and dropped his thoughts to a shamed whisper, *Gone to Illsbrook.*

"Open the gate!" a clear voice cried out, startling the sergeant. It was like a voice from his childhood. A young man. Two young men. Friends. Fiends. The Boys of Illsbrook. A two-man army. They had played where three rivers met. They had played at night. Night, when their mothers worked. Jay. That was his name. Jay. Jay the Swift. Koertig the Strong. Jay the Elder. Koertig the Young. Princes. "Open the gate!" He and Jay had hidden on the Illsbrook roofs and thrown clay shingles at the drunks as they stumbled through the gates of Queenstown looking for whores. That friend was gone now, but Koertig lived.

"The sergeant needs a medic!"

The voices mingled with the stars and set them in motion, or was Koertig turning? They wheeled overhead, and his head turned with them. The sound they made as they turned in the sky, chains on a pulley. The grunt of an ox, its constellation dragging the cosmos out of order. A flash of clarity cut through his fever, and Koertig knew the truth of the universe and the hidden gears that drove it.

"The stars, they do not move on their own!" Sergeant Koertig's dry voice rasped through labored breaths. "How wide, this Aurling threat!"

The fiends attending him understood Koertig had gained a secret awareness. This they would not allow. They offered him up to the mouth of a great beast. The stars fell away as he rolled through wide jaws. The teeth, each one larger than the largest man, hung overhead waiting for Koertig. He would not be consumed! He would not be eaten! The beast had taken his arm, and was now swallowing him whole!

Then despite his will, despite his strength, and despite his pride, Koertig screamed. Darkness overtook him, and the heat, the stars, and the devils were no more.

Father...

Koertig slept.

15

Harner

For two days and nights Olen had ridden Bakku's shoulders as he moved south along the Rückraadt Mountains. They journeyed mostly in silence save for the ravens that grunted at them from the treetops, or the random four-legged predators that turned tail and fled whimpering from their oversized prey. At the darkest of night, when the unbroken cadence of his footsteps willed her eyes to drift shut and her head to fall against his neck, he finally slowed. He found a stone overhang with a small dugout. He lifted her from his shoulders and placed her in the hollow. Then he brought his massive form to the ground and laid on his side, placing his etched and scarred back to her, sealing her off in her little enclosure, protecting her from whatever lurked in the night.

Hours later she woke to find herself being lifted upon great shoulders, and the journey began again. He had not spoken of a destination, but since their path south along the mountainside led straight to Kessel, she let him carry her away.

His wounds had all healed completely.

There were more squawking blackbirds here than ever before, and more frightened harts that flashed their white tails as they raced away. And as the trees thinned out and the mountain fields opened up, she saw why. Water. He tromped over the brush and pushed through to a grand stone jutting over a mountain lake. Two grey-headed ducks with bright yellow bills paddled away, murmuring angrily at the interlopers. Reeds circled the clean and clear pond, and a light breeze rippled the surface. There would be food here and lots of it.

He set her on the stone and dropped his pack. The large sack may have been full after he ransacked Millthrace, but it was now nearly empty. He reached deep inside and pulled out the battered tin pot she had seen him pilfer. He handed it to her and pointed to the lake.

"Yes sir," she said, mockingly, and took the pot to the shore. She sat on her knees and splashed cool water on her face. She licked her lips and tasted the mineral-rich water. It was fresher and cleaner than the chalky water of Lowtown. She scooped a handful and drank. Beyond the lake the plains stretched out below, far down the mountainside. Such a huge world, so much bigger than she ever imagined. Wide-winged flyers circled the prairie below looking for their morning snack. She too needed to eat. She looked back at Bakku. He whipped a jagged stone at a line of bushes along the forest edge. Then he loped over and dug through.

At the base of the mountain clusters of forests grew, but farther east the trees and prairie grasses fell away to a flat and lifeless wasteland that stretched to the horizon. The Ode, she thought, looking over the drab and foreboding expanse. She had heard of the Ode from travelers. It was a wide sand and stone territory deprived of rain by the tallest peaks of the Rückraadt. The Iron Road cut through a western dint in the Ode. Only the hardiest or most desperate traders ventured that lifeless trail, and not all made it out alive.

She wondered if Koertig was alive.

She dipped the pot in the lake and was reminded of washing pots in Millthrace. Her sisters would be at the river right now. Beautiful Lysa, nervous and excited that her adoption was nearing. She would have a hundred questions for Haggart as she cleaned. Ellery, so thin and so tall, and so quiet, working harder than everyone. And Maggie. Little Maggie with her black jar.

She wondered how long until they all forgot about her. Word would get back that she had escaped. They would say the monster helped her. Philippa would tell them the witch and her pet monster were going to come back and—

Bakku grunted, and she snapped out of her fantasy, for that was all it was, a fantasy. She would never go back to that city, not if Haggart did not want her. She had parents to find, a real family, and she knew where to find them.

She lugged the full pot back up to Bakku who already had a fire going. He had pulled a fat dead rabbit out of the bushes and bit into its belly, tearing back its pelt with his teeth. He scraped a horny fingernail along its underside, rupturing tissue. Then he swirled a thick finger inside its belly poking out noodle-like innards. A week ago she would have been sick watching him, but now she was starving. She made sure he did not waste any useful parts.

She set the pot on the fire as he snapped off the rabbit's head and tossed it far into the lake, then he dropped the rest of the hairless hare into the pot. She sat next to him and held her palms near the flames. He pulled his sack near and dug inside, feeling around. He pulled out a small round something. It was the onion she had given to him. He crushed it between thumb and forefinger and sprinkled it into the pot.

"You saved it," she said, smiling at him. He did not smile back.

An eagle circled the lake as they waited for the pot to boil. The bird hung effortlessly in the sky on outstretched wings, silently watching the water. It tucked its wings and arrowed straight into the mountain lake. A quick struggle on the surface and the eagle rose again, a silver trout flapping helplessly in its talons.

"Can you talk?" she asked, as Bakku sat beside her. "I mean more than one word at a time?"

He did not respond. He only sat staring at the rabbit as it churned in the pot.

"I hope Edwin got away. He was also in my cage," she said, but Bakku sat statue-like on the mountainside. "I thought he could tell me more about Aurlings and my magic, but he didn't know much." Still no response. "I mean, how do Aurlings lose a baby? If they're so smart and strong and magical, then the one thing I think they could do is not lose their children."

She meant this as a sort of jest, but the stoic Aurling stiffened even more.

"I don't know why you helped me," she said. "But thank you. Maybe I could have gotten out of that cage, but I never would have gotten away from those soldiers." She plucked at the grass between her crossed legs as steam rose from the pot. Then she said the one thing she had tried not to say. "I think you killed that man. Koertig."

Bakku turned his great head towards her. His eyes, so large, and manlike, compassionate and mournful. She had seen these eyes in the old men of Millthrace who had somehow outlived their wives. They were the eyes of someone just waiting to die.

"Sorry," she said.

He pushed the rabbit under the steaming water with his bare fingers.

"Try it like this," she said, pressing a stick into the pot.

He pulled his finger out and sucked on the stock. "You. Must. Go," he said slowly, deliberately, his voice shaking the ground.

"You keep saying that," she said and thought perhaps he was not a messenger from her parents. "Food first?"

Bakku nodded slowly, but did not look at her.

***

Edwin continued on through the forest, kicking leaves high with broad jaunty footsteps. He would never tell anyone about the wild larvae he had swallowed, but at least he felt alive, awake, and energetic. He had a full belly, and an even fuller purse. And after three days lost in the haunted forest, the thinning trees told him he was nearing the edge of Ma'alabrad. Once he made it out, he could buy secret passage back to University. There he could live frugally off the stash of silvers, just writing his memoirs, finishing his dissertation, and attending only the best traveling lectures. And if his observations ever pulled him away, well, he now had the purse to travel in style and comfort. He almost welcomed the idea. He had a light skip to his step as he rounded a tall hill and came face to face with the broken gates of Nerikan Prison.

"Oh no," he said, and fell to his knees.

He ducked behind the mound. "Only you, Edwin, would march straight into the one place you were trying to get the farthest from." He peeked around the hill at Nerikan. It was as he had left it. One gate lay on the ground atop the moldering remains of a wolf-boar scion. The other gate still hung half-hinged against the granite wall, and one giant iron falchion still hung over the entrance. The Brennan ironworkers had not yet arrived to do their repairs. A vaporous rot, hot and nastily sweet, like a plagued man's final exhale, vented from the deep below.

For a man whose world was made up of coincidences, he had long ago given up the shock of special things happening right at the moment of his arrival. Therefore, the otherwise nervous scholar was not too surprised by the sound of voices in the woods. He stayed back behind the hill, observing.

They came from the northwest, Millthrace's way, in a group of three. Two had tall walking sticks and small packs strapped to their back. All three had thin sabers hanging from their belts. The man in front was shorter than the rest, with finely combed black hair and dark features. He also carried a saber, but his was pure gold.

"Mayor Brynn!" Edwin whispered, and nearly called out. He was one of the few rational and educated men he had met in the waterwheel city. Brynn was a man that could be reasoned with. And now with the excitement of the beast's attack on the city far behind him, perhaps he'd welcome a dialogue. The fact that Bakku had abandoned Edwin to rot in the woods proved they were not in league. Brynn would understand that.

Brynn and the two men marched up to the black hellmouth of Nerikan. They peered deep within, seemingly unaffected by the stench. Brynn called out into the black burrow, shouting commands to some unseen subordinate, his words echoing back to Edwin. Again Brynn called into the vast cave, calling someone or something to his side. After several moments of this, a new sound drifted out of the lair. It was a flurry of clicks, thick in the air as if made of substance not just sound. He felt them, like a thousand tiny insects traveling up his arms, his neck, and then tickling his inner ear. He batted his ears and thrust a thin pinky deep inside.

The mayor stepped back into the clearing as the clicks thickened. The two men took up their weapons and stood by. At the gatemouth, a shadow, tall and thin, separated from the darkness and skulked into the light. Black-shelled legs, jointed backwards at the knee, gave the creature a forward lean, as if ready to leap and run. Thin upper arms hung below its shoulders, but they widened at the forearms and were also covered in a roach-like shell. Its fingers were long, dexterous, and fearfully clawed. Its torso was of a man, but its back was cased in a horned beetle-like husk. The face was a confused mixture of man, rat, and insect. Its jaw man-like, but with two long incisors jutting upwards. The nose, stunted and upturned, allowed the teeth to slide freely over. The skull sloped backwards as on a rodent, with a thick horn curving out of the crown. Black saucer eyes, pupilless and stationary, were held distant from the sun. Loud clicks, like dry twigs snapping in rapid succession poured from its mouth. It was a gore, the Nerikan guardsmen. Many more of the same appeared behind it.

Brynn chastised the creatures loudly, berating them for Bakku's escape. He grabbed the first beast by the head and slapped his palms over its eyes. A pale light emanated from his palms, and the gore screeched in pain. Brynn tore his hands away, and the creature blinked widely. Gone were the wide lidless plates, and in their place now darted man-like orbs, with pale white sclera and searching black pupils.

"I have given you the light," Mayor Brynn said, as the other creatures obediently lined up for their transformation. "Come out of the darkness!" He pressed his palms against more gores, and sent them out of the shadows, their new eyes for the first time wide and searching. "Find him and bring him back to his chains."

Edwin sat nervously behind the mound as the mayor altered the creatures. He scratched-off Brynn as a possible savior from his never-ending ordeal. None in this world has suffered such as Edwin. It was a lament he had made much of his life, but after an ogre, a cage, and now Nerikan gores, Edwin's lament was finally true.

Find him and bring him back to his chains. It was Bakku he spoke of. He was ordering these creatures to hunt him. Edwin was certain the ogre could protect himself, but he was no longer alone. He was also sending these creatures after Olen.

He peeked around the hillside again as Brynn finished transforming the gores into sighted hunters. Then without ceremony or celebration, Brynn and his men abruptly turned and marched straight back the way they had come, leaving the gores to their new eyes.

The gore Brynn had touched first twisted its neck, searching the forest, blinking often at what must have been confusing visions.

"At least that infernal clicking has stopped," Edwin thought, as the gore scanned the tree tops, the ground, and the stones that surrounded the doorway. At one point it even seemed to turn its eyes right towards Edwin's vine-covered nook, but showed no sign of recognition and turned away.

Then, perhaps dissatisfied with its gift, it sent a flurry of clicks into the woods and waited stock-still as echoes mapped the overworld. Edwin shivered as unseen fingers tickled his neck. The gore jerked its head to the side and looked directly at the wayward Observer. Its new eyes now focused on Edwin, and its new brows sharpened. Then the scion gore screamed out a brutal call.

Edwin dropped behind the hill, rolled to his feet, and darted away into the woods, never looking back, never wanting to see the horrible gores right on his trail.

***

Olen thought of direction as the rabbit boiled. She had a general idea of how to get to Kessel. The mountains trailed off to the south, and the town was just beyond the mountain's end, near a wide river. So as long as she followed the mountains south, she should eventually find the village she had come from. The only question was, if Bakku left her, would she stay in the mountains or first make her way to plains and fields below. There were wild creatures in the mountain forests, but

Raiders stalked the fields. She was not sure which one to fear more. She could hide from a Raider party, but mountain predators could sniff her out before she knew they were trailing her. She could do this on her own, she thought, but it sure would be easier if Bakku stayed...at least a little longer.

The rabbit and onion stew finally reached a boil and Bakku let it cook for a few minutes more. When some unknown measure of time was finally reached, he abruptly grabbed the fire-hot pot and gulped down the entire rabbit. She fell back stunned, hungry, and outraged. Only then did the ogre speak.

"Still. Hungry," the gluttonous cow lamented, an entire hare sloshing inside him.

She sat with severely crossed arms and one foot tapping harshly on the stone ground. He furrowed his brow in question.

"That rabbit was for both of us!" she yelled, her words echoing off the mountain peaks. "Never mind. Go!" she said. "Take your tin pot and your ravenous appetite and leave."

Even during the most desperate times at the Ward they had always had food to share, and even if there was very little, not one sister took more than another. When they feasted, they feasted together, and when they starved, they suffered as one.

He seemed surprised, as if sharing was a part of his past that was forgotten in his long stay in Nerikan. He also seemed embarrassed and hurt. He grabbed the still warm pot and held it out to Olen. Pieces of onion floated in a cupful of broth.

"Onion soup," she said sarcastically. "Very nice." But she was desperately hungry, so she snatched the pot from his hands and slurped it up. There were a few tiny pieces of meat still in the stock. She finished it all and set the pot down roughly.

"Still hungry," she said, shaking her head.

"Always hungry," he replied.

***

Fever dreams had overtaken Sergeant Koertig as they had rushed him out of the woods. His world had fallen away to darkness, and he had slept for many days. After what felt like a hundred years of delirium, he woke to the aroma of freshly baked pretzel bread and the slow steady rhythm of chopping wood. *Chook, chook.* His eyes, crusted and weak, opened to a familiar yet unexpected sight. Hand-hewn logs were stacked and mudded up four walls, and rough cut joists spanned the shadowy cathedral-like ceiling. He lay in the cot he had known as a young man, and all around him the memories of his youth. It was his parent's cabin.

Winter winds blew in through cracked glass. As a child he had watched out that window at night as the city of Illsbrook twinkled far below. Distant sounds of drunken merriment had echoed up the mountain for much of his youth. The boy who grew up in hilltop hardship had grown to hate the sounds of Illsbrook and its depraved populace. The chopping continued outside. *Chook, chook.*

This cabin had burned years ago. He had been just twelve when he and his mother had been forced to flee to the wicked city below. They were hungry. They were penniless and had only the clothes they wore. His father had been gone for two seasons. There had been work in Illsbrook, for any healthy female.

Koertig sat up, his mind clouded in fog. The cabin had burned, yet here it stood just as he remembered. There the small stove, burning weakly, and the wooden barrels of rice and dry bean. A half-eaten knot of roped bread lay discarded on the table his father had built, and beside it lay his father's thin knife. His parent's bed, hardly large enough for two, sat across the room. Mother's books. Father's pipe. In the air, mother's sweet aroma, father's musk. He pulled off the blanket. A fleshy knot, twisted like the bread, covered his shoulder where his arm once hung. The knot was pink and painless. He had been healed. *Chook, chook.*

He wrapped himself in the blanket and moved on weak legs to the door. He grasped the familiar wooden handle. It was the same doorway he had stood in as his father had rode away for the last time. The elder Koertig had been a soldier in a clandestine army, a secret young Koertig had kept all of his life. This select group of men and women had been commissioned to complete Eisen's cleansing, generations after the last of the Aurlings had died away. As his father told it, a new menace had appeared to threaten their world. It was no longer creatures from beyond the veil, but men and women born of this land who had somehow taken up Aurling magic. They called them Demi-Aurlings, and it was his father's mission to end them.

Young Koertig had just turned twelve when his father had left the cabin that last time. He had boasted of the bounty they would receive. He would return with horses, he had said, and a coin of pure gold. Then he saddled up their lone mare, and rode off towards the city of Daegan.

Months later, and for many weeks after, Koertig had stood in this very doorway scanning the mountain trails for a father who would never return. On warm evenings he would sit alone outside watching, waiting, as his mother boiled tea indoors. She had days earlier ceased her nightly sobs, muffled under woolen blankets, and had seemed to accept that the elder Koertig was never to return. And so the younger Koertig had sat alone on the mountainside while colored firelight and music drifted up the hills from Illsbrook below. It was as if all the world had no regard for the missing man. *Chook, Chook.*

It had been a night like that when an unattended fire had leapt to the cabin's dry walls and then spread to the roof. In mere moments his father's home was a fiery mountaintop beacon, and Koertig and his mother were struggling down the hillside with nothing but the clothes they wore.

He now opened the familiar door to a snow-covered mountaintop. A dark figure stood in the blinding snowy whiteness, as if in a halo. His back was to Koertig as he heaved an axe over his head and swung it down against a log resting on an old wide stump. The hardwood split like dried clay and fell aside. This wide and muscular man, bestial in his winter furs, hefted another log one-handed and set it on the stump. Koertig stepped through the doorway, crackling frozen snow under his feet. The figure stopped chopping and listened. After a moment he returned to his labor. *Chook, chook.* He hacked the logs.

"Hello?" Koertig asked timidly.

Chook, chook.

Koertig called again, louder.

The figure thrust the axe into the stump, and stood up straight. Koertig could not move as the man turned his head. The profile of the father he had lost so long ago looked to the ground as if confused. The large man turned full around and faced his son in the doorway.

"Harner?" the large man asked. He was older than Harner Koertig remembered, yet the age lines in his face were contours of muscle. He had the thick leathery skin of a man raised in the wild outdoors. A wide moustache, wiry and grey, trailed down both sides of his lips. The rest of his face was clean shaven. He pulled back his hood revealing a thick shock of closely cropped black and grey hair. He smiled at his son. His teeth were full and white. "Harner, it is you!"

"Father," Koertig said, stepping forward. He had come home. He was years late, but he had finally returned, as only Koertig believed he would.

"Yes, it is I," the old man said. He gave his son a big hug and held him out by his shoulders. "You have grown!" The old man's face darkened as he felt his son's right shoulder. He pulled back Koertig's blanket. "I see you have taken a wound in battle," he said.

"Yes," Koertig replied. "The Aurlings have returned. I was not vigilant, and again they have come. Forgive me."

The two men stared at each other as the wind howled around the valley. Horns and drums from Illsbrook trickled up the mountainside. There was so much to take in from his youthful home, but he only beheld his father. The old man looked beyond him to the cabin.

"They are relentless, these Aurlings. They would have come nonetheless," he concluded, then asked, "And your mother? Is she well?"

"Gone to Illsbrook," Koertig replied, unable to hide his disgust. This common phrase was not merely an answer, but an insult. For it was understood in Eisen that a woman who had *Gone to Illsbrook* was a woman who paid her way by selling her body. And in Eisen, going to Illsbrook was a one-way journey.

The old man nodded solemnly. "I see," he said, looking down at the vile town, as if searching for the woman who was no longer there. "I was gone for so long," he said pensively. He nodded again, but this time with an air of certainty, "She kept you fed then. She did what she could."

This was not the reaction Harner had been expecting. He wanted his father to share in his disgust, to commiserate with his son in his mother's betrayal. She had been a fine woman, strong and wise until that night of the fire. She had read to him at night by firelight and tended him when he ached. She had been a pure mountaintop angel who had tainted her own life for measly shelter and cold bread.

"Father—" he began, but the old man cut him off.

"She did what she had to," he said strongly and jerked the axe out of the stump with one pull. He held it out to his son. Harner Koertig shook his head in disbelief.

"I cannot. I have no arm, father. Can't you see?"

"You can, son, and you will."

"I awaited your return for so long," Harner said. "But now I see you have gone mad."

Koertig's father hoisted the axe above his head and brought the blade down upon his son's shoulder, hacking off his left arm in one stroke. Koertig wailed, his shouts echoing across the hills, and stilling the celebration in Illsbrook. The old man kicked him in the chest, sending him backwards onto the snowy ground. Even as blood gushed from his open shoulder, his father placed a boot on his chest and hacked at his legs. *Chook, chook.* He chopped high at his thigh, cutting away the limb. *Chook, chook.* He hacked again, chopping away the other. The old man kicked the dead appendages down the cliff-side and returned to the woodpile.

Harner Koertig lay squirming maggot-like in red snow. "And the head!" larval Koertig cried. "Take that too! Take my neck and end this suffering!"

His father ignored his cries and calmly pulled up his hood, returning to his labors. He took a large block of wood and set it on the stump. With two swings the block was in pieces. Koertig lay in the snow, unable to fight, unable to do anything but writhe, screaming for death.

Chook, chook.

The old man chopped away as Koertig lay freezing. Harner pulsed his spine, trying to worm his way over the cliff and into a deadly freefall, but the pain consumed him. He surrendered and lay in the snow, staring into the sun through icy wet tears. He pleaded for relief. He pleaded for death. When neither came, the son of Koertig screamed for vengeance. The chopping stopped.

"At this point," the old man said, with a curiously playful voice as he approached and stood over his son, "You're imagining a hundred ways to kill me if you only had one finger."

Koertig growled at his elder, willing him to lean in closer so he could tear open his throat with his teeth. Any longing for the old man had turned to hate. His breaths were steady, strong, and steaming in the cold air.

"Imagine what you could do with a whole hand!" he said, smiling broadly. He offered his left hand. Koertig reached up and his own left arm appeared. They clasped hands at the wrists. Koertig's father pulled him to his feet. "And two legs!" He stood his son up straight on fresh legs.

His legs were back, and his left arm, but his right was still missing. Koertig wore full plate armor, a ball of steel spikes cupped over his wounded shoulder. His silver body gleamed in the mountain sun, a blinking mirror, a new beacon, sending a new message across Eisen. Harner Koertig has not been defeated.

"So I will say again, *I see you've taken a wound in battle.*"

"Yes, father. An Aurling took my arm. But I am still alive."

"Very good, my son. They have made a fatal error. By taking your hand—your sword arm—they have released you of the failings of many fallen warriors. Recognize you the fallen, in so great a number, who had opted for the brisk glory of a swordfight over the slow certainty of poison, the snare, or deception from within. Know you all of the foolish soldiers lost, flailing madly against impossible numbers, certain their courage alone would assure them victory."

"Yes, father" Koertig said, "I understand."

"And now look at your father," the elder Koertig said looking over the vast world below them, "and observe the man who believed his birthright and bravery were enough to overthrow the gods. By doing so, son, you will see yourself."

Koertig nodded at the man and thanked him. "They will not defeat us, father."

"Not this time, Harner. Not again."

The old man touched the spikes over his raw shoulder, and Koertig jerked awake in the Midtown infirmary. His back and shoulder spasmed, and he convulsed, arching his spine high off his cot. A yellow-haired girl in white tending his bandages moved her face into view.

"Sorry, sir," she said but continued pulling the gauze, "I just need to change your bindings."

He spasmed again and then fell back, panting. He was alive, the pain alone told him that. He was alive, and not defeated.

"It will hurt some, but it must be done," the nurse chirped, as Koertig bled. She eased the blood-crusted strips of linen off his shoulder, pulling away bits of fresh pink skin. He clenched his jaw and growled at the ceiling. "But it is very nice to see you awake," she sang, unaware of the torture she was inflicting. He gripped the cot with his left hand as she went in again.

"Your fever broke overnight," she said as she walked the bloody bundle of linen over to a small bin. He had seen her before, but he could not say where. She was homely like the inbred youth from Uptown, but they would never allow their children to work. She returned to his side and cut off long strips of fresh white gauze. He saw the wound for the first time. There was nothing more than a confused mass of skin and muscle. So vicious a wound, and yet it already showed healing. She wrapped it loosely.

He lay in an upper floor room that he had previously only entered to greet wounded soldiers. Heat from the stone fireplace drifted over his cot and warmed him. There was a smell in the air that reminded him of the Lowtown slaughterhouse, and he knew it was his own fresh blood he smelled.

His arm was gone but the urge to clench and release muscles remained. He imagined grasping the caregiver by the throat and a nub of bone moved under the mass, sending a shock down his spine. Father was right, he could no longer match swords against his enemies. That part of his life was over. If he was to defeat the Aurlings, he would have to use his head. She let a fresh strip slide over his open wound.

Koertig howled in pain as a tear escaped down his cheek, "Are you even a nurse!"

"Sorry sir," she said, dabbing his jowls with her apron. "I am midwife trained, but I have been learning healing under the physician. It is hardly morn and the doctor will not be in until sunup." Then she gave the tidbit he had not expected, and would have preferred not knowing. "I am from Haggart's Ward," she said proudly. "My name is Philippa."

And now the great Sergeant Koertig was left in the care of a Lowtown rat, he thought.

"Perhaps you remember, I helped your men catch the witch," she offered.

My men, he thought. They were his men, his soldiers before the attack, but now he was alone. That creature had taken so much more than his arm. It had taken away his command.

"The soldiers...did they survive?" he asked.

"All but one," she said somberly. "A recruit. Crushed. And there were many injuries."

She finished wrapping his shoulder and placed a thick folded blanket behind his head. She sat him up at an angle and held a small tin cup to his lips. "Medicinal tea. I had made a small pot each of these past few nights, hoping you'd awake. The physician scolded me for being so wasteful," she chuckled, "but I wanted to be ready for you. He says they are rare herbs that should dull the ache."

He sipped the warm tea eagerly. He had proven his strength and courage years ago, and many times throughout his life. Koertig was no delicate fop. But after such a wound he welcomed even the slightest relief. He finished the cup, and she laid him back down.

His tenure was over. His men, his title, and his power would all be stripped away. Any vengeance would have to be done alone.

She pulled the blanket up to his neck and smoothed out the folds, her hands resting longer than necessary on his chest. She spoke of his bravery and how she hoped to pay back the man who had given so much for his people. She did not see a broken man, she somehow still saw Sergeant Koertig. She dimmed one of the candles beside his bed and stood to leave. "I have tended you for some time already," she said softly. "And I will continue to help you, sir, as long as it takes."

He had lost his arm, but he had gained this woman, so eager to do his bidding. And this nurse had once shared lodging with an Aurling witch.

"Don't go just yet," he said, motioning for her to sit. "Tell me more about the Ward, dear Philippa,"

The Lowtown nurse blushed and returned to his side. She told about her home at the Ward. She spoke glowingly of such a dreadful place, rattling on about her sisters and the jobs they all shared, and how such work prepared them for adulthood. Everything she spoke of was about "someday". Someday she will do this, someday she will achieve that. He did not care about this girl's impossible dreams. What he really wanted was information about the Aurling child.

"Olen?" she asked and told him about the time she had caught Olen in the cellar stealing potatoes, and how the girl's clothes had magically changed as she brought her to Haggart.

"She knew about the girl, then?" he asked, his words sharp and accusing.

Philippa stalled and stuttered her way out of her admission. "No, no, she simply did not believe me when I told her of the girl's magic."

"It's not magic," Koertig said, shifting in his cot. "It's lies." There were two knocks on his door and the day workers came in to tend to him. The Ward orphan ducked her head at the sergeant and slipped away, her face red from the shame of betraying her Mistress.

16

The Twig

The next morning, an ambitious Olen led Bakku through the mountainside, pulling the giant man along by his not-so-little little finger. He had told her many times how he must be on his way, and that she must go on alone, but she had rejected those suggestions offhandedly. It was after he had boiled the rabbit that she had found the thing to keep him by her side. She had thanked him for the onion soup, and promised to pay him back. If he agreed to stay with her for one more day, she would make him a meal and it would be something better than rabbit or onion soup. He had agreed, and she had secretly began thinking of tomorrow's excuse to stay. She would feed him all the way to Kessel if that's what it took.

He followed behind her on the green plateau, crouched low as she tugged him along like an oversized pet. With every step they were nearer to her parents and some answers about herself.

After pushing through the latest patch of heather, Bakku pulled his finger out of her grip and stood up groaning, squeezing his thumbs into his lower back.

"You sound like an old man," she said and asked how old he really was.

He stretched his spine and craned his neck. "Old," he answered. "Even for Aurling."

"And I'm young for one, I guess," she said.

He shook his head, meaning she was not an Aurling, but her top rippled and changed color as if to prove her point. Bakku was unimpressed.

"No Aurling. Only two," he said.

She thought about this. "You, and who?"

Again he shook his head, "His name...it changes."

They walked along, side by side now, Olen stealing glances as he scanned the bushes for anything edible. A massive boulder, like a stone hut, lay in their path. She ran ahead and pulled herself up the many crooks and elbows onto the tall stone. Bakku walked by and they were nose to gigantic nose. She held his gaze and he held hers as he loped along. He pursed his lips and shot a wall of wind at her, blowing her back a step. She laughed and leapt onto his shoulders, clinging to his neck with one arm.

"Why did you come back?" she asked. "Why did you rescue me?"

He trampled brush as he walked and explained in his halting and broken speech that he knew they would place her into his prison. He could not let that happen. Then after a long pause he added shamefully, "And I was lost."

Olen laughed out loud and kicked her heels. "Lost? Edwin said you had lived here for years before they caught you."

He grunted in agreement. His voice rang clearer every time he spoke. Muscles in his throat, unused longer than she had been alive, gained back their strength, and words half-forgotten for over two-hundred years gradually reformed.

"Everything is different. Even the mountains," he said.

Far ahead they saw the faint outline of a river. Waterways meant food, and it had been over half a day since his rabbit stew. She did not have to ask. She knew they would head straight for it.

"If you *weren't* lost, where would you go?"

Bakku turned downhill and made for the river. "Daegan," he said, and set her onto the ground. "Daegan...to Calderra. At Calderra I will be free."

She held back as he lumbered down the mountain. His large feet kicked up stones that sent mini-rock slides rolling down. She stared at him with her hands on her hips.

"Daegan!? You want to go to Daegan!?"

Bakku stopped and turned back to her.

"We are going in *exactly* the opposite direction of Daegan!"

He gave a slow confused blink.

"Daegan is northwest of Millthrace," she said, and pointed over the mountaintops, "Just like it was two-hundred years ago! That has not changed. You are so far off your path, you might as well just come with me to Kessel first."

He looked between her and the river.

She spit laughter through her pursed lips. "I'm sorry," she said, and climbed down the cliff side before jumping onto his back. "You just cannot think without a meal in you, can you?"

"Always hungry," he grunted.

"Let's go catch some fish."

They hit a flat patch of ground, and Bakku took off at a trot. He moved quickly when motivated. Leather and glass goggles appeared over her eyes. Not an Aurling, she thought, but she could make goggles appear out of nowhere. She hoped Bakku's voice would clear up soon, because she still had a lot of questions. They hastened across and down the rocky mountain, sure to be boiling fish in an hour.

They stayed at the river all day, and ate three meals of fish and boiled snails—that is, Bakku ate the boiled snails, crunching right through their brown coiled shells. They sat around a small fire finishing off their dinner, the last of the day's sun an orange disc atop the horizon. They took turns passing the warm pot back and forth. He took moderate sips, saving plenty for her.

"No thank you," she said, and passed on another helping, patting her gut. It was a rare treat to feel this full. No wonder the Uptowners spent their afternoons laying under shade trees on long chairs. A full belly makes one sleepy.

Bakku gulped down the rest.

"Thank you," he said slowly, "for the fish."

She sidled next to him and dug her head under his arm. She rested her chin and arms on his crisscrossed tree-trunk legs. She liked him, this strange and giant man; and she thought maybe he liked her too. She had not really tricked him into staying, she knew that. For some reason, he had just needed an excuse not to send her away, and dinner had been a good one.

"Thanks for getting me out of that cage," she said, watching the sunset. "I don't really know much about Nerikan, just silly children's stories, but Edwin had been pretty worried. He said we would not have survived."

He nodded and checked the empty pot for any last morsel. He seemed to be thinking back on his many years. If she had been brought up as a proper lady, she would have known not to ask about unseemly things. But she was raised in the streets where she only learned by instinct, and by asking.

"What was it like?" she asked. "In Nerikan."

He searched again inside the empty pot before finally setting it aside. He held his hands before himself and showed her the clasps that still bound his wrists. "Chains," he said, sliding the circular hasp over stone-like scars. "Chains and bars. Darkness. And gores, always clicking, always biting, always. And me in chains."

She imagined herself chained to the iron railing of her little cot in Haggart's Ward, never going outside and exploring the Scape, only eating whatever her sisters brought her. In a month she would have been like a rabid hound, snapping at anyone who dared pass near her. Then she thought of this torture continuing for decades, centuries.

She shuddered at the idea. "Why didn't they just kill you?"

"Did not know how. Poison me, bleed me, foul the air, but Bakku never die. Sick and angry, but never die." He seemed to remember the torture, and added, "Then they starve me."

"Oh no," she said seriously. "They took away your favorite thing."

But starving him, he explained, had only made him howl. Gores may be the thing of nightmares, but they have very sensitive ears. If Bakku was to suffer, then they would too. They had yielded to his cries and began to feed him again. Only then did their master realize Bakku was more than just strong, he was neverending.

He poked at the fire, turning the burning wood.

He added somberly, "Then I become Bakku."

"Bakku who's forgotten his way to Calderra," she joked.

He did not laugh, and she understood it was too soon for jokes.

"Sorry," she said. "I don't even know that city."

He furrowed his brow in confusion and was about to say something, then he closed his mouth and looked away.

A cool breeze blew down the hillside and tickled her spine. Her clothes rippled and puffed out to a thicker warmer wool. She sat up and pointed to her new outfit. "Are you sure I'm not an Aurling? Because my new jacket says you're wrong."

"The Aurlings are dead," he stated and then grunted, as if ending the conversation.

"Fine. I'll see if I can find some more mushrooms," she said and pulled away. He was angry. She was sure his torture in Nerikan was worse than she could imagine, but he was free now. Soon she would be in Kessel, she thought as she pushed through some brush, and he would be in Calderra. She needed him to know that his old life was behind him now, and he could relax. Like his ever-clearing voice, she thought, he would just need some time. She climbed between two stones and stepped on a dry twig, *click click*, snapping it in half.

Her world went black.

The great Bakku roared and seized the cooking pot, leaping backwards in the air and blotting out the setting sun. Like a dark eclipse he spun in midair, a graceful yet terrible flight a creature his size had no right to make. He landed on one knee and fist, directly in front of her, the crush of air knocking her back. He held the pot high overhead, ready to crush, eager to smash. His lungs pumped out hot wet breaths as she held her hands up before herself, a pitiful defense. His head jerked from her to the forest edge then back again, searching. Gores, she thought. He searched for the clicking gores. She pointed to her feet and lifted a boot.

"Just a twig," she said, softly. "Bakku?"

He still panted, jerking his head from side to side, searching, uncertain, afraid.

"Look, it was just a twig," she told him, and reached down for the dry broken branch.

Bakku finally understood and dropped the pot and fell to his knees. He collapsed to his elbows and rolled onto his back. She placed a tiny hand on his heaving chest.

He had almost killed her, smashed her with the very hands that had saved her. This was why he had insisted she go on alone. Not just so he could continue on to Calderra, but because he did not trust himself. Nerikan had changed him. He did not just look like a monster, Nerikan had made him act like one too. And monsters could harm anyone.

She knew what he would say next. She had promised one last meal, then she would let him go. The meal was over, and it was time for her to go on alone. Kessel was due south, she could find it alone. Still, she did not want to leave him.

He lay on his back staring at the campfire smoke trailing high into the sky, a target and focal point for the world's ever-watching eyes. He rose to his feet and walked to the fire, stamping his bare foot into the flames, extinguishing them. He threw the pot and other small things into the large sack. When he finished tearing down the camp, he turned to her. She still stood between the two stones. Tears slid down her cheeks, sorry and afraid for scaring her giant friend. He would send her away now. She would be alone once again.

He walked over and knelt down.

"We go," he said, dropping his shoulder.

She drew her sleeve across her wet eyes and climbed up and onto his shoulder. He grabbed the sack and held tightly to her legs. He rose up tall, and they surveyed their world. Vast lands stretched out all around them, and even more distant domains lay hidden beyond their sight.

"I will take you to Kessel," he said. "There you will be safe."

They could go truly anywhere in this world and he could get them there quicker than swift Daegan stallions, but they were both drawn to destinations and destinies that she for one was starting to doubt. She would ride with him forever if only he would ask. She dropped her head against his cheek as he began his journey southward, a promised companion for at least a little longer.

***

Something spectacular happened to Edwin the Observer as he fled from the Nerikan gores. He had run blindly, chasing neither track nor trail, thinking only of putting space between his soft flesh and the gores' rigid claws. In his flight, the dense hardwood suddenly thinned and sunlight crashed all around. And with vitality from forest grubs still churning in his aged legs, he had run himself straight out of the woods and into a dry and dusty basin.

Still he hustled ahead over the buff-colored plain, shooting quick glances over his shoulders to the woods drifting behind him. The pilfered blanket hung over his shoulder, and with both arms he clutched the bag of coins to his chest. Defense of this sack was as sacred as saving his life itself, for this sack of coins promised a new and gratifying existence.

As distance between him and the haunted woods increased, muscles in his legs weakened and his heaving lungs became more difficult to satisfy. Soon his frantic pace decreased. He slowed to a trot, a hurried shuffle, and then finally a casual walk. And as soon as his sandaled toes had touched hard-packed sand, he had a general idea of where he was. He had studied Eisen maps closely enough to know he had run himself into the Ode.

A funny name for a desert, the Ode, but he understood it was based on the old tongue, meaning something to pass through, preferably as quickly and efficiently as possible. There were no villages in the Ode, no camps, no shelter, and no tri-city wells. There was only a sandy trail that brave or desperate merchants traversed between Millthrace and Illsbrook. He was not yet on that trail.

The Ode. The name made him think of a different ode, the kind he had studied in his youth. They were poems, bright and lyrical, though often drenched in yearning. It was his love of the ode that had first led him into the minstrel world. And it was his family's abhorrence of all things impractical that had forced him to abandon such foolery. He ambled along the Ode wondering if there was imagery in such a trope: a man walking through the embodiment of an art he once loved. He tried a few lines in rhythm.

"A bright and brilliant soul traversed the Ode..."

He liked it. A good start. And he had still a little walking ahead of him in which to refine it. He strode confidently ahead. He looked from sun to moon to mountaintop, gauging distance and setting his bearings. East was the best, away from the damned forest and far away from Millthrace. He marched on, churning words and phrases in his mind, and after an hour of walking across the hard sand he came upon a narrow but well-tread path. It was the Merchant's Trail heading southeast towards Illsbrook.

"And owed to greater skill, he found the road!"

Meh, he thought, needs work.

He re-checked the sun, half-hidden behind the clouds. He stood at the center of the road, turned to the southeast horizon, and marched straight for the city. Should be no more than perhaps a three-day's journey, he thought and licked his lips. His mouth was dry and tacky, yet he kicked his legs proudly with every step. The bright sun poked out from behind high clouds and beat down upon his bald head. He smacked his lips again, turning over the rhyming words in his head. He was suddenly thirsty. He had no water.

"Damn," he said.

Three hours later Edwin staggered with each dusty step. He was nearly bare, wearing only thin white underpants, and lazily dragging his robes. Atop his bald head was wrapped a torn section of the blanket he had stolen from the cart. The rest of the blanket had fallen to the wayside many hills ago. He still clutched the coin sack to his chest with one hand. Every exposed mound of bony flesh was deep red. There was not even a small tree to offer limited shade. He mumbled through white salt-crusted lips.

"Stupid. Stupid. Stupid..."

His feet slid forward in long sweeping steps, trudging weakly towards the horizon. The road rose up ahead in a tall mound that would take every effort to surmount. With his burnt skin, dry swollen tongue, and befuddled thoughts, he was only certain of one thing, he was still a long way from Illsbrook.

This time he surely would die. Not in the forest with rabid pig-dogs, not in a cage before a hellish ogre, and not on the run from hissing and clicking gores. He would walk until his aged legs collapsed below him and then he would shrivel up dead in the lonesome Ode. His aunts were right, he thought deliriously, poetry would be the end of him.

Something squeaked, and squeaked again. He thought perhaps it was his own joints seizing up. The sound was behind him, where even his last footprint seemed a hundred leagues away. He willed his body to cease its forward motion. It took every effort not to fall face first to the ground. He turned by walking his right leg around his left. His head only turning with his torso. He would have welcomed any traveler at this point, be it the Millthrace guard, a roving band of thieves, even the damned Nerikan gores, as long as they offered him some water.

An oxcart approached, its lazy amble only slightly more urgent than his own. A large white ox pulled a tall-wheeled wooden wagon across the trail. Five faces, browned deeper than Edwin's robe, were spread peacock-like over the front of the carriage, looking cautiously at him. Two shirtless boys, mere seasons away from manhood, leapt off each side of the cart and grabbed tall walking staffs; staffs that could easily double as weapons. Their hair was shiny black, as was all of the family's, and they seemed not to notice the heat. What appeared to be a mother and daughter sat in the middle of the cart, their hair and shoulders wrapped loosely in wispy white scarves. Atop the white ox rode the smallest child, a young boy of about five years. He sat just ahead of the shoulders where a yoke would rest, riding easily on the back of its neck. The small child pulled a leather rein, and the grand beast eased to a shuddering halt. A sixth person, surely the father, stepped off the back of the wagon and strode up to Edwin.

These descriptions were fascinating and all, for it was Edwin's need to observe. But what most transfixed his gaze were the two great barrels that sat at the front of the carriage. These people were traders on the Iron Road, and their cart was loaded for bear. Water most certainly sloshed around in those barrels, though if wine, he would not refuse a sip. Behind the barrels lay stacks of long thin crates, like the Millthrace traders used to haul fruits and vegetables. And behind it all, where the father had sat were larger crates, the contents of which one could spend a lifetime speculating. But those barrels!

The father shouted a word to one of the shirtless boys. It was a word Edwin did not understand, but a language he had once heard. They were Swarhee people from the distant east. He had not studied much this land's religions, and he himself believed only in his five senses, but what little he knew of the Swarhee he liked. They believed in a maker, and worshipped this deity devotedly, but they sought out their god via science and invention instead of what many called blind devotion. What brought them to trade on the Iron Road, he could not imagine. Again the father called to his son and the teen boy leaned his pole against the carriage. The rail thin but starkly sinewy boy dug in to the cart and pulled out a leather flask. He approached Edwin with a blank face and casually handed it to him.

"Thaaa..." Edwin tried to thank the boy, but sand grated in his throat. He sat the coins at his feet and sipped. It was water, cool and fresh after all those leagues. He drank again and let it fall through the hidden mechanisms of his interior. The family, seemingly in no hurry, let him slowly recover from his terrible ordeal. Again he drank as life returned to his body. He paused for breath and thanked the family properly. Then he poured some of the water into his hands and washed his scalded head and face.

The teen snatched back the leather and sealed it tight.

"Scitan heaf!" the youngest boy called out from the ox.

"Tomo!" the mother scolded her boy and covered her daughter's ears.

"Sorry," Edwin said. "I forgot myself there. I am not quite sure of your Swarhee language, but if you understand mine, would you have any food to spare for a kindly old gentleman?"

The father stepped forward. He was a hard-faced man, as so many of the travelers were. His boys obediently stepped aside as their father approached.

"Swarhee is a religion. We are a people. We are not Swarhee," he said. Edwin quickly apologized, claiming ignorance. He told Edwin that indeed they have food but their portions were low and the road long. He added that despite that, he would not walk by and let another man starve. He spoke lilting foreign words to his wife and daughter. They dug into the carriage and pulled out a palm-sized hunk of tough bread, a couple handfuls of dates, and two strips of jerked mutton. He said it was all he could spare. "I cannot save every beggar on the Iron Road."

"Oh!" Edwin said, as if remembering. "But I am no beggar. My name is Edwin, I am from University," he declared haughtily in his under-pants. "I have just become a bit turned around in my travels, but I assure you I am no tramp. In fact," he said, and pulled his robe off the ground and slipped it on, "For that flask, some more bread—the fresh stuff this time—and a small lot of essentials, I would be happy to pay you a fair price." He grabbed the sack of coins and held it aloft while tapping the bottom. The sound of the jingling coins drew the attention of every member of the family. Now they looked like the starving vagabonds, while he looked like the well-prepared traveler.

The young men grabbed their long poles and joined their father. Even the youngest child slipped off the ox and approached. Edwin pulled the bag to his chest and clutched it with both hands. In his head he called himself a fool a thousand times before he spoke aloud.

"And by 'fair price' I do not mean the *entire* sack of coins."

The traders' faces brightened, and they pulled in closer. Edwin pulled back a step, bumping into a boy, who held his ground.

"Coins and rocks!" Edwin insisted, clutching again his precious sack. "Mostly rocks!" So much trauma he had endured in Eisen, only to be slain along the Iron Road! He fell to his knees and pleaded with new-found energy, "I do not deserve to be murdered by common thieves!"

The father burst out laughing, his sons joining him. "Do not worry old man," he said. "If I was going to kill you, I would not have given you water."

Edwin laughed timidly while he tried to read their intentions, "Are you going to rob me?"

The father explained that any trader along the Iron Triangle who turns to thievery is a dead man within a year. It is the brotherhood of the road. If someone commits a crime, there is not a soul in Eisen land who will trade with them. They will starve, their family will starve, and all will be lost. "Don't be afraid of traders along the Iron Road, they will never be less than friendly to you."

Edwin rose to his feet. "Well that is about the best news I have heard all season," he said as he opened his sack to dig out two coppers.

"There is just one problem," the father said, and Edwin stopped, his hand wrist-deep in coins. "We are not traders."

The father flashed a blade out from the back of his pants and held it to Edwin's face. The bald man in robes smiled bitterly and held out the bag.

***

Olen and Bakku spent eight days trekking along the mountainside, slowly making their way south. Very slowly. When they happened upon small edible groves, such as bright patches of golden currant or collapsed trees coated in meaty chickenwood mushrooms, they would hunker down at that spot until every edible bite was gone. The more meals they shared, the more he seemed to accept her as his companion.

He had placed her backwards on his chest as they walked—her legs wrapped in his arm, and her elbows resting on his shoulder—so she could watch sentinel-like behind them. She asked him what the gores looked like and was surprised to find he did not know. Of course, there was no firelight in Nerikan. Two hundred years and he had never seen his jailers. She had seen no movement behind them all day.

He spun her around in his arms and showed her a surprise. Before them stood a grove of short thin-trunked trees. Their leaves were small and curled up upon themselves. Red fruit hung from the limbs, pulling the brown arms down in sweeping arcs. It was a wild apple grove. Bakku smiled.With a wide palm he held her before a branch. She plucked an apple, one of thousands.

"The rest are mine," he said with a wry sideways grin and set her down under the canopy. He lumbered over to a tree and reached in to the trunk. He wrapped his long fingers around the grey bark and shook. A red hailstorm erupted around them. She covered her head with her arms, and screamed and laughed as she ran circles around the tree.

They had feasted on apples all afternoon. She told him about the apple tarts they had had in the Ward, and her secret rooms under the city where she had found the coins. Bakku told her a little more about Nerikan and Aurlings, like how he knew she was no Aurling because all but one had been cast into Nerikan, and of those all but one had died there. But he had also told her something that proved Philippa wrong. She had said that all magic users had come from Nerikan, but he said that was not true. Nerikan was just a prison under a mountain, he said. And Aurlings all came from an impossible to describe place called the Ether.

"So they all came here and were killed?" she asked.

"Only some came," he said somberly. "Many more await their chance."

The ground was still more red than green as so many apples had been shaken free. He scooped an armful into a pile, and then smoothed them out, pressing an indent in the middle. Then he lifted her up and set her in it.

"You made me a bed?" she asked, as the sun fell down on the horizon.

"Comfy?" he asked, and she burst out laughing.

"Some words don't sound right coming from you," she said. "But yes, it is surprisingly comfy."

She lay with her back to him. He laid next to her. It reminded her of sleeping next to her sisters in the Ward, her so-called family.

"I never knew my parents," she said, as night fell over the camp. "So I don't really miss them, not like I miss Haggart and my sisters sometimes," she admitted. "Do you know what I mean?"

He did not.

"I don't know either," she said. "I always told myself I didn't like my sisters, but I find myself thinking about them all the time. I hope they found a good barker to bring in jobs. I can't imagine Ellery out there every day, cowering behind the stand as everyone walks by. I wonder if Lysa left yet for her new home and if she's happy there. And Maggie, I hope Gerda or Marta took my cot so they can talk to her when she wakes in the middle of the night."

She turned over on the piles of apples.

"I'm on my way to a place I always dreamed of going, yet if Mistress Haggart walked through these woods right now and asked me to come home—"

A hooting owl cut off her words.

"What if they *are* there?" she asked softly. "My parents. What if they are there, living their lives, not searching for me, not caring? What if they don't want me either?"

Bakku reached into his pack and pulled out a small burlap blanket. He laid it over her. She wrapped it around herself and thought more of what awaited her in Kessel. Sleep came eventually, but it did not last. Perhaps the bed of apples was not nearly as comfortable as she had thought, or the night air was cooler than expected, but soon she rolled off the pile and slid into the warm waiting arms of the sleeping giant.

***

Don't, Bakku told himself, as the child slept in his arms, and he doubted his resolve. *Do not let yourself be turned away from Calderra.* His mind had played the cruelest game when he had been in chains. It was a game in the form of a question that wormed its way into his thoughts frequently. The question was, "How old are they now?" And the images in his mind shook him to madness, seeing his children age and grow and slow and grey until certainly their time, and their children's time, and their grandchildren's time had long passed on. For only Bakku was forever, he had known that long before he had ever left the Ether. That was his gift, that was his curse. And only leaping into the flames of Calderra could halt his healing and stop his suffering and end this most cruel magic.

The sleeping child turned at his side and nuzzled her head between his chest and arm, a tiny action that washed away another decade of torture.

Don't, he told himself again, fighting the urge, the instinct that was growing inside him to forget his promise and live.

17

The Iron Road Chef

Edwin thought of marigolds as he stared at the knife. There was a family plot at Ulm where bright and musty marigolds blossomed over his family's generations. They were not the most fragrant flowers, these sunny blooms. Their scent had always reminded him more of a ripe tomato when he rubbed their fine leaves while kneeling beside his parent's plot. He had been but a child when they had both succumbed to the bloody cough. He had not even been allowed to see them when they passed, as he had been pulled away to his aunt's estate at the first note of infection. But he had visited their graves constantly over the years, especially on bright summer days when their marigolds were in full bloom.

He had always feared his own mortality, perhaps even more so than the average man, but had found a petal of comfort in the knowledge that he too would someday spring forth in that lush garden alongside his mother and father. But now this knife at his throat, and nothing but the desolate Merchant's Trail for many leagues. No marigolds for Edwin, only dust.

"Timo!" the mother shouted from the carriage. She held her daughter tight against her chest as her husband and three sons circled the traveler. "Timo, stop this!"

The face of the father, hard from years of constant travel under the sun, softened into a smile. He said a word to his boys, and they all pulled back and relaxed. They laughed a laugh Edwin remembered from his youth. It was the laugh the rich kids of Ulm made after they had tortured him about his lineage and had then been scolded by their parents. It was a laugh that said "Very well, the game is over, but we won. And we own you now."

"First rule of the road," Timo said, as he moved over to the carriage. He instructed his wife to fill a good sized bag for the traveler. "If you are not tough, you better at least act it." He dug into a small box and traded his knife for a short dagger. He showed it to Edwin and told him he was not giving it to him, he was selling it, and he would not let him leave without it. "What I said about the traders is true, they won't harm you, but near these roads are faceless riders who will snatch not only your purse but steal away your soul."

"Raiders," Edwin said, understanding.

The woman handed her husband a large sack. Many fine and fresh foods had fallen into that bag. The man pulled two small hooks off another sack and told Edwin he was buying those also. They could be used for fishing, but also for mending robes at night. He hooked them onto the sack, and finally tossed in a small jar of ointment for his sunburnt skin—something he craved nearly as much as the water. Then he carried the bag over to Edwin and held it out. Edwin grabbed at it, but the man pulled it back just out of reach.

"Now your final test, Edwin. Here we stand in the heartless Ode. I have just saved your life many times over. I have given you water. I now give you food, wine, protection, and a means to support yourself along the way. It is up to you now, friend, how much you offer me for my assistance. Any price, I will not refuse you."

Edwin was quite impressed. This vagabond had outdone the University scholar in every way. The old man dug into his purse and pulled out a handful of silver honors. It was many—many—more times what the same bounty would be worth in the city, but under the circumstances it seemed fair. He gave the man the coins, and was fascinated to see neither Timo nor his sons drool at the price they had just received. Six silvers were surely more than they would earn on the entire trail, but they acted like it was just another fair trade. The family went back to their carriage, and the teen boys helped their younger brother back on to the ox.

"One more thing," Edwin said, holding aloft two more honors. "Perhaps these University robes are not the wisest garb for a city man hoping to fit in."

Moments later Edwin stood in his new clothes and waited until the family cleared the rise ahead. He wore dark grey pants with deep pockets on the front and side, and a light grey tunic with a leather bootlace woven up to his collarbone. He scratched at the fresh white hairs growing on his neck and chin, and dabbed white ointment on his nose.

Alone again, he pulled a yellow sunfruit out of the full sack and bit through its bitter skin. His cheeks and jowls screamed as tart juices splashed across his mouth. In a moment it was pure heaven. He marched ahead along the Iron Road and walked up the tall rise thinking perhaps the wandering Timo had not gotten the best of him after all.

In time he reached the top of the hill and saw the land beyond. A wide clear stream flowed just half a click ahead. Along the stream sat an oasis of sorts for travelers. Eight traders had set up small sunshade tents and were selling their wares to each other. Others reclined on the soft riverside grasses smoking pipes and eating cheeses. The family he had just met approached the oasis. Timo held his arms out wide and spun around for his fellow tradesmen, smiling broadly, and proudly showing off his new University robes. The other tradesmen laughed and patted him on the back. A few bowed mockingly to their newly "educated" friend. They offered him wines and cheeses. He had his wife open a fruit barrel in return. Then Timo pointed over to white-nosed Edwin standing on the hill.

The travelers all pointed and laughed.

"Damn," Edwin said, and started forward.

They greeted Edwin kindly, though mockingly. Even their taunts were good humored. Tradesmen eagerly offered him "fair trade" deals for their common goods at outrageous prices. The old scholar just nodded and took the ribbing, walking past eager hands that patted his sunburned back.

His first notion of an oasis was spot on. This bend in the river marked the border of the Ode, and the one-third distance from Millthrace to Illsbrook; much further from his destination than Edwin had assumed. It was the last freshwater stop for travelers, besides a few oases well off the Iron Road. This was where the travelers rested up before the final push for the cities, and where they huddled together for at least the fantasy of protection against Raider hordes. The road ahead was still unforgiving, but the hardship of the Ode was now behind him.

One of the oasis men who had been smoking under a canopy waved Edwin over. He wore a long black beard down to his chest with short-cropped hair atop his head. His large white teeth were widely gapped and forced his mouth open in a perpetual grin. He wore a thin white robe down to the ankles, much like the women had worn in the carriage. A darker scarf curled around his neck and under his arm. Edwin could not place this man's citizenry by clothing alone, and his singular features betrayed no obvious heritage. He waved Edwin over again.

"Come! Out of the sun University Man!" His smile was wide, his accent thick. Yet the accent was an indistinct inflection of a man trying to sound foreign. He introduced himself as Marko.

Edwin sat next to him and thanked him for the shade. He waved off an offered smoke as the river trickled behind him. Edwin loosened the ties around his neck and pulled open the shirt from his sunburned chest. He took a swig from his leather and then dug through the contents of his dearly purchased goods.

"Do not worry, the shade is free my friend!" the bearded man said and laughed.

Edwin exhaled loudly, "I get it. I made a bad deal." He dug through the bag and pricked his finger on the fishing hook. He shook it off and sucked on the tiny wound.

"I will not charge you for bending the grass either!" Marko said, nearly falling to tears.

"If you do not mind," Edwin said, beginning to regret his choice of shade. He laid out a few of the vegetables. Were he still lost in Ma'alabrad or the Ode he would have happily eaten his meal raw, but here in the oasis he had options. He was going to make the best of it. The smoking man still smiled widely.

"At the risk of opening myself up to ridicule," Edwin began calmly, choosing his words wisely. "Would you have a boiling pot I could borrow?"

"Twenty silvers!" the man shot back without hesitation, rolling backwards laughing. "Twenty silvers!" he said again, pulling himself to his feet. Others at the oasis looked around cattle and tent poles to see the commotion. Marko tapped a donkey on the backside. It moved aside lazily. He reached under a tarp on his long cart and pulled out a deep two-handled pot. "No, no. I am kidding, here." He handed Edwin the pot and was thanked appropriately.

"What is that accent, Marko," Edwin asked, certain the answer would be elusive.

"What an accent, Marko, indeed!" he replied at full steam.

Very well, Edwin thought. Keep your secrets, just give me some shade.

Edwin built a fire outside the tarp and then went to the river for water. He thought of the fish hooks the traveler had given, no, sold him. Fried trout would be splendid after his day, but he would not risk the mockery from the men and women who would be overjoyed with his less than ample fishing skills. Vegetable soup and a little jerked mutton would be perfectly fine. He pushed the tall reeds aside and dipped the pot in the cool clear river. A small yellow bulb danced among the green shoots. "Could it be," he said, and plucked the plant. He abraded the leaves between his fingers and smelled. Mustard. A taste of home. He pulled a few more shoots.

Later, Edwin stirred the boiling pot as it cooked over the fire. He had added the mustard plant to the mix of potatoes, onion, and the firm legumes Timo had sold him. It sent an attractive fragrance all across the oasis, drawing in the other traders. They soon forgot they were supposed to laugh at the learned man who was out of his element and crowded about the chef at work.

"Mustard plant," he said, in answer to their questions. "But what would really bring it all together would be pepper willow."

They huddled closer and asked what that was.

"It is common around rivers, at least near University. I would look for some here, but," he trailed off intentionally. The men bit at his hook.

"Describe it," Timo said, his wife peering eagerly over his shoulders.

He drew a picture in the dirt. "It is long like this, with little furry buds at the top," he drew the image, and the men got excited. They knew the plant by another name. Timo sent his younger boys down to the river to search.

"Inside those pods are little black seeds that, when crushed, will make your driest potatoes taste like steak," Edwin said, remembering watching the chefs work in his aunt's kitchen.

The boys returned with more than enough pepper willow. Edwin popped open the pods. He crushed the seeds between two stones, and brushed the dark flecks into the soup. The travelers were entranced, but Edwin let his smile fall away while stirring, "It is just too bad we don't have any trout." Two of the men grabbed their long poles and ran. Not much later he was stirring a pot of thick white trout bisque. The travelers had supplied the fish, the wine for seasoning, powder for thickening, and even rich goat's milk for the cream. Edwin had only supplied a few spare vegetables, and he had the entire crowd of eight men, four women, three boys, and one little girl at his mercy. And Marko, who smiled proudly.

"Bowls," Edwin called out, and the line formed neatly behind him. He ladled each a bowl of the finest bisque they had ever eaten. He knew this because each told him so many times before the night was over. He made sure to leave plenty in the pot for his own aching belly.

Marko went to the river and pulled out two large leather flasks he had tied off to the shore with ropes. "Beer," he announced and gave that wide toothy grin.

He filled every man's cup, especially the chef's. The beer was cool and fresh. Nobody laughed at Edwin after that, and nobody mocked Timo's scholarly robes either. Edwin the Observer, Edwin the Historian, had a new name among the travelers. For the rest of that night every man greeted him with a smile and a pat on the shoulders, and simply called him Chef.

Edwin licked the last spot of wetness from his bowl as the sun went down over the far mountains. He had eaten in the finest restaurants of Cedar Bay; he had eaten with the most esteemed professors in the halls of University, and he had sampled the finest dishes from across the sea, yet as Marko handed over the freshly packed smoking pipe, Edwin had to admit that this was the best meal he had ever had.

"Thank you, Marko," he said, and lit the pipe with a burning reed.

"No, thank you, *Chef*," Marko said with a conspiratorial wink and laid back under the stars.

18

The Price of a Reed Cap

Olen watched as Bakku slept soundly under the mountainside apple grove. They had stayed three days under the canopy of trees, not eager to leave the abundant food behind. He lay on his back with his arms splayed out wide. His large head hung to the side with deep snores rolling out of his open mouth. Even though they had not seen soldiers nor gores since leaving Ma'alabrad Forest, Bakku had refused to build a fire. Olen pulled the thin blanket around herself and cuddled up deep into his side. She wondered why he looked the way he did. Edwin had told her about Aurlings, but he had said they looked no different than Eisen-folk. The only thing different was each man or woman's special ability, unique to each Aurling. But Bakku looked like a creature from a fantasy.

Clouds rolled in from the mountaintops leaving the sky starless and black. Hidden insects buzzed and chirped in voices many times greater than their size. Bite-sized creatures scurried from tunnel to tunnel on tiny paws before dark flyers could nab them. And distant beasts howled and hooted in neighboring woods. There were creatures everywhere, but she had the biggest one of all. Bakku shifted and slid his arm around her. She placed her arm over his, and kept guard in the hollow night.

The stars turned slowly as herds of bovine-like clouds meandered across the veil. In the darkness, she fell victim to Bakku's soft rhythm and let his hypnotic breathing match her own. Her head drooped forward and then kicked back, but it was just enough for the briefest of dreams. Just an image it was, Mistress Haggart in the Barrens, and she called out Olen's name. She shook away the moss and again set her watch on the night. He had not asked her to keep guard, she had just wanted to help, just in case. But again the easy cadence of his breaths lulled her to an airy calmness, and again her head rolled to her chest before jerking back to attention, but this time something else had awoken her. It was a sound. In her haze she was not sure if it was real or a dream. She sat still and listened. The night creatures had ceased their calling. Perhaps it was not a sound after all but the silence that had woken her. She sat up, still in the crook of Bakku's arm. He breathed the long inhales of a man lost in the profound depths of sleep. It was the thick of the night and with the heavy clouds she could barely see Bakku's face from a breath away. Then she heard it, a rush of clicks.

Like a gambler's wheel it started fast, ticking away in the darkness and then slowing to a stalking crawl before stopping with one last tangible *tick* that tapped the back of her neck. She batted at her nape as she spun around. There was silence. Then again, the rapid clicks, slowing, and a *tick* that this time tapped her chest. This touch was stronger, fuller. There were gores in the darkness, and they were creeping closer.

"Bakku," she said, pushing him in the chest. He rolled over onto his side and exhaled deeply, lost to his dreams. The clicks rushed through their cycle and tapped at her arm. She brushed at it like sweeping away a spider.

"Bakku!" she whispered louder in his ear. He did not respond.

The clicks came from nowhere, and everywhere. Behind them, beside them, above. She did not know if it was one, two, or a thousand creatures tracking them through the blackness. She wished for daylight so she could see beyond her nose. She pinched his sides, her full hand grasping a hide so thick and scarred that even awake she knew it would not faze him.

The clicks were livelier now and focused. They tapped all over her like poking fingers, one cycle beginning before another ended. Tap, tap, touch, tickle, slap. She wanted to see, she begged for light. She pushed herself out of Bakku's arms and stood as shuffling footsteps entered camp.

She kicked Bakku in the back of the head and screamed, "Bakku, wake up!"

He woke with a roar, and was answered by the ear-shattering hiss of gores.

She would never truly be able to explain what happened next. She only knew that the attack on the camp was the most frightful moment of her life, and wished more than anything else to be far away from here. So as Bakku roared and the gores screeched, Olen screamed also. Her skirt and vest blossomed into a bright white gown and brilliant dawn burst forth from all around her. It was no less than the noonday sun shining out from the center of their camp, and it all came from inside her.

The circle of gores collapsed backwards as if hit by a crashing wave. Their heads twisted away violently as if burning in Olen's light. Their hisses cracked into agonizing screeches. Ten of them were thrust to the ground by the burst, and they tossed their crude picks and axes blindly, missing badly. They flailed about in her white light, clawing at it as if it were a tangible foe.

It was like she had fallen into a well, with a wild wind circling around her. She still stood in her spot, but Bakku and the gores appeared thrust to a distant mountaintop, their shouts and screams distant echoes. The entire world seemed tiny and brittle. Tall trees were but garden greens she could pluck from the hillside, and the mountains themselves were little ridges she could leap over in a game. In her ears echoed a sound like in the depths of the pool in the Scape, dreamlike and muffled. And beside her a war was being fought by creatures like little toys. And as the battle raged on, her joints were rigid and locked, and all she could do was watch as winds whipped her now white and flowing robes.

Bakku grasped the chain in his right hand and whipped it. It wrapped around a man-beetle, and he flung it into a tree, snapping its back. The other gores regained their feet. Bakku grabbed one in his wide tough hands and tore its horned skull clean off. He clutched the headless gore's ankles and swung it like a man swatting flies. Gores fell with each blow. Once on the ground they were ended with a mighty stomp. Some scurried away back into the comfort of darkness, while a few of the bolder ones leapt at Bakku.

One made it through his swinging arms and latched on to his thigh. It bit deep into his leg with its finger-length incisors and sucked at the wound. Bakku howled and grasped at the gore, but it held strong.

Olen struggled to move an arm, a leg, anything. Finally her fingers flexed and that seemed to free her entire arm. She reached out, her arm stretching as if across leagues. Her tiny white hand grabbed a gore at the back of its neck and squeezed. It was an effortless pinch, quite nothing at all, but the neck snapped and the head dropped loosely to the side. She released the gore and it fell to the ground dead.

She looked at her glowing palm, pulling back across the ages. Light emanated from her hands, her arms, from everywhere around her. She felt no heat from the intense beams, and unlike the gores, her eyes had adjusted instantly to the brilliant glow. She felt strong, magically, fiercely so. And yet still she stood, unable to move, uncertain what was happening.

Bakku cleared the camp of gores and raced over to her. He must have stood right next to her, yet he seemed many fields away. He barked a word to her, but it was lost in the light. Still she glowed, a white beacon on the mountaintop for all of eastern Eisen to behold. Phantom winds blew all around her, out of her. He moved easily through the storm, unconcerned. He threw their supplies in the sack, and tossed in an abandoned gore ax, and still he seemed to be falling even farther away. She was drifting back, being pulled into herself and away from this world.

"Bakku?" She pleaded in a tiny voice as the world faded.

He searched the gore bodies making sure they were dead.

"Bakku?" she said again, as tears began to fall. Then a point of white light opened up ahead of her. The orb grew as it brightened. Through it she saw a field in summer. There were flowers with fat bees dancing from stem to stem. It was a beautiful land, if unfamiliar. She wanted to step forward, away from this terror and into the new land.

This Bakku saw too and he finally came to her. He reached into her swirling whirlwind of leaves and debris, grasping her around the waist and giving her a gentle shake. The swirling orb collapsed around the field and disappeared as the cyclone fell away. Her knees buckled, and she fell back into his palm. Her gown faded, and again she wore her patched skirt.

"We go," he said, slinging the sack over his shoulder and holding her to his chest.

Her head was hazy and her body numb. "Where?" she mumbled.

A flurry of distant clicks returned as the gores regrouped.

"Up," he answered decidedly and raced further up the cold mountainside.

⁕

The traders at the oasis brought around their mules and donkeys and strapped them to their carts. Most were continuing on to Illsbrook, but a few of them were heading northwest to Millthrace. Edwin, in his dearly purchased tunic and pants, helped the others throw ropes over their crates and tie down their goods. He asked about knots and was patiently shown the difference between the Maring Knot and the Maring Twist, which he still insisted were the exact same thing.

The sun was out again and shining brightly along the highway, but Edwin no longer feared the searing heat for he was now supplied for the long haul. Timo's youngest son, Tomo, came back from the river struggling with a large wooden pail, spilling more than he saved. Edwin rushed over and helped the boy. They hauled it over to the ox and let it drink before the long walk. The boy looked Edwin up and down as he walked backwards back to his carriage. It was his father's clothes that Edwin wore, a sale the boy probably did not understand.

All the men and women of the oasis were carted up and ready to get on their way, but there was one more trade to be made. Timo's youngest daughter went about the men offering reed hats for sale. Edwin had not seen her all day, and now he knew why. She had been at the river pulling long green reeds and fashioning them into wide brimmed hats. She walked around the oasis holding up her little finger, meaning one wedge per hat. Many of the travelers bought one—even those already wearing hats.

This reminded Edwin of Olen in the Millthrace square, slaving away her youngest years making trades with rough and ignoble brutes, all for a bent and rusted wedge. He had found himself thinking often of her, wondering if she truly had escaped. He hoped she had, and that Bakku had evaded the gores and taken her back to her parents. She had been kind to him in their cage, kinder and more accepting than anyone he had known at University.

Timo's daughter had one reed hat left and offered it to Edwin. He thanked her properly and pulled the coin sack off his hip. The bag was considerably lighter than when he had picked it off the soldier's cart in Ma'alabrad. The little girl waved her hands in the air to show he did not have to pay.

"For Chef!" the tiny girl said in that innocent childish octave, and handed him the hat.

"Oh, I couldn't," he said, practically overcome with emotion. "I can pay. It is alright, child."

"No, no," she said, waving her hand dismissively and turning back to her family. She called over her shoulder. "For Chef."

Such overwhelming shame he felt as the child walked away. Just days ago he would have called these people—any one of them at the oasis— brutes. Had they passed through Ulm he would have slammed shut his windows and rang the bell for the constable. He had gotten so late in life with no real friends to speak of, and for the first time he considered that maybe it was his prejudices that had failed to let these friendships blossom. He dug into his purse and pulled out a handful of coppers and wedges. He ran over to the girl and made her take the coins, which she did reluctantly.

"I insist!" he said, rolling them into her palm.

Timo chuckled lightly as Edwin placed the reed cap on his head. His laughter spread to his boys, and then his wife blushed as she too let out a little laugh. It was Marko in the cart behind them—reed hat on his head—who helped Edwin understand.

"It ends as it began, Chef? Oldest trick!" He burst out laughing and Edwin finally got it. That youngster had tricked him into paying more by toying with his emotions. He had been duped by a mere child!

"Heavens!" he thought. "She really does remind me of Olen!"

The old Edwin would have spit fire at the people for treating him so cruelly, but the new Edwin was different. The girl climbed into the back of the carriage and looked at him sheepishly. He looked like a fool with these green leaves hanging crookedly on his bald head. And as all of the oasis cackled and pointed fingers at him, Edwin the Chef, despite all of his cultured training, laughed.

"Well played, my child," he said, tipping his new cap as the caravan started forward. He then gave broad and fanciful bows to all who passed by, saying sarcastically, "I am so happy to have entertained you on your layover. Perhaps next time I will charge for such a show!"

A war horn cut through the laughter and merriment. The startled traders eased up their carts and looked towards the road to Millthrace. Atop the rise in the burning sun stood a regiment of seven soldiers on horseback. One held a broad sword high above his head. The lead horseman blew again the horn, an alert for the travelers to cease and wait to be inspected. Edwin pulled his reed cap over his face.

<h1 style="text-align:center">19</h1>

<h1 style="text-align:center">A Mote of Dust</h1>

Koertig lay in bed in the dispensary as orange morning light filtered through the slatted window. It was a kingly private room with a vaulted ceiling, but it smelled like a morgue. His large cot lay book-ended by tall tables, each filled with his every need. Two soft chairs crowded an inglenook by a stone fireplace, and a small wash station stood off to the side. A smaller cot sat against the wall behind him for the nurses who watched over him while he slept.

It had been twelve nights since he lost his arm, twelve nights lying in this bed. The ache of immobility gnawed at him. He stretched his legs, bending and flexing them. Then he raised his arm and worked his good shoulder, moving it in circles. Skin and muscle across his back tugged at his wound. A sharp pain cut into his right shoulder. He seized and dropped his arm to the bed, panting. This will never heal, he thought, and then forced the idea out of his mind. In fact it had already healed well ahead of everyone's expectations. He had seen men die from lesser wounds.

"Do you need something sir," a voice asked, as the girl in white hurried to his bedside. It was Philippa, the Lowtown midwife posing as a nurse. She had been taking on many more hours than trainees were generally allowed and was thus earning a generous pay for one with so little training. She was granted this honor at Koertig's request.

"Just sore," he said, fighting to control his breathing. He lowered his lids and slowed his breaths. Now calm, he looked to the girl. "It will pass," he said. "With your help."

With her help indeed. She was his arms and legs while he rested, scurrying about the city and doing his bidding. But she was also of the Ward, much like the witch that had escaped with the ogre. There were secrets in the Ward, secrets he would discover, with her help.

The heavy-set girl demurred. "I will do my best," she said.

"You always do," he said softly and found he meant it. She had a certain hard-working virtue. So many nights he had drifted in and out of sleep, always to wake and find her waiting, eager to work. Strange, he thought as he watched the orphan prepare his morning meal, how this girl strives to better herself, certainly knowing such is impossible, while his own mother surrendered so quickly and took that shameful walk to Illsbrook.

He thought of his mother and the choices she had made. "She kept you fed then," his father had said in his dream. "She did what she could." That was not so, Koertig thought, hating to doubt his father's words, even from a hallucination. Young Koertig could have kept them fed. Even a boy could hunt and kill, his father had taught him that much before he had left. Shelter had been her concern as they escaped the winter winds, but even in wicked Illsbrook righteous fools had raised firebrick temples to their deaf and mute deities. They surely would have offered a warm blanket and a dusty corner to lie down in until the bitter winds receded. Then mother and son could have journeyed west to Brennan, where honest hard work abounded. Had she not surrendered to the easy coin of lustful drunks, she would still be alive today, proud of who her son had become. They would have survived, much as Koertig survived now, bearing a wound greater than any man had ever suffered.

Philippa checked his bandages as he flexed his good shoulder and stretched his ankles. The wound throbbed and ached, yet it was the rest of his frame that now craved relief as healthy muscles ached to move.

"They tell me not to treat the wound, but to treat the patient," she said, moving to the opposite side of his bed. "I was not sure what that meant until now." She slid the blanket off his good side and laid her hands upon his shoulder. "How sore you must be after lying here so long. Try not to tense up, just let the muscles go lax." His instinct was to resist her, to pull away from her touch, but as she smoothed her hands over his shoulder and traced her fingers down his arm, the relief was instant and inarguable.

She swept around his good shoulder and squeezed softly down the back of his arm, pinching lightly at the elbow. It was a miracle of relief, as if a poison that had collected under his skin had been squeezed away. She pressed her thumbs into his forearm and pulled the tension down to his hands, where she drew it out by his fingers, even mimicking flicking the sticky tension off her fingertips and onto the floor. Koertig fell back as the soreness melted away. For nearly two weeks he had lain in this bed suffering with each waking moment, and for the first time he forgot the pain in his shoulder and felt something he had not expected: pleasure, deep and consuming.

He had been touched by women before, indistinct faces with their tiresome confessions of love, hoping to win over the great sergeant. The women of Midtown had not been interested in Koertig the man, only the status he could supply them. So he had happily granted them the one status they deserved: Koertig's whore. And there had never been a shortage of status seekers. Yet he had grown weary of these ladies whose touch had always left him drained, as if they had scratched away a part of his soul.

But this nurse's touch healed him, made him stronger. It was a feeling he was not accustomed to, and not prepared for. His mind drifted between wake and sleep. His body danced between pain and pleasure. His eyes fell shut as the nurse stroked him, and in those moments when they fluttered open, he caught her sneaking longing glances at his face. So she was no different after all.

She finished the arm and worked on his upper back. She moved her backside onto the edge of his cot, and asked if that was acceptable. He nodded. She wrapped her left arm around his neck and pulled him up off the sheets. With her right hand she reached behind and massaged the sergeant. Her cheek pressed against his, her full breast against his shoulder. Steady breaths left her nose and skimmed his ear as she stroked his back. She smelled fresh, cleaner than he would have thought possible. She was not heavily perfumed like the Midtown ladies he was used to. It was a lighter fragrance. Familiar.

"What is that?" he asked. "That scent?"

She ran the back of her hand down her neck, trailing her fingers from ear to throat, and then drew her hand across her nose. "Snowbell," she said. "It's a moun—"

"A mountain flower," he cut in. "It blooms even in winter."

"Yes. So strong, and yet so beautiful. Not many people know of it." She leaned in again and rubbed his back. The windows grew lighter and the city woke as she massaged him for the better part of an hour.

Snowbell was a mountain flower, indeed. It grew exclusively along the western slant of the Never-Ending Ridge, the very peaks of his boyhood home. He closed his eyes and was back in his family's cabin where his mother had sworn the snowbell bloomed only for him, a winter gift from the mountain itself.

"Are you of Illsbrook?" he whispered, as she rubbed his back.

"I was there as a child for two winters, but honestly, I do not know where I am from, sir." She massaged him a little more in silence. When she finished she laid him back down and smiled. "Would you like me to let you sleep now?"

"I could not sleep after that," he said, tenderly. "No dreams could match your touch."

He had not intended those words as a seduction, but as she turned away shyly and her cheeks flushed red, he knew that was how she had heard them. My but this truly is a confident warden, he thought. Were she a Midtown lady with even a chance at him, she would have used his kind words as an open door to his heart. And his bed.

Philippa turned back to him. "How about a story then?" she asked, laying the blanket over his chest and smoothing it out with a palm. "I am a very strong reader. I could fetch a book from the library if you would like."

Thankfully, she had not put him in the position to reject her advances.

Books. This brought back a memory to Koertig. That educator had brought books, and had received many more from the mayor. There was talk of Aurlings in those books. Just a few nights ago he had no use for books, and was only vaguely aware of the city's library. All that he had ever known of the Aurlings was from the few words he had stolen from his father. But now he needed more. He needed knowledge, strategy. These books might tell him where the Aurlings came from, why they were here, and most importantly, they might help him understand how over two-hundred years ago men were able to capture and cage a creature like Bakku, while he and his men were utterly destroyed in one brief battle.

"Yes, Philippa, that is a great idea. I would love a story. But I want to hear a special one. Do you know where Mistress Egg rents out rooms?"

She nodded quickly.

He pushed himself up with his left arm. There was but little pain following the massage. He told her she would need some coins and asked for his purse. She objected saying that she would never take money from him, not only because it was forbidden, but because she was indebted to him for securing her this position. She then pulled five coppers out of her apron pocket and said that as long it was no more than that, it would be her honor to pay.

"Very well," he said, "but if you find you need more, come see me. It will be our secret."

She nodded again, noticeably excited to share a secret with the great Sergeant.

"Now, go to Miss Egg, tell her you understand the educator has left some books behind and you would like to purchase them. Propose three coppers for the bunch. She will quibble for more. Then offer her the five, which she will accept."

"How do you know she will accept five pennies?"

He fell back onto the bed and adjusted himself comfortably, "Because Mistress Egg is a foul drunk who gets no pleasure from books. Five coppers will set her up at the Eagle and Trout for the whole night. Now hurry back, I want to hear those stories."

"Yes sir," she said and made to leave.

He reached out and grabbed her hand. "Please, call me Harner."

She smiled a wide pink grin and said, "Yes, sir." Then she dashed out of the room.

He lay alone for the first time since his injury. Snowbell lingered in the air. She would be back for more coins. Miss Egg would squeeze every hack out that warden. He pushed himself to the edge of the bed and eased his feet onto the cool floor. With one great thrust he pressed himself to sitting and cried out as a shock tore through his shoulder. He leaned on his arm panting, before pushing himself to standing. He wobbled and staggered ahead to a bench where his clothes lay. Within the pile he found his purse and removed three pennies. Then he hobbled back to his cot, his head swirling, and lay back down. She would be back soon. She would bow her head and shamefully ask for more coins, and when she looked up he would already be holding them out to her. She would ask how he had known and how he had gotten across the room and back. He practiced the casual smirk he would give her.

***

Philippa practically glided through the Midtown maze of tall row houses before pausing at a bench outside Miss Egg's. The sun shone brightly and the scent of sweet bread was in the air. Mornings in Midtown had always made her belly ache as the bake shops sat their pastries and jellies on wooden tables for quick sale. On past mornings she had only ever hurried through this borough on her way to some latest undignified chore. She surely never had the coins to buy any of the breakfast sweets, and even if she had paused to inhale their aroma, her man's tunic and mended skirt would have signaled the shop owners to guard their wares from the poor girl from the Ward.

But now she held a small collection of coppers and hacks that were all her own. Not money to be shared with her sisters, not coins to be placed into some community pot, but her own hard-earned coppers to be spent as she wished. And with her clean white apron over a new blue nurse's gown, she passed through Midtown not as an interloper, but as a fellow, an equal. And it was all thanks to Sergeant Koertig.

"Please," she whispered in a soft mimicking voice, "Call me Harner."

She flushed and surged with life, throwing her head back and laughing aloud at her crazy luck. Good things were finally happening. And even with the ever-present rumble of the Skywheel and the Old Mill churning away, she wondered if all of Millthrace also felt the awesome thumping of her own beating heart.

She leapt to her feet and spun around to Miss Egg's, her skirt whipping around her. Then smiling wider than perhaps she ever had before, Philippa Cree knocked on the door.

***

Olen held on as Bakku ran and climbed much like he had after first escaping Koertig's army. He was frightened. Even though he had decimated the small black army, their attack had stirred something within him, and she knew he wanted to get them both far away. He moved steadily up the mountainside, his energy revived. He had told her he was taking them over the top of the Rückraadt Mountains. It would take them off course for Kessel, for now, but he had said it was the only way to elude the gores. She had not seen nor heard the gores since leaving the forest a day ago. "Take me anywhere," she had thought. "I will go." But she had only said aloud, "Okay."

A sharp gap in the peaks was their target. The trees thinned out behind them, and lush heather blanketed abundant stone. From here and beyond their only food would be what they carried, which was apples.

The incline up the Rückraadt sharpened and for the first time his steps were slowed, but still he walked, and still she held on. Muscles in his shoulder stretched and contracted as he pulled himself over boulders and his thick neck pulsed as he pushed himself along. And still he carried on, dauntless and constant, always peering ahead to the next obstacle, never looking behind. And this was what he did for an entire day, walk and climb and walk some more. Colder air met them as they ascended. The warm woolen jacket again rippled and spilled down her back and arms. She told him she wished she could make a coat for him also.

"I am fine," he said, but his voice lacked conviction. The snow-filled gap through which they would pass still seemed leagues away and higher up the cliff-side than they could possibly climb. But still he plodded on, and still she trusted him. His breaths became heavier as they climbed and the first snows began to fall. After a day of running and climbing, he was finally wearing thin.

A large nook loomed up ahead, a deep black shadow cutting into the stone. It was a natural cave along the mountainside. She tapped him on the shoulder and pointed to the refuge. He moved with newfound vigor to the tall triangular cavity. He set her on the ground and backed himself in, wedging himself against the deep back wall. He opened his sack and pulled out some firewood.

"Let me," She said, snatching away the kindling. "You rest."

Again he did not fight her. He leaned mountainside and was asleep at an angle before she ever struck the first flint.

An hour later Bakku awoke when the boiling apples reached his nose. Olen shook her head at this. A screaming girl and a gore attack in the middle of the night had barely roused him, but boiling apples jolted him to consciousness.

He seemed confused about where the water had come from, but the words would not come.

"There was snow just up the mountain," she said, as if admitting a crime. "I'm glad you didn't wake up when I was gone. I wouldn't want you to miss me." She smiled and handed him the warm pot. "You first. I'll eat the next batch."

He inhaled deeply over the steaming pot and sipped at the cider. He dug his thumb and finger in the pot and pulled out a soft and puckered apple, handing it to her. It sizzled and burned in her palms. She tossed it from hand to hand and blew on it as he lifted the pot to his lips and poured the whole thing into his mouth, apples, cider, and all. She ate hers a little more leisurely, and was again reminded of apple tarts at the Ward.

She then refilled the pot with snow she had piled outside the cave and set it on the fire. She sat next to him and rested on his crossed legs. "So you lived with those things, those gores?" she asked. It was the first time they were able to talk since the attack.

He scooped fresh apples out of his sack and dropped them in the pot, "Ugly."

She laughed and agreed wholeheartedly that they were indeed quite ugly.

"Smaller," he said of the gores, as he moved the apples around the pot with a finger. In his broken speech he reminded her that he had never seen a gore until the mountainside attack. He had been chained in complete darkness. And now that he saw them, they seemed smaller, less frightening than before. "Brittle," he added, which pulled a laugh out of them both. He thought long on his words while Olen pulled his finger out of the quickly warming pot and stirred the apples with a stick. Then he concluded, "I can handle gores."

"You sure can," she agreed. "Well, I didn't have gores, but I had Philippa, and that's almost as bad."

He asked her to explain what a Philippa was, and how it was almost as bad.

She told him how Philippa had always hated her, and how she had never known why. She mentioned the incident at the laundry, but besides that she didn't know where the dislike came from. She traced a finger over the scars on his forearms as she told how Philippa would report her to Miss Haggart over every little thing. When she snuck out at night, when she tricked the local boys into doing her chores, even that time when she had traded a loaf of raisin bread for a silver bracelet she had convinced the guy was worthless. "She never let me have fun!"

Bakku spoke no words. He merely plucked apples from the pot and chewed.

"Don't look at me like that," she said, feeling shamed. "I know, I know. I wasn't perfect, but she could have just let it go. Instead she got all motherly, thinking she could turn me into some proper lady or something."

Bakku tossed a few more frozen apples into the water. They sat in the warm cave as outside winter snows fell. "I don't know," she continued. "Maybe she didn't like me because I didn't like her. None of us did. We all knew she would never find a home, and I guess we didn't want to be a part of that, because what if we were next?"

He still spoke no words, neither convicting nor pardoning her. But something was on his mind, she could tell. "Say something!" she finally blurted out.

"You glow?" he asked.

She looked up and said, "I guess we both learned something new that night."

"I have seen that light, your light," he said.

"It was like a doorway," she said. "There was a field on the other side."

"Yes, a doorway," he said, stirring the pot with his finger. "A dangerous one."

* * *

Koertig had expected Philippa to struggle and fail in purchasing the Observer's books. But his nurse had returned swiftly. And when she pressed open his door with her backside and hauled in the stack, he had been at a loss for words.

"I'm impressed," he said, as he stealthily tucked the coins under his bedding.

"There's more," she chirped before rushing back out.

She had returned with another stack just as the day-medics arrived, so she had given her report and went back to the Ward. But it was now evening again in the infirmary, and she was back at his side. She sat on his bed and read from one of the old tomes as the fireplace crackled and candles burned.

"But this does not make sense, sir, I mean Harner," Philippa said, holding open a thick leather-bound.

"Just read," Koertig said, sipping again from the medicinal tea. "*I will make sense of it.*"

She slid a finger over the page as she read, "*The seeds of the universe exist in the Ether. All things that are, can only be because of their seeds. See what I mean?*"

"I am sure it will all make sense in time," he said, trying hard to keep his patience.

He had never had a woman sit so close to him, her thighs pressed against his hips, without her wanting, nay expecting more. Yet this warden had seemingly grown familiar with the sergeant, and appeared hardly aware of their closeness as she absently adjusted his blankets and handed him his tea, all while reading aloud.

"*All things certain or intangible have their seeds in the Ether. Every element, every emotion. Every mineral, every desire. Every action, every sensation is seeded in this hidden world,*" she read, in a school girl's diction.

"The people," he said, pushing himself to a higher seating. "Is there anything about the people?"

She brushed his hair behind his ear with a finger and scanned ahead a few pages, "Yes here, *An Aurling grows around this invisible seed, like a raindrop forming around a mote of dust. They take shape and spring to life, full masters of their chosen seed.*"

"Strength maybe," he said, mostly to himself as he tried to work out his thoughts. She asked what he meant. "That creature that attacked me. Perhaps he owns the seed of strength, or maybe size. Power. Outside of his brute force he didn't seem to be, well 'magical' at all."

"And Olen?" she asked.

"Hmm? Oh, the girl. An illusionist perhaps? A shape-shifter? I do not know." he said, remembering. "The menagerie had passed through Illsbrook once, you would have been too young. They brought bizarre creatures from all over the world. Most of them were bones, common beasts crudely mudded and glued to appear fantastic. But there were live creatures also. My friend Jay and I each paid two hard-earned coppers to enter a wide tent and see...a shape-shifter!"

She brightened and clapped her hands in front of her mouth. "How wonderful!" she exclaimed.

He held his thumb and forefinger apart. "This big," he said, with a broad white smile. "They called it...*chameleon*. It shifted from green to light green."

"Oh no," she laughed along with him.

"Two coppers, wasted. Had I my knife, I would have sliced off the useless creature's head," he said, mimicking the cutting motion in the air.

"No, don't!" she played, as he laughed. "Oh, the poor little creature!" She clasped his hand in hers and held it to her chest, staying the imaginary execution. And for just that moment he forgot he was a wounded soldier laying in a hospital bed. For that briefest moment he was a young man making a lady laugh. A lady of Lowtown. His smile faded as a shadow passed over him. He pulled his hand free.

"I was just as unimpressed with that chameleon as I am with that girl," he said.

She smiled politely, but it seemed forced. Perhaps a little camaraderie for her old bunkmate after all, he thought. She returned to searching through the stack of books. She had found many leather-bounds in Edwin's room. Most of the books were from the library, but there were also Edwin's University texts, and a few children's books with grand tellings of the faerie tales. One of the old story books had fine drawings, hand painted, after every five pages. He watched as she turned the pages.

His shoulders ached again and he craned his neck. She leaned forward to adjust his pillows. She reached behind his head, again her breath on his face, and again the faint scent of snowbell—

The door clacked open, and a soldier marched in unannounced. It was City-Corporal Martz, Koertig's number one. Martz halted when he saw the Lowtown nurse leaning over his commander. She sat up immediately and jumped off the bed.

"Terrel!" Koertig said happily, welcoming the intrusion. Philippa excused herself and sat on the small cot in the corner. She hung her head and paged through the painted book. "I see you've recovered!" Koertig said.

Terrel Martz had been the first to attack the creature when it broke into Millthrace and also the first injured. Koertig had liked to joke that he never played favorites: after Terrel Martz, all of his men were equal. He loved the man more than anyone since his boyhood friend in Illsbrook. Because of this, Koertig had felt horrible shame that he had not been ready when Bakku had first ravaged the town.

"My body has recovered, sir," Martz said, stalking the room apprehensively, not looking at his commander. "But I fear my shame has not. I should have been with you that night in the forest."

This was why he loved Martz. So few men, even within this grand army would feel shame for missing an absolutely futile battle. These two men were one.

Koertig asked him not worry himself over such things, but he could see there was more. Martz struggled to look his commander in the eyes. He had never been unsure of himself before, but now he walked nervously around the room avoiding Koertig. He stopped in front of an open window. The sun's low evening rays shone upon the fresh blue emblems on his chest.

"I see," said Koertig, deflated, but understanding. "Well, congratulations on your promotion Sergeant Martz. There is no one in my company more deserving." Koertig meant the words he said, but it still hurt to say them. "Are you here to tell me I have been relieved of duty?"

"No, sir," Martz said. "I understand you will be made Lieutenant Colonel...an honorary rank, with retirement to follow immediately."

"I believe you mean City-Lieutenant Colonel," Koertig said, adjusting himself in his bed. "Nonetheless, that's a fine title—were it not an honorary award, of course."

Martz stood uncomfortably in the room.

"Pardon me, Terrel. My constitution is not one for hospital beds, and my attitude is reflecting that," Koertig said. "So what is your first act as head of the army? Killing the creature I assume?"

Martz became animated and approached the bed, for the first time addressing his commander directly, "That's just it, sir! The council forbids us from hunting the ogre! Instead, they recommended sending two small forces to patrol the highways to Brennan and Illsbrook. The rest of the army was to stay within the city and protect its walls."

"A wise decision, Martz, even if I prefer a bolder move. Our forces may defend all of Eisen, but this city will always be our first priority."

"Perhaps, but it is *who* they sent into the field that worries me." Martz listed off the soldiers Mayor Brynn and the city council had enlisted. Among the names were Koertig's greenest recruits along with the veterans holding the most dubious records. Koertig found this odd but not completely unheard of as it left their best men to defend Millthrace.

"That may be so," Martz agreed, "but some of the men see a different tactic. They think Brynn does not truly want them found."

Koertig found this preposterous and Martz admitted it sounded strange, "But strange things are happening, sir." He leaned in conspiratorially, as if not wanting his nurse to hear, "Raiders, sir. They've reappeared in the fields, snatching indiscriminately. Women, children, disappearing from caravans."

"And Brynn sends out no hunters?"

"He scoffs at the idea! Calls the Raiders *hardly a concern.*"

Koertig considered this new information, wondering what kind of leader could care so little for his own people.

"Harner," Philippa said, drawing a curious look from Sergeant Martz. "Sorry, I mean Sir. I found something you might find interesting." She held the colored plate out for both of them to see.

20

Edwin's Bounty

Edwin could do nothing but wait in the scorching sun as the soldiers on horseback strode slowly down the Merchant's Trail, kicking up clouds of tawny dust as they plodded along. Timo grumbled about their tortoise-like pace, while Marko slapped a hand on Edwin's shoulder and again gave that conspiratorial wink. When the soldiers finally arrived, Edwin found a regiment of stiff-faced boys acting like men. They were led by an older thin-armed commander whose striated muscles and bumpy red nose reminded Edwin of the mathematics professors at University. There was something about moving numbers and hash-marks around a dry slate which lent itself to fermented indulgence.

"Names, homes, and occupation," the commander said with an arrogance bordering on disinterest. His chest-plate hung loosely-bound at his sides, freeing his bloated gut. His sword lay tucked behind him in his saddle pack. An iron helm also hung from the pack, as he donned a lighter non-regulation leather bucket-hat for sunshade. He rubbed his temple lazily with his thumb, as if fighting a headache.

He was the very model of a mathematician, Edwin thought.

The younger soldiers, more eager to look the part, were properly geared and held their swords in their hands. Two pack-mules trailed behind, loaded for bear along the Iron Road.

Timo spoke for his family, and the other traders followed suit, calling out their names. Each person answered "trader" for their occupation, and each one of them claimed the highway as their home village. One of the boy soldiers checked and rechecked a sheet of paper every time a name was mentioned. Edwin knew his name was on that sheet and pulled his reed hat down to his nose. He searched his mind furiously for a fake name.

"Marko Meloon!" the bearded man next to him called out. He smiled that wide toothy grin at the guards and tipped his reed hat respectfully. "Famous trader!"

"And what makes you famous?" the old guard asked grudgingly.

"Beer!" Marko trumpeted. "I trade beer and wine!"

Edwin spoke next, though the guard was still engaged with Marko. "Reese Hammond," he lied, remembering the cook from his aunt's pantry. "Village of Grimm. Trader...and chef."

The guard brushed off Edwin and edged his mare closer to Marko. "And how stocked are your supplies at this outpost, wine merchant?" He asked.

"Ohh, very low," Marko said. "Not much left. I must keep it for my long journey."

It was at moments like this Edwin felt the whole world was a fellowship of fools, toddling about without a thought in their mind. *Just give the man a damned drink, and he will be on his way!*

"You are talking to a man with the wealth of Millthrace at his disposal," the sun-haggard guard announced, as he scratched at his stubbled neck.

"Very low," Marko said again, somberly. "Very dear to me."

"You are very fortunate, Mister Meloon," he said arrogantly. "For the luck of a coin toss, our most brutal legion was sent west. Had it been them journeying to Illsbrook, they would have already taken all of your precious stock, and your head. You will find me considerably more reasonable." He held up his hand for Marko to wait, and then addressed all of the travelers. "We are looking for two," he said and went on to describe Olen but made no mention of Bakku. When he spoke of Edwin, his descriptions were painfully accurate. But Edwin, with his dearly purchased tunic, pants, and new reed cap, not to mention his slightly thinner frame and sprouting white beard, no longer matched the descriptions of the escaped Observer.

"He is an educator of sorts," the old dipsomaniac continued, "and a fancy-man it seems."

Marko slapped Edwin's shoulder and bent over cackling. Edwin considered giving himself up, if it somehow meant Marko could be arrested too.

"And should any of you locate him, I assure you the city will reward you greatly."

None of the men spoke. Timo had told him there was a brotherhood among travelers, and "Chef" had been accepted into the pack. But his heart sank when the old soldier reached into his pocket and pulled out a wide yellow coin, a rare gold manor. Timo looked nervously to his wife who shrugged her shoulders. Even Marko's smile impossibly grew wider. A golden manor would take an entire family off the highway for a year, two if they were frugal. With one gold manor they could sell their carts and set up a real shop in any one of the cities.

The old guard held the glittering coin aloft, letting the greedy fantasies evolve in the travelers' minds. One word, one pointed finger, and the coin would be their own. To hell with the Iron Road brotherhood, a golden manor could transport one so far away from this nomadic life, they wouldn't care about some unspoken oath. Yet all the traders stilled their tongues.

Edwin had actually allowed himself to believe these crude nomads would not reveal him, but he slayed that fantasy as the old soldier skimmed his thumb over the manor's yellow face. The coin slid apart, revealing a second golden manor.

The gasps were audible and sustained. The tradesmen and women, indeed even the children, were as if they were staring at the face of a primal sun god, brilliant and yellow, promising them all of their desires. A more attentive guard would have noticed the one man who did not drool at the wealth held before him and instead, had his skin fall white as blood and bile drained to his bowels. Edwin knew one day's fellowship would not be enough for any of these men to refuse such a bounty.

"Two golds, for the arrest of the escaped prisoners," the soldier said.

Silence among the traders.

He held the coins aloft for a full minute, letting the desperate worshipers soak up its radiance. Still, nobody spoke. The old man dropped his arm and tucked away the coins.

"Now," he said to Marko. "About this beer and wine."

"Very rare!" Marko shot back. "Two gold manors!"

All of the traders burst out laughing, and even Edwin forced a chuckle, though inside he felt like vomiting.

21

A Good Pasture

Olen sat alone deep in the cave hugging her ankles as Bakku hunted for burnable wood. It was summer below, but a winter-like storm blew over the mountains. They had stayed two nights in the hollow, waiting for the weather to subside, but the icy winds blew harder each day. The latest fire had burned down to embers, and she shivered while wrapped in both Bakku's travel sack and her enchanted coat. She thought of her last winter in the Ward and how she and Maggie had shared blankets and a cot to stave off the frigid nights. It was strange, Olen thought, how harsh times like freezing and starving in the Ward become such sweet memories over time. She shivered again and wondered how her memories of today would ripen.

Once the storm let up they were going to risk the summit. He thought he could make it in one day, morning to night. Once they were over the top they could drop down into the Mecan Plains where they would be warm and safe from the searching gores. The gores would never be able to follow them over the mountain, he said. He would see her safely to Kessel before moving on to Calderra alone. She thought of just going along with him.

The large Aurling returned with firewood. He poked his giant head into the cave. "No gores?" he asked.

"No gores," she said through chattering teeth.

A thin layer of snow lined his shoulders as he built up the fire at the mouth of the cave. With sticks he rolled an old burnt log, now just orange coals, to a spot on the ground between them. He squeezed into the hole and sat with his back to the wind, practically sealing off the outside world. The cave warmed quickly. He let a massive shiver roll up his body like a dog out of the river. Water splashed on Olen's face.

"Sorry," he said, but she saw the half-smile he tried to hide.

She had still not gotten used to him. He was a glorious creature, impossibly strong, resourceful, honorable, and yet at times even child-like. He was funny, or at least he used to be before being locked away. He still scared her a little; he had a temper that flared up from time to time, but she was sure of one thing, she liked her giant Aurling friend.

"Do all Aurlings look like you?" she asked.

"No," he said. "I don't look like me either."

Perhaps if her brain was not frozen she could have made sense of his words, but at this elevation and in these temperatures, she had no idea.

"Aurlings look like you," he said, his wide lips forming words more easily now, "And your friends, and your enemies, and everyone else you have not met yet. I looked like them too."

Suddenly she understood. She jumped up and let the sack fall to the ground. "You're a scion!" she gasped.

He nodded, but showed none of the excitement she did. "Aurling scion, yes."

He sat her down next to him and told the tale of an early Aurling, among the first to arrive. His gift was the ability to combine living things, selecting only the parts he chose, thus making an entirely new creature. A curious gift indeed, but to this Aurling it was nothing more than a jest, as he gave the world ridiculous combined creatures meant only to entertain. His creations grew larger and more fantastic, but were still of little use. His experiments became tiresome and the Aurling grew bored. So then he began to experiment on men and women.

"Regular people?" she asked.

"It is how he made the gores," he said. "And what you call Raiders."

He said they were all his slaves, these creatures, each mindlessly following orders. Gores were his crude servants, while Raiders he left with more man-like attributes, only bigger, stronger, and with a cruel heart that could inflict any atrocity without shame or care.

She was even more impressed now with her sister Samantha's escape from the Raider horde knowing they were creatures worse than the gores.

Bakku explained that when changing men and women had lost its charm, the man had started his experiments on other Aurlings. No one knew if he was trying to control the Aurlings, make them stronger, or even steal their strengths. But what he ended up making was something he could not control.

"You," she said.

"Me. And as soon as I realized I was strong, I escaped." He said and poked the orange coals. "But he lured me back, promising to return me to my old skin. In truth, he wanted to end my life. And when he found I would not die for him, that's when he locked me away."

"Is he dead?" she asked, and then added softly, "Did you kill him?"

Bakku patted her head and let out a sad smile, "He is still out there somewhere, hiding away, waiting for his gores and Raiders to track me down, and hoping Bakku does not find him first.

"And that's why you're going to Calderra, to search for him?"

"In Calderra, I search only for peace."

Black wings flapped in the storm behind Bakku. Vultures circled high above the mountains. He followed her gaze and craned his neck backwards. "Scavengers," he said. "Looking for meat."

"Yeah, probably us," she said.

He nodded in agreement.

"I was kidding!" she shot back, but he did not acknowledge her.

He mashed around the bright orange coals, and the cave warmed some more. She let her thick coat melt away to a thin jacket.

"When I am gone," he said in a serious tone, "You must never again reveal your light."

"I didn't reveal anything," she explained. "I got scared, and it just happened. But why shouldn't I?"

"Because then he will find you," he said, "And I won't be here to stop him." He took the sack from Olen and tore two large holes near the opening. He sharpened a twig with the gore ax and tied some twine to it, creating a makeshift needle and thread. Then he went to work sewing the sack.

"Who did this to you?" Olen asked, as he worked. "Who is the other Aurling?"

"He called himself Brynn."

***

Koertig stared in wonder as Philippa held open the University book. Sergeant Martz stood behind him, peering over his shoulder. On the painted page, green and yellow brush strokes dragged wild vines out of the spine. These vines curled into an elaborate script above and below the image that read, "An Aurling brings new life to the world." Blood red lines in the middle of the page framed a tall doorway with flat sides and a rounded top. Floating in the upper left corner of the doorway was a white dove mid-flight. On the bottom right sat a sleeping rat, its tail curved around itself. Between these images stood a man holding both hands in front of himself. He wore purple robes and was flanked by two kneeling men in red. In his hands he held a creature Koertig had never seen before. Neither rat nor dove, yet both at once. Wide wings spread over a sleek rodent body. Piercing bird eyes looked out of a beakless pointed face. It stood on thick rat-like hind legs, limbs too heavy to allow easy flight. Perhaps a flaw in the Aurling talent.

Yet, it was not the winged scion that made Harner's blood run cold, it was the skill of a long dead painter. For the image of the man holding the blended creature was expertly defined on the page, and it was clear the scion master was Mayor Janus Brynn.

"It is a striking image, sir" Martz said, unconvinced. "But can we convict a man over a painting in a book?"

He defers to me, Koertig thought. He is not ready for command.

"It's more than striking," his nurse cut in, "It's Brynn. There can be no doubt."

And she defers not enough.

"There can be no doubt," Koertig agreed. "Perhaps the rumors are correct Martz. Maybe Brynn does not want his creature to be found."

"But sir, if they are in league, why did he have him destroy his own city? And why torture the creature for so long in Nerikan?"

Koertig quietly sifted through the particulars before answering.

"We do not need to know all the answers," he said finally. "What we do know is a traitor has infiltrated our ranks, and it is our duty to stop him." He pushed himself to the side of the bed and sat up, refusing the nurse's aide. Martz moved to his side. Koertig pressed his palm onto his soldier's shoulder and rose to standing. He still wore his sleeping gown, tied loosely behind his neck. He was barefoot and his hair disheveled, but on rising he still cast a noble form. "This wound, I need just a little more time. We will expose Brynn."

"And if he resists, sir?" Martz asked, surely knowing full well the answer, but needing to hear it from his superior.

"We have sworn an oath. It appears Mayor Brynn is an Aurling interloper. And Sergeant, I believe we already have a prison for Aurlings."

Martz nodded severely and saluted Koertig. He gave a quick bow to Philippa who reacted awkwardly. She gave an unappealing curtsey to Koertig's number one as he left the room. The amputee had gained another far-reaching arm, he thought, as Martz darted out into the street.

"He will gather a small army of loyals," Koertig said, mostly to himself.

She placed a thin blanket over his shoulders. He nodded politely and leaned against the window frame as Martz rushed across the street.

"A coup?" she asked.

"A putsch," he said, moving unsteadily back to the bed. "A quick decisive blow." She helped him sit back and held his head as he lay onto the pillow.

"Is it possible the mayor knew of Olen?" she asked. "And the old man?"

Aurlings, Demi-Aurlings, and jumbled scions, he thought, as she brushed his hair back and set his pillow. Somehow they had all infiltrated his city, and he had not known. This was why his father had come to him in his dream, to warn him. She reached for the tin cup of medicinal tea and held it to his lips, cupping the back of his head as he drank. It wasn't just the ogre he had to hunt down, but every last Aurling in Eisen. Only then will he have completed his father's tasks.

"Sir?" she repeated. "Did Brynn know of the others?"

"Mayor Brynn seemed more surprised by the girl than any of us," he finally answered, as she moved to the window and clacked shut the wooden blinds. "I think until now he too believed they were all but extinct."

She lit a candle by his bedside, and another by hers. It was evening again. She would soon move to her small cot in the back and silently watch him as he slept. If he woke, for even a moment, she would be there asking if he needed something. This act would begin as it did each night with the same three words.

"You should rest," she said, laying the woolen blanket over his legs.

"Soon," he replied. "But I am a bit sore yet. Perhaps you could?"

She told him it would be her pleasure and sat on the edge of his cot. She loosened the strings around his neck and he stopped her.

"Not my shoulder, please, my legs. They were so tender I could barely stand."

She said she had been a fool and apologized for neglecting his legs for so long. She folded the blanket and set it aside, then she rolled his gown up to his knees. She started at his feet and squeezed away the bad blood that had pooled there.

It wasn't that she was ugly, he thought, as she worked in candlelight. It was that she was not at all pretty. Ugly, one notices. Beautiful, one notices. But were she not his nurse, he didn't think he would notice her at all. She slid her cupped palms past his ankles and up to his calves, her strong hands pulsing and pulling as they went. He thought of a joke his boyhood friend Jay had made about the plain girls. *They all look the same once you blow out the candles.* A lock of her hair fell loose from its bindings and trailed down his leg. She blew it aside and continued. It fell again, and she let it hang, brushing back and forth as she massaged up past his knees. Her hands were warm, her hair tickled his thigh, and her breaths blew against him in some unheard primal rhythm. She kneaded him right up to his waist, and then stopped abruptly, pulling her hands back. She looked to Koertig, and then back to what awaited her.

She had seen him before. For days she had helped him clean. But she had never seen him ready for her. He had grown accustomed to her healing touch. Grown to the point where he craved her strong hands. Tonight, she would heal him more.

He held out his hand. She appeared frightened, embarrassed, and he would later insist, intrigued. But she only looked at him, saying nothing, doing less. A mistake, he thought, and was about to pull back when she placed her warm hand into his and nodded. Koertig gently pulled her onto the bed.

***

Hardest for Philippa was keeping it secret. Koertig had never actually told her not to tell anyone about what they had done by candlelight, but some things a girl of Lowtown just knows. She had tried very hard not to give any hint about her night in his bed, but the next day at lunch as her sisters quietly sipped their soup, Philippa could not resist occasional outbursts of laughter at every silly slurping sound. And as all the faces looked to her, even the confused visage of Mistress Haggart, she simply shrugged her shoulders and kept eating while laughing into her spoon. These and similar surges of laughter escaped her all day as she waited for nightfall, and her next evening of tending the injured soldier.

He had been so gentle. That too was a secret. All of Millthrace saw the hardened sergeant, but he had revealed another side to her. He had held her not like a sword, not like a weapon of war, but like a precious thing he had feared to shatter. And with his one hand he had touched her, sliding his fingers over skin and cloth, pausing at buttons and bows, awaiting her aid. Wordlessly and fearlessly she complied as together they worked to strip her of the shields that separated them.

Much later, as the candles burned down and the night carried on, he had still held her, long after the burden of delicacy demanded. When she had finally slipped out of his bed to return to her own, she had paused to watch the sleeping sergeant. "Is this your true face?" she had wondered, as Harner slept blissfully serene. Gone were the sharp and focused brows that lowered when men disappointed. His jaw, so rigid and proud, hung loosely now, his lips parted in slumber. Perhaps, she thought, this is who Harner can be when he's not being Sergeant Koertig. Perhaps all he needs is someone to show him harshness does not equal strength, and that he can be a strong sergeant while also being a good man.

The following afternoon she washed up early and donned her stunningly clean and pressed white nurse's bib and blue gown. No white bonnet today, she thought as she pulled the snarls out of her ropy blonde locks. Thick yellow hair was the one great gift this cruel world had bestowed upon her, but she had always kept it braided and wrapped around her brow. Not today, she thought, as she raked her long tresses. Even she had forgotten how dandelion yellow her hair was in the sun.

She left the Ward and skirted around the dust-covered tradesmen who were tearing down tents and the mud-caked oxen clomping across the Square. Up the Midtown stairway she flew and then through the maze of Midtown until she entered the stairs below Koertig's room. She touched her hair one last time before scrambling up the old staircase. At the top she entered Koertig's room without knocking. He was seated at the side of his bed, whispering to Terrel Martz. Without turning his head he said, "If you enjoy clomping around like a breeder cow, I know a good pasture. Some tea for us both, and gently up the stairs this time."

"Yes sir," she said and backed out of the room, unsure what she had done wrong, and when.

22

Sailor's Shore

Edwin thanked the traders at the Oasis as the soldiers disappeared along the long lonely road to Illsbrook. Only after they were far beyond worry did the families remount their beasts and pull their carts back onto the dusty Merchant's Trail. Marko had reloaded his leather flasks and small barrels onto the cart after the soldiers had left. He had indeed made a good price on the wine, but nowhere near the two gold manors.

Edwin happily accepted an offer to travel with Marko Meloon and his burro. Taking haven in the horde, as the saying went, even if it meant partnering with the buffoonish trader. Marko had only a small cart and a stubborn donkey named Sonny, so they would have to walk to Illsbrook. His feet would be raw in a day, but as long as he had food and water, calloused foot pads were cheap tuition for a journey home. They both wore bright green reed hats as they set out.

They quickly lost sight of the traders that were heading back towards Millthrace, while most of the other travelers journeyed ahead of them to Illsbrook. The Illsbrook caravan held tight for a few hours before the faster beasts of burden pulled ahead. By midday Edwin and Marko were alone on the Merchant's Trail. As they walked in silence, Edwin formed a map and itinerary in his head: seven day walk to Illsbrook, a boat to Ulm, and a carriage to University. He could be home in eleven days, maybe twelve. And most importantly, his bag of coins was still in his grasp.

The sun was high and bright, yet Edwin felt cool and refreshed.

"You laughed Marko, but this reed hat was quite the investment. It is cooler than a wine cellar under here," he said, tugging at his brim.

"Bless and honor the children," Marko said in a casual voice at a reasonable volume. "A curious aspect of a flawless con is, even when one is taken for a fool, they do not always come out the worse. Those are the best ploys, for the fools rarely seek retribution."

Edwin stumbled to a halt. A few hours ago he had accepted travel with Eisen's most annoying man, but now he seemed to be walking with a peripatetic University philosopher. Even his giant toothy grin had subsided into a calm smile.

Marko moaned, and rubbed his sore jowls, "I need a new act."

"What is going on here?" Edwin asked as he stepped back a pace.

"You say you are a University man," Marko said casually, as if he had not just transformed into a different species. Sonny twisted his ears at the men and slowed to a halt. When no one complained, the donkey flapped its lips in what could only be called a sigh and hung his head. Nothing green grew out of the Merchant's Trail, so he merely stared at the ground as his master continued, "Does old man Stokes still haunt the literature halls?"

"I mostly studied history, but the name sounds familiar," Edwin replied, still befuddled. He slid a hand over his clothing, surreptitiously patting at the many pockets in Timo's tunic and pants, trying to recall where he had stashed his dagger. "I warn you, if your plan is to sack me—"

"I liked Stokes, but he was a tough one. Always with the rote memorization."

"*You* are a University man?" Edwin asked dubiously, certain he was the only Hulblich man foolish enough to travel this far north.

"I had a few good years there, but the world called me away."

"Yes, I know what you mean," Edwin said, holding his distance.

Marko, if that was his real name, picked up a long stick and gave the mule a brisk tap on its hind end. The animal brayed and lumbered forward, the heavy cart chunking and lunking after on the hard road. Marko followed his pet with Edwin trailing behind.

Marko turned and walked backwards, a cheery countenance as he detailed his history. He told Edwin that he too was of University and named off the proper halls. He even knew of the tiresome library cats and which tall windows allowed the brightest sunbeams for them to roil in. He said he had studied the sciences, among other things, but he had never quite felt enamored with the lessons. "The stage had been my one true love, and I had found that life among the company men in the theatre was more rewarding than anything in a lecture hall. Once I had left the school, I followed the traveling troupes to Eisen," he waved his arms open wide, dramatically, "and in Eisen I have remained."

Edwin felt a little less troubled about whatever con this man had been playing and let the distance between them diminish. They strode down a long bend in the highway and headed due east, again walking side by side behind Sonny. A tall green forest on the horizon promised shade and fresh game, if their hunting skills were sharp.

"So you are an actor?" Edwin asked.

"Oh, I did a few shows from Brennan to Illsbrook," he said flippantly. This man, who spoke like any gentleman of Ulm, explained how he had loved the stage, but it had left him starving. He had found he earned more between shows—odd jobs, or maybe a quick song and dance— than he ever had in the theatre. "Outside of Illsbrook nobody took in a performance anymore, and inside Illsbrook the Guild took most of the profits. So one day, I never pulled off the highway, and just kept on traveling."

"But clearly you never stopped acting," Edwin noted, as he brushed dust off Sonny's thigh.

"Ah, very good University man!" Marko said, a hint of his old personality coming through. He said he had created his most successful character while on the road, a crazy merchant named Marko. And it was not intentional either. If he had come upon someone he had not felt like doing business with, he had just started talking like a half-brained nut. "Funny thing is, people were *more* eager to trade with 'Marko' than they ever were with me!"

"And who are you?"

He ignored the question and continued. "It is because they just assumed they were smarter than Marko. It's kind of like you and the girl with the reed hat. After your success with the cooking pot, it never occurred to you a small child could out-duel your vast intellect, did it?"

"I wouldn't say she out—"

"Same thing with Marko," he cut in. "Nobody thinks an idiot will best them in a trade, but Marko wins...every time! Did you see how much that soldier paid me? And for my oldest skin!"

They walked ahead. The tree-lined horizon barely seemed any nearer as they pounded their feet on the dry clay road. Edwin tried to make sense of the two Markos, not quite sure which one he preferred. The old Marko was as crazy as they come, but this new Marko had a devious tenor. He thought his sleep would be less secure tonight with the new Marko in camp.

He seemed intelligent, learned even, but Edwin did not believe his story of University. It was quite rare for students to drop out of University. Edwin would only look at himself for proof. Students only went to University if their family's money stores were adequate. Even if their grades weren't quite passable, it was nothing a handful of silver honors could not remedy. So for someone to walk away without papers and find himself a trader on a desolate Eisen highway, something quite terrible must have happened. Or more likely, he decided, it was all another lie.

"Why are you telling me this?" Edwin asked. "Your livelihood depends on maintaining your secret, yet you just spoiled the game. I will have you know that if you try something in the night, I am not against defending myself."

Marko showed no signs of offense, he merely kept on walking. He said that Edwin the Chef indeed was the only man on the highway who knew the truth, and then added, "I am not merely giving you this information, Edwin my friend, I am trading it. It is what I do."

He let his donkey walk ahead as he turned on Edwin. "I have told you the truth about Marko, an artist painting the edges to distract from the center. Now you tell me the truth about Edwin. Truly now, why are soldiers offering two golden manors for an historian's hide?"

He could tell him the truth. He could speak of Aurlings and gores, and a little girl who could change her look at will. He could talk of his escape, twice, from the haunted forest, and the journey that had led him here. He could tell Marko everything, but he knew how crazy it sounded, and he did not know how the man would react.

"You should know," Edwin began, and hesitated. He owed Marko a fair trade secret, so he offered up one he had held for a very long time. "You call me historian, but that is not quite true. My historian's degree, like yours of science, can be found somewhere in the halls of limbo. If I were to be honest, the one title I have truly mastered is that of minstrel."

Edwin talked about his early years, when music and song had filled his home. His parents had been free of the invisible social restraints that seemed to bind those of Ulm, those arrogant tea-sippers who would rush their carriage past the faire, curtains drawn and fingers in ears. Education, etiquette, and discourse politic was all they had valued. To don the leggings and prance about with lyre in hand was tantamount to the fool.

"But I adored it, every strum and verse," he said, walking casually now with Marko. "I found I had a talent for writing and performing odes, which is not too far removed from your drama-craft."

He explained that he had been forced to abandon his song after his parents passed, and he was sent to the strict quarters of Ulm Academy, then the Welter Bay Junior Institution, and finally the vast stone halls of University.

"I must admit," Edwin continued, "I also deeply enjoyed my book learning. I admired my professors and saw myself someday donning their gilded robes, but I truly loved my parents' song."

Edwin said that after his parents had succumbed to the cough, he had been passed between three aunts and an uncle, each one quickly discovering some terribly urgent reason they could no longer foster the precocious youth. It was in that time he had found it easy to sneak away to the faire, neither aunt nor uncle monitoring his whereabouts. Then afterwards at night, as candles burned and young Edwin sat alone in his upper floor room, he would read adventure books and scratch out lyrics on dearly purchased parchment.

"I had no formal training, so each lyric danced to the same sing-song tune in my head, but I had found endless variety in the verse." He said he would dress as a commoner and escape to the faire. There he would sing his songs to whoever would listen. "My family, when they finally found out, well, I was nearly cut off. And not just from the coffers, I mean at the neck!" he said and looked to Marko guiltily. "Nobody at University knows. But I was good."

"Sing me an ode," Marko said.

"One of my own? Well, let me think," Edwin lifted his cap and scratched his head as he walked. Then without introduction, soft lilting words drifted forth.

By waxen fire I hold you dear, too close, too close
You speak to me of life so clear, lands froze, kings rose.
Vast worlds pass as we sit as one, cruel hate, hero's fate
Our story has but just begun, night's late, tales wait.

The two men walked as Edwin finished his song.

"A love story?" Marko asked.

"Of sorts," Edwin responded, cupping his hat to his chest. "It's part of an early work of mine. An ode to the books of my youth. A time when reading was a nightly joy. Oh the adventures I had simply clutching those folios near the fire!"

Marko's face brightened, and that wide toothy grin returned. "Not the story I was looking for, my friend, but a good one nonetheless." He slapped Edwin on the back and said, "Two men of the arts. We will be rich!"

23

Stupid Gores

Olen paced the empty cave as strong wet winds blew against the adit. She had woken to an absent Bakku, who had at least set a strong fire before abandoning her. She warmed her hands by the flames while searching the mountains high and low. It was early dawn and the world was turning from black to a misty grey. She was debating whether to track him through the storm when his hazy figure lumbered through the gale like a ghost ship at sea.

He ducked into the cave without greeting and lifted his burlap sack.

She said, "I thought you had disapp—"

He scooped her up in remarkably warm hands and placed her gently inside the sack. He lifted the bag over his head and slid his arm through a strap he had sewn during the night. He had stitched a sort of a trader's pack that hung high over his shoulder and down his back. She poked out of the bag and stood like an arrow out the top of a quiver. She crossed her arms and placed her elbows on his shoulders, resting her chin on her forearms.

"We climb. Very steep," he said. "Very cold."

Earlier he had held her legs when he had run, but to scale the Rückraadt he would need his hands. He could no longer hold her, so he had made a satchel that could. And when the chilling highland air turned her lips to ice, she could duck inside for warmth. He had done this for her, she thought. Last evening she thought he was only mending holes but he had been fashioning a protective carriage, for her. It was a strange sensation, much like when he had first come back and rescued her, to know you lived in another's thoughts. People had done kind things for her in the past, but only in trade. Bakku did things like this that let her know he thought and cared for her even when he was getting nothing in return. And now he wanted to carry her over a dangerous and icy mountain to safety.

"I trust you," she said, and they started out immediately.

He first walked back the same path he had come through in the storm. The winds had calmed some with the slowly rising sun, but still they bit at her face. He seemed eager today, almost impatient as he hurried forward.

"Why are we leaving so early?" She asked. "We haven't even eaten."

He pointed ahead to a dark tangle on the ground. A bird, large and twisted lay in a heap of feather and bone. One crushed wing hooked under its frame while the other lay splayed out wide. Together its wingspan was nearly as wide as Bakku's. A long beak with rows of razor sharp teeth hung open in an eternal scream. A dead eye, forever open and manlike, stared at her. And even without the spark of life behind it, the eye looked disturbingly aware.

"Scion vultures," he said. "They have followed us all along."

It had flown low in the night, he told her, and he had been waiting for it. It was Olen's own words that had tipped him off. They had not seen any wildlife this high in the mountains at all, and no meat-eating scavenger would waste its precious energy scanning the mountaintops. She had jokingly said maybe the vultures were searching for them, and she was right.

"It flew low," he said. "I caught it with a rock."

"It wanted to eat us?" she asked, as the corners of her mouth turned down in disgust.

"When I got this one, the others flew off," he said. "These are not scavengers, they are messengers."

He adjusted the shoulder pack and she shuffled her feet.

"We have not had meat since the river," she said. "Are we just going to leave this thing behind?"

He walked over to the carcass and kicked it over. Bones and tendons lay exposed to the air, as if it had sat rotting for a week. Fungal meat hung off the bones leeching a grey-green foam.

"It's rancid!" she said, pulling back.

"Made to decay quickly," he said. "He wanted it to leave no trace of itself."

"Who wanted that?" she asked.

"Janus Brynn," he said and turned up the mountain. "I was a fool. He has found me."

* * *

They had entered a pattern, Philippa and Koertig, a pattern that left her aching for nightfall. He would greet her coldly as she began her long shifts. She would clean him, feed him, and tend to his wounds as medics and soldiers came through. She would speak when spoken to, often disregarding his gentle curses of the Lowtown folk, or quietly reasoning away his barking rebukes when her service was less than perfect. But as the sun fell low in Midtown and they were left alone in the upper-floor room, she would clap shut the wooden blinds and his words would take on a gentler tone. And she would once again feel desired by this desirable man. They had been lovers for two weeks.

"Thank you, dear Philippa," he said, as she handed him his evening tea. He palmed the tin cup and inhaled its honeyed steam.

She had placed folded blankets behind his head and back and helped him to sitting. He dipped his head at her, a silent command to sit also. She eased herself to his cot and straightened the blankets at his hips.

"Tea was the one thing my father and I disagreed on," he said, taking a sip. "He favored the boiled-bean infusion Swarhee-folk choke down twice a day. I prefer to sip the essence of Eisen's own green leaves." He handed her his cup which she made to set aside, but he said no and told her to drink. She held the wet lip of the cup against her own and sipped. "In that way alone," he continued, smiling contentedly, "I took after my mother."

She chanced asking him a question about his parents.

"Both gone," he said, letting the words drift away like candle smoke. "One a victim of Aurling magic, the other a casualty of indiscretion."

Even during his twilight calm, she dared not equate them both as orphans. To Koertig, an orphan was more than a parentless child. It was an unwanted and unnecessary issue from an inferior line. Koertig may be parentless, but he was not unnecessary.

"Father and I agreed on everything else," he continued, "including the need to eradicate the Aurling menace." He said his father had a vision he had failed to achieve. He had been a warrior who hoped to end wars, a compatriot who believed in the wholesomeness of this land's people, and a wise man who saw in Eisen the great land it could be. "I believe that is still possible, Philippa. Once the Aurlings and all their impurity is gone, I envision a time when sheathed swords shall maintain the peace."

She held the tea to his lips and he sipped. He closed his eyes and intoned as she set the tin on the table, seeing with prescient surety the shared night before them.

"I had thought simply joining the army would satisfy my father's memory, but Philippa, he haunts me," he said, reaching out for her shoulder. He said the elder Koertig knows of his son's failure. He knows how he blindly let the Aurlings and Demis infiltrate the land, and how he was so quickly defeated by just one. As he spoke, he slid his fingers behind her neck and traced his thumb over her ear. "It is my father I see when I dream, and it is his vision I fight for. I must defeat these creatures. Until then he will forever haunt me."

She sat silently as he spoke, guiding his hand with a shift of her neck, a turn of the arm. This to Koertig was a conversation. He spoke lovingly of his family and achievements, she sat quietly transfixed. She was okay with this, even happy at times. To be allowed to sit beside Harner Koertig as he stroked her and spoke of his greatest hopes and fears was something she never would have fantasized about just two short months ago. So certain was she of her role as a mute witness that she did not even answer when he asked her a question.

"I said, what haunts *you*, Philippa?" he asked again. "Is there a ghost in your life, like how my father haunts mine?"

She did not answer right away, though she knew her ghost immediately. She took his hand off her shoulder and held it in her lap.

"All I ever knew was my father," she said finally, her two fingers stroking the blonde hairs on his forearm. "Haggart says I was too young to remember him, but I do, to a degree. Images, sounds. I remember big hands," she said, holding up Koertig's own large hand. "Big hands lifting me up, and a wide belly that I kicked at with bare toes. Hickory," she said cheerily. "He must have worked in a smoke house because to this day the smell of hickory..." She drifted in her thoughts and shook away tears. "His voice," she continued. "In my dreams I still hear his voice, thick and echoey, like we're in a tight room even in the vast outdoors. It's just my name, but he says it in a way like no other. 'Philippa' he says, and each time it's like he is trying it out for the first time, and falling in love with it."

Koertig listened quietly as she spoke, and when she finished, he reached over his body to the bedside table and again offered her his tea. "You must have been very special to him."

They had entered a pattern, Philippa and Koertig, a pattern every morning she told herself she should break. Hours of cold disregard from Koertig melted away in the quiet evenings as he sat her on his bed-side and spoke of his dreams. Koertig at night talked of wild mountain flowers, and youthful springs in Illsbrook. He had a vision for Eisen she could easily believe in, and a vast beating heart buried below years of soldierly indoctrination. And most importantly, at these times, Koertig showed her a kindness and attention like she had never known. Night-time Koertig was a man she could love, she thought, as he placed her hand on his chest. But even as he pulled her in, and she resisted not a whit, she knew that in the morning, icy shame would greet her from her lover's eyes.

She would let him have her again, and for another night she would let herself believe she could one day have him too. She lay beside him and spoke of her time in Illsbrook as he rolled his thumb over her bottom lip.

And in this pattern, two months passed.

***

Olen stood in the sack, leaning on Bakku's shoulders as he hiked up the mountain. When the rocks got too steep, she ducked inside as he climbed to the next crest, pulling himself up with strong arms. When his pace evened, she popped backed out to his shoulder. They had entered the snow caps and could see the crests ahead. He was making for a dip in the mountaintop where they could slip through to the western lands. It was so bitterly cold already that she was glad they would not have to climb all the way to the peak. A winter storm blew snow in their faces.

They reached a valley-like bowl that rose right up to the crest. The snow collected here year-round and was deeper than they would ever know. Bakku's heavy footprint sunk knee-deep with every step. She ducked into the sack as it dragged in the snow below her. She was curled tightly inside clutching the pot and shoving aside frozen apples, while wearing the warmest clothes she could imagine. Her coat transformed between hides and furs she had seen traded in the square, searching for one that would trap in her heat. Now a bear skin jacket, now otter pelt slacks. Still the winter chill sliced through to her bones, and still Bakku climbed, nearly naked to the world, laboring ahead. There would be no camp in this weather. There was no stopping now and no turning back. He had to make it over the top.

And this was how they climbed for the entire day, Bakku plodding up the wintry mountainside, the icy winds blowing him back. He trudged slowly, and when it was vertical he climbed, forcing out grunting breaths with each pull. She poked her head out of the sack and was blasted by a sandstorm of frozen mist. The world was a white-out swirl with hints of grey on the horizons. The warmer lands far below were lost in the blowing snowstorm.

"Stay down," he called through the gale. "Too cold."

She ducked back inside as winds whipped against the sack like flags in a storm. Bakku's heavy breaths were soon replaced by anguished groans as he forced his legs up the snow-packed mountainside, his icy chain banging against ice and stone. Winds blasted against him, forcing him back, but he kept moving forward. With slow plodding steps he strained on, while Olen bounced around inside the large sack and tried to stay warm. The cold picked its way through the porous burlap, setting her teeth chattering, and her temples aching. She wished for a fire and a rest to settle her stomach and head. Just a small camp for an hour or two, not long. She would make the fire herself. She kept these thoughts to herself as Bakku suffered up the mountainside. He growled, forcing strength into his legs and arms.

She could not have done this alone. She would have been captured or killed by the gores that first night, or would have fallen away to whatever world her magic had opened up before her. Only Bakku could have gotten her over this mountain, and for that she was not ashamed. She had always been independent, trying her best to live by her own set of rules and tending to her own needs, but some things she just had to admit she could not do. She only hoped there was a way to pay him back.

And still he climbed. Time and direction disappeared from her reckoning as she tossed about. There were sideways jerks as he reached for distant grips, and quick weightless leaps as he flung himself over rifts. All along she banged and bobbled in the frozen sack as the hours edged by more slowly than she had ever encountered. There was a great moan and a vast upward lift as he crested one of the lower peaks. He shuffled ahead on smoother footing, groaning with each step as the burlap sack buffeted against her.

Words mingled with his moans, distant words, confused. She lifted her head out of the sack and was blinded. They had broken through the clouds, and the sun was brilliant and wide. She wore a fox-fur hood and riding goggles. Ice formed quickly around the corners of her glass.

"What did you say?" she called out, yelling into the harsh winds.

"I did not give up," he said through stuttered breaths, but it no longer sounded like Bakku. Snowy crystals had formed around his eyes and nostrils. His mouth hung open as he gasped for air, and his lips were white with frost. The world was a whiteout of snow and sunlight, and she was freezing in the blazing sun. Still Bakku moved forward. His voice was weak, childlike. Still he climbed. "They chained me, but I did not give up," he said.

"That's right!" she yelled at him. "You are unstoppable Bakku! You never give up!" And she thought maybe that was why she cared for him so. He had suffered for centuries in that prison, compared to her brief time in the Ward. And yet he still fought to survive, much like she had always held on to her dream for something more than the orphanage.

"So many years," he said. His eyes were wild, as the ice had seemingly seeped past his scarred flesh and frozen his mind. Ragged layers of frost-bitten skin, like frayed hems from her skirt, hung off his fingers and palms. His feet were lost in the snow. "I rubbed the chains at my ankles," he said proudly, but sounding near death. "That was all I did. I did not care how long it took. How long was it?" He asked, turning his head to her. His eyes pleaded with hers as the winds whipped at his long ice-covered ropes of hair. She hardly recognized him.

"Over two hundred years!" she shouted, saying the words but finding it impossible to truly fathom such an expanse of time. Two hundred years in chains, while she had lived twelve in practical freedom.

"Two hundred...two hundred years," he repeated, as if trying to make sense of the words himself. He trudged ahead and climbed. "I twisted the chain for fifty years, and then one day," he made a snapping motion with his hands. "Three more chains to go! But I never gave up. They did not know, stupid gores. They would come. Clicking and biting," he said, pulling himself over a ledge as nature's fury ravaged them for their trespass. "But they never checked my chains. I was patient. Two hundred years, four chains, and the stupid gores did not know. When my hands were free, I started on the bars. I never gave up!" he shouted defiantly, as if to Brynn himself.

"And you never will!" Olen called out, the chill wind taking her breath away.

The ground leveled out and the winds eased. The mountain dropped down below revealing green fields far beyond. They had reached the crest. The colorful lush lowlands stretched ahead to the horizon.

"Stupid gores," Bakku said and started down the slope.

Olen's body screamed for her to get out of the cold, but she refused to listen. She wrapped her arms around Bakku's frozen neck and gave him what little warmth she had left.

"Stupid gores!" she agreed and kissed his jowls.

24

Willingly

Harner Koertig sipped his morning tea and felt vigor in his bones. Nearly three months after the city-sergeant was first rushed to the dispensary, he had recovered enough to finally journey outdoors. His legs were stronger every day, and he told Philippa nothing heals like Eisen's fresh mountain air. She helped him down the staircase and held open the door as he walked past.

"Hurry back," she said, holding on to the door like a sailor's maid watching her lover escape to the sea. "And do take care."

She wore a severely pressed nurse's gown and a new white bonnet that, in the revealing sunlight, appeared costume-like and absurd. She tries so hard to blend in with the Midtown folk, he thought, but she will never hide who she truly is, an orphan of the Lowtown Ward. And she had revealed even more during their nights. Her kin, what little she knew of them, were vassal-class laborers. Slave-like workers who toiled for feed instead of coin. It would take more than a new uniform to clean such a taint. It would take Koertig.

She stood in the doorway waiting for him to dismiss her.

"Come along," he said, waving her in. "You wouldn't want to miss the coronation."

He was to be made City-Lieutenant Colonel this afternoon, an officer and a member of the city's ruling council. Sergeant Martz had been correct. The Aurling Brynn had sent Reeve and Graeme, his closest advisors, to his room with the plot. He would be given the promotion at a public ceremony, at which time Koertig was to make the surprise announcement of his retirement. There would be no dishonor, and the city promised him an officer *and* a councilman's pension, in perpetuity. Thus the pantomime. They encouraged him to spend his days in travel exploring this great land he had suffered for; he could even take his nurse. They had smiled the entire time they spoke.

"One quick moment," Philippa pleaded and ran back inside to grab her small pack of necessaries. When she came back, the two explored the wooden labyrinth that was Midtown. She strode beside him, moving confidently with so few others around. Each tall row of wattle and daub buildings was like an alley, disappearing around sharp corners or stretching like covered bridges over clefts in the mountainside. There was very little commotion outside these wooden structures with mudded walls, as little commerce happened in the alleys of Midtown. They strode under timber footbridges that linked balconies, Philippa tickling green vines as she passed. She would have been a pleasant lady, he thought, had she not been born so low.

They then followed the call of a distant flute straight into the Midtown square. It was smaller than the Lowtown square with fewer vendors, but the merchandise and foodstuffs were of a higher quality. The minstrel paused his strumming as the sergeant entered the market.

Constant bed-rest had done little to harm Koertig's physique. He stood tall above most of the townspeople, and his muscles had retained their solid mass. His soldier's uniform was long gone, and he now wore loose dark blue pants with low black boots. His top was merely a white undershirt with a mid-length sleeve and an open chest, a scandalous show for a man bred outside of the Lowtown class. The right sleeve had been cut off high over the shoulder and deep below the armpit. His wound was only lightly bound in gauze, with large mounds of scarred and twisted flesh showing through the shirt. *Look at my scars*, he silently dared the townspeople, *see the hurt I have taken for you.*

They approached a vendor who held out a bright green pear. Koertig nodded and Philippa reached in her purse for a coin. However, the vendor waved her off, saying it was a small price for the sergeant's suffering. She took the pear, and the vendor nodded respectfully.

He would not need Mayor Brynn's damn perpetual charity.

The minstrel's song returned to the square as they walked. They toured the borough passing by open storefronts. He wanted gasps and awed whispers. He was not disappointed. They stopped at a fountain above the Oiskonn River. He cupped his palm underneath the spout and lifted a handful of fresh water to his lips. The Skywheel churned behind them, with children and travelers being lifted high above the city. Philippa pulled a small carving knife out of her purse and sliced the pear, holding it out to him. He insisted she eat some too. Every man and woman that passed by stared at the special couple.

He was making a show of it, letting them recognize the good man he was. They would know Philippa was one of the Ward, and they would see the kindness he meant by sharing his food. Midtowners had no hate for Lowtown rats; they pitied them desperately. They simply did not want throngs of them invading their clean borough. They needed to see that their new City-Lieutenant Colonel was a kind and caring man to all of Millthrace.

The curse with the Aurling Brynn was that he had actually managed the city well and was truly valued by all three levels of class. Koertig could easily overthrow the man, even with only one arm. But he could not risk losing the people.

They next took a walking tour of lush Uptown, where the wealthy— lounging under canopies, smoking long pipes and eating when already sated—offered their respects. Even here she held her head high and dropped greetings to the townspeople as if they were equals. So this is how high you hope to climb, he thought. Were it bravery he would have been proud, but her aspirations were pure foolishness. He didn't know whether to admonish or admire her.

They then journeyed back down to the dusty air of Lowtown, stopping at the Well. He checked the bob and saw that the water was quite high today. This troubled him, as it did all. He rested on a bench and was pleased to see the youth scatter from one-armed Harner just as quickly as they had done from the old Sergeant Koertig. Tradesmen dipped their head to the sergeant and many tipped their caps. Then they turned back to their haggling, cheating, and worrying about the river.

He pulled a folded slip of paper from his pocket and handed it to Philippa.

"What is this?" she asked, cheerfully surprised.

"That is how to catch the Aurling Bakku," he said. "Swords and spears just make him angry, but this should stop him."

"I see," she said. She read the note and looked at him questioningly, as if wondering what she was supposed to do with it.

"It is for Martz," he said. "Give it to him without a word. If that creature comes back I want him to be ready."

"Yes sir," she said. "And what of the Mayor?"

"What of him?"

"I know you want to expose him," she said, folding and then refolding the note, getting the edges right before putting it in her purse. "But you must consider what he offers you. You will want for nothing...for the rest of your life. There are not many who can say that."

He let her speak, and in his mind he saw himself climbing the Never-Ending Ridge and seeking out the remains of his father's old cabin. He could rebuild it in much the same style. Millthrace would sponsor him, and he would once again be home.

"What sense is there in fighting a battle you would surely lose when he promises you a long and comfortable life instead?" she continued "Accept your reward, and leave Brynn his damned city. This is not your father's war."

"Never speak of my father!" he shouted, snapping out of his day-dream and silencing the traders. Moments ago she was the bold social climbing rat from the Ward, and now she seeks compromise and easy solutions. "Look to your own actions! How can you ask me to accept his bribe while you sent your own sister to her death?"

That one hurt her, it was obvious. She shook her head disbelieving him, but inside she must have known it was true. A woman shopping at a stand nearby replaced her goods and slipped away.

Philippa covered her face in her hands and whispered, "She's not dead."

"Not yet," he replied.

A barker returned to the call-and-answer dealing of the square. Traders and shoppers resumed business, peering sideways toward Koertig as they moved.

He placed his hand on her knee. She turned away, but he pulled her back, speaking calmly. "Perhaps you are right. I am not the soldier I once was. Even if I have to face Brynn, I will not be able to do it alone." He pointed to the large building down in the Barrens near the river. "That was a military dispensary long ago," he said of the Ward. Scrap wood covered holes in the roof, and the siding was warped, pulling nails out of the foundation. Boards covered broken windows in the basement. "It was much nicer back then."

"Haggart's place?" Philippa asked, looking up. "Yes, I had heard that."

"I prefer my current accommodations much better," he said softly, leaning in.

"As do I," she said, wiping away her tears.

"I will not expose Brynn," he said and pulled on her knee until she looked at him. "But I cannot stop him from exposing himself. If he makes an act of war against this city or its people, I will have to fight him. And if that happens I will need you with me full time. Do you understand what that means?"

"Yes," she said. "I will have to leave the Ward and stay with you."

"No, dammit!" he said, and she shook her head questioningly as confusion and shame washed over her. "No," he said more softly, "You don't *have* to do anything you don't want. I only want you with me *willingly.*"

She let out a breath and wiped her wet cheeks. "I am sorry," she said, sniffling. "I misunderstood." She rubbed her hands over her cheeks and then down to her mouth wiping away the emotions. "Of course I am with you willingly."

"I know," he said and stood with a purpose. "Well! I believe we have a ceremony to attend." But the girl did not stand. She sat with her hands on her knees, staring at the patterns in the wooden floor, still sniffing away the tears. She took a breath and words formed on her lips. *Say it* he thought. *Give me your ultimatum. Demand to be treated like the lady you are not, and see how fast I cast you back to your rat's nest. Test my spirit, and find your own resolve on trial.*

She smoothed out her skirt, nodded to herself, and then stood. "I'm okay now," she said. "I just needed a moment." She reached over and adjusted his shirt, pulling the cut sleeve away from his wound. "I want you to know it's alright, these things you say. I know the suffering you have endured, for this city, for its people." She smiled softly and checked the buttons on his shirt. "But I also know the good of your heart. If you need to vent your anger from time to time, you have earned that right. That it is mistakenly directed my way, I understand and allow that also. That, Harner, is what I do willingly."

She patted his chest twice and grabbed her parcel off the bench.

"Come," she said pleasantly and took a step near the Midtown stairs. A merchant pulled aside his cart for the Lowtown nurse, and an Uptown barrister gave her a quick nod as he passed by. As if ordered by some unheard command, crowds on the stairs ambled aside and opened a path for the tall nurse with the blonde hair and rigid spine. "Come," she repeated, sunlight rising behind her, as she smiled proudly at the statue-like soldier.

Koertig followed.

25

❧

The Plan

Most roads on the Iron Triangle were well-traveled. A merchant leading his train from Millthrace southwest to Brennan could hardly pass an hour without trading "hulloes" with the driver of a swift carriage or heavy wagon heading north. That same merchant, turning east onto the Brennan-to-Illsbrook Glory Road would never be certain where the towns ended and the prairies began. Life thrived along this southern highway due to its place alongside the Wide Galenic River. Over every hill and around every corner, small communities formed. Some had names and makeshift administrations—like Kessel and Grimm—others were no more than semi-permanent tent villages with ever-changing monikers. Brennan to Illsbrook travel was teaming with life. Not so on the dusty Merchant's Trail between Millthrace and Illsbrook.

With no permanent communities along the way, and only rare encounters with fellow travelers, voyagers on the Merchant's Trail often suffered from a loneliness reserved for sailors and the incarcerated. Men and women traveling this lonely road often found their thoughts drifting to fantasy. After days on the silent trail, Edwin again ached to be back in the bustling halls of University.

Plaited river reeds in his hat had finally begun to jostle themselves free and dangled in his face, tickling his cheeks. He lifted the dry brown cluster off his head. The lattice-worked leaves unwove in his hands like a basket with a torn slath. He let the nest-like clump fall to the roadside and watched it as he walked ahead. An unusual sense of melancholy came over him as he moved further and further away from the lump of dead grass. It had served its purpose and was now left to rot on the lonely road.

Marko pulled his donkey cart off the Merchant's Trail and traveled down a lightly worn path. The flat and well-marked road gave way to ruts in a field that snaked back towards the trees. "Trust me," he told Edwin, when asked why the detour.

Things were getting greener again, the further they journeyed away from the Ode. Edwin marveled at the sheer variety of low vegetation in the wide fields, and tried his best to make quick notes of the unique flora.

"Prickle Pear," Marko said, as Edwin touched the low spiny plant. "Don't eat it. Deep bitter roots, but at midnight its leaves swell with water. It's not satisfying, but enough to keep a man alive. Spider Weed over there," he said, and pointed to a mesh of crooked brown stalks. "Don't eat that either."

Edwin walked off-trail and plucked a thick green stalk. "Sparrow-grass!" he declared. "We have this in Ulm. Certainly we can eat this?"

"No," Marko said.

"And why not?"

"I do not like Sparrow-grass."

Marko and Sonny pulled ahead on the barely visible path, and Edwin quickly followed, grabbing handfuls of green as he went. He liked his new title of chef, and as long as he was stuck in this land, he was going to do his best to live up to it. The thin trail ambled east into a dense woods.

"Southern half the Twins," Marko said, as they neared the forest. He explained that the Twins were two similarly shaped woods. Seasoned travelers knew this path led to a small lake just inside. Sonny pulled the cart with vigor he had not used on the highway, practically skipping like a child. "He knows," Marko said enthusiastically, patting the donkey's rear end. "He remembers."

They moved through the chestnut and poplar forest, Sonny pulling the cart around tall thin trunks. Just a few moments later the woods opened up, and the path angled down to a thin pebbly beach. Marko unhooked Sonny and let him wander over to the tall sweet grasses.

"Do you want to make the fire or catch the fish?" Marko asked.

"I would love to perfect my fishing skills," he answered, rubbing his belly, "But I am afraid my hunger cannot wait that long. I will work the fire and trust the fishing to you."

As with most of the untamed lakes and rivers in Eisen, it did not take long to bring in a healthy catch. Marko, a fine chef himself, took care of the dinner duties, and encouraged Edwin to rinse his feet in the lake. Edwin did him one better and dipped his entire aging body in the cool waters.

As he floated naked in the still pond, Edwin considered his tenure at University. He had grown up with the aristocrats of Ulm, a fine and proper group, but also a people whose most profound questions regarded the age of wine. He had wanted to know about the age and ages of the world. He dove under the waves and kicked to the surface, shaking the water out of his grey hair and newly formed beard. He had attended classes dutifully, but due to his need to observe, he rarely finished a project. He had learned so much but had accomplished so little. At first he was going after an education; now he was afraid he was merely chasing a title. His degree had been his passion, but at some point a man must rest. At some point a man must live.

He thought of Olen again, the girl who lived openly and freely. He had never quite shaken her from his head. She still lingered there, demanding to be observed. *It is because you never completed the observation,* he told himself, before diving under again. Bakku had broken up the observation, and white-livered Edwin had run away. Before he let himself fall into a shame session, a euphoric thought entered his mind. If he still felt her, then she must have survived. And then a more endearing revelation. *I will be drawn to her again. The urge will pull me away to I don't know where, but there she will be.*

He swam to shore, and Marko greeted him with a drying rag before leaping into the waters himself. After toweling off and digging out his ears, Edwin found his wet clothes by Marko's cart hanging on a line. Marko had washed them clean. On the ground sat a neat pile of all of Edwin's goods. The washing had surely been a feeble excuse to rummage through his pockets. But all of his possessions were there in the pile, including his coins, and even the small dagger that sat atop it all.

After Marko's quick swim, they supped quietly on a fishy bisque as the still-hot sun set behind them. Sonny wandered around the shore, lazily unimpressed by the two naked men. Marko had refilled their cups with ale and packed his wooden pipe with tobacco. The aromatic brown leaves had kept their moisture during the long journey over the arid highway, but they lit as if dry when Marko held a flame near the bowl. Thick grey plumes rolled out of the pipe as he puffed away. He passed it to Edwin who thanked him and inhaled. It was sharp at first, then a soothing calm as he exhaled. They lay back on their folded robes and watched the sky as they smoked.

"So I still don't understand," Edwin said, only mildly aware of his nakedness. "Who is Marko Meloon?"

"Marko Meloon is tolerable," he said cryptically, as he did most everything. "What is an Observer?"

"Oh, it's a bogus degree," he freely admitted as he inhaled. "One created only as a humorous slight for the old University man. Perhaps they expected spitting outrage, but instead I had accepted the honor, ceremony and all. If they thought they could ridicule old Edwin, well, they had clearly not been so thorough in their studies."

They smoked in silence until Marko offered up dreamily, "I do not plan to stay on this road forever, Observer."

"Hmm?" Edwin asked, mid-inhale, feeling his rapid thoughts calm for the first time in a long time.

"Trading," Marko said. "I have saved a bit here and there. Not enough, of course, but more than your average trader along these routes."

"Hmm," Edwin nodded in agreement as he took another puff before handing it off to his companion. "Rather dangerous, though," he said, his head swimming in beautiful fumes, "Carrying that kind of coin...around and around this crazy circuit."

Marko smiled that wide grin he had created for his character, but which had also become his own. He rolled on to his side and faced Edwin. The two men lay bare in the warm and setting sun. Not since sneaking away with the minstrels had Edwin felt so unashamed about his body. University had taught him so much, but it had also taken so much away.

"My money doesn't travel with me," Marko said. "The big merchants in all three cities do their accounting with moneychangers. I have joined them!"

"You have investments?" Edwin asked, as if it were the craziest thing he had ever heard. Wandering tradesmen do not invest, they suffer for every coin. Surely many of the families in Millthrace's Uptown had savings, but for the most part all of Eisen's investments were held by wealthy Hulblich financiers. Even Edwin lived only by the dividends his family spared him. "Foolishness," he concluded. "Only the wealthy have investments."

"And so does Marko!" he said proudly, and rolled onto his back. "One in each city. The granaries of Millthrace, the ore burners of Brennan, and the Illsbrook ferry. Very small amounts in each, compared to their usual clients. Scattered silvers here and there. To them, my money is hardly worth the ledgers they are written on."

"Then you are a great actor indeed my friend, to convince even the great Brennan iron works to pay you dividends. They are a name I had heard quite often spoken in my library. Only the deepest pockets are allowed to unload into their coffers, yet they welcome your spare silvers. Why?"

"Because they think I am a fool!" Marko proclaimed laughing, and then added wryly, "And moneychangers are always greedy! They guard my silvers for free, and even add a copper or two of their own twice a year. All because Marko Meloon is an idiot who will either lose his ledgers, forget about the money altogether, or get his fool hide killed on the Iron Road! They are the fools!"

"Safe keeping and easy profit," Edwin said absently, but he had his eyes on the pipe in Marko's hands. Marko passed it over. "Marko Meloon, I believe you are a genius!"

The sun fell below the tree tops, and dark shadows crawled over the camp. Edwin puffed away thinking he may never wear clothes again.

Marko's face hardened as he turned back to Edwin. "But like I said, I do not want to do this forever. It is time for me get off this road and go home."

"To University?" Edwin asked.

"Welter Bay, just north of University," he said, pushing himself to sitting. He pulled a small burlap sack into his lap and offered Edwin a dried date. He thanked him, but no, as Marko continued, talking through his chews. "I cannot go home just yet, I need a little more. You see, I did not just leave the school to act. I left to make my fortune. I am almost there, and once I have made my money, then perhaps...perhaps she..."

His focus drifted off, and for the first time Edwin saw through his façade. He was acting out a prepared bit. Shall we call it *Marko the Lonely Heart*, he thought. Show a sensitive side, tell a woeful tale of lost love, and then reel in Edwin the Dupe for a grand score. The pipe smoke was sweet, but it would take more than that to fog his mind. Edwin was on his guard. He also pushed himself to sitting, crossing his old white legs in front of himself. Marko wanted him to press the question, so he did. "She?" Edwin asked, with the proper interested inflection.

"There is always a *she* in everything we do, isn't there?" Marko asked, nudging Edwin conspiratorially as he took back the pipe.

Any calm from the smoke and ale fell away. Edwin felt sick, like Marko was preparing something, and he was not quite sure if this something was a small ruse, or something that could leave Edwin penniless and left behind. Or worse. Sonny had wandered to the far side of the pond. *Well,* Edwin comforted himself, glancing at his nude companion, *at least I know the man is unarmed.*

Marko took three deep draws on the pipe before handing it back. "Suffice to say, my ledgers are not quite up to snuff for a lady of her upbringing, which is why I hope you trust me now and are willing to tell me why drunken soldiers are looking for you." Marko set the pipe behind himself and pressed on. "Why does an untitled Historian carry such a big price on his head? And who are you running from on the Iron Road?"

And there it was. The reason why all this game. This was why Marko had asked him to travel together. This was why he had pulled him off the highway to this hidden lake. This was all part of Marko's plan to claim the golden manors for himself.

"Are you going to report me?"

"Of course not," Marko said. "We are partners now. But I do want my two gold pieces! And before we can top those guards and get our coins back, I need you to be totally honest with me. Tell me everything, and I will be able to set up the perfect fiddle. It is what I do."

"Wait, wait!" Edwin said, thinking he had felt so good just moments ago. The swim, the bisque, the ale and smoke. And now this foolishness! It felt suddenly cool in the darkening woods and the rough ground hurt his bare backside. "But if I help you, then why do you get both gold manors?"

"Because there are four golden coins," Marko said, with a smirk, and then challenged Edwin, "Tell me why there are four."

Edwin ran through his head everything the drunken soldier had said, as Marko went to his cart and pulled out a pair of sleeping packs. Warm knit blankets were wrapped in tough deer skins that would soften the ground. He sat one at Edwin's feet. He pondered Marko's question, but he came up empty. Then as Edwin unfurled his pack he remembered something the soldier had said. "*Our most brutal legion was sent west!*" Edwin exclaimed.

"Indeed! And when I sold him his wine," Marko continued, "he told the old fool Marko Meloon he is to go to Illsbrook where he will wait for word from Millthrace. He praised his good luck in being sent to

Illsbrook, where a handful of coins and the proper authority can get a man anything—anything!—he wants."

"Which is exactly why I despise that filthy town," Edwin added, remembering his one brief previous visit, a visit that had both formed and confirmed his mindset about all of Eisen.

"Me too," Marko said. "He then laughed and told me about the other regiment that had drawn the Brennan assignment. *'Let them choke on Brennan's black fog'* is what he said." Marko grinned.

"The other regiment," Edwin said slowly, as Marko's plan dawned on him. "So the other regiment must have two golden manors also!"

"Four gold pieces guarded by the worst troops in Eisen. We will take the gold from Illsbrook, and then Brennan. After that—assuming they didn't send a third troop to Ulm—you can retire at University, and I can go back to her. Now Edwin, what is your story?"

This Marko Meloon was a wise one indeed. Devious, yes. Trustworthy, he wasn't quite sure. But he was a smart man, who quite possibly had studied at University. Two gold manors each, Edwin thought, and had to admit it sounded more than a little inviting. But he would have to trust the man, something that was uncomfortable for Edwin. He would have to explain about the girl and her magic, and also that thing inside him that pulled him around the world. He had never even explained it to his aunts.

Edwin rolled out his deerskin and pulled the blanket over his shoulders. The two men sat in the darkening woods as Edwin made his choice. He told Marko Meloon everything.

His rewards for speaking came early and often, as an enthralled Marko paused the speaker and tore into his cart. He dug amongst his goods and returned with treats for them both. Whether it was hard cheese, or his special stash of pipe weed and wine, Marko shared happily as Edwin told his tale.

"Fascinating!" Marko said, after he told him about Olen. "If I could change my appearance at will I would have every pocket in this land emptied in a month!"

"Well, she has not quite perfected her skills, and she is just a child," he said, and a certain melancholy fell over him. He missed her. It was more than an unfinished observation. He missed his brief companion who had listened to him, spoke with him, and let him teach her. And there was more. She had a boldness about her, a confidence that he had never attained. Perhaps his entire life would have been different had he been born with her self-reliance and conviction.

He continued on in detail about all he had seen, and how he too had been accused of being an Aurling. He told Marko that it was ridiculous of course. He had an intuition that lured him, but that's all it was, a certain informed instinct. Marko pressed him for a few more questions on this, though Edwin assured him it was of no consequence.

As Marko built up the fire, Edwin then spoke of how Bakku broke them out of the cage, took the girl, but left poor Edwin behind. He told him about stumbling upon Nerikan the second time, and how Mayor Brynn gave the gores sight. He told everything and every detail including his meals.

"Yes," Marko agreed, "Grubs are very good. Try crickets too. Very good roasted."

Edwin rubbed his belly. "Right now I couldn't possibly eat a thing. I am completely stuffed, and I must say a bit foggy from all of the smoke. But that is pretty much it. Everything after that you are aware of."

Marko lay back on his deer skin and looked to the starry sky. Edwin could almost hear the gears in his head turning and locking into place. He pushed Edwin's story through his scheming mind, searching for the scam or scams that would work best. It did not take him long to find one.

"They are not looking for you," he said, to Edwin's surprise. "That commander knows it too. Two gold pieces is a high bounty for even the worst criminals. Mayor Brynn is offering up a reward he never intends to pay. That regiment we saw was not the best Millthrace had to offer. Brynn is keeping his best men in the city."

"But why?" Edwin asked.

"I do not know, and what happens in Millthrace does not factor into our game," Marko said. "I am only concerned with Illsbrook and Brennan and getting our coins back."

"*Back*, you keep saying *back*. What do you mean?"

He sat up and crossed his legs, facing Edwin. He then went into great detail of what must have been his philosophy of life. He said that one must convince their mind that whatever they want is truly theirs, and that someone else has stolen it. Once they do this, they will have every fold in their brain working for them. "You won't be haunted by those voices saying *this is wrong* or to *just let it go*. You will tell yourself you won't stop until everything is put right and you have your things back. That is what we must do to get our coins back."

"I don't know about this," Edwin said, not ready to launch a new career of deception and intrigue. He still just wanted to get home, with or without the gold. "We both have our little stashes of silver."

"Which you *got back* from Koertig's overturned cart, if I remember correctly?"

"My goodness you are right," Edwin said, staggered by Marko's revelation. "How quickly I had come to think of it as *my* money!"

"It is your money!" Marko demanded, as he stood. "You earned it for all of the dishonor and suffering they subjected you to!"

"Yes!" Edwin said and stood with him. "They are lucky all I took was a small bag of coins!"

"And have you counted your money recently?" Marko asked, placing a hand on Edwin's shoulder. He told Edwin that he had seen how quickly he and his coins get separated. He promised he would get him to Illsbrook with silvers to spare, but travel on any *safe* ferry to Kessel, then a carriage down the highway to University, would leave his purse barren. "Does Edwin the Observer have any aunts left willing to give alms to their poor nephew?"

Edwin hung his head, ashamed. "At this point they wouldn't let me past the front gate." And he was not just being dramatic. His benefactors had allowed no coin for his latest adventure, so he had forged a promissory note; a note he had quickly redeemed before even reaching Millthrace.

"Listen, my friend," Marko leaned in close. "I saw what you did at the oasis, gaming the others to make your bisque. It is why I chose you. You and I are the smartest, most talented men on this entire highway, and it is a blessing we found each other. We cannot let that go to waste."

He wanted to believe Marko. He wanted to think someone in this world thought so highly of him. But a lifetime of mockery and disdain had taught him to resist.

"Before I accept anything, I need to know your plan," Edwin said.

Marko placed his hand to his chin and walked the camp thinking out loud. "We have a dubious regiment ordered to holiday in the most decadent city in all the land. They have to stay there and spend their city's silvers until they are called home. Or!" He snapped his fingers and rushed up to Edwin, "Heaven forbid they actually capture the fugitive and must return to their barracks! Imagine how terrible that would be!"

Marko said no more and just stared at Edwin as his smile slowly grew into that wide toothy grin. Sonny finally ambled back from the far side of the lake and walked up to the men. He sniffed at them both then hung his head and let his eyes drift shut. In a moment he was standing between them, fast asleep. Marko gave Edwin all the time in the world to figure out the plan for himself.

"Oh no!" Edwin shouted, waving off the idea and startling the donkey. "No sir, no way, no!"

"Think about it!" Marko pleaded, following Edwin as he paced around the fire. "The last thing they expect to do is actually capture you! I will turn you in; they will have to pay me!"

Edwin saw himself back in a cage, journeying back to Millthrace or Nerikan, but this time without curious Olen to share his misery. "And once you have the golden manors, how do you expect to release me from their grip?"

"I haven't figured that one out yet, but so far it is foolproof!" Marko said. "And besides, you are forgetting something important. These guards are not looking for you, but the gores sure are."

Edwin stopped. "Don't try to scare me," he said, but his voice betrayed the fear in his gut.

"Surrounded by armed guards just might be the safest place, until I break you out."

"And how do I know you won't just leave me?"

"You don't. You will have to trust me. And as a sign of my good faith," Marko rushed over to his cart and pulled out a small leather wallet. Inside were three small folded papers, which he handed to Edwin.

"Your ledgers," he gasped, and checked the others. He read the bottom lines. "Marko, I am impressed. You have indeed done well in your trade." He read them over again. Unless they were the highest quality fakes, they seemed absolutely genuine. He held them back out to Marko, "But I am clearly not Marko Meloon. You are too well known to these men. Even if I forge your signature they would never—"

Marko cut him off. "I do not expect you to take my money! You will be locked up in Nerikan! This is just to keep *me* honest. If I don't get you back from the guards, I will never be able to retrieve my fortune. Even with my gold pieces, it won't be enough."

"For *her*," Edwin said sarcastically.

"For the love of her," Marko concluded.

Edwin thought about it. Marko's ledgers could be fakes, yet somehow he believed them to be true. He had secretly counted his money earlier. The bag was still weighty, but he was mostly down to coppers and wedges. At the rate he had been losing cash, he truly would not have much left to get him back home, let alone to settle down and write his dissertation. But perhaps that was something he no longer wanted.

He thought again of Olen and how she had lived her life so freely. An ogre that had torn apart an entire city had come for her in the night. Instead of covering her face and cowering in a corner, she had trusted the creature and let him carry her away to a new life. Whatever life Edwin had been living, it truly had not been his best. Cowardice, anger, and an unearned arrogance had ruled his days and left him bitter and alone. Here he was at a crossroads with a chance to break free from his old ways. But he would have to do one thing. He would have to bypass reason for faith.

"I will trust you," Edwin said finally, snapping the first of many chains that had bound him for so long. A refreshing bolt of courage surged through him. "But I want a different plan for Brennan!"

"Already working on it!" Marko said, slapping the Observer hard on his shoulder.

***

She had almost told him, Philippa thought as she led Koertig to his inauguration. When he had barked at her, she had almost shouted back a secret. But she had not wanted it to be an angry thing. She would wait until nightfall until a kinder Koertig appeared.

He swept past her taking the lead, and she saw his bandaged shoulder, white strips without a hint of pink. He had healed so quickly, so completely. He may even had been released earlier than today had his wound not appeared so gruesome, for in truth, he had not bled in many nights. This was his special day, and she would let it be for now. Perhaps tonight, she thought, as she trailed behind, watching him stalk proudly to the Midtown square. Tonight he would learn that this month, she too had not bled.

26

The White Owl

It took most of the day for Bakku and Olen to get below the snow caps. They were still further up the mountains than Millthrace traced, and higher still than the eagles flew. But the harsh storms were far behind them, and the breezes were now miraculously warm. They had made it. Bakku had.

He lumbered ahead, trancelike from exhaustion. Then for the first time since scooping her into his sack and racing uphill, Bakku's feet touched dry stone. Juniper bushes dotted the ground here, low and compact, like the fountains of Midtown. The trees were Whitebark Pine, with sturdy trunks as white as the snow. Olen's hands rested on his wide shoulder, and when he first touched the dry mountainside his muscles fell slack and he slowed to a stop. His great task was over, his body finally spent. Bakku collapsed to his knees and laid a palm on the ground. She crawled out of the sack and leapt away as he fell to his side. His heavy lids lifted once more, his eyes rolling sleepily until landing on Olen.

"I'm okay," she said.

His eyes closed, his mouth fell open, and his entire body sagged onto the ground as he fell into a deep sleep. A faint barely-there light shone out of his frost-bitten wounds as warm blood flowed in. Already he was healing. Grey skin turned bronze, and pink scabs grew over cuts on his fingers and knees.

She dumped the wood, food, and other random things out of the sack, and then gently laid it over his shoulders. They were high above the Bluestem Prairie southwest of Millthrace. Tall bright grasses, blue like a summer sky, swayed along the lands far below. Since leaving the city, every time she had opened her eyes there were new lands to see, new wonders to marvel at. Bakku shivered in his sleep. She got to work on a fire.

"How many times are you going to save me, Baboo?" she said quietly, as she piled sticks. And then she realized she had said it. Baboo. A name children call their fathers. A word she had never been able to use. She had thought that when she found her father she would use the word, and that it would feel natural to say it simply because she was his daughter. She had never guessed it would slip out so naturally to someone else. Maybe words don't know their own definitions, she thought, maybe they only know their feelings. Maybe anyone can be a Baboo. Maybe anyone can be a Tanta. Maybe not.

"Bakku," she corrected herself, grateful he was still asleep.

She lit the kindling and brought the fire to full flame, heat touched her hands and face. She scanned her surroundings. There was no movement on the ground or in the sky. She snuggled up next to the snoring Bakku and slept through the night.

When she woke the next morning, she found Bakku sitting up straight. He was rubbing the sleep out his eyes and yawning. His face, hands, and feet were deeply scarred, but healed. He smiled that sideways grin that made her laugh.

"Don't say it," she said. "Hungry?"

Bakku nodded, "Always hungry."

She gathered their sparse supplies. A small pile of apples remained, but their red skin had turned soft and brown. Bakku ate one anyway. She could find some shoots and other greens around the camp, but Bakku needed more. She needed more.

"I'll hunt," she said, grabbing the gore ax. The head was similar to the hatchets woodworkers in the cities used, but the handle trailed down and curved into a canine-sharp poker. It was top-heavy and awkward, but it was their only weapon.

He asked her if she knew how to hunt, or what to do if she actually caught something.

"I will learn," she said and leapt down some rocks to the pines below. Before she entered the woods she checked on her friend. He sat cross-legged in a morning sunbeam, happily eating rotten apples.

Olen sat in a grey-green juniper amongst the pines watching the ground for anything with legs. Further down the mountain there would be deer and rabbit; here the best she could hope for were weasels and chittering pine squirrels. But that would do. Bakku needed meat. Baboo. She pulled one leg up onto the branch and let the other dangle. She wore her faded skirt and heavy boots from Millthrace. She let the tickle race up and down her spine. Her clothes rippled and tightened. Grey pants and an olive top now covered her. She pulled a loose hood over her head and was all but invisible.

During quiet times like this, she had found herself saving stories: the gores, the apples, and the frozen mountaintop. It was something she had always done, ordering tales in her head, readying them for when she found her parents. But now she thought of the Ward and her sisters. She imagined telling Samantha—who was always cold even in summer—of Bakku's mountain climb and watching her shiver the whole time. She wondered what Clara with her morbid wit would say of the crushed gores. And as for the apple trees, she was dying to tell that story to Mistress Haggart.

She had forgiven Haggart, she realized. The Mistress had been good to her and given her a home when her own parents could not. She had fed her and clothed her as best she could. What a shock it must have been to find out a girl living under her roof had these strange powers. It was rough when Haggart spit at her and abandoned her, but all things considered, Mistress Haggart reacted better than those that had surrounded a younger Bakku.

Her thoughts drifted as a large white bird dropped out of the sky and soared under her limb. It glided in on outstretched wings, a wing-span wider than she was tall, sweeping low and searching. A hunter, just like she. Its ashen wings curled and pulled it up to a thick branch just a tree away, where it perched soundlessly, its pure white back to Olen. She slid the gore ax out of her lap and held it aloft. The bird ruffled its snowy feathers and pulled its wings in tight, as if wrapping itself in a snowy white blanket. Two tufts like bright white ears grew out of each side of its head. It was an owl, angelic and pure, still awake from a night of hunting.

She could hit it. She knew she could. She assumed she could. She would only have one chance. She held the ax in her right hand, easing her arm higher, as the bird again flexed its wings, settling in and prac-tically sighing an exhale. It was ending the hunt and ready to rest. All she had to do was throw it. Those snow white feathers would be stained red, but she and Bakku would have their meat.

She had caught and cleaned fish before. She had watched hungrily when Bakku had skinned the rabbit. But this bird was different. She could not do it. It was just too marvelous. Beatifically it perched, its back straight on the branch. This world needed beautiful creatures, like this owl, like Bakku. They would eat bruised-apple soup after all.

"It's your lucky day," she whispered, and called across the treetops. "You're just too beautiful!"

It spun its head completely around. And as it locked its eyes onto her, she stifled a scream. The white bird's eyes were wide and frightened, and as familiar as her own, for they were not the eyes of an owl, but of a woman. A line of feathers circled an oval patch of bare skin, skin that was light brown and stretched over a chin and cheeks. There were lips, pink and full, as if ready to speak her tongue, and a nose hardly differ-ent than her own. But it was the eyes that held her. A woman's eyes, a mother's eyes. Eyes in shape and color, but wiped of all self-awareness.

These eyes revealed a mindless hunter, unaware its essence had been stripped away, altered, and reformed by Janus Brynn.

Then the face that was woman-no-more screeched. It was a fierce cry like a monstrous screaming eagle that clawed deep into Olen's ears and made her temples ache. The cry tore through the woods, wailing through the trees longer and louder than its avian lungs should have allowed. Olen dropped her head and covered her ears as the painful screech echoed. Then it turned its head and leapt into the air, thrusting out its white wings.

It was a spy. A scion. An owl touched with the soul of a woman. It called to its master. It had found the girl. It had found Bakku, and now it was returning to Brynn. It flapped its wings, and without thought, Olen just reacted. She launched the ax. The black cleaver spun as it flew across the pure green expanse and struck the bird high in the back, thrusting it off course. It flapped harder, even rising up slightly before its right wing finally dropped loosely to its side. Then the she-owl circled twice, gliding helplessly as it fell to the ground, dead.

The woman's dead eyes stared at her from beyond this world, and she finally understood the horror of Janus Brynn and the threat he was to her and her Bakku.

Much later she tracked her way back to camp and found Bakku sitting right where she had left him. She carried the owl over her back. An imagined saddle bag hung off her other shoulder. The bag was full. She flung the bird down in front of him. The woman's face stared up at them both.

"Scions," she said and saw his reaction. He had given so much of himself to get them over the mountain, and Brynn was already ahead of him. They were not free, and never would be.

The face reminded her of the ladies from Uptown, soft with small features. It could have been the face of a woman she had seen in the city, someone who had secretly slipped her a wedge when the men were not looking. It had the skin and muscles to smile and laugh. Eyes that could have been intelligent and caring. Bakku turned the dead bird face-down.

"Others?" he asked, looking to the pines.

She shook her head, knowing this discovery was very bad for them.

"We can't eat it."

"I wouldn't want to," she said.

Bakku looked at the dead scion. "It's not her fault."

It's not your fault either, she thought, but she saw the concern on his face. There was a madman out there, making these creatures and sending them out, and somehow Bakku seemed to think he was responsible. She could tell he had seen beasts like this, and probably much worse in his time. He was an experiment just like this owl, just like this woman. He picked up the corpse and walked far away from camp into the tall heather. He dug with his hands and placed the body in the ground face up. Then he folded its wings over its chest, and scooped the dirt back over. He came back to camp and sat down staring at the fire.

"He is still doing this," she said. "Brynn is still making scions. This woman," she said, her thoughts drifting off as she looked at the small burial mound. "She could have been someone's mother."

He turned his large head to her. She was challenging him, and he knew it. He was strong, and the more he ate the stronger he got. He must be able to stop Brynn, make him pay for what he's done.

"Calderra," he said, with a finality to his words. "Calderra is the only way to stop him."

"Running away stops nothing!" she demanded. "If you run away, Brynn will continue with his scions forever."

"No. Not forever," he said, and rubbed his wide hands over his head. He wore scars on his skin, but his face showed a greater pain, a curse he carried along through his long years, a curse that haunted and plagued him. "Only Bakku is forever."

"I'm sorry," she said, sitting next to him. "Well then, maybe I will just go with you to Calderra and help."

"No!" he said, his words knocking her back. He calmed and lowered his head. "You go to Kessel. Find your family."

"We can't let him do this," she pleaded.

"In Calderra," Bakku said. "I promise you. It will mean the end of his games."

Bakku pressed his palms into the ground and rose to standing. He grabbed the pot and moved uphill to fill it with snow. He returned to camp and set the pot on the fire.

"Apple soup is fine for today," he said.

"I said I would feed you, and I will," she said.

She opened the saddle bag and dumped out a collection of brown roots, mushrooms, hazelnuts, and a few green husked walnuts. He picked through the pile and one by one tossed the roots and mushrooms into the pot. A short round mushroom with a grey cap he pulled off the pile and showed it to her. He shook his head and tossed the cap behind him. With a flat stone he bashed open the nut shells, sprinkling the nutty brown and white meat into the soup. While he did this, she picked through what was left of the apples, and tossed in the few good pieces she could save.

"Probably not the best meal, but it will have to do," she said.

Bakku looked at the unusual soup hungrily, "Very good meal."

Later, they ate on the low mountainside as the sun continued across the sky.

"This is our thing, I guess," she said, scraping her finger inside the empty pot and sucking on it. "Eating."

He did not seem to follow.

"Food is our connection," she explained. "It's like Maggie—she's one of my sisters—she and I share this little finger wave," she curled her index finger at him. "I don't know how it started or really what it means, but we do it, and it feels good. It's just something we share. But if someone else waved at me like that, it wouldn't feel the same." She set the empty pot down and ran her hand through the walnut shells on the ground, searching for any edible pieces they had missed. She found a small chunk and popped it into her mouth. "What I mean is, even if I find my parents and make a new home in Kessel, it won't be the same. It won't feel like home, just like eating won't be the same without you."

He seemed to think about her words as they sat in the foothills of the Rückraadt. He lifted his hand, a palm wide enough for her to rest on, and curled his index finger at her, up and down, up and down, slowly as a wry half-smile spread over his face.

She spat air between her lips and burst out laughing.

"You look ridiculous, you must know," she said as she rolled on the ground. "You just like to prove me wrong, don't you?"

Bakku shrugged his shoulders and smiled.

"Fine," she said, in mock anger. "Go to Calderra, see if I care. You're right, I won't miss you at all. Not when I eat, not when I sleep, not even when I need to reach tall things!"

He placed his palm over her head and mussed up her hair. She pushed him away laughing. They then sat on the hillside watching the sun fade, and she let her head fall against his lap. She did not want him to go to Calderra, and she no longer cared about Kessel. If he asked her to ride his shoulders beyond it all to the distant frontier, she would climb up on him and never look back. But he did not want that, at least not yet. A thin trail of smoke rose on the distant southwest horizon.

"Brennan," he said. "We have traveled far south."

"The Iron City," she said.

He pulled the clasp back on his wrist and rubbed the scarred flesh. He had broken his chains, but he would never be able to remove those clasps.

"We should go there," Olen said.

Bakku turned to her with a confused look on her face.

"There is food there, real food," she explained, motioning to the shells and scraps scattered by their fire. "And there are also ironworkers in Brennan. They can cut off those shackles."

He turned his manacles. "They would alert the guards."

"No they won't," she said confidently. "Men will do anything for the right price, even if that means taking the shackles off a monster—"

Bakku grunted stopping her cold. She cursed herself for saying that word as he looked away with pained eyes.

"You're not a monster," she said, apologizing, and feeling like a fool.

"I didn't mean it that way. I hope you know that. Sometimes words just..." she did not know what to say. "Bakku, monsters are scary and mean, and little girls like me are afraid of them. You are gentle and kind, and with you around I am afraid of nothing. You are not a monster."

He grunted his assent, but she knew she had hurt him. She would pay any price to take that word back. There was nothing in her that wanted to hurt him.

"Let me hire a smithy to take off those shackles."

He did not respond. Oh god, for so long he did not respond.

"I have no money," he murmured.

"I do," she replied, digging into her shirt. There in a small hidden pocket was the coin. It had survived all this distance. She pulled it out and showed it to Bakku. He had been locked up for so long money had lost all value. He showed no signs of being impressed.

"Edwin says this is as much as *twenty-five coppers*! Any blacksmith would happily cut off your chains for just a part of this."

He looked at the distant smoke of Brennan.

"And Brennan is on the Westing Sea," She continued. "I'll find a workman who will remove your chains, keep it secret, and we'll still have enough for seafood dinner."

The deep indents in Bakku's brow smoothed out. "That coin is worth that much?" he asked.

"Much more," she said. "Any man would take that offer."

"A full dinner?" he asked.

"The fullest," she said. "You deserve a full, big, fresh dinner, with everything you can imagine included, and I am buying! If we go to Brennan, for the first time we can fill you up."

"Very well, we go," he said and stood up. He grasped his one remaining chain, jerking it free of his clasp and letting it fall to the ground. "But only to give you a good meal. I do not care about these shackles. They will be gone soon enough."

The broken chain lay in pieces on the ground, and she marveled at how strong he had become. He swung the sack over his shoulders and knelt down next to her.

"I can walk," she said, starting off downhill towards the Iron City. "You've carried me for too long."

Despite the smoke on the horizon, Brennan was still a great distance away. They trekked slowly down the mountainside and through the thick and varied woods that lined the Rückraadt Mountains. Over the days they paused at vegetable meadows and slept near small ponds, always eating what they could and resting when able. She had stopped counting the days, and had forgotten the weeks, for as long as they were together she was in no hurry. There had been no more white owls or looming vultures searching the skies, and for now, Bakku had stopped talking of Calderra.

Though she had lost count of time, she felt a month had passed since they had cleared the snowcaps. Sadly, despite their slow pace, they actually reached the bottom of the mountain and stood facing the edge of the Mecan Plains. Brennan's stony outline was much clearer now. A shallow river and the Iron Road crossed right in front of them. Hiding behind trees and thick foliage, they saw a small caravan of traders heading north towards Millthrace. Donkeys pulled three long carts, as men and their families walked alongside.

"Migrant traders," Olen said. She had seen them in the city. They had no home, besides the highway. They just forever traveled the triangle working when there was work, trading when they had goods, their numbers always growing. "That's probably just one family."

She counted over fifteen men, women, and children in the caravan. Two young boys ran along the wide stream skipping stones. The mother called them back to the road. They lacked most comforts, but life was not miserable, family supplied all.

"Those aren't iron workers," she said. "We will have to go to the city. Only a smithy will have the tools to free your bindings. We will wait for dark, when the highway is empty. Then we'll go."

They both sat back in the woods and watched the travelers walk by on the highway. They waited much of the day, just sitting in the woods off the highway. She did another run through the forest and found some purple grapes for Bakku. They were too bitter for her, but he chewed them happily. As he sat and ate, she saw the huge muscles flexing in his arms. He was getting bigger, stronger. It was nearly impossible to imagine, but the hulking beast that had broken into Millthrace must have been—in a strange way—a withered form of his true self, starved in the halls of Nerikan. He smiled at her, grape skin coating his teeth.

She laughed, and he laughed with her.

The first signs of sundown set across the land. It was not blackness, but for the couple that had waited all day, evening shade was dark enough. They waited for a small carriage to pass out of view, and then she stood.

"Looks clear," she said. Then it came, the sound they should have known would come. A flurry of clicks shot through the woods, untraceable, coming from every direction. Their journey, their impossible climb over the mountaintops had not stopped Brynn's scion army. It had only delayed the inevitable. They had found them. Another flurry of clicks and Bakku rose also.

"We've got to get to Brennan!" Olen said. "Even if you have to run in the front doors!"

He slung the sack over his back, and she leapt on to his shoulders, then he dashed out into the twilight plains as the first invisible fingers tapped against her neck.

27

Shield or Sword

Koertig stood off to the side near the Midtown fountain as Mayor Brynn introduced City-Sergeant Martz as the new head of the Millthrace Guard. He heard not a word the Aurling fraud spoke in the terraced square, as his mind turned over and over Philippa's words. Terrel Martz took his assignment respectfully and thanked the mayor. Polite applause rippled through the mixed crowd. *Allow.* That was the word she had used. She said she had *allowed* him to speak to her that way.

Most Midtowners had closed their shops for the ceremony and had gathered around the square. The minstrels had set aside their lyres and lutes, letting a different actor take the stage. The few Uptowners who could be bothered attended briefly, dressed in their finest. Among these crowds snaked the seamy Lowtown tradespeople. Never the type to miss a sale, these traders worked the crowd, distracting the others from the show—for that was all it was, a show put on by an Aurling mole. *Allow.* She allowed nothing. Yet he had followed her up the stairs when she had beckoned, and had felt a strange pride as the merchants stepped aside for her. Not for Koertig, but for her.

Mayor Brynn thanked Sergeant Martz and directed him off the dais. A flock of grey green waterfowl passed over the square, aborting splashdown on seeing the crowds. Brynn then spoke glowing words of praise about Sergeant Koertig and called him to the dais. But Koertig stood transfixed on his nurse.

Brynn called again and mimed clapping for the crowd to follow. As they applauded, Philippa stepped to his side and clasped his elbow, walking him to the mayor. Brynn handed her a cloth with a golden brown emblem sewn into it. It was the mark of a council member. She slung it over the front of Koertig's belt and faced the emblem forward. When the clapping subsided, Mayor Brynn asked Koertig if he had anything to say. He did.

"Thank you, Philippa," he said politely, as she stepped back into the crowd. Old Lowtown acquaintances looked at her admiringly. "I would not have survived these torturous weeks without you. I am forever in your debt." Old women and young girls saw the warden in a new light. She was no longer just a broad-shouldered pot-washing orphan, but instead a model of the perfect class-climbing lady. "As indeed I am in debt to every man, woman, and child in this great city."

He looked out over the crowd. All these faces had no idea of the Aurling standing just a few paces away. Brynn looked out over the crowd also, smiling broadly. She had asked him to accept Brynn's bribe. For a moment he had even considered it. With an endowment from Millthrace he could have revisited the Never-Ending Ridge, perhaps even building a cabin where his childhood home once stood. And he could have taken Philippa along on his travels. But then the damn fool of a nurse slighted his father, something no one may do, man or woman.

"You may not know this, but my father died in service for this land. It can be said now; he was killed defending this land's purity from the Aurling menace. I too would have given all, had it not been for my soldiers, my men, my brothers."

Brynn's face cracked ever so slightly. *So you did not know that I knew,* Koertig thought. *There is much I know, Aurling.*

"Yet in a way, I must give all. For you see, this army is my life but it is a life I am no longer fit for."

And there it was, a small exhale from Philippa, relief that she had controlled her patient. And from Mayor Brynn also, muted pride his master plan was falling into place.

"What battle can a one-armed soldier win? He is limited. Does he choose sword or shield? For no longer can he wield both."

"Let us be your shield!" a soldier cried out.

"And I, your sword!" another from the rear.

Koertig held up his hand to silence the crowd. A nervous Brynn did the same with both hands. Koertig spoke again, his voice commanding.

"I would rather the Aurlings take my life than allow any of our Millthracian sons to receive my wounds! I would rather the Aurlings steal my soul before I send our boys to battle in my stead! If I cannot fight, and if I cannot defend, then I must not lead!"

The soldiers cried out in rounds of disbelief. The townspeople also shouted their dissent. They were loud, they were frightened, and they were angry. Koertig was angry also.

"Damn the man who asks others to fight and defend while he sits back and reaps the rewards. For that is not a man," he said, turning towards Brynn as the Aurling's smile faded, "but a devil in disguise."

The mayor's eyes widened like those of a frightened cow. Koertig stared into his soul, and Brynn knew that Koertig knew.

Then a whisper at his feet. "Harner, no," Philippa said. She shook her head slowly, and he knew then what he had to do. He admired her attempt to guide the life of a Koertig, even though she failed horribly.

"Which is why I must resign my post of Lieutenant Colonel," he stated calmly, and stopped the crowd before it could roar its displeasure. "But I shall do this only after I complete my original task. I was asked to deliver the Aurlings to Nerikan. That duty is not complete! I will hunt the three creatures and deliver them to hell!" Then he added casually, glancing towards Brynn, "And should I find any others along the way, I'll toss them in too."

Soldiers and townspeople rushed the dais and congratulated the new Lieutenant Colonel, as Brynn and his men disappeared into the crowd. Women placed cloths around his neck and men crowded around him offering their left hand to shake. Even the Lowtown rats who had feared him all their life pushed through the crowd and laid hands on the man. But his nurse held back, her once glowing façade now frightened and dim.

Here's something you did not allow, he thought and smiled.

28

The Orange Clay of Illsbrook

Edwin had seen the adobe shops of Illsbrook on the horizon at dawn, and by midday they were inside the bustling city. It had been nearly a month since he first swam in the lake at the Twins, and even longer since he had run a blade across his chin and cheeks. His beard had come in full and white. With that and the clothes he had traded from Timo, the old Observer was unrecognizable.

"Honestly, I do not believe I have gone more than two or three days without a shearing since I was a young man. It is just not something men in our circle do," he said, stroking his white hairs. "But you say it looks good though?"

"Very good!" Marko said in his fully annoying character voice now that others were around. "Like a Grandpa!"

"Pugh!" he spat out.

"People trust Grandpas!"

Marko had not cut a straight path to Illsbrook. Instead he had pulled off the Merchant's Trail countless times following nearly invisible foot-paths down valleys and tight canyons to hidden huts and dens along the way. So populated was this desert, Edwin had thought, if only you knew where to look. And at each stop he was welcomed by familiar friends who each called him by a different name. Marko in turn replied with a character unique to each buyer.

As they walked, Marko had instructed Edwin on the ways of trading, which is to say, the ways of swindling. He did not use that word of course, but Edwin understood he meant it nonetheless. Marko had created little maneuvers, acts perhaps, he had found worked best for every situation. And he had given each of his schemes cutesy names such as the Wobbly Swap—a dizzying quick-handed trade where the buyer is not quite certain what, if anything, you just placed in his sack; or the Red Fox Feint, which as far as Edwin could tell involved completing half of a trade, and merely running away into the nearest woods. When asked what he called his maneuvers with the wine-loving soldier at the Oasis, he responded matter-of-factly, "The Inhibitive Dangle."

He had also explained to Edwin his plan to free him from his jailors after receiving the gold. Perhaps Edwin truly was the world's greatest fool, he thought, because the plan was simple yet elegant and seemed completely foolproof. He still was not eager to do it, though.

He worked Marko's scheme through his head as they led Sonny through the busy Illsbrook market known as Princetown. Multi-storied adobe buildings with carved-out windows and doorways packed the city, though it seemed every resident and traveler was out in the streets. Open exterior stairways of dry tan clay led to the upper floors, where myriad faces, from the darkest black to the palest white, looked down at the bustling market. Ropes were strung from rooftop to rooftop, with faded and torn flags of every color dangling below. There was no faire or holiday this time of year, the flags were merely to add to a general sense of perpetual merriment. A heavy orange dust quickly covered Edwin's toes as he moved through the crowded city, bumping elbows and rubbing shoulders with blurry shapes and colorful shadows.

"Tuck in," Marko warned, and Edwin protected his sack of coins.

The sights and sounds reminded Edwin of the Mayden Faire held each spring in the towns outside University, he even heard the distant sound of minstrels across the river. Tradesmen barked wildly, waving colorful flags and blowing horns to draw attention to their small corner of dust. Vendors here were on a downward track. They accepted un-reasonable offers and unfair trades, just so they could revel in one more night of debauchery. But that did not make them complete pushovers, for if they thought they were cheated they would take back what they lost, along with the right eye of the person who took it from them.

"Never tempt a man who has nothing to lose," Marko whispered as they angled through the crowds and into an open corner.

"What's the wares, old man," A grisly bearded trader growled to Edwin. He sat on the lower step of a tan adobe staircase. Another younger man sat atop the stairway with a wide-brimmed hat pulled low over his brow. His feet hung over the side and a thin and battered sword lay in his lap. The grim trader cleaned his teeth with a long knife. "I've got river-melon in trade, old man, so what's the wares?"

Edwin mumbled a nervously as the obnoxious Marko cut in.

"Manure!" he declared. "Fresh from the mayor's office! He's just giving it away!"

Edwin laughed uncomfortably, and Marko pulled him along. The grizzled trader grunted and moved on to the next passer-by.

"Never stop when someone talks to you," Marko said. "That's how they get you."

"Get me?" Edwin said. "He did not get me!"

Marko pointed to a tall three-storied building. "Adele's Tap. We made it!" He walked over to the busy tavern and strapped Sonny to a post. "You stay here, I have friends with ears inside. And no trading!" Then he walked through the open doorway and disappeared.

"Get me?" Edwin said to the air and patted down Sonny's back.

He found his initial impression of a faire an apt description for the Illsbrook square. Besides the many vendors, entertainers also filled the market, dancing, singing, and doing their tricks for hacks and coppers or a bite to eat. If they had not appeared so desperately sad and low, he would have approached one and paid for a song, but their leggings were torn, and their lutes out of tune. Still they performed, and sang and danced for an unappreciative crowd. Numerous people came by and asked what his wares were, but he passed on any offers.

Soon Marko returned with word that the soldiers had moved on to Kingstown, the one Illsbrook borough Edwin had visited long ago. The city was divided into three boroughs, much like in Millthrace. But instead of a city separated by its classes, the districts of Illsbrook were divided by their vices. The northwest borough of Princetown—where they were now—was the center for gamblers hoping to strike it rich. Queenstown to the east was where men went alone at night looking for pleasurable company. And to the southwest, Kingstown was where the drinks flowed easily, and each tavern had a show or a song every night.

The three boroughs sat on the three shores where the Wide Galenic River split, with three long bridges connecting the townships.

"I have been thinking about your plan," Edwin offered. "And it's a great plan. Wonderful even. But I was thinking, you say I have changed my look lately," he stroked his beard and continued. "So maybe these guards have no idea what I look like. What if we just say you are Edwin, and let me turn you in?"

"Won't work," Marko said, as Sonny stepped ahead slowly.

"Why not?" Edwin demanded.

"Because of that," he said, pointing to a public notice board against the side of Adele's Tap. Among the old and tattered notes were two freshly tacked notices proclaiming a reward for capture. Edwin easily recognized his face and old robes. The artist had captured his eyes, with the deep-set crow's feet. His sketched-self looked tired and angry with shaded half-moons under his eyes and a furrowed brow. The corners of his mouth were turned down.

"I was not a happy man," he mumbled.

A group of laughing women brushed past him and jostled him back to sanity. Each poster mentioned a reward of pure gold. All around the busy square snaked hungry townspeople, so eager to beg and steal. What little it would take for them to turn in this wanted man. He was just glad the poster did not say "dead or alive." He hoped they were aware of that.

The drawing of the little girl looked back at him. She wasn't so bad, he thought. She had listened intently as he had spoken to her about the Aurlings. His stories must have drifted—as everyone told him they did—but she had made no signs of being bored. He had only wished he had had more to tell her. He would have made an excellent teacher. He hoped she was still on the loose. Of course she was, he thought, he still felt pulled to her, and she had that beast to protect her.

"Wait," Edwin said, catching Marko's attention. "Where's the beast? Where is Bakku?"

Marko rushed over and quieted him. "Do not draw attention! If someone else turns you in, we do not get the gold!"

Edwin did not hear him. "When the soldiers met us at the oasis, they only asked about Olen and me, not Bakku. And now, these posters. You don't think they captured him, do you?"

"I do not know, and unless you can get me two gold manors for him, I do not care. Let us go."

"She and I are nothing," Edwin said. "You said it yourself, they aren't really looking for us. But why aren't they looking for that creature?" Then he realized, "Oh that poor girl! If they have captured him—or worse!—then she is out there on her own, alone in the world!"

"Then you can send her your half of the reward. Keep walking!"

"We have to find her," he said, pulling Marko back. This was no longer that thing in his bones that sent him from observation to observation. This was the need to do the right thing and help someone in their time of need. He had grown up alone, but at least he had his aunts and uncle's reluctant support. Olen had nothing. They must help her.

"We?" Marko asked.

"Yes, we," Edwin said, a new bold conviction behind his words. "We will go find her." He held Marko's gaze until the crazy trader backed down.

"Gold first?" Marko asked. Edwin agreed.

29

Bakku Falls

Olen clung to Bakku's neck and watched behind him as he thundered across the Bluestem Prairie. He held tightly to the back of her legs as gores spilled out of the forest like beetles from an upturned stone. But instead of scattering like frightened bugs, the gores converged on the two. The black-shelled scions wore leather bands crudely wrapped around their eyes, cutting out the light. After she had blasted them on the mountaintop, they must no longer have trusted their fragile eyes. They sent clicks across the prairie.

A scream from the treetops and a large grey vulture with fleshy wings flew out over the field. It screamed again and two more flyers approached from the north. They had long beaks with razor like teeth, much like the one Bakku had killed in the mountains.

Bakku's powerful legs pounded across the deep prairie as she banged against his shoulders. The air and ground swarm gained on them, clicking, hissing, and screaming. She pressed her palms against her ears, but the probing clicks dug through her skull. He reached the Iron Road and pounded straight across it, crumbling the old highway.

She counted three winged scions and fifteen gores, taller than men, but much smaller than her Bakku. They were swift predators, but Bakku was also fast. A wide but shallow stream cut across the path. He ran through the stony waters without slowing. Water splashed into her face. The gores followed close behind. One of the slimy black creatures tossed a crude hand axe, hitting Bakku in the left shoulder and cutting a small wound. He pulled her off his shoulders and cradled her in his arms, protecting her.

He splashed across the stream and pulled away from the Nerikan guards. He ran through deeper waters, but still his powerful legs churned ahead as if unimpeded. She had seen him climb the mountain; she knew he could run all day.

And then he slipped.

Perhaps it was a rock, or a dip in the river bed. Maybe a gore's aim had been true and his axe had knocked the giant creature off balance. She did not know why; she only knew that Bakku's right leg collapsed underneath him and he fell tumbling into the stream. With his last breath before falling, he tossed her far down river into a deep swirling pool, away from the gores. She cartwheeled in midair, his arms still reaching out after her, his face apologetic. She hit the water on her back and went under. The last thing she saw was a blanket of gores overtaking her Bakku.

She dropped to the bottom of the whirlpool as the river pressed against her. She was back in the Millthrace sewers diving for coins as her back scraped against the rocks. The surface was a mere body-length away, but a league it seemed as the swirling waters held her down. She curled her legs underneath herself and kicked herself free of the eddy.

She burst through the surface and spit up a lungful of water. She heaved for air and pushed herself to shore, raking aside the thick reeds. Gasping, she pulled herself to dry land. Upstream a foamy storm raged in the shallow waters. The colossal Bakku whipped about in the river, casting great arcs of water as the gores tore into him. He rolled and churned, like a sea beast trapped in a maelstrom. Gores clamped on to his huge frame and hacked at him with the axes. A black bug dug its rat-like incisors into his thick arm. He howled and tore the gore away, stripping away a mouthful of flesh. Another gore turned his axe and jabbed the spike into Bakku's lower back. Blood spilled out of the deep hole and painted the river red. The gore latched onto the bloody wound with its mouth, sucking in deep inhales of Bakku's blood. Above it all the three searchers circled, screaming with delight.

Olen ran upstream and chucked a river stone at a gore. She pegged it in the back, but it only slowed the creature for a moment. She called to Bakku, but he was too deep into the battle to hear.

He tore away gores and crushed them in his hands, but there were just too many. Two gores latched onto his back and chewed into his ribs. He slammed himself backwards into the stream, crushing them. Their lifeless bodies rose to the surface and washed away. Another gore detached from Bakku's left leg and pushed itself away from its foul feast. It reached the far shore and ran back across the plains, blood dripping from its mouth. It had gotten its fill. As it raced away, a flying scion flew after it, and then overtook it. The gore followed as it led it away.

Bakku fought the dwindling number of scions, and slowed down himself, and still Olen tossed her useless rocks. The battle was wearing him thin. Dead gores, with crushed skulls and torn appendages, floated past Olen, while those who had fed rushed away from the fight, following the path of the scion birds. Bakku grew pale as the onslaught continued, and his grasping hands grew weak. He pulled a gore off his arm and snapped its neck, then he just let it drift out of his open palm. He could fight no more. He swung at a gore but missed badly. His momentum spun him around and his knees buckled. He fell back into the stream, and lay there lifeless, unable to fight.

Two gores remained attached, their mouths pressed against his skin, their bellies swelling in and out like bellows. Bakku lay back as the rushing waters coursed past him. He only made weak attempts to push away the foul suckling creatures. They drank freely, and then simply pulled away when they were done. Of the fifteen that had attacked, six had survived. When they were gone Olen waded into the stream and crossed over slick rocks.

He lay dying in the running waters. His head bobbed in the wake, and his eyes—grey and motionless—stared to the sky. His skin was pale and his breaths came in short panting huffs. Yet the wounds were already closing up. He was no longer bleeding. His head fell to the side and water rushed over his face, he was lifeless. She waded beside him and tried to lift his mouth and nose out of the stream. She pressed with all her might against his giant head, but it barely moved. Air bubbles rolled out of his lips, and water seeped in. She pushed again, groaning aloud and pressing with her thin legs. The large head moved slightly. She pressed harder, crying out fiercely and straining every muscle and tendon in her young body.

"Don't go, Baboo!" she cried, forcing her legs against the rocks. His head rolled on the slick stones and turned skyward as she leaned backwards against his temple. She braced her legs on the stony stream bed, not letting his face fall back into the water. He choked and coughed, spitting up a lungful of water. He opened his eyes and sucked in deep breaths, laying there as the waters swirled around him. His large eyes rolled across his face to the little girl holding his head out of the water. He looked as if he did not recognize her.

"Olen," he said, his words slow. "I heard...a voice...a voice."

"It's me," she said. "It's alright. They are gone."

He struggled through a couple quick breaths and said, "They will never be gone."

He rolled onto his bulging belly and pushed himself up to sitting. She helped steady him as best she could. The waters swirled around them. He felt his wounds, already scars in his thick skin. She too touched one of the holes left by the gore.

"Gores are bloodsuckers?" she asked.

"Gores are whatever their maker wants them to be," he said, shaking away his dizziness. He took a handful of water and washed his face. "When it is only one biting you, it is not so bad. After a hundred years or so, I hardly even noticed. But this was different."

"They are not trying to catch you, are they?"

Bakku shook his head. "I don't know." He angled forward and tried to crawl to shore, but his eyes rolled back, and he fell limply into the stream. He awoke quickly and pulled himself back out. He crept to the shore, elefant-like, on his hands and knees. He rolled onto the ground and lay back on the green shore grasses. She climbed out and stood next to him. His eyes fell shut, and his head fell to the side, fast asleep on the reedy shore. Rest, she thought, I will watch over you. She pulled the gore axe out of the sack and climbed onto his firm round belly. His breaths quickly fell to a soft easy rhythm. She sat cross-legged on her friend and watched all directions as the night passed over them.

At dawn, his breathing shifted and his eyes slowly opened.

"No sign of them," Olen said, sliding off his belly.

He sat up and looked at the river. His eyes were tired and held barely open. He reminded her of a sleepy Maggie.

"If you're thinking about food," she said, "Don't worry. We are almost to Brennan."

He nodded at that and rubbed his freshly scarred wounds.

"Why do gores want your blood?" she asked.

"They do not. They have no want. They do this for their master. Janus needs my blood, and he has sent gores to get it. They have been pretty successful in their purpose."

"Why does he want your blood?"

"To live," he said, strength flowing back into his words. "To live like I have lived. To never die," he said. He rubbed his palms into his eyes. He had been no different from any other man when Brynn had found him, he explained, except he was strong and aged very slowly. Any wounds healed quickly, and his body stayed young and powerful. Janus had been a jealous Aurling, never satisfied with his own skills. "It was when the first Demi emerged that he formed a plan."

"Demi?" she asked.

"Demi-Aurling," he said, touching her head. "Like you."

He pushed wet hair out of her face and explained Demis were just regular people who had gained Aurling powers. Even the true Aurlings had not known such things were possible until it happened. That was when Janus learned it was possible to transfer Aurling magic from one person to another. And that was when he started his experiments.

"On you," she said.

He nodded, explaining how Brynn had thought he could separate from Aurlings the very thing that made them special, their seed. He had already shown he could take the venomous fangs off of snakes and place them in purring kittens. These and many more experiments led him to believe he could take an Aurling's gift and make it his own.

His plan had been to divide and conquer. He would take the essence that is Bakku and transfer it down to lesser more controllable beasts, hoping eventually to transfer it to himself. But Bakku had held tight to his seed, and Brynn's experiments not only failed, they made Bakku stronger. With every test it was Bakku who absorbed the essence of the other, always adding to his bulk. He continued to grow until Brynn had no choice but to lock him in chains.

"Only then did he find he did not need my seed to extend his life, only my blood."

"So all this time he has known about you locked away in Nerikan?" she asked.

"It is my suffering that has kept him alive. The gores did their job well today, but it won't be enough. For the first time in over two hundred years, Janus is facing his own mortality. He won't just let me slip away. He will forever hunt me." He sat up as color returned to his face. "But now I'm certain of one thing, the gores are not after you. And for that I am happy. You will be safe in Kessel."

"I'm not leaving you, Baboo," she said, unashamed. She had chosen him. Whatever he wanted to be to her—friend, father, or just temporary foster—she would have to accept, but she had chosen him to be her Baboo.

He patted her head. "It is the only way. Calderra is where I go, and I go there alone."

"He will follow you!"

"He will not," he said, looking at her. "Not there."

She fell down to the ground and collapsed onto his lap. "I don't even want to go to Kessel anymore," she said. "Either my parents will be there, or they won't. I no longer care. And what if they are alive? Why didn't they fight to keep me?" she asked, and looked up at Bakku.

He stroked her hair and looked to the horizon. "You came back for me, Baboo, and you didn't even know me. Why should *I* have to find *them*?" she asked.

She broke down into tears. He rubbed her head and let her cry.

"Find them," he said softly. "Forgive them. They will want to know you. They will be proud to call you daughter."

He sat like a great statue built by men to worship. He stroked the back of the crying child whose head lay in his vast lap.

"Who are you?" she asked. "I mean, besides Bakku, besides an Aurling and a scion, who are you?"

He rubbed his temples and ran his wide palms over the back of his head. "I am...I was...a man. A worker, a husband." He smiled at her, "A father."

She looked at him, her face asking the question. He nodded sadly.

"Long ago, before I looked like this, I helped men build great things."

She asked him why an Aurling would work, especially hard labor.

"You have to understand where we came from, the Ether," he said, and he looked beyond her to the sky. "In the Ether, life was formless. We were creatures of light. Mere ideas of what we truly could be." He said that they were each powerful in their own way, these Aurlings, but indistinct, simply influencing their power onto the world below. But when the crystal veil that had separated their worlds cracked, they found they could slip away from the Ether and take solid form. "When I came here, I finally felt the glorious tug of weight. For the first time I had found myself limited, and I reveled in it! It was like for all of my life I had been falling, just flailing in the wind, but here I had landed and could walk, run, leap into the very sky I had climbed down from!"

"The Ether must be just the opposite of being bound in chains," she offered.

"I have lived both extremes," he said. "Pure and limitless freedom is in itself a prison."

He stood up to his full height and flexed his arms. "Here I found I was strong, and I wanted to work my muscles. Burn them. I wanted to lift heavy things, and break thick branches over my knee. I wanted to climb and run until my lungs ached. I wanted to know the borders of what this body could do; I wanted to know my limits!" He gave her a wry smile. "Those limits were hard to find."

She watched with wonder as Bakku spoke, adoring him even more.

"My greatest task was Bran's Wall," he said proudly, pointing to the north. He explained that such a wall they had not even intended to build. Instead, he had been hired on to dig a trench. He and other workers had been commissioned to build a canal across the isthmus known as the Melle just west of Daegan. It was to be a new shipping channel to allow commerce to flow through Eisen. He had dug and lifted soil and stone for years as the gash formed across that strip of land. He had created a deep valley wide enough for the largest ships to course through. All that was left was to cut away a channel through the Caraway Mountains, and let the seas flow in. Many years he had spent in those mountains pounding spikes and splitting boulders other men shied away from. "It was there I made my best friends. It is still those mountains I think of as home. And it is through those mountains I will pass unseen into Calderra."

Olen sat cross-legged on the ground, her tears stilled.

"Sig Bran's madness halted the project. The fruit of my labor, acres of fractured stone, were piled and mortared into what came to be known as Bran's Wall. But by then, Janus had found me and lured me away to my fate."

He sat back down in the grasses and patted the ground next to himself. She sat next to him.

"What you need to know is I—the old me—didn't know who I was until I came here. When my thoughts were no longer shared across the Ether, they truly became my own. I hoped I could stay here forever. Little did I know my wish would come true."

"And what of me?" she asked.

"I believe you have done what Janus could only have dreamed of. You have absorbed an Aurling seed and become a Demi. Your gift, it is a pathway you opened up, much like the one that allowed me to travel here."

"And my clothes?" she asked.

"Seeds are curious," he answered. "Even Aurlings do not fully understand them. But we do know they change depending on the host. The ability to open your doorway, you get that from the seed; while the power to change your look, the seed gets from you. Brynn's seed allows him to change living things, while he gives his seed the ability to read people, gauge their loyalty, truthfulness. It is like this with all Aurlings and Demis."

A dusty cloud appeared on the northern horizon. It was a carriage traveling south down the Iron Road. Bakku moved over to the tallest patch of Bluestem and lay back as the family trekked down the lonesome road, unaware of the watchers in the far-off field.

"Go with them," he said, and quickly held a hand to silence her protests. "Go with them to Brennan. Eat there and rest. Kessel is not far away."

"I want to go with you," she insisted.

"I know," he said.

The carriage moved along the highway. Two oxen pulled along the wagon. Three women sat on the wooden carriage. Two men and two boys walked alongside.

"I will come find you," she said.

"No," he said, loud enough to silence the bugs and birds of the prairie. "Do not ever. You will turn Janus's gaze your way. He must not know what you can do. When he can no longer find me, he will begin again to fear death. The doorway has been sealed for a lifetime. If he knows you can open it, he will use you to send himself home."

"Then let's do it," she demanded. "Let's send Brynn back to the Ether. Then he won't be able to harm either of us anymore."

"He will go back to the Ether, but he won't go alone. He will carry you along. You are not an Aurling. You will not survive."

The caravan neared the river. She did not know their names, but she had seen them before in Millthrace.

"You have to go," he whispered to her.

"I don't want to," she said.

"Go."

"No," she pleaded.

"Go, or I will turn myself in," he said, stopping her protestations. "Brynn wants only me."

He would do it, she thought. He would stand up and announce himself to the travelers, or he would walk straight into Brennan like he did Millthrace. He would sacrifice himself to Brynn in trade for her freedom. He would do it. He would commit himself to Nerikan torture just to save her brief life. He loved her.

"Please," he begged her, his eyes wet. "Let me go on alone, or I will have to do it."

She ran over to him and hugged him around the neck. "I love you, Baboo," she said as tears rolled down her face.

She stood up and took a few steps towards the road. She turned back to the giant laying in the grass. He curled his long index finger at her twice, and she curled hers back. A ripple rolled up and down her body and her clothes blurred. She now wore the weathered skins of a child who had been lost in the wild. Then she turned and ran across the stream, kicking up water and calling to the carriage. The family saw her and pulled up the reins on their oxen. She crawled to shore, hiding her tears behind river water, and jogged up to the family of traders on the Iron Road.

30

⊛

An Aurling and a Fool

Koertig paraded through the square as a new vigor surged through him. His nurse-maid forged a path through the frenzied crowd. Townspeople cheered and patted him on the back, every man wanting to lay a hand on their new Lieutenant Colonel. *I will be more than that, soon*, he thought.

He let himself be pulled back into the dispensary. Philippa shut the door behind them and led him up the stairs. He was dazed with excitement. It had been a rogue Demi-Aurling that had killed his father and sent his mother to a life of prostitution. It was an Aurling that had taken his arm. And now it was another Aurling—within the very city walls he had sworn to protect—that had infiltrated the administration. And he had just made the first foray into a war that would end them all. Philippa pulled him through the doorway and into his room.

"Did you see his face?" Koertig said aloud, the hunt still in his blood.

"Yes, sir," she said, as she moved about the room stacking their things. Koertig hardly noticed as he spoke to the closed window.

"It was as if he stood there naked, his whole life exposed!" he said, wishing his father had been there to see his undefeated undaunted son.

"I did see it, sir," she said, as she tossed their things into blankets and tied them up in make-shift carryalls. "His guilt was obvious. You

255

were right." She sat piles of clothes and toiletries by the door. Then she gathered up the books and set them there also. "What pleasure does he get from such sickening experiments?" she asked, holding open the painted book plate of Mayor Brynn and the scion bird.

Koertig's mind cleared and he finally noticed her labor. All of their things were piled at the front door. "What is this?" he asked strongly.

She set down the book, "We have to leave, do we not?"

"What are you talking about, woman?" he asked, confused and angry, stomping over to her, rattling the walls. "You would abandon Midtown for such a petty menace? He'll be locked away by the week's end!"

"Harner...Sir, the things you said. He is an intelligent man. Do you really believe Brynn will just sit back and let you bring him down?"

"Come for me then!" he shouted, realizing he had been wrong about her. She was no stronger than the rest of the rats. She was as weak as his mother had been, choosing to run away from hardship. But not Koertig. "Let him try his worst!"

She then spoke to him in the most condescending tone, like a mother instructing a feeble child. "Let this be Martz's war," she said, slowly and steadily, as if she had been born among the wise. "Guide Martz, tutor him, but you cannot join the fight. Koertig's days of war are behind him," she placed a hand gently over his wound. "You are Harner now. Follow a different path."

He grabbed her shirt just below the neck and pulled her in. "We stay here. If the mayor finds the courage to confront me, then let him," he growled, as she pulled back ever so slightly. "I cower from no one, man or beast. You see only a broken man, but I am not broken" he said, and pulled the sister from the Ward in tight and kissed her on the mouth. She came back with a full-mouthed kiss of her own, sliding her arms around his back. His wide hand grasped her behind her neck, his thumb on her cheek, as he pressed her face into his. There was very little love in Koertig's kiss, but there was fiery passion. She matched his desire with her own, and they tore at each other.

The front door kicked open and two men, Reeve and Graeme, stormed in. Mayor Brynn strode in calmly behind them, his hands gripped behind his back. Koertig pushed Philippa to the floor and took a stance, but Brynn's men engulfed him and flung him backwards onto his cot. The Lieutenant Colonel fell with a thud and grasped at his shoulder, hissing in a deep breath. The men pulled out short daggers and held them to his throat. Philippa inched backwards on the floor and sat against the far wall. Brynn approached her gently and held out a hand. She looked to Koertig for guidance.

"My lady, please," Brynn said kindly. She took his hand as he helped her to her feet, and in that moment Koertig hated her.

Brynn surveyed the room. Their possessions sat in a pile. "Leaving perhaps?" he asked. "I am not surprised following your actions today." He saw the stacks of books. Edwin's book sat opened to the drawing of Brynn. "Ahh, so this is how!" He studied the image and held it up for his men to see. "Is that really how I look?"

"The only way out of this is to kill me," Koertig said, knowing that even with his wound he could take down one of the three before their daggers overwhelmed him.

Brynn ignored him and paged through the book. "I knew that educator would be trouble the moment he came to me," he said to his men. "Didn't I say that?" Reeve and Graeme nodded in agreement, still holding their daggers to Koertig's throat. "He holds a curious seed, that Demi, and he is not even aware of it. I try to be generous, I try to be welcoming, and this is what I get." He slapped the book's covers together and set it down as he approached the bed. "I am not going to kill you," he said to Koertig.

"Then you're an Aurling and a fool," the Lieutenant Colonel replied.

"You are only half right," Brynn said calmly. He assured Koertig not only did he not want him dead, he most indeed wanted him to complete his task. Then, as if he were still master of this town and not an Aurling mole, he gave Koertig his orders. "You are to find Edwin and the girl and toss them into Nerikan, even kill them if you please, as long as it is inside Nerikan's walls. That will lure Bakku back in, and he will once again find himself in chains. I will then depart from these lands, and the city will be yours. You will rule Millthrace for the rest of your short, natural, life."

"You lie," Koertig said, wanting to snap the man's neck.

"My offer is true," he replied. "And as proof," he said as he approached Koertig. He reached inside his robe and pulled out a small glass vial. A thick red liquid painted the inside. Graeme and Reeve held the soldier tight against the bed as Brynn tore open the stopper and clutched Koertig's cheeks, forcing open his jaw. Then he poured the gooey fluid into Koertig's mouth. The smell was worse than the toilet pits at the Eagle and Trout, and reeked of decay. He spit and smacked but some of the liquid slid down the back of his tongue. Strength surged through him, and he easily cast Graeme aside.

"I had gifted you many precious drops already," Brynn said, capping the vial and returning it to his pocket. "I thought I was rewarding my finest soldier. Little did I know that soldier foolishly believed himself to be my enemy."

Aurling magic, Koertig thought, and realized why such a brutal injury had not killed him. He should have died that first night. And if not then, then any of the many days he had lain in that bed. His wounds should have festered, his skin should have grown black and hard like a fire-charred tree. He had seen men die from lesser wounds, yet Koertig had survived, and quite quickly healed. It was not his strength of will that had sustained him, it was Aurling magic. And he should have known.

"The tea," Koertig said, realizing the truth. "You placed it in my tea!"

Brynn nodded, and Koertig shouted an accusation towards Philippa.

"I didn't know sir," she pleaded, nearly collapsing to her knees. "I swear!"

"You are alive because of me, and I ask for so little in return," Brynn spoke calmly, almost lovingly. "Return that creature to Nerikan, and take this city as your own for as long as you desire, yea, even as long as you shall live. You will never see nor hear of me again. Then, as time gears your essence into its final station and your worldly instrument fails, remember me then, for on your deathbed you will cede power to the grandson of Janus Brynn—a man who will bear a striking resemblance to his grandfather." Mayor Brynn smiled and cocked his head at Koertig. "Order will be restored, and we both will have gotten what we wanted. Do you see how reasonable I can be, Harner? If you had only chosen to work with me, I would have granted you your seedy desire for power long ago, and we could have avoided this public..." he searched for the word, "performance."

"Why would I take orders from an Aurling?" Koertig asked, hating the vitality flowing through his veins, the deep pain disappearing from his shoulder, and the confusing knowledge that a few drops of Aurling filth had made him feel so alive.

"Because it is what your family has always done," he said firmly and waited for the reaction. The stoic Koertig gave none, for he had already realized the truth. This was the cabal. These three. An Aurling and two Demis. These men had hired the mercenaries that sent Demis to Nerikan. It was Brynn who years ago had sent his father to fight a creature he could not possibly defeat. It was Brynn who was responsible for his father's murder. And it was because of Brynn's guilt in his father's death that he had promoted young Koertig so quickly through the ranks.

"I will kill you in your sleep," Koertig hissed.

"I doubt that," Brynn said calmly, and waved Philippa over to him. "Come dear."

Koertig laughed. "Take her! Do you think you can turn me by threatening a Lowtown rat?"

"A rat?" Mayor Brynn said, and looked Philippa over. He held his hands over her face and then moved them down her shoulders and arms. "Don't fret child, I won't hurt you." He brought his right hand in and hovered it over her belly. "I see. How thorough you have been in your patient's recuperation, nurse."

She hung her head, and Koertig saw the shame of her secret revealed.

"A rat you say?" Brynn asked, taunting Koertig. "Very well," he concluded, and thrust his palm onto her stomach and pressed his fingertips deep into her flesh. She gasped and recoiled, but Brynn held her steady. He kneaded the flesh underneath her shirt and turned his hand against her stomach. A stark bluish-white light flashed from his palm, and Philippa cried out in agony. Like a whip he pulled his hand away, and she fell back clutching her tummy. Brynn, sweating and exhausted, turned to Koertig.

"Then the son of Harner Koertig will be a rat also!" Brynn said, fighting to maintain his composure. Graeme rushed to his side and steadied him as Reeve stood over Koertig's cot, his dagger still in his hand.

Philippa wailed in the corner holding her stomach.

Koertig had not known. She had not told him. "How long," he asked. She only shook her head. He turned to Brynn. "With one arm I will tear you to pieces."

"If I die, then your son will truly be a rat."

"It can be undone?" he asked.

"One wonders," Brynn said arrogantly.

"I will kill her instead!" Koertig cried, as Philippa crawled to her feet. "I will kill them both!"

Brynn motioned to Reeve, who pulled away from Koertig. "By Spring, your bloodlines will be laid bare for all the world to see. It is up to you what shall be born of your rage. Focus your revenge on Edwin and the girl, and you will live out your life the hero and leader of this land, never seeing me again. But if you harm Bakku or conspire against me, even I won't know what fruit that shall bear."

He motioned to his men and they swiftly left the room. Philippa sat in the corner, tears streaming down her cheeks.

"This was your plan," Koertig said, accusingly. "You tricked me into being your bull stud!"

"Tricked you?" she asked, with newfound strength in her voice. She stood. "I tricked you? And how many times were you *tricked*?" She walked over towards Koertig, still clasping her stomach. "How many times did you drag me to your bed? How many times did you assure me as I pulled away? All I did was *allow* you to practice your insatiable lust. You were the one who tricked me. You made me believe in you."

She dug through the tied-up blankets and pulled out her things.

"What are you doing?" he asked.

"I am going back to the Ward."

She separated their things and made to leave. She grasped at her stomach and wept as she opened the door. She stopped and turned one last time towards Koertig. "Come away," she said, tears streaming down her cheeks. "Come away with me, Harner! Away from Millthrace! Away from the Ward! We'll go back beyond Illsbrook to the Never-Ending Ridge and start afresh. There will be no Aurlings and no war, just us. We can do this Harner. We are allowed to be happy."

The sergeant coldly shook his head, and she fell against the door. After several fractured breaths she stood again and pulled at the handle.

"Wait," he said, reaching out to her. She paused. He pushed himself to the edge of his cot and asked innocently, "How can I trust that the child is mine?"

She gave him one long last look lost between sadness and rage, shaking her head in disbelief. Had he been born a gentleman, he would have known the offense behind his words. Had he been a trusting man, he would never have spoken them. But he was Harner Koertig, a man without fault, pity, or shame, as his question hung in the air between them.

Somehow his words had stopped her tears, and her desperation washed away. Like Aurling magic, she stood revived before the sergeant. "You confuse me with your mother, Harner," she said coldly, straightening her spine. "But *I* am no whore."

She slammed the door behind herself and ran down the stairs.

Koertig fell back exhausted.

31

Kingstown

Edwin and Marko led the donkey over the bridge into the Kingstown district in Illsbrook. The town was less densely packed, and shade trees grew out of grassy plots. With the bustle of Princetown behind them, the quieter Kingstown reminded Edwin of the University parks he had walked through, trailing peripatetic academics. A familiar minstrel's tune caught his ear, and the words of a song thirty-years removed came flooding back. He found the songster in his bright leggings and billowing shirt singing along the shore, plucking on an eight-stringed lute. He wore a cupped hat, too small for his head, and sang a song of veiled ribaldry. Edwin giggled at the carnal wordplay.

"That takes me back to my younger days," A delighted Edwin said to Marko, but his partner was on the hunt for golden coins. Edwin, less eager to seek out his jailers, insisted on a quick diversion. "Dear minstrel, I beg, an oration if you would. Do you know," but he trailed off, hesitant to say the words aloud. He leaned in and whispered in the performer's ear.

The man genuflected dramatically and laid his lute against a tree. He leapt spryly onto a stump and declared, "The Playful Lover at the Gates of Sin."

Edwin snickered like a mischievous child, covering his mouth and ducking his neck. Oh! He felt so close to home now that he was with the minstrels. Marko seemed to feel nothing but unmoved.

The performer began his address, his waving arms and swollen chest as much a part of the show as his voice, "Down, Cerberus! Heel! Tis not a thief afoot before your gate! But Hero's face thus led by fragrant bait!"

Edwin giggled and elbowed Marko. Marko was unimpressed.

"I seek not to acquire your conquered hoard!" he cried, pleading yet flirtatious. "More sinful goods, Great Bitch, are my reward!"

"Tis one of my own," Edwin whispered to Marko.

"You were wise to pursue history," Marko whispered back.

"Oh! Woolen beast, indeed, I see thy snarl! For I was led here by thy very gnarl!" the minstrel continued, bolder now. "Resist my hand? Sweet Pup, thee craves it too! Concealed desire betrayed now by thine drool! Oh! Shameful Pooch, astern yet in thine jail! To bare white teeth, yet hide thy soft brown tail!"

Edwin tittered like a child hearing a dirty word.

"Did you also write bawdy limericks?" Marko asked as Edwin mouthed along to his old lyric.

The performer leapt from the stump and stood proudly before some invisible maiden. "Now, down Cerberus, heel! Unchained! Unleashed! Thy lonely shift is done! Obey my will! And with thy Master, come!"

Edwin, who had chuckled shyly at every pun, now applauded madly and raised his palms to the air. "Yes! Yes!" he cried, laughing and reveling in the oration. "Perfectly bawdy!" The minstrel nodded to Edwin and picked up his lute. He strummed a chord and sprung into his next song. Edwin dug in his pocket and pulled out a coin. He flicked the copper penny off his thumb and high into the air. A quick duck of the head and the singer caught the coin in his hat without skipping a beat. He nodded to his benefactor, dropping the coin in a bucket, and carried on with his song. Smiling broadly, Edwin rejoined Marko and walked into the city.

"Don't do that with the gold pieces," Marko said.

"Well, not for a one-man show," Edwin replied dryly.

Edwin patted Sonny's rump, and they pressed on ahead.

Street performers, cleaner and more talented troops than in Prince-town, sang on the corners. Unguarded coin-buckets sat at their feet. Cheerful music flowed out of plentiful adobe taverns. The locals here dressed no worse than Millthrace Midtowners, clean and bright, and held hands while dancing in circles. Marko stuck his head in bar room windows and asked cryptic questions about sentries in the city. Most townspeople did not want to be bothered, but some pointed the duo deeper into the city. They came upon an open square where the bulk of the citizenship bustled about, eating, drinking, and talking. Fire-stoked grills were built along the walk; in one a whole pig rotated on a spit. Beef and lamb legs hung from beams over a fire pit, and ladies sliced off the cooked portions and laid them on plates with bread. Chickens ran about wild, as many more fried in vats of oil. This was not the Kingstown he remembered observing many years ago. That had been before the city had expanded across the riverbanks and split into three boroughs. With the gamblers and whores cordoned across the way, he found Kingstown to be quite a wonderful place.

"I fear I may have misjudged this town," he said to Marko. "Had the city been like this on my first visit, I just may have stayed."

At the far end of the square a two-story pageant wagon sat boarded up, waiting to be unfolded for the evening performance. Beside it, a five-poled tent stood over rows of tables and chairs. The guards from the highway sat alone at these tables. The young men, still in armor, were gnawing on turkey legs, beans, and corn bread; while the head guard wiped his neck and brow with a damp rag. He had obviously just come down from a long and adventurous night.

"Before you do this, remember to ask them about Olen," Edwin said to nothing but air, because his partner was no longer at his side. "Marko?"

Marko was already across the square and hurrying over to the tent. He approached the dining guards. "Oh no," Edwin lamented. He had not liked the plan from the get go, but now he hated it. He was putting a lot of trust into the dubious trader. Marko greeted the guards and approached their leader. The head guard waved him away and rubbed his forehead. Marko was not deterred. He pulled a small tin flask out of his shirt. He pointed to it and spoke many words, surely explaining its worthiness. The commander grabbed it and downed a long swig. He winced and hissed through his teeth. Marko encouraged him to take another drink and he did, repeating the hissing sound. He handed back the flask, and Marko tucked it away in his shirt. The commander offered him what was left of his plate, and a thankful Marko sat down and ate. The commander sat next to him and they talked like old friends.

"Any minute now, Sonny," Edwin said to the donkey, "Those men are going to rush us. And when they do, I expect you to stay calm."

The pack animal lazily chewed grass as its eyes stared idly ahead.

"Good donkey," Edwin said, watching the guards while rubbing Sonny's long ears. "You will like University; it's nice and boring." Then he realized something he should have known all along. Marko and his donkey were not joining him on his journey home. They were partners only in this hunt for gold. *What is this sting?* Edwin wondered, as he imagined the two parting ways, shaking hands and journeying on down separate trails. *Is this the wound all persons take when losing a friend?*

The patch of grass below Sonny was bare when Marko finally returned. His wide Marko Meloon smile leading the way. Edwin had unpacked and set up a small shop, still hoping the cunning Marko had pounced upon a different scheme. He sat on the cart tapping a soft rhythm on Sonny's backside. As Marko neared him his smile faded and turned to stone. He kicked a large burlap sack into his hands.

"We go to Brennan," he said, and threw the pack back into the cart.

"Why?" Edwin asked.

"The money is gone. They spent it," he said. "The bulk of it anyway." There was no hint of Marko Meloon in his voice. It was the voice of a man who might be named Marko, or might be just about anyone else in this world. Whoever he was, he was angry. "Drunkards!" he exclaimed, as he tore down the thin awning and rolled it up. Then he raised his index finger right up to Edwin's nose, "Never trust a man with a vice! He will only ever feed his own needs!"

Edwin should have felt relieved, but he was confused. "So we leave?"

"No stopping except to feed and rest the donkey," Marko mumbled to himself as he packed.

"Did they say anything about the girl?" Edwin asked. Her pull was still there. He had felt it soften over the past few days, but still the need to observe her lingered.

Marko continued packing the cart and was angrier than Edwin had ever seen him. He slapped the harness over Sonny's shoulders and jerked the leather straps tight. He cursed under his breath. Two men wandered in Marko's path and were angrily shoved aside by the trader.

"Marko!" Edwin said, and he finally looked up. "What do they know of the other two?"

Marko's fire cooled. "He asked how I knew of the creature," he said in a softer tone. "I told him I had been in Millthrace when it had attacked the front gate. I had to promise him never to speak of it again."

"And the girl?"

The soldier had told Marko he had received a birded message just two days ago stating the girl was last seen in the Mecan Plains moving south towards Brennan, while the creature was heading north alone. *They are no longer together.*

Edwin rubbed his growing white beard, a new habit he had picked up quickly. *Terrible*, he thought. *This is terrible news.* Olen was alone, and she was being hunted. She was a resilient child, but even she would not survive an entire army. "She's all alone," Edwin said, feeling the need to help her grow inside of him. But it was not his gift commanding him. This was not some misunderstood and irresistible drive within him telling him she needed help. This was Edwin Ashdown the man, for once in his life wanting to do what's right, despite the danger ahead of him. "We have to find her!"

Marko placed a hand on Edwin's shoulder, calming him.

"Finding the girl is now essential," Marko said mournfully. "It seems you have made some good friends on the road to Illsbrook." He pulled Sonny by the bit. He faced him to the city's southern gate and smacked his backside. "And out of kindness, they have killed you."

A confused and frustrated Edwin demanded he explain. Marko

spoke under his breath as he said Iron Road nomads had testified to the guards they had found Edwin's withered corpse just off the Merchant's Trail about a sevenday walk north of town. "They had described the old man perfectly right down to his scholarly robes. The old historian had made a fair game of it, fleeing half-way across the Ode before the elements did him in."

"But that's absurd," Edwin spat. "It must be some other gentleman!"

"It is nobody!" Marko shouted, drawing looks from the crowd. He quieted and whispered to Edwin. "Don't you see? It is the tradesmen. They have welcomed you in. They thought they were doing you a favor."

"So that means I'm—"

"Dead," Marko said, pulling ahead with Sonny. "And Bakku and the girl are on the other side of Eisen. So in one short month these worthless soldiers spent more than a whole gold piece on themselves."

"And that's why you said Olen is essential!" Edwin exclaimed, running after him. "You cannot claim the bounty on a dead man, so you want to turn her in instead!"

"Yes," he said flatly. "If they have not captured her already."

They left the city walls and saw the bridges to Princetown and Queenstown. Flat-bottomed boats were loaded with logs from the Euloren Woods to be delivered to Brennan. Pole-barges were being pulled upstream by Oxen.

"Then what am I supposed to do?" Edwin asked, already knowing the answer.

"Go home," Marko said, and pointed to the boats. "Edwin the Observer is dead. You are free. Take what coins you have left, float downriver to Kessel, and jump on the first coach to University. The painted ladies and fine men will thrill at your stories of adventure! Go!"

Indeed Edwin was free. Brynn, Koertig, not even the gores would be after him now. This madness had all been just another observation. Until the next urge to wander grabbed a hold of him, he could write in his books about the masquerading trader and the Demi-Aurling girl. His part of this adventure was over, while Marko and Olen's continued.

"You promise the child will be safe?" Edwin asked, watching the boats in the river.

"I wouldn't dream of allowing them to hurt a child."

"And you promise to free her once you get the gold?" Edwin asked.

"Within moments," Marko assured him.

"Very well then," Edwin said decidedly. "I am going with you."

Marko asked why and was met with Edwin's wrath, "Because I will not let you cage that child for even one moment!" he shouted, no longer caring who heard him. "Any decent man would be scheming to protect the girl, not his pocketbook! And besides," Edwin concluded pompously, "I will not sacrifice to you *my* gold piece!"

Marko seemed to like that response but still insisted his plan was the only way to succeed.

"There is no plan!" Edwin said. "You haven't even figured out how to free her yet! We are still days away from Brennan. Even if we march day and night, they will have captured her before we arrive. What we truly need is a plan that convinces them to turn the girl and the coins over to us."

Marko listened as Edwin pondered. Then the aged scholar snapped his fingers.

"The Magistrate Machination!" he declared.

"Never heard of it," Marko said.

"I just invented it!"

"Too wordy," Marko said dryly.

"Can you learn a new character before we get to the city?"

At this Marko stopped and appeared intrigued. No, he appeared beyond intrigued, he appeared utterly enthralled. Edwin was learning quickly with this traveling trickster. It was not just the monetary reward, it was the game itself he loved. The wide Marko Meloon grin spread across his face. Two gold manors and a new con, he could barely contain himself.

"What character?" Marko asked eagerly.

3 2

The Caraway Mountains

Bakku had lain amongst the tall grain as Olen splashed across the stream, leaving him as he demanded. She climbed into the carriage and sat next to the women. He knew she thought only of him, yet unlike him, she never turned back. Olen knew not to give these strangers even a hint something lay hidden just off the Iron Road. She would survive, smart and strong as she was. The family welcomed her in. He did not know if the ride was just to Brennan, all the way to Kessel, or ever further away. But he knew they would like her, and when they found out she was alone, they would ask her to stay.

Once she and her carriage had passed beyond the bend and was nothing more than a dusty blur, he rose. He stood in the Bluestem Prairie, alone for the first time since taking her from her cage. Saffron grain flowed around him, brushing a soft rhythm against scarred flesh. A gentle touch from the land he had claimed as his home. A questioning chirp, the soft song of a yellow darter, balancing on the stem of a purple gayfeather, asking who was this large interloper. A four-winged angelfly buzzed past, pulling along mellow scents of soil and sage.

This was why he had stayed in this world, the sensations of life. Of living, not just being. And she had reminded him of another sensation, one of his very distant past. It was a sensation saved for parents in this world, a special gift they received while expecting none. That gift was the unashamed closeness of an embrace that can only come from a child. He still felt her arms on his neck, holding him, needing him, asking him to stay.

He turned west and headed off towards the Caraway Mountains. He would travel the mountaintops northwest, past Bran's Wall and the Melle. From there, the fires of Calderra awaited his all-too mortal flesh. The end of all things was near. It was the only way. By ending his life, he ended Brynn's. By stopping Brynn, he saved Olen. By burying his seed in the volcanic fires of Calderra, no Demi-Bakku would ever arise. He could do this now, knowing it would set her free.

***

Philippa closed the parlor doors behind herself. Haggart sat quietly in her chair, reading a small book. She had not been back to Koertig in three days, and every day she grew stronger in her conviction to never return. Despite the terror and shame it brought her, it was time to tell the mistress about what was growing inside her, and how Brynn's magic may have altered it.

She sat in the white wing chair, and just stared at her wringing hands. She had found her words in the hallway, but now they would not come.

Haggart turned a page in her book and asked, "Do you know why I keep this house?"

"I guess I never thought of it," she answered, pouring them both tea from the green ceramic pot sitting between them. "You've always just been the Mistress to me."

She folded the soft tome and set it aside, accepting the warm cup. "Thank you," she said and sipped. "It's not exactly the most profitable venture, housing lost girls."

It was evening again, and the girls were all in their beds. It was quiet in the Ward, save for the occasional creaking slat overhead as a sister shifted in her cot.

"Good thing for me," Haggart continued, "I was never interested in making a profit, only in making a difference." She set her tea aside and offered Philippa a flat oat biscuit before continuing. "I keep this house, this rotting cursed home, because even this is more than I was afforded as a child. You see, I was abandoned also, cast out of Grimm at a very young age. I had made a simple mistake, a joke, but it frightened the locals so much, even my parents, that they didn't hesitate to send me away."

She poured some more tea into both of their cups.

"I was alone for a long time before I found a home to take me in. It was then I knew someday I would make a home of my own. And in that home I would accept all children who came my way. I would not let silly superstition or naïve fears guide me. I failed on that promise when it came to Olen, but I will not fail again." She looked straight at Philippa, "Any child, no matter what, is welcome to refuge in my home."

She knew. She knew about her and Koertig, and she knew about the curse Brynn had laid upon her growing child. She did not know how she knew, but she knew.

"I am frightened for this child," Philippa admitted, as a tear fell.

"That is a fear of all mothers," she offered with a soft smile.

"I was wrong, Mistress. I was wrong in thinking he would change."

"He was wrong not to," Haggart said. "He is angry now, because he realizes his mistake. And he is enraged knowing there is nothing in his soul that will allow him to admit and correct it. He still expects you to be the one to return, to be the one who kneels."

"I love him," Philippa said and looked to Haggart as if asking if it was okay to feel this way. "But I don't ever want to go back to him."

Haggart set down her tea and grasped her child's hand, "You don't have to do anything you don't want."

33

Koertig Rises

Koertig marched down the wide stairway to Lowtown, mirror-like armor over his chest and head. A spiked silver pauldron girded his injured shoulder. He carried a spear that felt weightless. He slammed the butt of the spike into the boardwalk and halted. He was pain free and strong with a fury burning in his soul. Koertig was ready for war.

Soldiers raced past him, his soldiers. A command he had thought he had lost. Koertig had lost nothing. His men carried bright torches along with tall spears and long swords as they spilled into Lowtown and down to the Barrens. Koertig had sat alone in his room for a week, waiting, festering. He had anticipated Philippa's certain return, even playing out her groveling words. By his fourth night alone, anticipation had turned to outrage. By the seventh night, he had roused his army.

"Surround the building!" he called out, following his men to the Barrens. The shadowed moon was in crescent on this clear night, but the stars were bright and plentiful. "Cover the windows! I want them all accounted for!"

For those seven nights he had heard again every conversation he and Philippa had shared. At first she had bowed to him, calling him sir, begging to tend to his every need. She had worshipped him, and like any devout, she had let her god command her. But it had all been a lie, an act to get him to lower his guard. He had let her become familiar to him, a comforting presence even. And only then, when he was least defended, did she attempt to control him.

In the Barrens, Martz relayed Koertig's orders and waved at his men to take up positions around the Ward. Small shaded heads peeked out of the windows, while taller shadows ran behind them slamming panes and dropping curtains.

This too was an act of control, her fleeing his room, her still refusing to come. It was a standoff, an act to see who would break first. Unfortunately for Philippa it was a game with only one possible outcome. As he had gone over their many conversations, he remembered one in particular. Early on she had revealed that her own Mistress had known of the magical child living inside the Ward and had done nothing. Well, he thought, once Haggart the traitor is evicted and the Ward closed, Philippa will have no choice but to return and tend to him once again and—

And there she was, the unmistakable frame of his shameless nurse, the soul-stealing moll, peering out of second story glass. She pulled the curtain and moved aside. *Last chance,* he thought to her, *don't make me do this.*

Martz set his men in groups of three around the windows and doors of the old run-down dispensary. The soldiers dropped their torches and lit small bonfires, a crude lighted pathway leading away from the Barrens and back to the Square. Muffled voices of frightened girls slipped through the warped wood siding, questions and hushes from the young and old. Wine-wasted locals ambled out of the Eagle and Trout, speculating drunkenly on the ruckus. Filth before him, filth behind, Koertig shuddered at this filthy burg.

He marched up the fiery dirt path to the Ward as the front door pulled open. Mistress Haggart took a cautious step outside, searching the faces of the soldiers. She squinted in the bright firelight and pulled the door shut behind her. Koertig heard one of the wards slide the lock into place. *A metal bolt will not stop me, Philippa.*

Mistress Haggart stepped into the circle of firelight, her hands up defensively.

"What is this, Terrel?" she asked the younger Martz, but he deferred to his leader.

Koertig spiked his spear deep into the soil and marched forward through the ranks. He approached the old woman whose home had been the shame of Millthrace since before he arrived. He stood before the mother of rats and spoke.

"The child, Olen Marine," he said. "How did she come to you?"

"How do any of the girls come to me? Adulterous men who tend not their seed," she said and was met with the back of his hand. She fell to the ground and grabbed her cheek. Gasps came from behind the walls of the Ward. She climbed to her feet, still rubbing her face. Every blow she took was one less for Philippa, if she was wise, he thought.

All of the patrons and much of the staff now stood outside the Eagle and Trout. Others from Lowtown had slouched out of their hovels and stood gathered along the steps at the Lowtown square.

"The girl?" Koertig asked calmly.

"It was an errand woman," she answered, a red gash had opened on her cheek. "A migrant on duty from Kessel. The child's parents had been killed, and she was tasked with finding the girl a home."

"And when did you know she was not of this world?" he asked.

"She is as real as you or I," she said defiantly, and again was met with his hand. Her head snapped to the side, but she did not fall. Murmurs rumbled through the onlookers.

"When did you know you were harboring a Demi-Aurling?" he demanded.

"This is not about Olen Marine," she spat out. "I know what you did to Philippa. Is that what the great Koertig asks of his nurse, to bed him while he heals? We offer a caretaker, but you expect a concubine. When the beast took your arm," she pointed below his waist, "he should have snapped that off too!"

Koertig grabbed her by the throat and pressed his fingers deep into her fleshly neck. Her windpipe closed and thick veins popped out along her collar. Her eyes bulged, and her mouth fell open searching for air.

"Leona Haggart," he snarled. "For knowingly harboring a Demi-Aurling, you are expelled from the great city of Millthrace, never to return. Your wardens will each be examined and removed also, but should any show Aurling traits, they will be delivered directly to the Nerikan mines."

Through pursed lips and fading consciousness, Mistress Haggart forced out a final challenge, "Greet them at the gates of Hell, you one-armed deviant." Then she scooped her hand under her apron, pulled out a small bent dagger, and thrust it at his throat.

Had he another arm, he would have knocked the tool away. Had he a sword, he would have sliced off her hand. Had he been more cautious, he would have expected anything. But he had not, so the shiny bent knife came at his gullet. Pain and glorious death, perhaps, but no. A hollow metal-on-metal thump pecked against his chest as Martz's spear ran straight through the old woman and etched a small wound in Koertig's armor. Haggart looked down at the wet iron wedge jutting out of her chest, and fell forward, scraping the spearhead down the front of Koertig's silver chestplate. She collapsed to the ground, red ribbons of life flowing out of her chest, feeding the barren soil. The tiny dagger rolled out of her hands. She stared widely ahead as if focusing on some distant object.

"I always knew she was special," she whispered to no one, as life escaped her. "From the first night she stayed with me...she slept," Leona Haggart smiled as her final breath exhaled, "She slept in golden robes..." Then Haggart spoke no more.

Koertig tested her with a soft toe, but she was gone. His army stared at him, uncertainty on their faces. They were good soldiers, the city's best, but under Koertig they had seen very little combat.

"A blanket," he asked quietly, and one of his men edged through the gawking crowd and into a nearby building. Koertig waited quietly in the watchful starlight until his man returned and covered the body. Sounds of shuffling feet came from inside the Ward.

"Men of the Millthrace guard," he said somberly to the troops. "This is not the way we had planned it, but rarely is there an encounter without the unexpected. Had she not attacked, she would still be alive." He moved past the troops and paused near Terrel Martz. Koertig touched his shoulder and gave a thanking nod. "We were to shut down the Ward and evict the wretches and waifs. This incident makes it all the more important. What we know: These people have sheltered at least one Demi, possibly more, and they are willing to *kill* to protect them."

A guardsman asked if they should raid the Ward.

"No, I will not risk my men to their treachery," he said, approaching the building. He jabbed his spear through a window, shattering the ancient glass. He placed his back against the wall and called through the jagged pane. He ordered them to exit the Ward, but in return heard only the hushed whimpers of children and soothing murmurs from an older girl. "Exit this building immediately!" he ordered, but the girls stayed inside.

Already frustrated, he pushed away from the building and strode over to the fire, stepping over Haggart's covered body. He pulled out a torch and handed it to the guard. "Burn it. That will make the rats flee," he said. "And let something better rise up where vermin once crawled."

The guard hesitated. Koertig pushed him from behind. The soldier took the flame and ran at the Ward. He tossed a high arcing lob. The torch cartwheeled and smashed through an upper window.

"Burn it all!" Koertig cried out, and his men launched their torches at the building.

The dry wood would not resist the flames. It was as if the old timber had held fire inside itself all these years and was finally letting it burst free. Long boards cracked and popped. Wooden shrapnel flew over the retreating soldiers. Roof beams creaked and bowed in the erupting hellfire that boiled the air. Within moments the entire building was an inferno as black smoke rose high above Millthrace, blotting out the moon and inking the stars that watched.

"Watch the doors!" Koertig called out to his men, trampling the grounds as he shouted. "Watch the windows! Catch them as they flee! Gather them all in front!" *Especially one,* he thought. *Especially one!*

But none of the children escaped the flames as the Ward fueled its own destruction.

Townspeople moved nervously, not sure what to do. Two men rounded the Eagle and Trout carrying large wooden buckets. They saw Koertig's army and the madly pacing Lieutenant Colonel, and they knew this was not a fire to be doused. They set the buckets down beside the Well.

"Flee you rats!" Koertig cried out, stamping the Barrens, mad with rage, watching the doors for Philippa. "Come to me!"

The upper floor buckled, like a great horse falling to a knee. Iron crashed as beds fell through. The old patched roof failed next and fell in upon itself, pulling in the south wall with its collapse. The townspeople were silent as they watched the blaze. Koertig stormed about yelling at the flames.

"Why don't they run?" he screamed manically, but none dared answer him.

The walls fell in, the roof collapsed, and the Ward and everything within it burned to ashes. And as the flames of Lowtown raged, a desperate Koertig fell to his knees and cried out, "Why doesn't she flee?"

34

Pickled Fish

The canvas walls billowed with the breeze coming off the Wide Galenic River. Edwin had been to this river many times over the years but always on the Hulblich side. The traces of lead flowing down the vast tributary had always smelled to him like butcher's blood. He smelled that now as he bargained with a plump and nearly naked man in the village of Kessel.

Kessel was the last small town along the Wide Galenic before entering the large metropolitan city of Brennan. Strong storms had slowed their passage, and after four days on the road, Edwin was eager to hurry on to the Iron City. He was certain Olen was in need, and he and Marko were going to help her. It felt good to be on the opposite end of giving.

Marko had led him into a five-poled tent behind one of the many wooden huts that made up the town. Stacked crates, piled sacks, and goods of every kind were strewn about the place. The portly man lay on a pile of stained pillows eating pickled ocean fish and drinking Marko's fresh ale. He was shirtless atop the endless pillows. Too bloated for pants, he wore a canvas kilt below his waist. His skin was stained brownish yellow from his chin to his belly. His name was simply Leo.

"I would offer you some," he said to Edwin, indicating the fish, "But I do not hate you."

"I see," Edwin said, not understanding.

"He means you won't be able to stop eating, just like himself," Marko explained from behind a curtain. He scraped a thin blade across his neck and wiped away long black hairs.

"Ahh," Edwin said, and focused back on the reclining trader. "Then, I thank you. What we need are clothes of the gentry and ruling class."

Leo lazily fished another fillet out his wooden bucket and sucked on it between cheek and jowl. His eyes rolled back as if in ecstasy. "So good," he said dreamily. "But yet it makes one so thirsty." He drank from the ale pouch and addressed Edwin. "Clothes of the gentry. Which city?"

"Millthrace," Edwin said.

"Millthrace," Marko echoed.

Leo pulled out the fillet and dipped it back in the brine bucket. "That should not be too difficult, and for a reasonable price." The slippery fillet wiggled in his fat fingers as if it was still alive. Leo forced it into his mouth.

Marko wiped his face and joined Edwin. His neck was clean, and his beard was gone, except for a finely trimmed mustache and short black chin hair. A sharp jawline and strong muscles lined his neck. He was a handsome man, more so than Edwin ever would have guessed behind that long beard and exaggerated grin. He was even calmer now as if shaving his face had cleared away Marko's bothersome character. His black hair was swept to the side, just as Edwin had described of Mayor Brynn.

"Why Marko," the sticky-fingered man said, "You look like a mayor-general already!"

Marko took over the trade and bargained with the recumbent gentleman. He and Edwin had discussed their needs and what they were willing to pay during their walk to Kessel. They had agreed they would not go higher than fifteen coppers, and that they could earn back about five or six by selling their goods afterwards. But Leo was a tough negotiator and the trade quickly grew heated.

"No coppers then!" Marko spat, after Leo refused his last offer of eighteen.

Edwin leaned in and whispered, "Don't offer him silvers."

"No coppers and no silvers!" he shouted, glaring an eye at Edwin. "Instead, we give you one barrel of pickled rock herring, fresh off the first ship in Brennan!"

Leo choked and fumbled for the ale pouch. He took a big swig and coughed into his hands.

"Insanity!" Edwin exclaimed, knowing the high price for such a delicacy. "Come now!"

"A barrel?" Leo asked, just as surprised.

"One full barrel," Marko said. "Off the first ship we see."

Leo sat forward and spoke like an educator towards foolish children, "Ships deliver *fresh* fish, not pickled. I have no need for *fresh* fish." He shuddered and continued. "The sweet stuff is made in the city, and it does not come cheap. Only time can cure a barrel of herring, and time my friends, is money. I wrote that," he said proudly, while covered in brine. "Are you sure you can do this?"

"Of course!" said Marko.

"Impossible," said Edwin.

Marko side-kicked at Edwin's ankles.

Edwin side-kicked back.

Leo pushed himself to standing. He was not much taller than when he was lying back. He put his hand out to Marko, and they both shook vigorously. He then offered his wet palm to Edwin.

He did not like it. Every silver, every copper, every item in Marko's cart would be traded away for a foolish game. It was a silly ruse to begin with, and even Edwin was no longer certain his plan would work.

"Trust me, Edwin," Marko insisted, and he heard the soft endearing voice of the Millthrace mayor coming through. So quickly he had mastered the tone. "We have come this far," Marko said.

Reluctantly, Edwin bowed to the sticky Leo, holding his clean hands behind his back. "I accept all terms of the offer," he said.

The deal done, Marko hurried out of the tent while Edwin stayed behind. "One more thing," Edwin said. "I am also in the market for leather-bounds. Histories and faerie stories if you have any."

Leo promised him the libraries of University, if given some time, but for now he only had two small volumes to sell. Edwin paid a hefty six coppers for the books, and met Marko outside the tent.

"Why would you agree to blow our fortune on a barrel of fish?" Edwin asked. "You should have offered nineteen coppers."

"And you should not disagree with me when I am trading! I could have talked him down to half a barrel!" Marko said, coming up to Sonny. "When the game is on, and Marko is dealing, your job is to agree with anything I say. The answer is always yes! Anything less and the plan falls apart."

"That's fair, but it always feels like you never let me all the way in on the plan."

"Because I don't!" Marko said and gave his raucous Marko Meloon laugh. "For example, why spend nineteen coppers when I can get a barrel of pickled fish for free?"

***

Bakku reached the lush green crest of the Caraway Mountains, and for the first time since leaving Olen, he stopped running. It was quiet here, his silent solitude only broken by the shushing leaves of ocean-side sumac and the faraway call of a lonely gull. Even during his long confinement in Nerikan he had rarely been alone. His beetle-like jailers had always been there, clicking, clawing, poking at his flesh, searching for new veins to open in his thickly scarred hide. It had seemed so simple then, the idea of ending his life. Weighed against endless torture, he had found the strength to do something he had naturally found abhorrent. But he was free now.

"No! You are not free!" he scolded himself and thought of Olen.

He was not free, because he now had the duty of protecting her, and she must never know the truth. She must never know that she was the reason Bakku must die. He would have given up his quest for death quite easily. He had discovered that not long after bursting free of the barrow. Just a few days back in the sunlight, and he had changed his mind. He would not leap into the flames of Calderra. Instead he would risk fleeing to some new and distant land, and live alone in peace until once again captured. But then he had met her.

Olen held a seed that connected their worlds. Brynn would use her much as he used Bakku. She too would be placed in chains, forced to open and close the doorway to the Ether at Brynn's will. And she would do this, suffering for eons in Nerikan, as he forced her to swallow the life-giving blood of someone she had once loved. And there they would sit, Bakku and Olen, forever chained, forever Brynn's slaves, and Bakku forever shamed for letting this happen.

He pulled the sumac aside and continued to Calderra. He trekked north, wading through wide-leaved plants. When travel was easy he jogged ahead with renewed vigor, but when the foliage overwhelmed him, he trudged ahead, bending a wide path through the leaves. For two days and nights he ran across the Caraway mountaintops.

He neared the isthmus known as the Melle where the mountains edged west. From this vantage could he see ships sailing south of him on the Westing Sea and far north on the Olmere Ocean. The outline of Bran's Wall tracked between these two waters in the field below, a grey contour atop the green grass. He was near the place of his greatest effort, a place he had once known of as home. He leapt down a few lengths of mountainside and pushed aside lithe tree trunks as he passed through. Moss-covered boulders lined the forest floor. He clawed off the lichens and rubbed his thumb over the edge of the stone. Still sharp. Still jagged after all of these years. They were remnants of the stone he had cut away from the Caraways. They were boulders unused in Bran's folly. He pressed ahead and entered a clearing.

It was a stony oasis, a dry grey refuge hidden among the lush mountain forest. The ground was level and flat here, and cleared of all growing things. Four huts of stacked granite stood much as he had left them, tall and wide with flat stones arcing up to a roof. They stood like stone beehives growing out of the ground. The huts were not beautiful, but the stones stood as true as the day they were laid.

Beyond the huts stood a wide cavity leading into the Caraways. This tunnel he knew reached nearly all the way to the Westing Sea, just one last span of stone holding back the waters. A month's more work with his pick and he could deliver that sea across the Melle. Not a month, he thought, that was who he once was. A day's work for Bakku. The time for such labor had passed; he had a new task now, which he must not delay much longer.

He slipped out of the forest and into the familiar haven. He felt the stone huts. They seemed so large back then, before Bakku was Bakku. This one, he thought as he touched the southeast hut, was his. He had built them all, but this one was home. He could not even make it through the undersized door anymore. A fire pit sat centered between the huts. It was black with fresh ash. He touched the cinders. They were wet. He knelt and swept a finger through the pit. Orange coals. The fire had recently been doused. He cursed himself.

"Away, devil!" a voice behind him called out.

Bakku rose up, tall above the stone houses, and spun around. A teen-aged boy stood in front of the deep mountain cave. He held a hatchet with both hands as he blocked the doorway. The muscular child stood boldly, yet the shaking hatchet betrayed a deep fear.

The boy commanded, "Leave us, fiend!"

Bakku lunged forward, unsure if this was one of Brynn's hunters.

The boy stepped back, righted himself, and stepped forward again. "I am not afraid to die to protect my family."

"Who are you?" Bakku asked angrily, as if to an intruder in his home.

The boy seemed shocked Bakku could speak. He still held the hatchet in both hands and held it up threateningly. "Burke," he said. "My father is Richard Burke. And if any of us are harmed, he will hunt you down and skin you, even if he has to travel all over this world to find you. I promise you this. Now leave!"

"Burke?" he asked, letting the name echo through the depths of his remembrances. Burke, a name he once spoke. A name that was once his own. A name he was no longer a part of. So many years separated him and this boy, so many generations. He had thought his family was gone, but here stood a Burke. Despite the eons that had passed and the generations, this boy was part of him.

"You are a Burke?" Bakku asked. The boy looked confused at the question.

"Just leave us," the boy pleaded, his false bravado fading. "Can't you see we have nothing for you? Let us live."

Shadows moved behind the boy. An older woman appeared next to him. She held a pole ax awkwardly. Two young girls came around her side holding small cooking knives.

"Leave here," the old woman demanded. "It's true. If you harm us, the men will hunt you. They will make you suffer. They will not give up."

"Yes," Bakku said confusedly, but he was not sure what he was agreeing to. "Suffer," he mumbled, searching the family's faces for traces of those he had once known, many births and many deaths ago. The boy, his stance, like one Bakku may have made before he changed. The woman, her mouth, maybe there a hint of the lips that had once smiled his way. And the girl, was it fantasy, or did she appear like a child from eons ago? What Brynn had done in a day, the natural order of life had done over the ages. Hints were there of the faces he had once known, but the conjoining of new lines and new blood had altered them to something new. Yet it was his family, he could not deny it. They were Burke, like Bakku had been, so long ago.

"Go away!" shouted the youngest child, a girl of no more than seven summers.

The Caraway Mountains rose beyond the family, leading into the Melle and Calderra. He would go away and let the family live in peace, as it had done for so many generations. But he could no longer head west. He had cut a wide path over the mountains and through these woods. He would be followed. This family, his family, would be found. Janus Brynn would know their heritage. He would make them suffer.

"Live," he said and nodded to the family. "In peace."

Bakku turned towards the eastern horizon. Towards Millthrace. He escaped back into the thick woods, dashing through the vegetation, letting tree limbs whip at his face. He cut straight downhill and into the prairie known as the Melle. Then he raced due east for all the afternoon, leaping over streams and pounding across the plains. Furry meadow fauna rose up on their haunches to stare in awe at this new larger faster mustang that thundered across fields on two legs. Then, for the second time in two hundred thirty years, Bakku blasted a gaping hole in Bran's Wall.

He was back in the hard scrabble flatlands of the Mecan Plains. Millthrace and Janus lay ahead of him. Only one family line would end this day, he promised, the line known as Brynn.

* * *

Olen had sat in the fields outside Brennan for days, delaying the inevitable. Her long journey had taught her how to survive with very little, but nonetheless she was hungry. She would have to go inside the city and buy food. Maybe she would spend a couple coppers to rent a cot for a night. After that, she would have no more excuses. She would have to go on to Kessel.

A carriage rolled out of the ancient stone arches, heading north to Millthrace or Daegan. A wealthy-looking family sat in the open-aired cart. In the back a small girl of about Olen's age watched the side of the road. She held on to the seat in front of her as she stood and surveyed the tall grasses of the Bluestem Prairie. The girl was dressed no differently than the men. She wore a white button-down shirt, with the cuffs rolled up to the elbow. Absent was the dress or skirt, as this child wore long pants in soft olive. On her feet were black boots with tall shafts wrapped snuggly above her calves. A dark belt around her waist held up her pants, but it also held a round metallic water canister and a large jagged knife. Olen barely felt the ripple, but knew her garb had changed as the carriage rolled out of sight. For the first time she wore something that felt absolutely right. If this was what Brennan girls wore, she thought, then she would fit in nicely.

Olen walked out of the grasses and stepped through the massive stone archway.

35

❦

Stilled

Koertig coughed and spat as smoke from the smoldering Ward blew into his face. Philippa was dead. She had chosen fiery death over another day with him. He knelt before the charred bones of the Ward. His eyes burned. She was dead.

Murmurs behind him, accusations.

He tore off his helm and cast it into the orange and red coals.

It was all gone. The entire structure had collapsed in, leaving just a charred footprint where the Ward had once stood.

Townspeople muttered, whispering about Koertig.

This was not his fault, not this time. He pushed himself to his feet, shaking and uneasy. She had brought this on. And she had doomed her sisters in doing so. *And his son.* No! Not his son, an Aurling aberration created by Janus Brynn. As he thought the name, someone in the crowd spoke it. The Mayor approached from Midtown, the very last to join the show.

A leather strap angled down Koertig's chest. He bit the free end and unbuckled the latch at his armpit. Salty brine on his tongue. The silver pauldron fell loose, and he caught it in his hand. He had seen a home burn like this before. His boyhood home in the mountains. It was his mother who had pulled him from the flames and carried him down the snowy path to Illsbrook. Even as she trudged down that frigid path she must have known the shame that awaited her. It was hardly two nights later they had found a room, and she had found steady income. Philippa had chosen a different path.

So offensive Philippa had found her lover, so unpleasant he had been to her that she had chosen her own death over the indignity of being with him. It was this very strength he had come to admire about her. He should have known she would not come out. He should have known she would not bow to his demands. All their nights together and he had not known her at all. He cast aside the pauldron.

The murmurs behind him grew as Brynn came down the Midtown stairway. Reeve and Graeme trailed the Aurling. The crowd opened soundlessly to let Brynn and his men through. Koertig snatched a spear off the ground and flipped the shaft onto his shoulder. He held it pointed at Brynn. The mayor stopped and held up his palms.

"What did you do?" Brynn asked, his voice an act of sincere concern.

"The Koertig bloodline is clean once again, *Aurling*," Koertig growled, calling out the mayor's secret for all of Millthrace to hear.

"The Koertig bloodline was tainted long before you came around," Brynn snapped back, no longer hiding behind his soft tenor. "There is nothing the son of an assassin and a whore can do to fix that! Both paid to spread their legs! One over the back of a warhorse, the other—"

Koertig launched the spear. Reeve held up his palm. It glowed a hollow light. The iron and wood weapon exploded, blowing debris back at Koertig and knocking him backwards. Brynn and his men stood unaffected.

The crowds gasped as the Aurling powers were revealed, and Koertig's soldiers stood discomposed. Brynn and his men remained calm as the townspeople muttered. After several measured breaths, Brynn addressed the people.

"I will no longer hide who I am," he called out to the hundreds of villagers who had gathered in Lowtown. "I was wrong to do so for so long."

"He is an Aurling intruder!" Koertig growled, blaming Brynn for all his pain.

"You call me an intruder, but what does that mean?" Brynn asked calmly, turning to the townspeople. "I am simply a traveler, much like many of you." He asked how many of the gathered were Millthrace-born and pointed out the very few. He called out neighboring villages, and then cities far away. He asked how many families had traveled north from Hulblich stock. There were Swarhee from far to the east, and those who had made this place home after sailing over the Westing Sea. "I have come from farther away," he continued. "And yet I too feel as though I am home."

He walked away from Koertig and stepped through the crowds, speaking to his fellow townspeople. "Some of what the old tales said of Aurlings is indeed true, but most is fantasy. Mere faerie tales to scare the kids. Aurlings did possess magics, but for generations had chosen to forego those gifts to live among you, as one of you!"

"Tell them the truth!" Koertig demanded. "Tell them you are the basest of murderers! That you hunted down and killed your own kind!"

"You demand that?" Brynn shouted. "You demand that of me, here at the still burning embers of our greatest tragedy? You, of supposedly untainted Eisen blood, have brought nothing to this city except pain and destruction!"

He marched around Koertig as if waiting to strike. Koertig stood alone, unmoved.

"Yes," Brynn continued, walking through the people. "It is true. I was active in what can only be called genocide. I said we have limited powers, and that is correct, but it was not so for all Aurlings. There were some with great strengths. And of those, there were many who used those gifts to wreak havoc in this world. Read the diaries of Sig Bran! The mere sight of one of these beasts, a terror even greater than Millthrace's ogre, sent him into madness! We have seen what just one of these creatures can do to our beloved city. Now imagine two, ten, one hundred of them battling it out for supremacy of our world!"

He stood on a small rise and addressed the crowd, "I was part of a small secret guard that hunted down those beasts and disposed of them in the only way possible. We cast them into Nerikan and let time be their judge. For that I am guilty, but I am not ashamed, for it left this beautiful land untainted by their foul desires. I am an Aurling, but I am also a man. I have helped you all make this city one of the greatest in all of Eisen. And if you will let me, I hope to continue."

Had he been waiting for a response, he never received one, for at that moment a certain hum that had permeated throughout the city since the day it was built faded away. It was a mild vibration that residents of Millthrace only noticed after leaving the city for travel or coming home after a long delay. It was the light pulsating heartbeat of a city run by water. The gears hidden in the Escapement slowed to a halt, and a dead calm seeped into everyone's bones.

"The bob!" a man shouted, pointing to the cork marker atop the Well. "It's gone!"

A woman ran over to the Well and dropped her flaming torch into the pit.

"It's dry!" she called back. "The river has run dry!"

***

Bakku stood high above Millthrace in the Rückraadt Mountains and shouldered another glass-black boulder over the cliff side. It tumbled down the mountain, blasting free more stone, and raining a deadly hail onto the Oiskonn River. Wide streams branched and found new flows around the city, while narrower flows stopped altogether. Still he heaved and pushed and tore stone from the mountainside, damming the city's lifeblood. By morning's light, not one branch of the mighty Oiskonn River would flow into or under the city.

He had eaten well during his escape and his muscles had grown larger than ever before. He clenched his fists and curled his banded wrists. Iron shackles burst open and fell to the ground. Truly unchained at last, he bellowed atop the mountain. Bakku was ready for war.

***

While the Ward had burned, flames had climbed into the sky, far over the tall walls of Millthrace. It was a beacon in the night for any traveler to see for leagues, and would quickly be the gossip of the Iron Road. But it was also a candle in the dark for deep places underground. Bright orange flames shone through the cracks of the Millthrace boardwalk and lit the world below. It shone down in beams like the sun after a storm. A line of shadows moved past these flickering rays, as whispered voices warned to stay out of the light. At the head of the line a tall, sturdy figure waved the smaller bodies ahead into the wide brick passageways leading them upstream, counting them as they hurried by.

"Twelve," Philippa exhaled, again wiping the flood of tears from her eyes. Black shadows pounded the boards overhead as townspeople raced to Lowtown to see the fire. Long ago Leona Haggart had warned her of Koertig and what would happen when he came the *next time*. She had chosen to disregard her warning. But when Koertig's soldier had slaughtered Mistress Haggart, she knew there would be no escape. It was a memory of sister Olen that had saved them. Philippa had quickly ushered the girls down the basement steps and through Olen's hatchway into the sewers.

The Ward was gone, Haggart was gone, and all because of Harner Koertig. She smoothed her hand over her belly and thought of the child inside. *Thirteen*, she thought. She hated herself for loving Koertig, and for knowing that deep down part of her still did. She had seen his true heart exposed long ago as he lay broken in bed. That was not the man who raged in Lowtown.

"Philippa?" a small voice asked in the darkness. Maggie came back down the tunnel. She was already dirty and wet. "Mistress Cree, are you coming?"

Mistress Cree, she thought as she crouched down next to the child. It was true, she was the oldest. She was the mistress now, and these children were her wards. She had once thought the Ward needed a protector, and that she would be that guardian. But it was no longer her silly superstitious fears of Olen that threatened them. Instead, it was Koertig and his entire army that stood between them and their very lives. *Very well*, she thought, she had once promised her life to protect these girls. Now she would hold on to that promise. She would get them out of Millthrace, all of them, and then deliver them far away from here.

"Yes, Maggie dear," she said, rising and walking through the throng of frightened girls, placing her hand on their heads as she went. She looked towards the gloomy underworld that only Olen had been bold enough to explore. The Lowtown flames faded to darkness just beyond. Philippa moved ahead into the forbidden Escapement and said, "Follow me."

36

The Price of Rock Herring

Mayor-General Marko Meloon rode into the sooty streets of Brennan on his regal ass, Sonny. His accountant and city administrator, Edwin, walked beside him. Brennan was like a city built by giants with its granite archways of disturbing heights. Edwin felt tiny passing through the great entry and seeing the monolithic structures within. Grand stone houses and citadels grew straight out of the Caraway mountainside, with the blasted-away rock scattered and stacked around the city in mighty huts and shops. Millthrace was certainly larger with its many boroughs, and Illsbrook more populace during the Faire, but there was nothing in this world as massively weighty as Brennan's grand boulevard, where even the street was paved in giant flat stone. Had he not been so pursued, the great Bakku would have rested nicely here, he thought.

They passed under the archway in colored robes purchased from Leo. Marko had matched Brynn's hair and mustache perfectly, and after just a few minutes at the glass, he had matched the mayor's facial expressions down to the soft smile, and even his gentle speech. Edwin had given up on his Graeme impression after hours of trying.

"You must have been the greatest actor in Illsbrook," Edwin said.

"Excuse me, Alderman?" Mayor Marko asked, lost in the character.

Leo had tossed in a royal purple riding blanket for Sonny once he saw their plan coming together. He loved a good scam and wanted to see it come to fruition.

Edwin led Sonny through the smoky downtown, looking around corners for a familiar little girl. He saw, and felt nothing.

Iron ore was the commerce of Brennan, and the heavy black clouds that hung low over the city were its consequence. Edwin had first smelled the city an hour out of Kessel, and thought the smoke would overwhelm him if he got any closer. But now that he was in the city, he saw how the smog hung far overhead in dark mists, and the air below was hardly worse than in the fields. Still he coughed when he spoke, which seemed to amuse the new mayor.

Many stared at the man of importance who bounced through the smutty boulevard on his donkey. Those who had traded in Millthrace murmured that they believed him to be the mayor. For the most part, the Brennan crowds accepted this news and turned back to their work indifferently.

The two-man parade marched under another set of granite arches into the market district. Edwin asked a vendor with a vegetable cart where he could find the fishmonger. He pointed down a tall stone alley.

"And what is the fishmonger's name again?" Edwin asked politely.

The vendor held up a green tomato, "Are you buying or not?"

Edwin tossed the man a wedge.

"Anders," the trader said and turned away.

Moments later Mayor Marko strode through the open door of the fishmonger's stone shop. "Ah, Anders!" he exclaimed, like meeting an old friend. Edwin followed close behind. It was more than a few degrees cooler inside the windowless hut. A thin but muscular middle-aged man with a white apron strapped over his belly stirred a barrel of sour cream. A dirty white rag circled his forehead, and he was shirtless under his apron. Mayor Marko gave him a big hug. "So good to see you again, Anders!"

The man pulled away and pointed a thumb over his back shoulder. "That's Anders," he said and went back to stirring the barrel.

A tiny old woman with even more wrinkles than years sat on her haunches in the corner of the shop smoking a long curved pipe. Edwin sighed.

"Anders!" Marko said, not skipping a beat, and moved over to the old woman. "How long has it been?"

The frog-like woman winced awkwardly at his hug. Her eyes were milky white with age. Mayor Marko raved to her about her rock herring. "It's become quite the favored snack at our council meetings," he announced. She set her pipe down and sidled away from Marko on wooden sandals.

"Anders," she called to the man stirring the barrel, "What the hell is this?"

"We should go," Edwin offered.

To Marko's credit, he barely slipped out of character.

"Vagabonds, mum," Anders said casually, as he hoisted a cleaver off a hook and slammed it onto a wooden tray. "Tryin' some new scam I guess. I'll call up the guards in a bit. Don't worry none."

The old woman settled back down in a different corner and relit her pipe.

"We apologize," Edwin said, taking a step back to the door. "Marko?"

Mayor Marko shot him a dark glance, and quickly softened back into character. "Vagabonds?" Marko said, digging into his shirt. He pulled out some folded papers and showed them to Anders. Anders raised a brow and nodded approvingly.

"Nice work," he said, pouring a bowlful of chives into the mixture. "It's the Mayor of Millthrace, Mum. I bet he's about to ask for some free samples, and maybe some overdue tax."

The tiny old woman laughed and showed her bare gums. Edwin tried to wave Marko out of the door, but Mayor Marko was undeterred.

"Hah, my good Anders," Marko said, patting him on the back. "You know as well as I, Millthracian taxes cannot be levied here in Brennan. I come merely for business. I would like to *purchase* one barrel of your finest pickled rock herring."

Now Anders was the one to laugh. "A barrel? We don't sell it by the barrel. You would wipe out my supply."

"And would that be so bad?" Mayor Marko asked.

"Yes it would. People come far and wide for my herring. And when they buy it by the jar, they also buy other things. Look around you. I've got pots, knives, cheeses, and pickled hocks. These things only sell when the herring sells. If I sold you a barrel, you would have to buy everything else too."

Marko smiled, "How much?"

"Marko, no," Edwin said. "It's not worth it. We'll pay Leo some other way."

"Let us talk," Marko said kindly to the shop owner, ignoring Edwin completely.

After just a few moments of dickering, Edwin reluctantly handed Marko his bag of coins. Marko separated the coppers, hacks, and silvers on the countertop and quickly counted them out. He slid all but two silvers back into Edwin's bag. He proudly presented Edwin with his last two silvers. He held out the bag to the shopkeeper, but before he let go he asked, "With delivery?"

"By my own hands," Anders said, grabbing the sack. He dumped the coins back on to the counter and quickly re-counted. All totaled it was just shy of thirty silver honors. He looked at Marko, "You sir, just bought yourself everything! Mum, we're going on holiday!"

"Huh?" the old woman said.

Edwin berated Marko as they left the store. "Two silvers! All I have left are two dull silvers!" He dug into his shirt and pulled out Marko's ledgers. "I demand you withdraw your investments and give them to me!"

Marko snatched the ledgers from Edwin and stopped in the street. He put his leg on a railing and opened the papers against his knee. He signed the bottom of each of page and thrust them back into Edwin's hands.

"They are yours!" he spat out and walked away.

He had done it. He had actually signed them over. Sixty-eight silvers total. "But this is more than I ever had! Why?"

Marko was already halfway down the paved street. "Because you forfeit the gold! You didn't trust me!" he called over his shoulder, and continued downtown. "And worse, *you broke character*! This partnership, it is over! Your act is a solo one once again, *minstrel*!"

And as Marko disappeared amongst the traders and ironworkers of Brennan, Edwin realized he didn't give a damn about any silver honors or golden manors. He cared about Marko, the dammed fool of a trader who he had never been drawn to, but hated the idea of leaving. He stuffed the ledgers in his pocket and ran over hard stone, chasing after his friend.

***

Olen stared at the massive walls within the city of Brennan and wondered if Bakku had helped raise them so many years ago. Then something on the stone caught her eye. Men with soot-covered carts walked around her and loud sounds of the city drifted right past her as she stood fixated on the image before her. Two thick posters, hand-drawn and detailed, hung on the cold granite walls. There were Edwin's angry yet frightened eyes, captured by a knowing artisan, staring back at her and looking lost. Next to him hung an image of a child that looked so much younger than she felt. Her hair was dark and stringy, and hung together in clumps. Her neck was thin, as were her cheeks, and the hollows around her eyes were dark. She looked poor but proud. She looked bold, more so than the old man.

She did not look like that anymore. The road to Brennan was rough, but Bakku had kept her fed. Her cheeks had filled out, and her clothes were clean and new, but her confidence was gone. She had escaped Millthrace determined to find her parents, now she felt unsure where to go or what to do. Somehow she had lost the brave child she had once been.

She could read enough to make out the words. These people were wanted. But something between the pictures and the descriptions was blacked out with a thick splash of paint.

A firm hand slapped down on her shoulder and held her still.

"Stay," a man's voice said.

* * *

Edwin found Marko at the docks. Five tall ships were docked at Brennan and were being loaded and unloaded. Mule trains pulled thick ropes through pulleys, lifting heavy crates high into the air. Brawny workmen pulled guy ropes and angled the crates to shore. Seabirds cried. Among the men crowded on the shore were the troops from Millthrace. Ten older soldiers, hard grizzled men with thick arms and wide jaws. They wore their armor with thuggish pride, and stuck their already bulging chests out farther when Brennan-folk walked by. They shouted unwanted advice to the dock workers and scolded younger men for running on the piers. They were the brutes of the Millthrace guard, and they would have been proud to wear that title. Marko peered over stacked crates watching the soldiers.

"Do they have the girl?" Edwin asked, as he sidled next to his former partner.

"No," he snarled. "And I can do this myself."

"Sorry about today," Edwin offered. "I panicked. What do you want me to say?"

Marko motioned to the men, "I want you to ask them which one has the gold."

Edwin scoffed, but saw Marko was serious.

"They would wallop me just for looking at them!"

A shoreman guided a shipping crate to the docks. It caught a mooring pole and burst open. Bright yellow and green produce poured out of the wide gash and spilled onto shore. The soldiers rolled over themselves with laughter. None offered to help pick up the mess.

"Fine," Edwin said, finally catching Marko's attention.

"Really?"

"Yes, I will do it. I owe it to you," Edwin said and stood up, ready to walk to his death, or at least a fine thrashing. "Just tell me one thing. Is there really a girl back home?"

"What do you mean," he asked, as Marko Meloon slipped from character.

"Before I go to my demise, I want to know...is this a love story, or one of greed," Edwin asked calmly. "If you lied to me, I forgive you. I simply need to know."

"Edwin, my friend," he said, in a voice as true as he had ever spoken, and absent of all deception, "I have never lied to you."

They stood nose to nose studying each other's faces, looking for truth behind the lies. This was the first man Edwin had ever chosen to befriend. He had found himself comfortable with him, happy, even trusting him with his life. But even so, Edwin wouldn't believe Marko Meloon if he said it was cold in winter. Here stood his chosen partner, an unabashed trickster who now swore Edwin was the one man he has never deceived.

"Bullshit," Edwin said and marched down to meet the guards.

37

Fireflies

The river had stopped flowing. "Aurling treachery!" Koertig cried out and leapt at Brynn. The two fell to the ground and rolled in a pile of clawing arms and kicking legs. Koertig was vastly stronger than the mayor, but with two good arms Brynn quickly pulled free and got to his feet.

"Lock him up!" Mayor-General Brynn called out to the army, all of which hesitated. "Lock this man up, now!" he demanded.

The soldiers looked to neither Koertig nor Brynn. Instead they all turned towards Sergeant Martz who had quietly watched it all unfold.

"Martz!" Brynn called out. "Order your men!"

Koertig rose to his feet, proud of his army, proud of his sergeant. "Yes Martz, order your men."

Martz threw down his spear, and pulled his sword out of its sheath. He held his sword aloft. "To arms!" he cried out, and slowly lowered his weapon to the face of Brynn. The roar from the army was deafening as his men hoisted their swords and spears, and as one they charged at the Aurling politico. Koertig too grabbed a spear and advanced.

Reeve waved an arm in a circular motion, and the air rippled around him, Brynn, and Graeme. They ran to Midtown and dove for the alley shadows. A blurry protective bubble surrounded them, much like Koertig had seen in the Ward girl. Then Graeme held his hands high above his head, and crashed them down around himself, pulling darkness from the sky, blotting out the three men as they ran. And as the brief deep darkness unfolded, and Koertig's eyes refocused in the encroaching firelight, all three men had vanished, and the alley was empty.

***

Twelve orphans were lost in the mossy black Escapement. Philippa had taken them as far as she could before the orange light from the burning Ward had faded away to darkness. The younger girls had moved ahead warily, speaking rumor of ghouls and evil creatures that crept in the Scape.

They had long ago jumped the streams at Midtown and left behind them the last air vent to the upper world. They had wandered in blackness for the past half hour, turning back from barred passageways, and circling around through previously traced paths. She had thought she had found a new tunnel when the water stopped flowing down, but soon all of the tunnels were dry. She pulled the girls back out of the dark brick tunnels and into the wide underground. The Midtown boardwalk was far overhead. It could not be seen in the utter blackness, but footfalls clamoring above let her know it was there. Moving her hands in the shadows she found a rock wall facing Uptown. Her long arms stretched high, but the next level was out of reach.

She sat the girls down against the wall, and told them she needed to rest. Clara and Lysa comforted the younger ones, who did not understand and just wanted to go home. *Where had you gone, Olen?* Philippa asked herself. She knew her sister had been able to get anywhere via the Scape, even outside the city walls. She had seen the map on Mayor Brynn's wall while she was nursing Koertig, and she damned herself for not studying it better.

For the first time since the fire, the girls had stopped moving and the silent whispers began. Leni, too young to fathom such horror, asked Philippa about Mistress Haggart. Renata spoke also, saying they should go back before Haggart came home. They had all seen it, but not all understood. It seemed just moments ago Haggart had been telling the girls to get away from the windows and to stay calm. She had remained cool as her home was surrounded, and had even straightened her top in the mirror before stepping outside. "Lock the door," she had said, her final words to Philippa, not "Goodbye," not "I love you," just "Lock the door." Moments later, Philippa and all her sisters had watched as Mistress Haggart lay bleeding to death on the dry Barrens. Since then they had only seen darkness. The only possible image still in their minds was Haggart lying on the ground, as Philippa knew all too well.

"We need some light," Philippa said aloud, hearing tears in her voice. She swallowed hard, shook her head, and spoke more clearly. "We can risk it. If they thought we were down here they would have already torn the boardwalk apart. We will find just a little light, and then we can find a way out."

No one had a candle or a match. Of course they were unprepared. It had been bedtime. They had all been getting ready for sleep. Most were in their bedclothes.

A small hand tugged at Philippa's sleeve. "Mistress Cree?" the little girl asked.

"Yes, Maggie?" Philippa said, recognizing the voice.

"You promise you won't be mad?" Maggie asked.

"Mad at what?" Philippa asked, wondering how she could ever be mad at one so young.

"You need some light," she said, and a tiny dull puffball of light, no bigger than a pea appeared out of Maggie's upper back, curled up over her shoulder, and faded away as it danced into the sky. Another small fuzzy ball came out of her belly and curled away too. Then another popped out of the side of her head.

"I call them fireflies," she said ashamedly, as soft glowing spheres drifted out of her skin and swirled around her before fading away. The younger sisters snatched at the lights, which faded in their hands like soap bubbles. "I'm sorry," Maggie said, "Mistress Haggart said not to." Then the little girl wagged her finger and copied Haggart's tone, "*Under no circumstances!* That's how she said it."

"Fireflies," Philippa said, watching the girl light up their edge of the room. "Haggart knew?"

Maggie nodded, "She said if anyone found out—"

"She'd spit at your feet and send you away," Philippa finished for her, as a deeper more sorrowful shame filled her soul. "She'd have to, to protect the rest of us."

"Do you think she's mad?" Maggie asked, as more light danced around her tiny frame.

Philippa pulled the little girl in and hugged her tightly, weeping into her faded white bed clothes. "No, Maggie. Mistress Haggart would understand. I just wish I had." And as she held the girl who just this morning she would have called a witch, dancing fireflies floated up into the Escapement's sky. And in the unworldly glow, Philippa saw hanging from the Uptown ledge Olen's knotted rope.

38

The Golden Manors

Edwin marched up to the lounging guards like a shortchanged trader. Tall wooden ships clunked their hulls against long oaken docks, as brass bells clanged limply in the humid breeze. Gulls cried as they dove from mast to sea.

"Very well, men, let's have it!" Edwin said, putting his hands on his hips.

"Go away before I bust your skull, gramps," one of the men growled.

"Not without my reward," the smaller Edwin demanded, undeterred.

A stocky guard moved past and rammed his shoulder into Edwin's, sending him twirling in his ministerial robes.

"How's that for a reward, milord?" the soldier asked and slapped palms with his crew.

Edwin regained his balance and composure and straightened out his clothes. Then he asked in his most piqued voice, "Are you not the mighty guards from Millthrace sent here to retrieve wanted criminals, or are you merely the local dog-catching crew?"

The soldiers rose and gathered around him. Marko peered over the crates. He did not appear likely to burst onto the scene and take over, so Edwin continued, less certain of himself.

"Because if you're searching for criminals, I have one of them here."

"Where, here?" a guard asked, unconvinced.

"Well, actually *right* here—," Edwin said, offering himself, but was cut off by a brutish voice behind him.

"Look what I found," a wily but gruff soldier said as he marched down the planks from the city square. He dragged a small girl by the scruff of her neck. She kicked and clawed at the muscle-bound man, and caught his forearm in her teeth more than once. He hoisted her in the air by the back of her shirt, and held her an arm's length away. "They warned us she was a fighter! I bet she could take Otto down, best two outta three!"

"Watch yer mouth, Walt, or I'll knock ya into the sea," the chubby Otto shot back.

"Olen!" Edwin gasped, forgetting his character. It truly was her dangling there before him. After all these months and all these leagues, they were back together. He had found her! Forget about Walt, Edwin felt justified in taking credit for this one. He had not been forced by some phantom drive to seek her out; he had made a plan to search for the girl, and now here she was! He looked over to Marko behind the crates and beamed. Marko angrily waved him off.

She stopped fighting the guard and looked up. "Edwin the Observer?"

"Historia—"

"You look like a grandpa with that beard. I don't like it." she said, swinging lazily in Walt's grip.

The circle around Edwin fell open, and the eldest of the soldiers looked between the old man and the girl. The older guard demanded an explanation. Edwin identified him as the leader, and certain money holder.

"She is with me!" Edwin stated pointedly. "That is what I have been trying to tell you! I captured this...ragamuffin along the highway and brought her in to Brennan. That is when this brute—Walt, you call him—stole her from my grip, saying there was no way a commoner was going to get his reward! Well, Walt the Difficult, I may be common, but I caught her, so the reward is mine!"

"Reward," Walt asked. "What in Nerikan's chains is he talkin' about Emmet?"

Emmet, Edwin quickly noted. *The leader's name was Emmet. Short fat Otto, and the muscular Walt.*

Captain Emmet stumbled for his words as his troops watched him curiously.

It was Marko, master of all the swindles, who seemed to understand Emmet's scam. He came quickly around the carts and praised the rough group of soldiers.

"Mayor Brynn!?" Edwin said to Marko's admirable delight. "Is that you?"

Mayor Marko thanked Edwin for his help in tracking down the said ragamuffin and then asked the soldiers if their captain had kept them well fed on their long sojourn.

"We've been starvin' our arses off in this damned smoky town," the rather obese Otto said, drawing a concerned touch from the kindly mayor.

Emmet finally spoke up, "Now just one minute. This is not Mayor Brynn, he looks nothing like him!"

"Oh ho ho," Marko laughed and sauntered right up to the head guard. He patted him strongly on the cheek, an act a breath away from a slap. "Same old Emmet! Don't worry, you have done well and shall be rewarded accordingly. But for now, Walt has the girl, so give him his coins."

"Yeah," Walt demanded. "Gimme my coins!"

"Ay!" Otto shouted. "What about us? We worked just as hard as Walt, here!"

"Yeah," the rest of the troops called out, and demanded Emmet give them a share.

Marko winked at Edwin and encouraged him on.

Edwin shouted above them all claiming it was he who had found the girl, and it was he who should get the reward. Then he slapped his thigh and declared, "If it were not for me, none of you would have even known about the gold pieces!"

Walt dropped Olen. She landed on her hands and knees and skittered away as Walt advanced on Emmet. The Millthrace guardsmen all jumped to their feet and circled their leader. Dockworkers who had been watching the altercation sensed the chill in the air and quietly slipped back onto their ships, or farther into the city.

"Gold pieces?" Walt asked, craning his neck as if inspecting his leader and truly seeing him for the first time. "They gave us golden manors?"

Mayor Marko leaned in and cheerfully added, "Two of them! And more for expenses!"

Otto stalked Emmet next, "And you were just gonna keep 'em for yourself, as we starved eatin' nothing but jerked beef?"

"Show us your purse!" Edwin demanded, in the boldest voice he could muster. He was seconded by all the Millthrace guards.

Emmet slipped a couple fingers inside his waistband and pulled out a small pouch. He untied it from his belt loop and held it high above his head. "Two gold pieces for reward," he finally admitted and was met with angry shouts. "And twenty more silvers for expenses."

Emmet tried to explain himself as he backed slowly to the docks. He said they claimed to have only eaten jerked beef, but they had also imbibed on whatever spirits these ships had delivered. His soldiers stalked him step for step, the small bag of coins dangling just out of their reach. Emmet said they had already gone through ten of the honors, and had nothing to show for it but hangovers, bruises, and worthless trinkets from overseas. "I kept the money from you, not to rob you, but only so we would have some left for when we were called home!"

"Are you saying you don't trust your own men?" Edwin asked, so deep into his character he truly felt like the coins had been pilfered from his coffers. The guards shouted in agreement as they pursued their leader down the long pier.

"I will trust my men in battle, even to the death!" Emmet said, as he backed away. "But with gold, I trust no man—"

"Not even yourself!" Marko shouted triumphantly, to the hurrahs of Edwin and the soldiers. Together Edwin and Marko emoted dramatically as mayor and mercenary, working the soldiers into a manic frenzy, while plotting on the fly for the gold. They were flawless in their act and worked off each other, feeding openings and taunts that the other man ran with, fully in character and fully convincing; the greatest two-man show in Brennan.

***

In the growing commotion Olen sidled next to Edwin, his eyes fixated on the dangling purse. Had it been a hunk of steak, he would have been drooling. She kicked him in the shins, breaking him free from the trance.

"What the devil?" he said.

"Be ready to run," she said.

"Not without our money," Edwin's friend shot back.

"*That* money is going into the sea," she said, and their heads turned. "Don't worry about your gold coins, I will get them. But when that purse goes in the water, run!"

She moved between thick legs and drawn swords as the coup escalated at the docks. Emmet had backed away as far as he could and was nearing the end of the piers. Sea water crashed against the docks, and gulls squealed overhead. His men were now left to shouting and demanding their reward. Only Olen knew Emmet had them right where he wanted them. She was the only one not surprised when the captain spun around and launched his coin purse deep into the bay along the shores of Brennan. She had seen this act so many times before on the streets of home. All ten troops of the Millthrace guard leapt into the cold waters right after their reward.

"Go," she yelled to Edwin, who struggled to hold his friend back from diving in also. He pulled the man away and dragged him into town as guardsmen dove deep into the waters after a prize that truly was not there. Captain Emmet tried to run away, but Olen leapt in front of him.

"How will I get home?" she asked, pleading desperately with the guard and tugging at his shirt.

"How the hell would I know," he said and tossed her aside.

When Olen sat up she held in her hand the tiny pouch that had been hiding inside Emmet's shirt, just over his heart. She stuffed the gold coins in her pocket and ran after Edwin.

39

Bakku's Wound

Koertig kicked in the doors to city hall. His men raced past him and held their torches aloft in the empty room. Gone.

"Look for hidden doors," he ordered. "Tear down walls if you have to."

He raced up the stairway to the briefing room. It too was deserted. Everything of Brynn's had disappeared from the city. His home, his office, even his private rooms below the Eagle and Trout were all emptied. It was the same for Reeve and Graeme, tables, chairs, everything they owned had somehow escaped the city, unseen.

He tore open the shutters from the empty meeting room and looked down on Midtown. His men had taken over the city, going door to door searching for the three Aurling moles. The river had ceased flowing and all of the waterwheels were still. The Ward was gone and the fires in Lowtown were under control. Philippa was dead, and it was because of him.

It had happened again, he thought, not wanting the memory to surface.

He saw rooftops through the shutters, and shadows of his men leaping over the spans. He thought of Illsbrook, and his wasted youth. At night he and his friend Jay—no longer boys, but still not men—had leapt across the adobe roofs of Queenstown. They had laid under the stars, high above the filthy city streets, and talked about joining the army. And when the sounds had ceased below them, and drunken men trundled out of their mothers' bedrooms, still tying up their braies, the boys had peered over the roof edge and chucked pebbles at their heads.

But Jay had had a couple years on Harner, and his thoughts had matured before his friend's. So as young Koertig sat alone on the adobe rooftop trying not to hear the sounds of the double betrayal, he stoked his anger and hardened his resolve. His mother and friend had combined their fates in an unconscionable act a mere pebble to the skull would not amend. In Queenstown, murder of cads and whores was apathetically investigated. And as young Koertig lay under a sky of watchful stars, he twirled his father's knife in his right hand. By morning, Harner Koertig was far away from Illsbrook and utterly alone.

And alone he remained for all those years until a nurse from Lowtown took up his care. Even now, after she was gone, he found it impossible to sort his feelings about her. She had been everything he was taught to dislike. A penniless orphan bred of the lowest class, she had hardly even been gifted with the looks to draw a poor man's eye. However, he had been drawn to her. The days were longer when his nurse was not around, the pain in his shoulder more severe. And even when she rejected him and fled to the Ward, his desire surged for the girl who had the strength to walk away. She never would have *gone to Illsbrook*. Philippa Cree would have found a different way. He loved that about her, and now she was dead. He had killed her.

He slapped the shutter shut as footsteps pounded up the stairs.

"Sir," a guard said, as he rushed into the room. "It is Martz, trouble uptown. The beast. He is back."

"Round up all the men!" Koertig said, his words angry. "And I mean all the men! Not just the soldiers, but every man in this city. Soldiers to the roofs!" He turned to leave and saw Mayor Brynn's golden sword on the wall. He tore it down and fed it into his belt loop. Then he ran to Uptown, hoping Philippa had given Martz his note.

By the time Koertig reached the back wall of Millthrace, a massive tree trunk had already been flung through the rampart. The mended wall was again damaged and split wide in the middle, but no Bakku. There was silence as all waited for orders or for something to happen. They did not have to wait long.

A carriage-sized boulder exploded through the barricade and smashed through a two-story home, rolling to a halt on the Uptown walk.

In hushed tones Koertig ordered his men to retreat behind a row of homes, "Stay back! Let it approach!"

They gladly obeyed and withdrew behind their Lieutenant Colonel. Koertig checked the skyline and saw Martz quietly ordering his men among the rooftops. Just out of sight, he knew the men were dipping their spears in laburnum pitch, and readying the nets. The back wall of Millthrace lay open wide.

The ground shook and the walls rumbled. Koertig held steady. Then Bakku leapt into the borough, roaring. He bellowed a call that shook the city. He thundered past the rear buildings, dragging down supports and collapsing upper floors under Martz soldiers. He grasped a beam midstride and launched it at the Skywheel. The log cartwheeled through the sky and crashed through the crosswise supports, shattering a carriage and dropping the tall structure to a slant.

"Janus!" Bakku roared, swinging his backhand into a fine linen shop, smashing windows and doors.

Koertig stood alone in the streets, just around the corner and out of the beast's view. A hundred armed men stood far behind him, many more lay hidden above. The creature plucked a granite goddess from the dry fountain and flung it deep into Midtown.

"Janus! Here I am!" Bakku yelled. "End this!"

"I am here!" Koertig said, and the monster turned towards the sound. Bakku stepped forward, and Koertig drew the golden sword.

"Is it you?" Bakku asked, fiery hate in his words. "Is this the face you've chosen, Janus?"

"The Aurling menace Janus Brynn has left this city a coward," Koertig said coldly, holding the point of his sword out at the creature. "I am Harner Koertig, Lieutenant Colonel of Eisen. I am to return you to your prison."

"I come only for Janus," Bakku said, undeterred. "Once he is mine, you may have your city."

"That is the same proposal the Aurling Brynn offered for your tainted soul. I will accept no accord," he said, stepping forward, the golden sword held out before him. "You are an Aurling scion and a menace to this world. You will return to Nerikan Prison where you will await your compatriot, the former Mayor-General Brynn. In the black halls of Nerikan you may do with him as you please, but neither of you will ever be allowed to leave."

"I will have Janus if I have to tear down every wall of this city!" Bakku demanded, and smashed his fist through the wood and stone of an Uptown abode.

"And I will have you back in your cell, even if it means delivering your corpse!" Koertig replied.

Bakku threw his head back, waved his arms out wide, and laughed. "Death! I welcome it! Do you not know? Did Janus not tell you? I am Bakku! The monster who forgot how to die!"

Still Koertig held the golden sword out before himself. The yellow tip never wavered as the mighty creature feinted and yelled.

"There was a girl," Koertig said, and Bakku ceased his laughter. "An orphan, known to tear about the sewers." The creature pounded his right and then his left fist into the thick boardwalk. A shuffling came from the rooftops. "You seemed to have taken a liking to her," Koertig said. Bakku raised his head slowly and stared down the one-armed man. He seemed to recognize Koertig then and understand the wound he had survived. Koertig smiled and nodded at the monster. "If you cannot die, perhaps she will take your place?"

It was the push the creature needed, and he reacted as Koertig had hoped. Bakku launched himself down the alley. A hailstorm of poison-tipped spears flew from the rooftops and jabbed at the beast. The heavy weapons rained down on Bakku and cut at his flesh. Some spikes fell to the ground, only grazing his thick skin, but many dug deep into his scarred hide. Martz sent out a call from the rooftops, and webbed shadows flew overhead. Thick-roped nets covered in pitch flew down and landed on the creature. Bakku swung at the netting and wrapped himself in the sticky trap. Another call, and another flurry of spears shot down, cutting deep ruts in the ogre. He roared and clawed but only worked the pitched-covered nets into unbreakable knots. He wrestled with himself trying to break free of the bindings, but the poison seeped into his blood and slowed him. Then the footmen on the city streets were upon him. They jabbed their poisoned spears into the beast and hacked at his thighs with their hatchets. The monster bled, and its bright flesh turned grey. He swung at the city men, but the sticky web held him. They jabbed some more at his scarred flesh, hacking away chunks of hide. The beast weakened and slowed, and his eyes dropped deeply. He flailed weakly now. His arms wound tightly in netting. With one last push, Bakku tore at the web over his head and then dropped. He fell to his knees, nearly unconscious. He dropped to one arm. His eyes rolled, and his breathing came in short bursts. His knees buckled, his arms gave way, and he collapsed deadweight to the ground. His head lay down on the boardwalk, and his eyes focused as if staring through cracks in the wood. A brief smile crossed his lips, and then Bakku fell unconscious and resisted no more.

Koertig calmly walked up to the sleeping beast, admiring his capture. Bakku lay on his side like a sleeping child, its shoulder as tall as Koertig stood.

"You will find you can and will die, Aurling, even if I have to take you apart piece by piece." And with one left-handed whack of the golden sword, he lopped off Bakku's giant right thumb.

***

Philippa helped all of the sisters up the rope and then climbed up herself. Maggie and her fireflies led the way across dry river beds and over crude driftwood bridges, the dancing fireflies lingering long enough for each sister to pass. They found more sewer tunnels heading farther uptown and ran inside them. Up ahead the brick passages looked different. She asked Maggie to wait and then moved up to look.

The tunnels branched and widened. She entered the wider tunnel and looked ahead. Then she saw the vast room that waited.

"In here," she motioned to the girls, and they all went in.

They had found the back wall of Millthrace. She had Maggie jog around the perimeter, and the images she revealed confirmed Philippa's thoughts. They were at the back end of Uptown, at the part of the city highest up the mountain. This must be where Olen made it out, but she could not figure out how. She searched for an exit in near darkness, and then looked up. The dark Uptown boardwalk hung high above their heads, far away from Maggie's fireflies. But all it took was just a tiny glint off of a metal fin, and Philippa's mind filled in the rest of the edges around the old waterwheel, so many stories above.

"Oh my goodness, Olen!" Philippa said. "You climbed up there?"

All of the girls saw the faint horizontal crack between the board-walk ceiling and the mountain ledge above. The great Oiskonn must have flowed over that ledge and powered that wheel for ages, but now it was dry and the wheel was still. It was the only way out, and one of their own had already made it through.

"We are safe here for now," Philippa told the girls. "But at first light we climb."

Moments later, as the girls huddled together for warmth and com-fort. The ceiling above shook violently. The girls heard, but did not see, as Bakku crashed through the back wall, and battled for his life right above their heads.

***

As blood had spilled from his wounds, and poison clouded his mind, Bakku had felt himself falling away. He had collapsed to the boardwalk, and sleep called him to rest. He knew he would not die. He knew he would wake. It had happened before. His thoughts drifted, and the pain drained from his wounds. He would awake in Nerikan and start again his long sentence. But Olen would be safe. No creatures would hunt her anymore. He would let the gores feed forever, knowing little Olen was all right.

His head fell to the boards, and he moved no more. His large eyes fought to stay open, but darkness flowed over his mind. He peered downward through the uneven boardwalk and saw faint light below. He hoped it was not a trick of the poison as he saw his little girl, his Olen, happy and safe, dancing below in the light of fireflies. He smiled and remembered no more.

40

Faerie Stories

Edwin ran with Marko and Olen through the smoggy streets of Brennan, laughing. His aging legs and aching lungs launched him through alleyways and squirreled him past locals, his robes flapping behind him. He had found Olen and Marko, captured the gold, and left the Millthrace guards splashing in the bay.

"Remember," Edwin said through labored breaths, "I earned back my share of the gold!"

"Fifty-fifty," Marko said, as they sprinted past marketplace traders, jostling their wares.

"Hey! What about me?" Olen demanded. "I'm the one who actually got it!"

They ran towards Sonny who stood tied near the granite arches leading out to the Bluestem Prairie. Marko unhooked his donkey and pulled him about face. Sonny stepped quicker than any donkey had ever moved, as if he understood their need for swiftness. He clicked his hoofs on the stone and scurried ahead. Olen and Edwin cackled as they ran.

Edwin had never cared much for animals, pets especially. There were the infamous library cats that prowled the University archives. Edwin had always seen them as just one more distraction from his already overdue studies. He felt the same about dogs who found it a daily delight to violate their superiors with their probing wet noses. But he had grown accustomed to Sonny. Sonny moved when asked, stopped when told, and otherwise simply chewed his grass, quietly observing the world, much like himself. He truly liked the donkey, which was why his heart ached so badly when the spear entered Sonny's hind quarters, buckling his legs, and dropping the beloved pet to the ground.

The trio skidded to halt just past the Brennan arches.

"Sonny!" Marko cried out and fell to the donkey's side. The spear had struck high on its back end near his spine. Sonny bleated as Marko pressed against the bloody wound.

The crowds behind them parted and Captain Emmet emerged. "Hand me back my purse!" he demanded.

"Hand me your life!" Marko roared to the guard, shaking the massive granite walls of the coastal city. For it was not the voice of Marko that forced the crowds back a step and stilled the stunned merchants. It was the unmasked voice of a man who had given up a violent past to become Marko Meloon. It was the fierce voice of a warrior, a commander of a vast forgotten army. Edwin saw the ferocious passion of the man who had since become the lonesome trader. Even Emmet pulled back instinctively at the commanding shout. The story of University and his time as a performer was just one more lie in the character that had become Marko. For that brief moment, Marko commanded all of Brennan, and all of Brennan obeyed.

Sonny convulsed and his eyes fell shut. Marko's brow softened, and he placed his arms around his dying companion. He held Sonny and whispered in his ear.

The rest of the thuggish Millthrace soldiers pushed through the crowd, soaking wet and furious. Emmet pointed to the trio and ordered his men ahead, wary to attack Marko alone. "The girl took your gold!" he called out, and then said those words Edwin would always remember, "Kill her."

Otto launched his spear straight at Olen and she screamed.

Edwin leapt in front of her, but was cast aside by an unknown force.

He was thrown to the ground as a smoky black tempest erupted around him, Marko, and—

Olen...

Where she had been now stood a tiny angel in white, glowing brighter than the summer sun and more fiercely than the Brennan ironworks. She was encased in billowing robes of radiant starlight and her long raven locks flowed majestically around her. She stood entranced, her arms out to her sides, unconsciously guiding the twisting black cyclone that surrounded them and funneled itself high up over their heads. It was no less than a tornado, and they all stood safely in its center.

The smoky whirlpool had cast aside the iron-tipped spear, sending it harmlessly to the ground. Edwin helped Marko to his feet as they both shielded their eyes.

"I have seen this," Edwin said, coughing on a mouthful of dirt. "In the books. I have seen this before. Olen!" He stood in front of the girl and waved his hands in front of her face. Her lifeless eyes stared through the swirling clouds. "Give just a little more, child. Let it flow."

Her face turned away from the twisting wall, and she looked upon Edwin. She looked confused, as if she did not recognize him.

"Do not fight it!" he told her. "It is good! Let it flow out."

Another burst of light rippled through her robes, and a rolling wake traveled up the coiling spire.

And then it happened.

An orb appeared before them, nearly as tall as Edwin. Brilliant white clouds swirled within. The clouds darkened as dust and debris from this world were sucked into the vortex. A ripple shot through her cyclone, and the clouds within the orb cleared. Like a seer's glass, a world appeared floating beyond the sphere. Tall colorful grasses waved in a vast prairie. At the edge of the lowlands stood a cluster of huts, aged and brown. And beyond the huts, a river flowed, and a wide tent village sat along its bank. It was Kessel, and it was mere footsteps away. Edwin pulled Marko away from Sonny. The donkey lay motionless on the ground. Marko clutched at him as Edwin tossed him into the ball-like portal. Edwin followed and traveled through to the other side.

Olen still stood in Brennan, angelic in her light. He called after her begging her to follow, but she was locked in. He stepped back through the sphere and held her shoulders. He slowly turned the girl, not daring to jar her free from her trance. He pointed her at the opening.

"Are you ready?" he called out.

She murmured an incoherent response.

"Walk with me." He held her hand as his white beard whipped about his face. She stepped forward, blindly following him. "It is just like stepping through a doorway," he assured her, and pulled her through. As she entered the sphere, the cyclone fell away and he could see the people of Brennan standing in awe. In a few steps they emerged into the open air outside of Kessel—at least a two-hour walk from Brennan. The orb still sat open, though now it appeared to be Brennan beyond the sphere. "Release it," he said gently.

Her eyes refocused, as if waking from a deep sleep. The glowing ball began to wane.

"Wait!" It was Marko and he was at his knees by the orb, peering back into Brennan. A large shape was coming through. "Sonny!" he called out. The donkey pulled itself through the orb as the walls collapsed around it. "Hurry!" Marko cried, as Sonny struggled to walk dragging its hind leg behind, the spear still sticking out of its back.

"Olen, can you hold it just—" Edwin said, but she woke in his arms, dazed. The sphere collapsed around Sonny like a horrible spider web encasing its victim. Olen's bright clothes faded to rags. "No!" Edwin cried out, and she finally saw.

She pulled her elbows back and burst forward again with heavenly brightness as an even greater cyclone erupted. The tunnel widened, and Marko pulled the donkey through.

"Okay child," Edwin called through the storm, but Olen shook her head.

"I can't—" she said and grew impossibly brighter. The storm raged on with even greater speed, churning the orb into a blur. No longer did Brennan show through the bubble, but a much more distant land. The image blinked and a frozen wasteland emerged. "I—" Olen said, trying to break free from her own powers. The image through the storm flashed again and a barren rocky plain shown through. Then the child let out a cry Edwin would remember for the rest of his life. It was pain; it was fear, and it was complete loss of control.

The orb flashed once more, and a crystalline shatter echoed across all of Eisen. Through the doorway a black void appeared. Edwin observed firelights, distant pricks of yellow against the veil. They moved slowly yet haphazardly in the darkness. He sensed awareness in these points of lights and a sudden realization someone had broken through into their world. They turned now and converged, unifying their movement. From the distant vault they approached the light of Eisen. Hundreds, now thousands of firelights, racing towards Olen's gate.

Edwin shook the child by the shoulders and called her name. He pulled her in to his chest and danced her around, finally breaking her trance. Again her light faded, and the bubble collapsed, just as the lights neared the entrance. The storm ended and the world calmed. Brennan was far behind them. Olen, Marko, and even Sonny were safe. Edwin laid her back onto the grass. She was unconscious, but she was alive.

Townspeople from Kessel had gathered around the three. Among them was Leo. He was shirtless and a sticky mess of herring and brine.

"Quite the show," Leo said, waving one of his men over to check on Olen. He was a healer of some sort and placed his ear to her chest. Leo waved another man over to help Edwin to his feet, and offered his own hand to Marko. "Sorry about your donkey. I have someone who will help," he said. "Did you get my fish?"

***

Olen hugged Bakku's neck as he strode through the Caraway Mountains. Over the far horizon, flutes and lyres and angel voices sang their welcome. They were nearly to Calderra, nearly to their forever-home. He had come back for her, yet again. She hugged his neck as Bakku walked through the bright summer day. But his gait was wrong; slower, shorter strides. And even though he smiled, he struggled to carry her. He stumbled, and Olen jarred herself awake. She awoke inside a large wooden hut in an unknown village. She was being carried childlike around the room's four corners. The man carrying her murmured in her ear and patted her back. She raised her head off of Edwin's shoulders. He gave a strained smile.

"I can walk," she said, wriggling her way out of his arms. "Where are we?"

"A friend's home. In Kessel," he said, helping her to the ground. She tried to stand, but her legs felt wrong. He eased her over to her bed. "Do you remember what happened?" he asked.

They had been in Brennan, she remembered. She was captured. She had seen Edwin, he had looked so old. Soldiers. A donkey. The gold! She dug in her pocket. "Where is it?" she demanded.

"It's okay," Edwin said, fanning his palms at her. "I have the gold manors, and your silver. Marko and I have agreed it is *all* yours. Rules of the road. You completed the swindle better than we did. We just hope you find it in your heart—"

"Keep it," she said. "I will need no coins where I am going. Bakku says there is no currency in Calderra, and even if there was, he and I are better off surviving on our own."

Marko stuck his head in the door.

"I heard voices," he said. "Oh, you are awake!" He welcomed himself in. He offered her a glass carafe covered with threaded reeds. She drank the cool sweetened water.

"After the gold," Edwin continued, "what do you remember?"

She did not remember much. There was light, and wind. Darkness. After that all she remembered was waking up in this town.

"Kessel? Did you say this is Kessel?" she asked, and he nodded. "Mistress Haggart says I am from Kessel! I was just a baby. She says my parents are from Kessel."

She had made it. She almost wanted to laugh. It had been one heck of a journey but she had made it from the Barrens of Millthrace all the way to Kessel. She wanted Bakku to know. He would be so proud of her, so happy. It just felt strange to say it, but she was in Kessel. The most mythical place in her mind.

Edwin pulled a travel sack from underneath her cot. Inside it was an old leatherbound. "You have had quite the adventure since we parted ways, Olen Marine. I too have had a rather exciting journey. I have been collecting books along the way and educating myself on this land's strange history." He paged through the tome and folded back the cover. He held a painted plate out to the girl. "Does this look familiar?" he asked.

It was an image of man. His hands bound behind him. He stood on a burning pyre, tied to a stake. Townspeople surrounded him, faces angry, frightened. They held red fire on torches. The fire at the foot of the pyre and all of the torches swirled in a tempest. The burning man appeared in a trance with his head up and his eyes rolled back. A churning ball of fire and wind swept around him and shot straight up to the heavens in a swirling column of light. Ahead of him an orb opened up to foreign land. The plate was titled, "The Devil is Cast".

"This is what I saw," Edwin said. "This is how you saved us."

"Minus the fire," Marko added.

Olen grabbed the book and studied the plate.

"This book," Edwin said, tapping the page. "This book I purchased here in Kessel. It contains the town's myths and legends. This is the story of the execution of an Aurling, not far from this very spot. You have the same magic as this man. And now you tell me you are from this city."

"Is this my father?" she asked confusedly, as she looked at the man writhing in agony.

"Not possible," Edwin answered quickly. "This man died over two hundred years ago. But I believe he left something. Something an infant girl happened to find."

The door opened again, and Leo walked in. "The price was cheap," he said happily. "I bought off everyone in town for just a copper each. That will be forty three coppers," he said, and held out his hand.

Marko balked and tried to work out a better price, as Olen studied the image. This was not Janus Brynn torturing an Aurling like he had Bakku. These were regular people throwing torches and shouting.

The hate on their faces is what she saw most as they burned the magical man.

Edwin got between Marko and Leo and handed over his final two silver honors. "Keep the seven coppers against future debts," Edwin said, and muttered that somehow he was not surprised he was once again penniless. "I believe we will have a few more favors to ask. For now I am merely satisfied no one will speak of our unique arrival.

"Can I hold on to this?" Olen asked about the book, and Edwin nodded.

41

Rope

Dawn's light fingered its way through the Uptown boardwalk and into the underworld. The children of the Ward had risen before the sun and had searched every corner of the room. Philippa lay back against a boulder staring up at the pylons and beams that led out. She could not have these girls climb that high, nor expect them, hungry and scared, to have the balance to tip-toe across to the exit. If even one of them fell—

"No," she said, shaking off the thought. But they could not go back either.

The younger girls played in the still moist sand and built tiny homes out of the silt. They moved with the sun and stayed under its warm beams as the yellow rays traced across the floor. She would climb, Philippa thought. She would climb alone to the top beam and make her way out of Millthrace. From there she could find help while keeping her sisters safe in this shelter. She would send food down, somehow. This was the best way, she decided.

She was jerked out her thoughts by the sound of a heavy iron gong. *Donng!* The sound reverberated throughout the stones and ironworks. Everyone froze in place. Even the workers above stopped moving. No one knew what it was, until a little voice came from a nook in the rock where the water had once crashed over the falls.

"Sorry," the unseen Maggie said.

Philippa threw her arms out and patted down the air, telling the girls to be still and quiet. After a few moments the footfalls began scraping again across the boardwalk, and the sawing and hammering above resumed.

Philippa ran across the room and climbed the small rise of slippery rocks in front of the recess. The stones were smooth here. Maggie stood in the hollow just out of the sunlight looking embarrassed.

"It slipped," she said, and pointed to the large iron knocker that lay on the ground, angled against two massive iron gates. The doors sat deep in the recess and seemed to lead even deeper under the Rückraadt Mountains. On their surface were etched three circles connected by double lines.

"I tried opening it, but it fell apart," Maggie said.

The iron ring was half Maggie's size and probably many times her weight. Philippa felt the broken hinge on the ring and on the gate. Its jagged edges crumbled under her strong fingers.

"This is one very old doorway," Philippa said, studying the gate. "It must be a way out."

The rest of the girls had gathered around her now and were looking on. They had not eaten since dinner at the Ward. A way out meant food.

"We have to open it," Philippa said, running her hand over the doors. The other gate had a similar iron loop. The rusted edges of this ring had lain against the gates for so many years. They had fused with the door, making the whole thing one. She tugged at the ring, but it did not move at all.

"Rope," she said, turning to her wards. "We need rope. Your hems, your sleeves, those who brought robes and blankets; we need to make a rope long enough for us all to pull, and strong enough to move those doors."

"That won't work," Maggie said and dashed back towards the tunnels. "But I know what will!"

"Wait," Philippa called to her, but she was already gone. This child with her rogue independence was starting to remind her of Olen. She smiled at the thought, realizing how not long ago she would have meant that as an insult. She wondered if these were the only two special sisters Mistress Haggart had harbored.

"Tell me, sisters," Philippa said, "It is no longer time for secrets. I need to know, do any more of you have a special something, like Olen's clothes and Maggie's fireflies, that Mistress Haggart asked you hide?"

She had not thought anyone would speak up, and none did, but one girl—Icha, her head still wrapped in her Swarhee scarf—turned away in shame. *My god, Haggart,* she thought, *how did you find them all?*

It was only moments later they heard the quick and hollow steps of Maggie racing back up the brick sewer, sparse fireflies leading the way. She rushed into the room dragging a long knotted rope behind her.

"Olen's rope from Midtown!" Philippa said.

"Yeah," Maggie said, "I had to cut it, so I guess there's no going back."

"Fine by me," Philippa answered, and checked the ends. One end of the rope had fluffy frayed edges, while the other was black and crusted. She looked at Maggie.

"By cut it, I mean *burned* it," Maggie said, giving Philippa a look that asked if she was in trouble. Philippa just smiled.

"Good job, Maggie. Let's go!" She took the rope to the door and tied it tight around the edges of the iron knocker. She tossed the rest of the rope to the sisters who all lined up and pulled it taut. Then Philippa, closest to the gate, closed her fist over a knot and called to her girls, "Pull!"

***

Olen had grown tired of Edwin asking her to stay in bed and rest. She was eager to explore the town and her past. When he had finally left her hut in the morning, she had climbed out of the only window and stood before the Wide Galenic River. Edwin had told her the water smelled like blood, but to her it was more like rotten eggs. She could not imagine why her parents, or anyone, had chosen to live here. In all of her fantasies of Kessel, she had never thought it would smell so bad.

Near the shore was a measuring bob just like in Millthrace, but unlike in Millthrace this bob was ignored with tall reeds growing all around it.

She walked the town, moving past tented shops pitched between mossy-green willow trees, their long branches hanging like damp rags. The more permanent structures were here on the river side of Glory Road. The field side was for the Iron Triangle merchants to set their carts and make a few sales as they passed through. She stayed river-side and pretended to be interested in the wares but slipped into conversational questions about a family named Marine. Nobody had answers. She approached a group of older women hanging laundry on a line and asked about the family name.

"Really, you don't remember anyone with that name?" she asked, after they offered no clues. "It could not have been more than ten or eleven years ago. Maybe travelers who left a baby behind, or one of your neighbors who already had too many children?"

"Honey, look around you," the oldest woman said, and pointed out the sparsely populated village. "There is no such thing as too many children around here."

She turned back to the road and found Leo standing behind her. His face was dark and serious. "Follow me," he said, waving her along.

They walked silently and slowly across town. He eased himself along unsteadily as if walking was a rare burden. They reached the edge of town where the elegant willows gave way to heavy oak. He led her on a short path between the trees. The woods opened up into an overgrown meadow. Shoreline reeds reached into the meadow, and yellow moths danced about. Stone slabs stuck out of the ground in crooked angles.

"Over here," he said, and led her past the gravestones. He pulled vines off a granite marker, crudely etched, lacking even a novice stonemason's skill. The name scratched at the top simply said, "Maring."

"Maring?" she asked. "This is wrong. My name is Marine."

"It is not wrong," he said softly. "Yours is the name they gave you, as they began a new life."

Below Maring two names were thinly engraved, "Oma" and "Kavil".

"He came from over the Westing Sea," Leo said. "Sails and rigging were his specialty. She had fled her Swarhee clan in the east. Water was her obsession too, but not for sailing," he said and placed a hand on her shoulder. "Oh, she was always every day taking her little notes on the Wide Galenic; temperature, color, and depth."

Olen remembered the shoreline bob and understood.

"He had given up the sea once their child was born. One or two circuits along the Iron Road to sell his wares, and then they planned to settle south of Ulm. He had mended many of our tents and shown us how to tie them down to resist even the strongest storms."

Olen rubbed her fingertips over the lightly etched names. Oma. Kavil. Her parents. She had found them. Somehow she had found them. For years in the Ward she had dreamed of this reunion, and of all the many ways she had imagined this meeting, she had never played out the version in which they were already gone. All those years that she had thought of them, spoken to them in her mind, they had been lying here in the ground. She forgave them then for not coming for her, for not sending rescue. She had not been unloved and unwanted, she had simply been an orphan. Philippa had been right. All along Philippa had been right and she could finally admit that to herself.

"I'm an orphan," Olen said, and somehow those words were no longer tainted. They were not bad words, only sad words. There was no shame, no dishonor; just a tragedy beyond anyone's control.

She tore away a knot of weeds binding the gravestone and pulled it back to vertical. She then packed handfuls of dirt and stone behind it, keeping it upright.

Oma and Kavil Maring, she thought. They had names, and with those names came images. They were no longer magical wizards from another world. They were people just like everyone else. She saw her father now, riding tall upon the gunwale of a sailing ship, one hand grasping the rigging as the wild sea winds blew his hair, waving to the woman on shore. And now her mother, dark brown eyes, nearly black, peering coyly at him through her scarf-wrapped head, a notebook in her hand, waiting impatiently on the Brennan docks. And in that moment Olen truly had found her parents.

"Hi Mom," she said, curling her arm around the stone and resting her forehead against the cool granite. The tears were not painful, they were a relief, the release of a deep ache she held in for so long. "Hi Dad. I found you," she said, as a deep exhale escaped her soul. "I know you didn't mean to lose me, but I found you," she said and wept openly against the stone.

I have so much to tell you.

She stayed at the grave, trying to remember the stories she had saved, trying to remember her previous life when all she thought of was escaping the Ward and searching out her real family. But the only thought that kept racing through her mind was how she wanted Bakku to know. *I found them Bakku,* she wanted to yell. *You won't believe it, but I found them!*

A victory, however small, for the child who was now once again alone. She sat back on her heels and wiped her arm across her eyes. "How?" she asked Leo, without looking up.

"They were too trusting and had drawn evil eyes their way," Leo continued. "When all you do is sell on the Iron Road, desperate ones take notice. Someone had found out the Marings were stockpiling silvers. They were finally heading south to Ulm when they were attacked just outside of Kessel."

Leo's face changed, like a cloud rolling over the sun.

"It was not hard to find the killers. I have many friends along the highway," he said proudly but then hung his head. "We left their carcasses for the crows."

She saw it pained him to bring up the memory.

"And what about me?" she asked. "How did I get to Millthrace?"

Leo shook free from his dark countenance. He smiled at the girl. "Oh, I guess that would be me," he said. "You were found unharmed in your parent's wagon, and two days later I had recaptured your father's purse." He waved her to her feet and leaned on her shoulder as he hobbled out of the meadow. "I knew of a woman in Millthrace who secreted away weird children."

"Hey!" Olen shot back, and Leo quickly apologized. He explained that in his vernacular, *weird* was not a disparaging term.

"Somewhere between a quick-talking side show illusionist and an actual cackling Nerikan witch is where I would place the weird ones. Middling magic users, if I should say it concisely. Your swaddled robes," he added, "They had changed color three times the first night we had found you! So, away you went to Millthrace, and I funneled your coins along at a regular pace."

"Wait," she broke in to his tale. "Haggart secreted away *magic users*? Do you mean she knew about me?"

"Knew about you? Child, once she learned of you, she *demanded* I deliver you!"

He again leaned on the child, struggling to maintain his balance. They walked back through the town and found Edwin and Marko standing outside Leo's tent. Olen could not help but notice the ship-like rigging. They all greeted each other kindly. By the look on Edwin and Marko's faces, they already knew where Leo had taken her.

"It is alright," Olen said. "I just needed to know."

Edwin knelt down and gave the girl a long hug while Marko patted her head. She fought the tears, bracing herself against the fact that in a short span of time she had lost both birth parents and also a surrogate mother and father.

"I have made a decision," Olen said, as Edwin pulled away. "I am going to find Bakku. I am going to Calderra."

"Calderra?" Leo said aghast. "Why ever would you go there?"

"It is where Bakku has fled to," she explained. "A land west of Bran's Wall."

"Child," Leo said, "Calderra is not a land. Calderra is Fire Mountain. It is a molten pit of liquid inferno. An open bowl of churning viscous flame!"

Edwin explained softly, "Calderra is a volcano."

Olen finally understood why Bakku had not allowed her to follow.

He had left her behind so he could leap into the fires of Calderra and finally end his suffering. He was strong and was granted exceptionally long life, but he had always known that in the end he was flesh and blood, and flesh and blood can be destroyed. And with Bakku utterly destroyed, Brynn would lose his immortal elixir and die also.

"We have to stop him!" she said.

"It appears he has already stopped himself," Marko answered.

Edwin explained, "Word on the highway is there has been a disturbance at Millthrace."

"Bad things are being said," Leo said and hung his head. "Terrible things."

"What do you mean *disturbance*?" she asked.

Marko cut in and gave it to her straight, "Bakku has been captured. Brynn is missing, and Koertig and Martz have taken over the city. They are sending Bakku back to Nerikan Prison."

Olen nearly collapsed. They had captured him, again. Only she knew the true horrors and suffering he had endured in Nerikan, and she could only guess at what he had not told her. He had broken free the last time. After many years of quiet resistance he had broken his chains and fled. They would not make the same mistake again. This time, his sentence truly would be eternal. Forever alone in the darkness of Nerikan. Forever at the mercy of heartless gores. Forever suffering while she ran free. She pulled away from the men and turned back to the road.

"What are you doing?" Edwin called after her.

"I don't know," she said. "But I have got to try something."

"Wait!" he called out, and she stopped momentarily. "Don't go!"

"Why?" she said, looking back on the men.

"Because," he paused and looked to Marko, unsure of himself. Marko encouraged him and motioned him to speak. He did so begrudgingly. "Because we have a plan."

Olen turned full around and saw Marko smiling broadly. Edwin had his face deep in his hands and was massaging his temples.

"It is a damn fool plan, for a damn fool brigade," Edwin murmured, and then dropped his hands and thrust his head high. "And the worst part is, I think it will work. I cannot even talk *myself* out of it!"

"It's a good plan!" Marko agreed.

Leo waved his fingers at one of his helpers who pulled two horses from behind the tent.

42

The Blessington Branch

Thick wooden wheels, each as tall as a man and bound in iron, creaked and groaned as they slowly rolled over a roughly hewn stump in Ma'alabrad Forest. "Easy! Easy!" a worker shouted, guiding the carriage ahead. Six wheels in all skirted the low-slung flatbed as it inched ahead its heavy load. It was the haulage of the Brennan ironworkers, normally used for transferring massive loads between the cities. But the only iron this load carried—as axe-men felled trees and cleared a wide berth ahead—were the thick iron chains around the arms, legs, neck, and chest, of the Aurling Bakku.

The tall wheel cleared the tree base with a thump and rattling of chains.

"Ahead again!" the worker shouted, as the next wheel rolled up the stump.

Koertig rode along on the flatbed, grasping a pole for balance, one foot perched on the thigh of the sleeping beast. Bakku's labored breathing increased, and a guttural moan rose out of his throat. His muscles, lax for so long, tensed and throbbed.

"Martz," Koertig said absently, and his sergeant relayed a call down the line. Two old men in red robes and long salt and pepper beards scurried over to the rolling giant. They mashed together a green and brown mixture of leaves, roots, and a foamy liquid. This they placed in a small bellows with a spear-pointed end, and jammed it into Bakku's belly. One squeeze of the bellows emptied the mixture into Bakku, sending him back to listlessness.

Were this a parade, Koertig thought, there would be no one left to watch it, as every able-bodied man—and some not-so-able-bodied—had joined the caravan. The ironworkers, with their broad shoulders and wide faces tended the iron cart as it was pushed to its limit. The Millthrace guard rode amongst the parade, their silver armor gleaming in the light. A swift-footed militia of bowmen dashed in and out of the woods, on the lookout for wolf-boar and other scions. Far behind it all, and at a safe distance, rode the uptown gentry in covered wagons. The men smoked long thin pipes and chuckled inside their carriages, while the ladies—in their finest—peered through dainty curtains at the wild forest. Following the wealthy were the poor Lowtowners, carrying all of the essentials that the Uptowners could ask for. The rivers were dry in Millthrace, and much of Uptown destroyed. There was little for the townspeople to do but follow the great train and watch Koertig.

No one had accused him, he thought regarding the burning of the Ward. Once Brynn had revealed himself and vanished, it was as if all of Millthrace had forgotten of the Ward and what had transpired. Koertig had not forgotten.

"Get those trees down," he demanded of the axe-men. They moved ahead and continued their hard labor. There are many wonders of this great land, Koertig thought as the workers smoothed a pathway, but who would not marvel at how the long and wide road to Nerikan was built in a day?

They rumbled and clanged ahead.

＊

Two strong horses galloped along the short grasses of the Mecan Plains. They were mud-brown with spotted white patches on their hind quarters. Olen rode one alone, living out a fantasy she had dreamt about while tending Schmid's stables in Millthrace. Her body bent forward, her head up and focused. Alongside her, two men shared a mount. The man in back grasped the reins while the man in front clutched the horse's neck and screamed.

"Slow down!" Edwin yelled, as he bounced about. Marko pulled up on the reins.

Olen swung her appaloosa around and came upon the men. A warm wind blew her black hair about. She wore the pants and shirt like the girl she had seen outside Brennan. One gold coin was gone. She had insisted Leo take it for the horses, and for the care he had promised to give Sonny. Money meant nothing to her if she did not get to Bakku before he was thrown back into Nerikan. She had then thanked him for sending her to Haggart so long ago.

"Please," Edwin pleaded. He had doffed his Millthracian ministerial robes for the same pants and shirt he had purchased from Timo. "Even walking, these fine horses will get us to Millthrace in good time. I could not take one more field at this gait. Every bone in me aches, every bone! I beg you."

Olen looked worried, but Marko seconded Edwin. "We should be able to see the city's skyline soon," he said, his words weary, but not without hope. "We know Koertig is making a slow go of it, and the ironwood trees of Ma'alabrad will halt him even more."

The men's horse blew hot air out of its nose and shook its flank.

"Ride with me, Edwin," she said, sorry she had pushed the beasts so hard for the third day. "Let the horses cool."

Edwin slid down the side of the brown mare, nearly kicking Marko in the face as he fell to the ground. He got to his haunches and flexed his back and neck before standing. He grabbed the front of Olen's saddle and made to pull himself up.

"Behind me!" she said.

"Ah, yes," Edwin said, hefting his frame onto the horse. Settled onto its back, he searched around for someplace to lay his hands, before awkwardly resting them on her shoulders. Olen smiled and wished Bakku could see her. They walked north along the Mecan Plains, just west of the foothills of the Rückraadt Mountains. The sun had started its long descent to the horizon.

Marko, a fine and natural horseman, sidled alongside her as she searched the horizon for signs of the city.

"I understand the first part of your plan," she told him. "But when you catch up to Koertig, what do you expect to do, take on the whole army?"

Even Edwin laughed at that and patted the girl's shoulders.

"The whole army?" Marko asked. "Little girl, that is the easy part! You stand before the talented Marko Meloon, and the brilliant Edwin Ashdown! Together, we *are* an army!"

The men laughed some more and patted shoulders across the gap. Where had all of this confidence come from, she thought. Edwin had even forgotten his saddle sores as he chuckled at the thought of being outsmarted by the Millthrace army.

"Ashdown?" she asked, peering over her shoulder, as Bakku had done to her so any times.

Edwin bowed politely, "Of the Blessington branch, but don't spread it around. You will see more palms than a diviner. Come now, milady, to the city!" He reached back and gently smacked the horse on its behind.

43

The Gate

Philippa wrenched the rope, pressing her feet into the rocks. "Pull!" she said again to the girls heaving behind her. Tiny arms and skinny legs strained as the girls pulled at the black gate under Millthrace. Some gave in, some still pulled, and a few were too frightened to help at all. Philippa relaxed and let the rope drop.

"Let's catch our breath," she suggested and placed her hands on her thighs, sucking in breaths. After her breathing calmed she continued, "If we want to get out of here, we're going to have to get that door open. And that means we'll have to work hard and squeeze every muscle until it hurts, and then just a little bit more. Icha?" She asked the girl who had recently celebrated two special days: her ninth birthday and her seventh as a sister of the Ward. "Remember when you and sister Olen snuck out at night and climbed the Skywheel?"

"I said I was sorry," she defended. "And Mistress Haggart already punished us rightly."

"I know, I know," Philippa said, calming the girl. "I only mean, it was *hard* was it not? You told me yourself that once you got halfway you both had to keep going because climbing back down was impossible."

"The moon had disappeared behind the clouds, and we couldn't see our own feet," she said. "So even though I thought my arms would fall off, we had to keep climbing."

"That's right. And Clara, I could speak of your trials along the Iron Road, and your will that kept you going," Philippa continued going around the girls, "Or Samantha, the only person I know who not only saw a Raider squad and lived to tell about, but snuck away from their very grasp! My goodness, look at this group of girls I have! We are not like the Uptown ladies with their umbrellas in the warm sun, and their little sneezes when they pass a bush!" The girls all giggled a knowing laugh that Philippa just adored. She sat down, and the girls fell in around her. It was nearly exhausting, this love she felt for her sisters right now. "We are different from everyone else in this city. We are strong," she said, pointing at the faces, "and smart, and brave, and we are survivors!"

She wrapped an elbow around Samantha, a true survivor even amongst them all, pulling her in and kissing her firmly on the top of her head.

"I may not know who put the gears in the sky, or how they wheel, but I do know this," Philippa said, touching their heads and pulling on their chins, "They turn for us! We did not survive pain and hunger and loss just to spend our lives sitting in wet sand. We need to get that door open, and to do that we need to be strong, real strong, and we need to do it together!"

She pulled the girls back in line and arrayed them in an order based on nothing but hunch. Clara, the second strongest she put at the back and asked her to sit on the ground with her heels dug into the sand. Then Maggie, the smallest of them all, stood next followed by an increasingly taller and stronger line of children: Leni, Samantha, Icha, Renata, Marta, Katia, Ellery, Gerda, Lysa, and at the front of the line, the strong arms and stronger legs of Philippa Cree.

The rope was already taut as she grabbed on. The girls were eager, they wanted this as much as she did. No more speeches, no more waiting. She dug her heels into the ground and braced them against a large stone. She whisper-shouted a word to her sisters and pulled back with her arms while pressing with her strong legs. The thick rope pulled tight and still Philippa and her girls pulled some more. As one, they strained against the ancient iron gate.

They heaved backwards again and a hollow metal on metal grind growled in the dark hollow. It had moved. It was just the slightest of movements, but this glimmer of hope gave new life to the girls. They pulled again and a heavy grinding, like the millstone at the Midtown granary, rumbled through the room. The black gate slid open, sucking in air and sand from the outside world. The girls dropped the rope and approached the gaping frame. Philippa dropped to her knees exhausted.

It was a tunnel, deep and black. It may have gone up to the surface, or it may have angled down, far deeper into the bowels of the world. She could not tell, as all she saw was the utter blackness that fell away like the endless dark of a starless night. They had to go in, and they had to be able to see, but she would not ask Maggie to lead the way.

"Cut the rope," she told her girls. "In strips this long," she said, holding her arms apart. She sent the girls to search the room for sticks or pieces of board. She would make torches. Maggie would lend them fire, but Philippa would lead the way. The little girls scrambled about, digging twigs and branches out of the moist sand. They had found a couple good ones when one of the girls called her over.

"Mistress Cree," Katia said, "I found something."

It was a small tin that had been buried under a boulder. Inside were little things, metal and glass. Presumably lost and found artifacts someone had gathered and saved. Someone who had nothing, and could cherish the simplest of things.

"These must be sister Olen's things," Philippa said, pushing a finger through the tin. "Let us hold on to this. She won't mind. And besides, I do not believe she, or any of us, are ever coming back."

Maggie tied a length of rope around a sturdy branch and pinched the twine between thumb and forefinger. "Don't laugh," she said, looking at her sisters sheepishly. The torch erupted in flames, and Maggie let out a series of rapid convulsive sneezes. She rubbed her forearm over her nose as she handed the torch to Philippa. "That happens every time."

"Thank you, Maggie. Now, to find our way out of here," Philippa said, and led the girls through the gate. "Everyone grab a partner and never let go of her hand." She turned back and eyed them sternly, "Never let go."

The dark path curved and angled worse than the Millthrace sewers, turning so sharply at some points that Philippa swore they were walking in circles. The rock walls were spikey and rough with uneven dimensions. Sometimes the girls shuffled forward as a tightly bunched group, step by step into the wide unknown like a many-legged beast, other times they were forced to pass one by one through tight fissures, sucking in bellies as they went. If this were a cave dug out by a professional crew, they had done a quick and dirty job.

The parade of twelve girls in bed clothes marched on, hand in hand, climbing slowly when the path rose, and scrambling quickly when it angled down. Philippa held Maggie by one hand, her torch by the other. They followed the jagged path for a couple hours, maybe more. The deeper they went, the more foul the air grew. At first Philippa thought the cave air was merely stale, but now she had to agree with the sisters, something rotten was among them. "It will get better the closer we get to the surface," Philippa promised, but it only got worse. The girls began to openly complain.

"Please!" Philippa admonished. "We could be walking into an army barracks for all we know. We must be silent."

The girls quieted and plodded along, many pulling their shirt collars over their noses as the stench grew. They had already changed out the blackened rope once, and would soon have to light another. That only meant a couple more hours of light. The walls smoothed out and the path widened ahead. Philippa waved her torch around to survey the tunnel.

"It's getting bigger," Maggie said.

"Almost like a room," Philippa agreed. They stepped forward and could no longer see the tunnel walls. Waving her torch only illuminated endless darkness. "Is there anything you can do?" she asked Maggie. "I want to see how big this room is."

"Sure!" Maggie said. "I've got plenty of fireflies!"

The little girl squeezed her fists and her eyes, scrunching up her face. Tiny balls of light escaped from her frame. They danced around and fizzled out, but not enough to light more than the group of sisters. Maggie clenched her jaw and squeezed again. "Just wait," she said to Philippa, "I can do better."

And she did.

A flood of fireflies streamed out of her body and carried around the room, like formless fairies scattering in the wind. From her head, her back, and her arms and legs the furry bulbs erupted. They circled out and about and spun away to every corner of the underground room. Her eyes were clenched shut in deep concentration, so little Maggie could not have seen what Philippa and the other sisters saw in the huge underground cavern. A wide room, as big as the Lowtown square, loomed ahead of them. The far walls held up a tall and jagged ceiling of glassy black stone. An unadjusted eye may have seen a small city of iron buildings, but Philippa saw clearly through the light. Row upon row of tall iron cages, some many times taller than herself, cluttered the floor. Hundreds of rusting and decayed black iron cells spread out in all directions. And laying at the bottom of each of the cells, glowing brightly in the first light of a hundred years, were the bare white bones of monsters. A massive skull, like a boulder, lay ahead of her. It was manlike, except for the eye sockets that hooked back in an evil arch.

She grabbed at her belly and backed away, realizing Icha's nightmare from long ago had been true: Philippa had led all of her sisters straight into Nerikan Prison.

44

The Thornapple Swindle

Olen may not have been the first to notice the front gate of Millthrace was wide open, but she was the first to say it out loud. Edwin and Marko shared a knowing glance and heightened their guard. The trio pulled their horses off the Iron Road and rode straight up to the city gates.

"Where is everyone?" Edwin asked, as he looked at the abandoned city.

Marko's answer was unheard by Olen as she saw the still smoldering ashes at the Barrens where the Ward once stood. She ran over as fast as her sore legs could carry her. Edwin started after her, but Marko held him back.

It was a pile of rubble. A black footprint of what she used to call home. It seemed so small, the outline of the large building she had slept in. How could walls this close have held so many? Then she thought of the many, her sisters, Mistress Haggart.

Edwin and Marko walked to the girl.

"It was Koertig," Edwin said somberly. "I did not tell you, because sometimes the things you hear on the road are not true, and this, even for Koertig...I did not believe."

"And my sisters?" she asked. "Haggart? Burned away?"

"I am sorry, Olen," he said, kneeling down next to her. Marko lowered himself to his knees also, and they held the little orphan girl.

She thought first of Maggie, with her bunk so close to hers. She envisioned the littlest sister clutching her black jar of fireflies as Olen's first tear fell. Then the other girls and the trouble they all got into. Sneaking out at night, picking the pockets of passed-out drunks. And then of course Philippa, the oldest sister who Olen had wished was—

She buried her face in Edwin's shirt. "I hated her," she cried. "Philippa. I wished terrible things for her. I might have wished this. What if—"

"No," Edwin cut in.

"But what if!" she insisted. "What if I wished this and it happened? You told me yourself you don't know what all my powers can do. Philippa, Haggart, my sisters who never said goodbye. I was mad at them all, jealous of them. What if?"

"No!" Edwin insisted, and held her out at her shoulders. "This wasn't you, and you know that. Only one person is responsible, and that is Koertig."

"He is crazy," Marko said. "That is why you must wait here. Edwin and I can do this."

"How?" she asked through her grief, staring at the charred ruins.

"Just get us through the mountain," he said and held the child again. The three travelers sat quietly in the wide empty Lowtown Barrens, as the girl cried in their arms.

A loud rapping cut through their sobs, and they all turned to a figure behind them. It was old Mistress Egg banging on the door to the Eagle and Trout.

"Open this fraggin' door you gob! Payin' customer!" she pounded the frame, unaware she was the last citizen left in town. "Don' make me climb in yer window!"

Edwin rose but was stilled by Marko.

"The Elmwood Hustle," he suggested, but Edwin shook him off.

"I was thinking Thornapple Swindle," he said.

"Thornapp—" Marko said in disgust. "You are not even wearing a hat!"

"I have adjusted it to suit my needs!" he shot back, pulling away from Marko's grip. He picked up Marko's sack and then dashed across the square and came upon Miss Egg.

***

"Dear Miss Egg!" Edwin spat out, startling the old woman.

"Wha?!" she said, nearly falling to the ground as she spun around. "You gonna open this place or what?"

"But Miss Egg, do you not recognize me, I am Edwin, the Historian. I stayed at your residence." He made a move to doff his cap, but grasped only air. Marko's faint "good god" drifted across the courtyard.

"Huh?" the old woman said, already tipsy from drinking at home.

"I believe I have left some things at your place. I would like to get them back."

"Abandoned goods are mine to keep or sell," came her surprisingly lucent response. "How much you got on ya?"

"Shall we retire to your abode and discuss?" he pulled two leather flasks from a sack. Her face and tone softened immediately. Edwin held out an elbow, which lady Egg grasped, and he led her back to her place.

***

Edwin had been gone for over an hour when Marko finally told Olen all he had heard about the Ward's final day. Haggart was the first. A spear through the heart. There was a rumor, he had said, that a girl named Philippa had been carrying Koertig's child, and the shame had led him to destroy them all.

Olen walked through charred beams that once were home. She kicked over pots and turned over boards, not sure what she was looking for. He said they had tossed torches in through the windows. Then they had just stood there as it burned. When they had left for Nerikan, the rubble had still been too hot to search for the dead.

Olen stopped him cold. "You mean they didn't bury anyone?" she asked. He shook his head no. She kicked over some more burnt debris and overturned a black panel. There was nothing underneath. "Then where are the bodies?"

Just then Edwin stumbled around the corner, dragging behind him a large sack. He swung his head in large sweeping motions looking for his two friends. When he spotted them, he pointed a jittery finger and smiled. He pulled the sack along over to Olen and Marko. He was beyond drunk.

He approached Marko and mimicked doffing his invisible cap. "See! Thorn-happle Spindle!" he said and dropped to his knees, then his palms, and then he passed out cold. The large bag fell open, spilling out his books on Aurlings.

45

And In Nerikan They Will Return

Philippa gathered the girls around her and turned their eyes away from the bone-filled cages. "Come close," she said and asked Maggie to dim her light. The girls were frightened and crying, but Philippa held strong. "Those are just bones. Bones of something from long ago, but now no different than chicken bones for the dogs. It is alright to be upset, but there is no reason to be scared. We must pass through here if we are to get outside. If we're frightened, then we'll do this frightened, but we *will* do it." She made sure not to speak the word Nerikan.

She had Maggie light a new torch. The little girl sneezed violently as Philippa hoisted the new flame. "Come on, sisters," she said, stepping forward. "Do not look in the cages, just look at me and follow close." Then she led the girls through the vast Aurling prison. She walked past cages, trying not to look inside, but her eyes disobeyed her many times as she caught glimpses of the caged dead. There were skeletons so twisted and bizarre that even alive the beast must have been a useless pile of flesh and bone, begging for death. These were the failed experiments of Janus Brynn.

Some cages housed the bones of large beasts, predators mixed with pack animals. Small bones on frames slick and sleek lay in smaller pens. Aurlings, Demis, and scions, cast into Brynn's mad prison generations ago. She mourned for their suffering, but she was glad the beasts were all dead. She hurried past the cages, the sounds of many feet scurrying behind her. "Remember, hold the hand of your partner."

A quick cycle of clicks circled the room and bounced off the stony walls before tapping at Philippa's chest and rattling deep inside her ears. It was just a sound in the air, but a sound with substance that touched her.

"What was that?" a young sister asked.

"I do not know," Mistress Cree said.

It came again, a rush of clicks. Invisible fingers drumming across her face and skin, searching her, sizing her up. The phantom hands seemed to come from directly in front of them. Philippa held the torch forward, but saw only darkness. Yet even the darkness seemed shiny and reflective in her firelight. Again the clicks, this time nearer, stronger, bouncing forcefully off her body. The girls whimpered, and hugged together.

"Do you want more light?" Maggie asked.

"Sure," Philippa said, not really listening. Something was there. Something shiny and black, moving slightly in the firelight. "But first...," she lobbed her torch into the darkness. It arced over the cages carrying red and yellow flame as it flew. As it came down, it shattered against the black chest of a man-sized insect, scattering red hot embers across its face and torso. It screeched and dropped to the ground patting at its burning flesh. Philippa had paged through enough of Edwin's books to know the image of a foul Nerikan gore. The girls screamed and an entire forest of brilliant fireflies burst from Maggie's chest. The vast cave erupted in light, revealing a dark tunnel cutting to their left.

"This way!" Philippa yelled, pulling the girls towards the passageway. She counted the girls as they rushed by, chasing after Maggie's light. All were accounted for. She rushed after them as the path angled upwards. She glanced back over her shoulder and saw the orange lights fading around the gore. It was slinking back into the shadows, not eager for another round with the sisters of the Ward.

They raced through the tunnels, Philippa matching her breaths with her steps, two breaths in, three puffs out. The way was wide and clear, and behind Maggie's light the girls flew longer than necessary to get far away. Finally, when her lungs and legs allowed no more, Philippa called the girls to stop and huddled around a sharp corner. She leaned against a wall, panting and holding her tummy. She slid down onto her backside and rested her head on her knees, breathless. Her stomach ached from the running, lack of food, and the tiny child growing inside. Then she thought of the gore and wondered if that was what Brynn had done to her baby. She violently shook away the thought and gathered her girls.

"What was that?" they asked, gathering around sparse firefly beads.

"Can you keep it up, Maggie?" Philippa asked.

"Funny thing is, it's harder to keep them in!" she said back. "This is actually kind of a relief."

"Good. Good Maggie," she said, stroking her hair. The girls asked again. "I believe that was what they call a *gore*," Philippa said and waited. A few of the brighter ones made the connection. "Remember the faerie stories about Aurlings and the prison they were sent to?" Some of the girls nodded. "That is where we are. But we are not prisoners, do you understand?" She pulled a young girl close, "Katia, it's like the jail in Midtown, remember? We go inside to do the cleaning and leave when we are done. It's like that here. We are not chained, and we will find a way out."

She sat on the ground as her breaths finally evened out. "We are going uphill now, sisters. We are closer to the surface. I can just *smell* it," she said, trying to convince herself it was not false hope.

"I smell it too," one of the girls said. "It smells like the sea."

"Does it?" Philippa asked, pulling the girl in. "I have never been to the sea."

It was Ellery, a young teen who kept very quiet. She was skin and bones with a long gaunt face. "My father," she said, pausing, "Before he died, he was a sailor. We lived on the sea near Daegan. I know we are too far away for it to be true. But I know that smell. It is the sea."

"At this point, Ellery, anything is possible," Philippa said. "And I will get us out of here, if I have to sail us out!"

Ellery smiled and nodded.

"Very well, then," Philippa said, while rising. "We can go now. But let us walk."

They walked ahead, again for what felt like hours, always choosing the widest path or the tunnel most straight. After that, they wandered on for hours longer, hoping beyond hope they were climbing out of the depths and not farther below. A slight rise in the floor continued forward, only to be met by the occasional brief downhill. The wide cavern was smoother now and mostly straight, yet a few slight corners kept them guessing their direction. The tunnels branched. Smaller caves opened to the left and right, and disappeared into the darkness.

Then a room. Maggie saw it first as her fireflies drifted into the alcove. It was nothing more than an open storage bay, but unlike everything else in this ancient cave, this one had crates. And within the countless crates were foodstuffs, shockingly fresh and new. There were even utensils, brooms, shovels, blankets and pillows stacked throughout. But most important was the food. "We can rest here," Philippa said, as she laid out the blankets.

They ate heartily, and camped out in this small nook for three days, maybe four, Philippa was not sure. But nonetheless they waited and relaxed and ate like they had never eaten before. She heard no more of the clicking gores, and besides the smell, she found the rest quite rejuvenating. When the stores had become low, and the girls grew antsy, they walked again the lonely halls.

They trekked ahead for hours, following the straightest paths. She wished for a sound or light to lead them, a map, or a crack in the stone that led out of the mountain, but what they found after marching through the endless tunnels of Nerikan was a fine wooden door that appeared freshly stained and lacquered.

"What do you think?" Maggie asked, sending fireflies around all of the edges of the elegant doorway. The reddish finish glistened.

"I think we did not come all this way to turn back," Philippa said. She grasped the round brass handle and turned the knob. The heavy door opened easily, soundlessly. She stepped in.

Brass oil lamps hung on the walls of a large furnished chamber, illuminating the room like dancing sunlight. Tall ornate tapestries, maroon and gold, hung from the ceiling, hiding most of the black rocky walls. Dark cherry furniture with golden trim sat in jumbled piles, as if a storage hall for a grand mansion. Tall cabinets and long chests, their drawers uselessly faced together, pressed against the back walls. Sturdy wooden armchairs with bulging red cushions were placed neatly around a small tea table. And a long oaken slab was clothed and dressed with dishes as if for a dinner party. She had never seen such opulence and in so small a chamber.

The long days had drained any remaining shock from her body, and Philippa just stared ahead like a lifeless corpse. It was the two men at the table looking over a map who seemed to have had the shock of a lifetime. A third man lay on a velvet-trimmed settee with a damp towel over his head. He had forced himself to his elbows at the opening of the door. He was pale and thin. All three men stared, mouths agape and completely dumbfounded, as a dozen children from the Lowtown Ward filed into their hidden bunker.

"May we come in?" Philippa asked Mayor Brynn and his two men.

***

Olen burned broken shipping crates that littered the Lowtown square as the sun fell low over the Millthrace ramparts. Nearly everyone she had ever known was dead and gone, she thought, while looking over the pit where the Ward had once stood. And soon Bakku would be gone forever too.

Edwin sipped tea and rubbed his throbbing head. It turned out Miss Egg was not the only stray still wandering the city. Scurrying shadows and echoing Midtown voices told her a few others remained.

Opportunists, scavenging abandoned shops and homes. Take it all, she thought.

In Lowtown, there was little left to take.

Edwin shook the cobwebs out of his head. "Can you believe she had sold my books for only five coppers," he complained. "And this she did not bother telling me until after both flasks were gone! Still, she was able to show me where to find them."

Marko paged through the leathery tomes while Olen sat focused on the remains of the Ward.

"But I can see nobody cares," Edwin said, and went back to rubbing his aching skull.

"These books are very specific," Marko said, pointing over the high walls of Millthrace to the mountains behind. "My goodness, I could find Nerikan in my sleep!" He drew long lines in the sand corresponding to markers on the mountaintop. "In my sleep!"

"Ah, yes, sleep!" Edwin said, laying down next to the fire.

Marko sat next to Olen and showed her the books. "Can you do it?" he asked. "You got us to Kessel. This is just a little further. Just get us close and we will free your friend."

"And then what?" she asked.

"Once Bakku is again out of his chains, well, you have seen him fight before!"

Olen did not like the plan because there was not much of a plan to like. Unchain Bakku and have him fight his way to freedom. She was not even sure he would fight at all. She still was not sure he had not sacrificed himself just to protect her. Brynn was hunting them, and Bakku's sacrifice would free her of Brynn's wrath.

"There must be a better way," she said, as two men walked in through the open gates of Millthrace, each man carrying one end of a long crate. She remembered the old man and his son from long ago. She had traded with them, potatoes for an onion. The younger man dropped his end of the box when he saw the empty and burned Barrens. Marko beckoned the fellows over to the fire with a kindly wave.

"Coffee," Marko said and poured warm brown liquid in a cup for the men to share. The older man took a long drink and thanked Marko by name.

"So it is true? All of it is true?" the younger man asked. "The creature, he has come back? And the Ward, the mayor, Aurlings…all true?"

Olen began to answer him, but the wise and patient Marko cut her off.

"Perhaps," Marko said. "Tell me what you have heard."

46

A Most Horrible Day

A gentleman from Uptown stepped out of his five-poled tent, and walked into the dense Ma'alabrad Forest. He wore a peach overcoat with a ruffled white blouse underneath. This journey through the ironwoods had taken much longer than he had expected, and he quite missed his bed. His nose was not accustomed to wild pollen, and he stifled a petite sneeze. The caravan still slept as the sun nosed over the horizon. The wealthy Uptowner walked deep into the woods, far away from prying eyes, or listening ears. He had never done his morning disgrace outdoors, and certainly never with witnesses. He found a quiet spot behind a honeysuckle bush where even the birds could not spy. He checked all around himself, lowered his pants to his ankles, and squatted like an animal.

He was past the point of no return when the bright ball of light emerged mere footsteps before him. It was at first a pinprick of yellow and white that grew, and then swirled about itself. In a flash it grew to twice his width, pulsed, and expanded again. The yellow and white washed away, as if clouds dispersing, and an image of the wretched Barrens appeared within. Much to his already staggering surprise, two men stepped through this crystalline ball and into Ma'alabrad Forest. One was a younger, tall and thin, gap-toothed man with black hair and dark features. The other was a shorter and older gentleman in robes with a full grey beard. They each carried large leather pouches over their shoulders. The men waved to someone unseen back inside the glassy orb. Then the circular enigma simply collapsed within itself and fell away.

The Uptown gentry-man hovered over his tainted mound as the two men looked about themselves and got their bearings. The darker man pointed towards camp, and they both set off in that direction, clearly pleased with themselves. As they walked past the squatting man, the older bearded gentleman spotted him and was taken aback. He quickly regained his composure, and in a voice with which this Uptowner had never been spoken to before, the old man scolded, "Have you no shame!"

Then the two men marched off to camp as the man in the peach overcoat finished his business. When he returned to his tent he woke his handlers and, despite his wife's protests, ordered them to tear down the tent and head out. He stopped in Millthrace only long enough to retrieve a few important items before heading south and settling in to a new life in Brennan. He lived many years after that, but always in fear someone would confront him about that most horrible day.

***

Koertig ordered the caravan forward. The Nerikan gates loomed through the forest, gloriously close, yet maddeningly far. In the tree-tops, ravens squawked and flopped from limb to limb, scolding the interlopers. Trees fell ahead, cracking and snapping like breaking bones. The path widened, but still, they had made so little progress today. The men were slower.

"Some mead, Sergeant?" a dark faced servant asked. He had the black hair of a tradesman, and the clothes of a Lowtowner.

"It's Lieutenant Colonel. Remember it," Koertig said. He waved the server away. He had no palate for a common man's mead. Philippa's medicinal tea was what he wanted. His shoulder ached mightily since leaving the city, and he struggled to mask the pain. Yes, he thought, Philippa's tea would soothe him, and her strong but soft hands on his back—

"Some beer for the Sergeant?" a grey haired man asked.

Koertig sighed heavily. He grasped his steadying pole and sat himself onto the mound of flesh that was Bakku's shoulder. "When I want beer, I will call for it. Until that time I want trees downed and paths drawn. Can you do that for me old man?"

"Sorry sir, just beer," the robed man said, ducking away.

"Wait!" Koertig called out, and the old man stopped. Koertig called him back and looked him over. "Are you of Millthrace?"

"Are not we all?" he asked, a bit too nervously.

"And your name?"

"Hammond," he answered quickly, stroking his long grey beard. "Reese Hammond. I trade in Lowtown."

"Yes. Yes," Koertig said, studying his face. "I have seen you there. Fill my flask."

"Of course, sir," he said, and poured his drink into the Lieutenant Colonel's leather.

A team of horses pulled a large root out of the ground, and the caravan lurched ahead a few more lengths. Damn this forest, Koertig thought, wondering if it would not be quicker to just slice Bakku into pieces and end it all. His thumb had come off easy enough, perhaps his head would also. He checked Bakku's wound. A thick scar had formed a lump where his thumb once was, but the finger did not return. They said he was immortal, but Koertig knew that any man that could be sliced up could die.

The cart lurched again, and Koertig grabbed the pole to steady himself. Bakku moaned deep inside his chest and inhaled a great breath.

"Martz!" Koertig called out, but his second in command did not respond. He called again, and a disheveled Martz rushed up to the giant cart.

"Sorry sir!" he said, straightening his gear. "Just sneaking a few afternoon winks."

Koertig nodded towards Bakku and set Martz to work sedating the creature.

"Seems everyone is a little slow today," Koertig said blankly, as he watched the workers saw lazily at a tall tree. "Perhaps I have pushed them too hard."

"Perhaps, sir," Martz agreed, as he knifed a hole into Bakku's side and poured the numbing mash inside. "Though I must admit, a bit of the ol' mead is more likely to blame." He laid fresh cloth over the wound, and capped off the poison. "It has not been in short supply, of which I believe we can thank you."

Koertig nodded blankly, only half listening. He shook free of his daydreams. "Yes, mead," he said. He reached for the flask the old man had left. "I would prefer a good wine." He opened the pouch and drank. It was cool, but bitter. It was not the freshest batch, but he was now thirsty, and when on the road one must take what offerings he can get. Koertig drank again.

"One more thing sir," Martz said, as he cleaned up. "This is the last of the poison. We really must reach Nerikan before nightfall or else we will not be able to control the creature."

This caught Koertig's attention, for he knew they had had more than enough to keep a whole army sedated. And just that quickly the pieces fell into place, as like the old waterwheels of Millthrace, the gears turned in Koertig's head. The mead. The beer. The old man. The Demi-Aurling. He almost rose and barked out orders, but he quickly steeled himself. The axmen at the trees sawed slowly, breaking often and wiping their sweaty brows. His troops sat about the forest and caravan relaxing and catching quick naps. And all of the townspeople had already retired to their tents and carriages, here at such an early point in the afternoon. Among the lethargic crowds, two men roamed, one black haired and one old and grey. They handed out cups-full of mead and beer to any and all takers, and never asked for a copper or wedge in return. "Poisoned!" he thought, throwing down his flask.

Koertig leapt off the caravan and jerked a long spear out of the ground. A Millthrace guardsmen slept next to it with his back against a tree. Koertig kicked him onto his side with an angry boot.

"Fools!" he yelled. "Do you not know you have been poisoned?"

The old bearded spy heard this and rose like a frightened hart. It was the damned Storyteller. Koertig saw it clearly now. He had to hurry. He had downed only a few sips, but they would have saved the strongest poison for Koertig! He sat the shaft of the spear over his left shoulder and grasped it in front of his chest. He ran across the encampment of sleeping and listless townspeople, charging after the old Demi he knew would not be immortal.

***

Mayor Brynn moved casually to the gentleman perched on his elbows on the settee. "Graeme, rest," he said affectionately, placing a palm on his shoulder. Graeme slid back on to the couch. He looked ready to fall into a deep slumber, fighting to keep his eyes open.

"He has had a strenuous week," Brynn said, approaching the girls, "As I assume you all have." He walked past them as if surveying the troops, touching some of the younger girls on the head warmly. Maggie ducked away. He came to Philippa, who still held her breath from the moment she entered the room. "Cree, I believe it is?" He asked formally, like he was greeting guests in the town hall. "Koertig's girl?"

She slapped him across the face and sent him stumbling backwards. The man at the map rushed to his side and held him under his arms. Brynn righted himself and eased out of the man's grip. "It is all right, Reeve. I deserved that." He patted himself off. "Your child is unaffected," he stated. "That is what you would like to know? It is true. I did nothing to harm him. It was simply a childish bluff. It was a chaotic day for us all, and I did not react to it well. I should never have frightened you like that. I am, most truly, sorry."

"Him?" she asked. "You called my child *him*."

"Yes, you carry a boy-child, and one of great will. Even as I sensed him he resisted me, in the womb, no less. The son of Koertig is strong!"

"He gets that from his mother," she said.

Brynn smiled and nodded, mockingly.

She knew she had often made excuses for Koertig's behavior. There was something she had seen deep inside the wounded hero that she had loved and hoped to nurture. But not with Brynn. Even with his soft comforting tones, she knew this was a man she could never trust.

Brynn indicated the crowd of young girls all vying for a spot behind their mistress. "From the Ward I assume?" Philippa nodded. "All of them?" he asked, and again she agreed. Everyone had escaped, except for Mistress Haggart. "And I again assume, it was one of your wards that got you here?"

She did not know what to make of this, and it must have shown on her face.

"A sort of hoodoo," he said, wiggling his fingers in the air, "Like Graeme here performed, before leaving himself so much worse for wear." He smiled a mayoral smile that in the daylight might have been charming, but in the candlelit darkness inside the Rückraadt Mountains disturbed all. "What I am asking is which of your girls bears the Aurling seed, because unless you walked in the front door, Aurling magic is the only way in or out of Nerikan."

The younger girls shuddered and turned to Philippa, whispering that frightening word, wondering. They may have strode past the white bones of scions, and fled from a hissing gore, but the nightmare inducing name of Nerikan still frightened deeper than any dark reality.

"I had found it best not to say that word," she admonished him. "They are but little girls, you must know."

"I do apologize, again" he said quickly and seemed to mean it. "Please children, understand, this place is not as the tale-tellers will have you believe. Faerie stories of Nerikan are not so much true, as they are meant to scare you away. This is a private place, not a frightful one."

"We have seen the cages," she said coldly.

"Very well then," he shot back. "It's a nightmare." He and Philippa stood in silent battle, a battle for virtue and honor she had been fighting all her life. The ancient mayor broke first. "Pardon again my rudeness, but these are desperate times. I only ask about the Aurling seed because we are a bit outnumbered here. Koertig has taken over the city of Millthrace. We do not dare leave this cave, yet we cannot stay here forever. If one of you bears a seed, a bit of magic, I might know a way to use it to—"

"There's a door," Philippa cut in before Maggie, Icha, or any of the others, frightened for so long, might speak up and offer a long-held secret at the hopes of getting out of this awful place. "An iron gate. Below the Uptown mill, and behind the falls. The waters have stilled, revealing the gate. It was abandoned. Rusted. None of my girls know any magic."

Brynn turned to Reeve who checked the map. He traced his finger over many lines, and looked up to his mayor and gave a somber shake of his head.

"A symbol on the door!" Philippa added, searching her memory. "Three orbs in a tringle, lines etched between."

"Hmm," Brynn said aloud, staring hard into Philippa's soul. "There should be no door there, yet she tells the truth. There is deception in her words, but all of the girls agree. They walked through a black door, into darkness and fear." He thought for a moment and approached Reeve speaking lowly, but Philippa heard the echoed whispers. "The gores, you think? No, even if they burrowed out their own tunnel, they never could have fashioned a gate. A doorway right into the heart of the city! We could take Koertig down from the inside. We wouldn't need Graeme to get us there. But where is it? Think!" He pounded his fist on the table, "Oh, it was so long ago!"

"Mister Brynn," Philippa said, breaking his reverie. He shot her an angry look. "I assume it is Mister, as the mayor has lost his city?"

"For now."

"If you would just ask, I could tell you where to find the gate."

"And you would remember your path through the endless twisting tunnels of Nerikan?" he asked snidely.

"Every turn," she said proudly. "And I'll add them to your map, in exchange."

"Go on," he said.

"For safe passage out and the truth about the Aurlings," she said. "No more faerie tales."

47

Into the Darkness

Edwin ran. He dropped the flask, called himself a damned fool, and ran. He peeked over his shoulder to see Koertig pursuing, and again called himself a fool. He should never have spoken to that man, that soldier's keen eye had been on him long before he was an active conspirator. He ran deep into the woods of Ma'alabrad Forest, sprinting past confused and sluggish axmen. They watched the deadly chase, too tired to help either Edwin or Koertig.

So many times on this wild adventure he had thought he had met his life's end. In the tree with the pig dogs, starving on the Iron Road, or when Timo had threatened to slice his throat. Each time he had met the end with anger and regret. However, something different overtook him this time. It was a certain gratification, a satisfaction in his life's ending if it meant another could live. He had lost his paunchy belly on the road. His legs had grown strong, and his once delicate feet had developed tough soles. But he was still an old man. His lungs ached, and his heart strained, but he had to stay ahead of that spear a little longer. He would never outrun the youthful soldier, but he could draw the man away. Run Edwin, he told himself. Run until the spike enters your spine. And if you still have a breath in you after, then crawl. Lead the soldier away from the camp and away from Marko. By the time this one-armed bastard takes your life, the incomparable Mr. Meloon will be gone.

Edwin curled around a still-standing ironwood and dashed towards the open gates of Nerikan. A worker stood near the entrance finishing off a flagon of ale. The bearded workman swallowed contentedly and fell to his knees. Edwin glanced over his shoulder; the soldier followed.

He had a sweet thought as he led Koertig away, that perhaps Marko would not disappear into the woods but into the ranks. Perhaps even now he was pulling on the armor of a sleeping infantryman, or pulling a blade over his thick black hair, shaving himself bald. *Oh you would love that ruse,* he thought, *joining the troops in the search for yourself!*

He tore through a tall stand of prickly stems that slashed at his face and arms. He curled around more trees, feigning left, but sliding right. Still the mad Koertig pursued, his spear balanced firmly on his shoulder. Two large tree trunks lay across his path, and Edwin leapt high above them. He was a young child of Ulm again, springing through the Euloren Woods on legs so powerful that a leap was no less than an eagle's flight. As Edwin flew over the barrier of trees, his robe snagged a freshly cut branch and jerked the old man to the ground.

He lay on his back tugging at the branch as Koertig rounded the tree. The mad soldier pulled the spear off his shoulder and approached. He placed a black and silver boot on Edwin's chest and stood over him, hoisting the weapon.

"For generations, my family has had only one job," Koertig said. "To kill Aur—"

A white blur flew over the downed trees and into Koertig. They rolled to the ground, and Marko Meloon came out on top, delivering rhythmic punches to Koertig's face. The spear rolled to a stop at Edwin's feet.

Of all the injury and injustice he had suffered along this damned adventure, here he was at another foul crossroads. He could watch his only friend die, or choose to no longer be an observer. He could flee from life, or pick up this spear and end one.

Marko and the soldier clawed at each other, rolling and scraping. The soldier thrust a knee, and Marko returned with a bite to his wounded shoulder. Koertig cried out, but his wail became a growl of anger. He grabbed Marko by the throat and rolled him onto his back, pressing all of his weight onto Marko's neck. Veins bulged in the mysterious trader's forehead. His eyes were wide, suffering. Edwin lifted the spike above his head.

"Let him go," his soft voice politely asked. "Let the man go."

It was a balanced weapon, if weighty.

"Do it!" Marko gasped between strangled breaths.

He gripped and spun the dry wooded shaft in his palms. How sharp the blade, how simple a slice it would make in this horrid soldier's back. "I will put this weapon right through your heart, sir, if you do not let my friend go."

Koertig turned his head slightly. He pulled his legs to sitting, and rocked his weight onto his heels.

"If you stand up, I will stab you," Edwin warned, but Koertig did not stop.

"Now!" Marko choked. "You must!"

"Yes, Storyteller," Koertig said, releasing Marko. The trader rolled away. Koertig pressed his arm to the ground and rose up on one knee. "There is no other way. Kill me, or die in Nerikan. Which will it be?"

"Edwin!" Marko commanded. "Do not hesitate! Do it now!"

"Yes, Edwin the Observer!" Koertig said, as he pushed himself to standing, a scar down his chestplate confirming the tales from the Ward. "Take me down."

The two men stood but a spear's length apart. Edwin held the weapon awkwardly above his head in both hands. Koertig, unarmed and disfigured, stood unafraid in front of him, his arm at his side, palm open. Now Marko, Edwin silently begged, run away now!

"What is your magic, Demi?" Koertig asked as he stalked. "Poison? Lightning? Divination?"

"I guess you could say the last one," he stammered, taking a step back. He lowered the spear to his shoulder and pointed the blade at the soft flesh below Koertig's chestplate. Only now it was heavy, awkward.

A useless tool in a fatal fight. "I didn't believe it at first. But I just always happen to be in the right place at, well you know."

"Give me the weapon, old man, and I'll make it fast."

"Kill him my friend," Marko pleaded as he got to his feet. "His banter is a game."

"I didn't want to be like this," Edwin tried, again stepping backwards, stumbling in the brush. "I just wanted to learn. But I picked up a little something along the way, an Aurling seed that leads me."

"Let me free you of that curse," Koertig offered, approaching confidently.

"Very well," Marko said, grabbing a thick log from the tree pile. "I'll do it myself."

He rushed Koertig, who spun quickly, smoothly, and slid a thin blade out of his hip. With a well-trained jab the knife went deep into Marko's gut, and both Marko and his club were on the ground. With action came reaction, and Edwin screamed a bloody war cry that sounded very much like a name. He thrust the spear into Koertig's left thigh, and kept pushing it through as red liquid drained from the soldier's leg. Still wailing, Edwin forced the spear clear through Koertig's upper leg and into the ground. The Lieutenant Colonel again fell to his knees, but this time he would not rise without help.

Edwin ran to Marko's side and helped him to his feet.

"Can you—" he asked, and saw Marko's shirt, no longer white, soaked red where the blade had cut a deep wound. A sheet of blood flowed from his side.

"I can walk," Marko said, wearily, "Get me away. I will not die in front of him."

"You will not die at all!" Edwin said, pulling him along at the shoulders. Together they limped away hurriedly, away from the soldiers, away from Koertig, and into the only sanctuary offered. The two men hobbled forward arm and arm, a trail of blood spilling below them, and passed beneath a mighty iron falchion and into the open mouth of Nerikan.

***

"There are no more Aurlings," Brynn said to Philippa. "They are all dead, at least as far as this world is concerned." He rounded the table and knelt beside Graeme. He carried a tiny silver goblet. He held the man's head up and poured a viscous liquid into his mouth. Philippa did not recognize the elixir, but by the man's reaction it must have been terrible. "Reeve offers you his ration," he whispered and laid the man back onto the couch before returning to his speech. "All dead that is, excluding myself and the one they call Bakku." He poured what little remained in the cup back into a tall sterling canister and then capped the top. The hollow sound from the slow drip told them all the container was more than half empty. Brynn and Reeve shared a nervous look.

"That cannot be true," Philippa tried. "We both saw Olen. And these very men before you. Do they not possess Aurling magic?"

"Demis," he said apathetically, moving around to the front of the room. He offered Philippa a seat in a wide red chair, which she took. The other girls gathered around her, leaning on the chair arms or sitting on the thick hearth rug. She pulled Maggie into her lap.

Brynn smiled at the children as he took a seat himself. Reeve quietly joined them for a sit as Brynn explained about the Demi-Aurlings. Demis were people of this world, regular Eisen folk, who happened upon an Aurling gift. But the true Aurlings, the travelers from a far distant world, were all gone. He paused as if remembering old friends. He smiled and added, "Many of their bones still lie within this very mountain."

Maggie shuffled around on Philippa's lap trying to find a comfortable spot, while the other girls looked around the large room. *Hide your fireflies*, Philippa's mind silently pleaded. *Hold them in, Maggie*, she thought, stroking the young girl's back.

"Why here?" she asked. "Why does this place exist?"

He said it all began with an Aurling woman, a dear friend. Her gift was in her eyes. They were not subject to barriers, as she could look deep inside of anything. She could tell a landlord how many mice slept inside his bedroom walls, what foods churned inside a fat man's belly, even which grave markers stood guard over empty plots. "She saw everything, except her own early demise."

Graeme rose from the couch and joined the group. He appeared as fresh and new as a young recruit. He smiled and nodded to Brynn, and then sat in a soft leather chair. Whatever had been in that drink had revived him completely. He crossed an ankle onto his knee and listened to Brynn's story.

He said it was no secret Aurlings could perish. For many of them, their bodies were no different than Eisen-folk and subject to the same fate. But what he and the others had not expected was, ten summers later, for a boy—a regular Eisen-born child—to emerge with the exact same ability as that woman. "He too could see through flesh and stone, wood and bone. And this boy lived in the same land, the same town, the very same home as where this poor Aurling woman had died in her sleep. That was when I knew that what we Aurling's possessed was not just magic, but a physical *something*," he grasped at the air. "Something that can be left behind, transferred, and mastered."

"And that was when you imprisoned your fellow Aurlings," Philippa said. "You rounded them all up in hopes of stealing their powers."

Mayor Brynn gave a dubious shake of the head and opened his palms as if confused. "Of course," he said, leaning forward. "It is only natural."

***

Olen walked the wide streets of Uptown. The tall wooden homes and stores stood empty; many of them damaged. A long balcony that had circled the third floor of a prominent home had been torn away at one end and lay on the ground like a ramp. Boards and beams lay scattered all across the boardwalk. Such a fight Bakku must have fought.

"Why did you come back, Bakku?" she asked, touching the collapsed rampart. The vast forest lay ahead of her. She was to wait two days, and at noon of the second day, she would open the gate again, and bring all three out, Edwin, Marko, and her Bakku. She understood what they had planned, and she knew it would not work. Two bumbling fools against Koertig's army. It would be the longest two days of her life.

She walked the boardwalk, hearing the echoes of emptiness below her feet. Here and there a small movement caught her eye, the trailing edge of a ragged jacket, a grimy clump of dirty hair disappearing around a corner. Looters. A dog ran across the street carrying a string of sausages in its mouth and wagging its tail victoriously. It carried its meal down the staircase to Midtown. She followed it down. The Midtown fountains were silent and dry.

She moved on to Lowtown and approached the gutted and charred remains of the Ward. All of her sisters were dead, she thought, as she pressed a tentative foot onto the burnt floorboards. Lysa, she thought. Lysa had been promised a home, perhaps she had escaped the flames and now lived with her new family. The walls had all fallen in, and many of the floors had collapsed to the basement. Little girls who had toiled away their childhood waiting for a chance to live were dead. Leni, the second youngest, but the shyest as she tried to learn Eisen words. Olen moved lightly across the strongest beams. Her sisters were all gone yet there were no bodies. The stone fireplaces still stood. The stone staircase to the basement held also. She wondered if she too would have died, had she still lived in the Ward. She jumped across a small gap and balanced on a thick beam. It creaked and bowed under her weight. Or could she have saved them? Could she have pulled Gerda and Renata from the flames and tossed them outdoors? The cluttered basement was even worse now. Boards and beams jutted skyward, and the metal frames from chairs and beds lay scattered below. Among the charred remains sat the heavy door she had used to escape to the sewers. The door still hung open on its iron hook.

"Open?" she asked aloud.

She had not left it open, and the only other people who even knew about the doorway were Haggart and—

"You got them out," she whispered, as images popped through her head of Maggie and Ellery jumping into the sewer. "You got them out," she repeated, seeing in her mind her eldest sister guiding the others through the flames, pulling them to the basement, and reassuring them as she dropped them into the hole. So very little time passed in the great world as she realized why the fire at the Ward had left no bodies.

She had not been needed here to save her sisters. That job was done by the strongest sister of them all! "You bungplugs are wrong. My sisters aren't dead," she whispered as joy swelled in her gut. Then she turned to the great empty city and shouted, "Philippa got them out!"

She crouched down on the beam and hung by her hands, then she dropped into the basement and landed on a pile of charred roof. She slid off the black boards and rolled onto the stone floor. She pushed aside boards and bed frames, squeezing through to the back wall. At the hole in the floor she took one quick look below, and then jumped in. She knew exactly where they would be waiting.

48

⸙

Light

Koertig sat on Bakku's cart as his men wrapped cloth tightly around his wounded thigh. Mid and Uptowners watched the great Koertig as he bled. "Off with your damn finery!" he demanded of the city folk. "Work for just one day in your life!" His soldiers and workmen were still recovering from the tainted mead, and he was out of the mash that had kept Bakku asleep. "If we don't clear these trees and get this beast locked away, none of you will have a home to go to!" A wealthy Uptowner dazedly walked by. Koertig grabbed him by the collar and flung him forward. "Grab a saw, an axe, a shovel. Just work!" The Uptowner hoisted the tool awkwardly. A young gentleman chopped feebly at a tree until the axe fell out of his limp grip. Two men worked a long saw through a tree until it got wedged. They stood there dumbfounded, waiting for instructions. "Pull it out and try again!" Koertig yelled.

Bakku shifted on his trailer. He was still out cold, but the juice was wearing off quickly. The trailer was close to Nerikan, just five more trees in the way. Koertig leaned back against the beast and exhaled as his thigh throbbed. The ogre tensed under his weight. *Just a drop,* Koertig thought. *A sip or two of Bakku's blood and this pain shall pass.* He slammed his fist onto the carriage and damned his thoughts.

"Chop them all down!" he demanded, and the Uptowners worked, as best they could.

***

Edwin led Marko down the dark stony hallways of Nerikan. Just a hint of grey sunlight still lit the way. Marko clutched at his side.

"That did not go as planned," Marko said.

"Nothing ever does," Edwin said, helping him along.

No one had followed them into the caves, but Edwin knew the biggest threat of Nerikan came from inside.

"I should have kept the spear," Edwin said, turning them around a sharp corner. It was all but black now in the prison halls. They tripped over large rocks and kicked at stones underfoot. "We have made so much noise already, and the gores, their hearing is so strong." The path shifted downwards. "I must say," he said, his voice wavering, "I believe if we get any deeper, this will be a one way journey."

Marko coughed and limped along, "For me, that is already true."

"Don't say that!" Edwin said, but he could not convince himself it was not true. They hurried along, feeling the walls for guidance. The cave broke away low to his right, and Edwin pulled Marko into a nook. The echoes faded and their voices sounded close and sharp. "I think we have found a little room," Edwin said, tracing the walls with his hands. It was a small empty dugout alcove, just large enough for them to sit down in and rest. Edwin eased Marko to the ground and wrapped his robe around his bleeding friend. In the darkness he felt around for the random stones that littered the ground, and he piled up as many as he could find by the entrance.

Marko laughed softly and wearily, "Are you sealing our grave, Edwin?"

"Trying to," he answered humorlessly through labored breaths.

"Do you think that will stop your gores?"

Edwin felt his way back to his friend in the darkness, "At the end, would you not want one minute more?"

"One minute more of pure terror?" he asked, but his words drifted out weakly.

"One minute more of life," he answered and sat back against the wall. He pulled Marko inside his arms and held him close like a child. "You sleep, my friend. And if the gores come, I won't wake you."

"Sonny...he will be good...in Kessel?" he asked, and Edwin said he would. "Go see him...will you?...He liked you."

Marko seized for a moment then relaxed.

There is something about the end of all things, as Edwin had discovered time and again, that brings a man to confession. It was no different for his only friend as he lay dying in his arms.

"I was there," Marko finally admitted softly. "In Millthrace. I saw you and the monster."

"I had assumed that quite some time ago," Edwin said and rocked him slowly. "It is why you befriended me so quickly at the Oasis. Even then you knew there would be a reward."

Marko stared at Edwin through the Nerikan shadows, seemingly eased knowing that Edwin had understood. "I'm sorry I lied, my friend," Marko said, as a wet cough hacked its way through his lungs. Blood sprayed onto Edwin's hands.

"About what?" Edwin asked, caressing Marko's scalp.

"Everything," he said, as he drifted away. "Everything."

Edwin stared ahead in the darkness, Marko in his lap. One arm curved under Marko's head, and a hand cupped over the wound. Blood, sticky and thick, coated Edwin's palm. They sat in silence as Marko fell asleep. Edwin counted the rising and falling of Marko's chest, hoping his dwindling breaths would never stop coming.

***

Mister Brynn continued his Aurling tale, as Philippa sat quietly, trying not to show her disgust. He explained that his gift was with the animals. He said he could change and create the beasts as he pleased, breaking them down to their individual parts and reassembling them in new ways. He said he had assumed it was only a matter of time before he located the seeds, separated them from their hosts, and made them his own. "One can never have too many abilities," he said. "But alas, time and time again I failed."

"At the expense of Aurling lives," she accused. She had wanted to understand Harner's hate for the Aurlings. She was beginning to understand his hate for this one.

"Aurling lives that were terrorizing your world," he shot back. "Give *me* the power of the wind, and *I* won't blow down your forests and sink your ships! Give *me* the power of strength and *I* won't crush your armies! These things were happening, child. Read your stories, they are in there. It was I who stopped them!"

"But not all of them," she said.

"No," Brynn replied, calming. "Not all. Bakku is what he calls himself now. A malapropism of the old tongue, a pun perhaps. Bakku: *strong, but powerless.* It is nice to see a man in chains retain his sense of humor."

Reeve and Graeme shared a smile and nod with Mayor Brynn.

He called Bakku the Aurling who would not die, and said that he had become quite obsessed with extracting his seed, wasting many years and many lives experimenting.

He spoke so openly and so smugly about his crimes, that she felt he had waited many lifetimes to make his proud confession. He told how he tortured the man, for that was what Bakku was when he had first discovered him, a man. He had tried to pare him down, reduce him to nothing but his Aurling seed. And as he talked of Bakku, he showed no concern at all for the man he had been destroying.

"Bakku had even more surprises," Brynn continued, "as time and time again it was *he* who absorbed the essence of the other and grew stronger. I blame myself for not stopping once I saw the monster Bakku was becoming, but the hunt for immortality is not a quest one gives up easily."

"Do the experiments continue?" she asked.

"Not for a lifetime," he said and stood from his chair. The girls sitting closest to him scooted nearer to Philippa. She reached down and with a soft touch urged them to sit behind her. Brynn indicated the dusty room. "This is quite the first time any of us have been back inside these walls since, well, pardon me dear orphan, but since long before your parents were born."

He explained that while he may not have been successful in his experiments, he had made an exciting discovery. He walked to the back of the room and opened the silver urn from which he had fed Graeme. He ladled a small scoop and poured it into the stemmed glass. The liquid was thick and red. "It turned out I did not need his seed, to enjoy its benefits."

"Bakku's blood!" she said, finally understanding.

"Indeed," he answered and drank it in one gulp, wincing as it went down.

Maggie made a disgusted face and turned away.

"You never do get used to the taste," Brynn said, shaking his shoulders. "I had achieved everlasting life. After that, I had found my constant research less rewarding."

Philippa asked about Harner, and Brynn looked her over with a smirk. If she had known how to use Maggie's fireflies she would have burned that smile off his face.

"A Demi killed his father, which in turn ruined his mother," Brynn said as he shrugged. But he added that revenge was not what fueled Koertig's hate. Instead it was his father's preposterous lies. "The elder Koertig had filled his son's head with such foolishness about purity and excellence that Harner had grown to despise anything that lacked perfection. Koertig's father had raised a son who would never find reverence in anything but his own flawlessness."

She had often wondered if Harner had loved her, as she had grown to love him. She now understood that the question could not be asked, because even if the emotion had been there, he never would have allowed himself to feel it. Not for her, not for anyone. When one can only love perfection, one loves nothing at all.

The doorway to Brynn's fancy room kicked open and a row of monstrous gores lurched in, sending the girls screaming and running behind the furniture. Brynn raised his arms as young girls hid behind him, grasping at his legs. Philippa leapt up and called the girls back to her. Nine gores knocked and reeled into the room, crude pick-axes in their hands. The hunched-over beetle-men had rags tied over their eyes, and navigated the room by sound, clicking as they went.

Brynn slammed down his silver cup and approached the creatures. "Damned slow-moving gores," he said. "Take off those rags!" he demanded, and the gores obeyed. Long clawed fingers slipped off the rags, revealing man-like eyes. The gores winced at the firelight and looked around the room. They looked at Philippa and the children, their heads jerking awkwardly.

"Put the young ones in the cages," Brynn said, and pointed to Philippa. "This one comes with me."

"What about our bargain?" Philippa protested.

"If the path to Millthrace truly exists," he said, "I will send back for your girls."

"What if I refuse?" she asked.

"Then there is a cell for you too," he said.

The gores jerked their heads at the girls and sent out a flurry of clicks. The sisters screamed back in a frightened pitch that jarred the gores. Again the clicks, and a vibrating rush of air blew over Philippa's face. A black man-beetle pulled her away from her sisters and held her near Mayor Brynn.

A faint and distant sound trailed in through the open door. The gores reacted first, jerking their heads about, trying to locate the noise. They hissed and clicked.

"Quiet!" Brynn said. "What was that?" he asked, but his men did not know. The room quieted and they listened. The noise returned. It was a horn. A war horn sounding the halls of Nerikan. Brynn stuffed silver utensils in his pockets as he sent Reeve to the silver urn. He poured what remained of Bakku's blood into a leather flask and slung it over his shoulder.

"Koertig, perhaps?" Graeme asked, as he ran back to the table and rolled up the Nerikan map.

Brynn thought about it as the horn sounded again. "He was a bold one," he said. "But would even Koertig dare a forward attack on this place? He could waste three lifetimes just wandering the corridors, lost, before he found any of us."

"Right sir, but I can think of no other reason why war horns would be sounding through our halls," Graeme said.

"Perhaps they are not war horns," Philippa added, drawing the men's attention. "I know Harner Koertig well," she said and touched her tummy. "He would very much like to see all of you in chains, as his duty requires. But for now something else motivates the Lieutenant Colonel."

"Impossible!" Reeve said, joining Brynn by his side. "Could he have captured the beast?"

"Then we are saved!" Graeme said. "And by our own rival!"

"Yes," Brynn said, lost in thought. "Perhaps it is true." Brynn barked orders to the gores, and the black creatures ushered the girls out of the room. The little girls cried and held out their arms for Philippa but were pulled back by the gores.

"Let me go with them!" Philippa begged, as two gores held her back. "You have your monster again, let us go!"

The last girl pulled out of the room was Icha, the Swarhee child. She looked carefree and confident as the beetle-like gore grabbed her arm. She smiled at Philippa, a playful grin. She shook her head and whispered, "Don't worry, Mistress Cree. Olen's coming for us, and she's bringing the light."

***

Olen dashed through the sewers and across the dry riverbeds of the Escapement. She had two days before Edwin and Marko would be expecting her, which was more than enough time to find her sisters. She raced up a small rise to Midtown, and then through more brick sewers, racing ever higher uphill. At the short cliff to Uptown she found her knotted rope missing from the overhang. This confirmed what she already knew; her sisters had been down here, and she was on their trail. The rope was just a convenience, not a necessity. She scaled the outer wall of an arched brick sewer. She placed the hard soles of her boots into the small gaps that separated the bricks and pulled herself up with her fingertips. She climbed this way until she reached the top of the tunnel. Then she ran along the top of the sewer and leapt a small gap to the stony grounds below Uptown. From here it was back into the dark sewers where she followed her well-known path. At the end she rushed into her favorite room.

The room was empty.

Footsteps, everywhere in the sand there were footsteps. They had been here, and they had explored the whole area. She ran to the boulder and dug at its base. Her tin box was gone. A sister had found it. Good for her, she thought, she could keep it. Strange how material things had lost their value since she had met Bakku.

"Where did you guys go?" she asked.

She walked along the dry river bed. Not long ago she would have taken this chance to sift through the silt, searching underfoot for those dropped things she had never recovered. She moved to the deepest part, which no longer looked so deep without all of the water. She let her boots melt away, and squished moist sand through her toes. Her sisters' footprints were different here. No longer haphazard, they were all in a row. The toes pointed in one direction. She followed the prints, and through the darkness she saw the open door to the underworld.

She climbed up the rocks and stood before the dark gate. "Could this be?" she said. It was too much of a coincidence. Marko had insisted the front gate of Nerikan was directly on the other side of the mountain. There was no other way in, he had said. She was certain she had found the back door.

"No," she said. "I didn't find it. My sisters found it!"

There would be gores, she thought. There could be any kinds of dark terrors waiting for her under the mountain. Two days, she thought. Edwin and Marko would be fine for two days, but Philippa and her sisters would not. She stepped into the black tunnel.

"Here we go Bakku," she said for encouragement, and closed her eyes. She thought of the time on the mountain when the gores attacked at night. She tried to remember the feeling, a tingling up her spine. She clenched her fist and remembered. She thought of Brennan and the spear flying at her. It was fright that had brought it on, and it was terror that made her lose control. She thought of Bakku and how he feared nothing, not even an eternity in chains to save the short life of someone he loved. *Be fearless.* She raised her head and opened her eyes. A brilliant white light erupted from her and lit the lost halls of Nerikan Prison. She looked at her glowing arms and smiled.

Then Olen Marine ran forward into the unknown; out of the dark, and unafraid.

49

Cages

A cavalry man again blew his horn deep into the darkness of Nerikan Prison. He had been sounding the horn from the front gates since the final tree fell and Bakku was rolled up to his fate. Soldiers and militia milled about working double time, recovered now from the poison and shamed from the easy mark they had proven themselves to be. Again the man blew his horn, the blast echoing down and back out of the long hall. Koertig lay against the cart, his bound thigh throbbing.

The ironworkers from Brennan had rolled another heavy cart along the same freshly cut pathway. This cart carried a different kind of beast. A domed brick furnace spewed black smoke into the sky as men worked bellows at its side. With hammer and fire they pried away the failed hinges and chipped stone away from the damaged gates. The massive iron falchion still hung over their heads. The caravan itself was smaller, as much of the Millthrace folk had drifted away after being forced to work. Koertig would remember their cowardice and sloth when he returned to Millthrace.

The cavalry man inhaled a deep breath and again blew his horn into the bowels of Nerikan Prison. A black hand shot out of the darkness and slapped the horn out of his mouth, breaking the man's nose and taking out two of his teeth. He fell to his knees and crawled away, cupping his bloody mouth. The ironworkers at the gate dropped their tools and backed away as the gore stepped out of the cave. It lurched on unsure footing and looked at all who gathered.

Koertig pushed himself off the cart and limped up to the Nerikan beast. Martz followed behind, a long bladed saber at the ready. When he reached the gore, Koertig motioned to Martz who took the small ax out of the gore's hand and tossed it aside. Koertig grabbed the gore by its neck and pulled it over to Bakku's cart, each stepping awkwardly. The gore jerked viciously in Koertig's grip but followed along.

Koertig forced its eyes onto the massive Bakku. "Here is your prisoner," he said, and the gore sent a line of clicks across the beast. It stopped resisting Koertig's grip and seemed pleased with its treasure. "I trust you will do a better job of guarding him from now on." Again the gore sent out a long row of clicks as it surveyed Bakku.

Martz called from the gate. More black gores were emerging from the darkness and walking out into the light. They tilted and pitched their way across the ground to Bakku, and then surrounded the cart, pushing and pulling at the heavy vehicle. It moved only slightly, but even more gores staggered out of Nerikan, their heads jerking from side to side and high to low. Ten, then twenty, then thirty gores crept into the clearing. They surrounded the cart completely, and some even crawled on top. One gore climbed onto Bakku's thigh and bit down onto his flesh, sucking at the meat of Bakku's leg.

The heavy cart rolled to the gates as Bakku began to come around.

"Get your prize back in chains before he wakes," Koertig admonished.

The gores clicked and pushed harder at the cart, as Bakku inhaled deeply. Chains dug into his chest. He opened his eyes as feet-first he entered the gate. The gores pushed and pulled and hissed and clicked. Bakku weakly lifted an arm and found it bound in iron shackles. Koertig sat rubbing his wounded leg and motioned for the ironworkers to get ready. Barrel-chested Brennan men worked the bellows over the portable fire. Bakku searched around himself, and he saw the gores. Then as he was hauled away to darkness, the once great Bakku rested his eyes upon the face of Lieutenant Colonel Harner Koertig, a man he had damaged but not destroyed. Koertig stared down the Aurling fiend as he passed into the cave and disappeared into the black halls.

"Seal it," Koertig said, setting the Brennan ironworkers to their task.

***

Edwin had counted thirty-four gores rushing past his little cave. He had grown accustomed to the dark and could see the black forms moving past his barricaded doorway. A loud war horn had been rattling his ears for the past half hour, calling forth all the underworld's black creatures. Thirty four gores chased after the horn, and not one had cared about the interlopers hiding in the nook. Marko slept next to him. He had lost a lot of blood and needed water, but they had none. His breathing was labored, but still he lived. For now.

"I should have studied medicine," Edwin said quietly, as he folded his robe and placed it under Marko's head. "Then I would know how to treat you, my friend." Another black shadow moved past the doorway and stopped briefly at the sound. It sent a rush of clicks into Edwin's room before scurrying on past. "Yes, yes, the action is at the gate, hurry on you mindless dung beetle." Thirty-five, he thought. Koertig's men will have them slaughtered the moment they stick their necks out of Nerikan. Edwin lay back against the wall, and tried to sleep.

Then he heard voices. Men were walking the halls. Orange light flickered off the passageway walls. Yet, it could not be Koertig coming to finish off the job, for the echoes came from deeper inside the mountain.

He checked on Marko. He was still alive, but his breathing and heartbeat had slowed. He crawled to the entrance and pulled enough stones away to peer into the halls. Deep in the cave he saw a torch and four dark figures standing around it. They were in deep discussion. He only heard parts of sentences, but certain words stood out. *Koertig's army, the creature, sisters.* Then a female voice protested and called one of the men by name. "Mister Brynn!" she demanded. "Let my sisters go!"

Brynn! He thought. The educated Aurling. They moved a step closer and the light expanded. The girl wore a white nurse's gown over a blue dress, and Mayor Brynn wore the royal gown he normally wore. Edwin marveled at how well Leo had done in fashioning the same robes for Marko. One of the two other men was dressed in black pants and a shirt, while the other wore a dark brown scholar's robe. The suited man carried the bright torch, while the robed man carried nothing but a water flask over his shoulder.

Edwin crawled back to Marko, "I am sorry friend, but the Elmwood Hustle demands a robe." He took his wrap from the sleeping Marko and gently laid his head on the stone floor. Then Edwin quietly removed the stone barrier and slipped into the dark hall. Keeping to the shadows, he sidled up to the group of four. As he entered the aura of firelight, he gushed at the men.

"Mayor Brynn," he exclaimed. "Thank heavens for your rescue!" He engulfed the mayor in a vast hug and buried his head in his chest. The two men shouted and tore Edwin away from Brynn. "Thank you all!" he said, hugging the suited man. "I thought I would languish in these dark halls forever!" He shook the bewildered man's hand and worked his way around the group, shaking hands and hugging them all tightly. "I under-stand now why you had to send me away," he said, still gushing and pawing again at the mayor. "It was for the greater good of the world, and especially for us Aurlings! Our secret had to be maintained."

Brynn shook off the old man, and his men pulled him aside.

"You are not an Aurling!" Brynn said, straightening his robes. "You are nothing more than an old fool who happened upon an Aurling gift you could neither understand nor appreciate!"

The men threw Edwin against the wall and pulled the girl forward. The back of his head hit hard against the jagged stone, and Edwin slipped to his knees. His world went dark for a moment as Brynn and the other three rushed away. They curled around a corner, and their torch light faded. Blood trickled down the back of his head and neck. He sat in the darkness, exhausted and dispirited, just letting the blood flow. Finally, he inhaled deeply and checked his spoils: a silver spoon from the mayor's pocket and the water flask from the robed man. "Fair trade for a bloody robe," he mumbled, and crawled back to Marko, with hardly even the energy to be proud of himself.

***

Olen ran ahead through the halls of Nerikan. Her clothes were tight and sleek, like she had worn to prowl through the city at night, but they were not black. She glowed a brilliant bright white. The walls and everywhere her light landed were brighter than the brightest day, and yet she felt no sting of sunlight. Far ahead down long halls she cast her light and rushed along, running without tiring, running nearly in flight. Fresh footprints of little girls kept her on their trail.

Long after she had lost track of time—had it been hours of running or mere minutes?—she hurried up a small rise where the walls widened. The cave tunnel fell away and her bright beams spread out far and wide. A vast cave lay open before her. The tiny girl in white lit the entire cave like a small candle lighting a great hall. The rough walls rose higher than the Skywheel, and the room was longer and wider than the Barrens of Lowtown. Hundreds of black iron cages littered the floor, separated only by gaps of a few feet. Within these cages lay piles of bones.

"Olen!" a girl's voice called out and echoed around the room.

A small child stood up inside a cage and waved. It was Marta.

"Olen!" Lysa said, and stood up inside her cage too. Then all around her little girls stood and called out, each one locked inside a cage with the bones of its previous tenant. She had found her sisters.

"Maggie!" Olen said, and moved from cage to cage. "Ellery! Samantha! You're all here!" She dashed around the room, touching hands with her sisters, counting heads and speaking their names. One was missing. "Where is Philippa?"

"Mistress Cree is with the mayor," Maggie said, grasping the iron bars. "He's a bad guy now." Then she smiled and jumped up and down in her cage. "She's having a baby!"

"I guess a lot has happened since I left the Ward," Olen said, smiling.

"Mistress Haggart is dead," Maggie added and quit jumping.

"I know," Olen said and held her hand through the bars.

Another sister called out for Olen. "I feel funny," young Renata said, pointing to her belly. "In here."

"Me too," Clara said. "Something's not right."

"Well then," Olen said. "Let's figure out a way to get you girls out of there."

As she tugged at the locks and felt around the bars for any loose fittings, pea-sized balls of light slipped out of Maggie's skin and curled around the tiniest sister.

"Fireflies?" Olen asked, poking at the ethereal orbs.

"Yeah," Maggie said with a smile. "The jar didn't work."

"Well, let's see if *this* works," she said, grabbing the iron bars. She had tried changing iron when she and Edwin were first locked in their cage. It had not worked at the time, but she had grown so much. What if these bars, she thought and squeezed her fists, were gauntlets? Like a wave washing over a shore, her arms, her hands, and then the iron bars rippled and changed. The two bars melted away and heavy gauntlets appeared on her hands. Maggie slipped through the gap as Olen cast aside her steel gloves. They clanged on the ground and reformed to long iron bars. Ten more, Olen thought, then Philippa.

50

Janus

Philippa struggled against Reeve. He had placed his hand over her mouth and held her behind a stone wall. They had reached the upper corridor and the tall doorway that led out of Nerikan. They had come around the corner too quickly and were nearly spotted by the figures at the gate. Brynn and his men had pulled back into the shadows, unseen.

"Graeme," Brynn asked. "Should Koertig and his army come through those gates, can you get us out of here?"

"Sir, only at the expense of his own life!" Reeve answered for him as Philippa broke free of his grip. "You've worked him so hard already, wasting his strength on tables and chairs and other useless finery! He could barely remove himself from this underworld, let alone all three of us!"

"Yes, yes," Brynn added. "I would never ask that of him." But the implication of his tone hung in the air.

Philippa stood quietly with them, also watching the gate, knowing he was out there. Forms moved about in the wide beam of sunlight. Workmen stepped aside, and a large wooden trolley rolled into view.

"A war cart?" asked Reeve, as he pulled a robe off his shoulder and stared at it blankly.

A large mass lay atop the wheeled machine. And over that mass smaller shadows crawled.

"It is swarming with gores, sir!" Graeme said.

The cart rolled into the vast cavern. Gores manned the carriage, pushing, pulling, and crawling all over the heavy load. Then the huge mass lying supine raised an arm. Chains tightened and clanged.

"It's the creature," Philippa whispered and fought off a smile. She would forever remember the shameful pride that washed over her at that moment. He had done it, he had captured Bakku. Her lover, the father of her child, and the biggest threat to her life, had faced the impossible and won. How quickly her love for the man overlooked the pain he had caused her, her sisters, and Mistress Haggart. Koertig's evil still lived in her mind, but for this moment she remembered a different man, a man who had shown her another side. The Koertig she remembered now had held her behind locked doors and stroked her hair as he spoke of his dreams. He had confessed to her his deep sorrow at knowing a wounded man like himself would never be more than a mascot for the soldiers he had once stood alongside.

And yet he had succeeded. He had captured the uncatchable, delivered him back to his prison. She still admired him in a way, this man who refused to be beaten. She was still fascinated by the ancestral confidence that had passed down the family line of warriors and into the heart of Harner Koertig. Her son would be no rat. For the Koertig line, that was impossible. He would be strong. He would be self-assured. He would be good. And among all of these thoughts, Philippa was certain of one more thing about her son. He would never meet his father. The Koertig line was strong, but flawed. From now on they will be men. No more warriors.

"It's Bakku," Brynn whispered. "Koertig has actually captured Bakku! Stay back, stay back. Let them bring him in."

The cart rolled through the gates and into the cavern. Enormous Nerikan gates clanged shut behind him. Loud banging erupted immediately outside. Philippa knew it was Brennan iron workers fastening the gate, sealing her in.

Darkness closed in on the tunnels of Nerikan. Graeme relit his torch, and Brynn walked out of the shadows and up to Bakku's cart. A gore leapt off the carriage and handed him a pickaxe. Brynn thrust the pointed end into Bakku's hip and dug a deep wound. Blood poured out. Janus Brynn sucked at the wound and swallowed mouthfuls of fresh Aurling blood. The creature bellowed and shook in his chains. Brynn drank again at the wound, dark red blood rolling down his cheeks. He pulled his face away and sucked in deep breaths, clenching his fists as if flooded with vigor.

"Welcome home, my friend," he said to Bakku. The creature turned its head the slight distance its chains allowed. It saw Janus Brynn standing just a body away. The creature's eyes widened, recognition at the man who had had gores do his bidding for so long.

"Janus?" Bakku asked, his words a sleepy slur.

"Burke?" Brynn replied. "That is your name, is it not?"

"The girl?" Bakku asked, and Philippa knew he meant Olen.

"You mean the gatekeeper?" he said matter-of-factly, wiping his bloody chin. "Yes, word travels quickly from Brennan. You were wrong to hide her from me." Then he added casually, "We will have her by week's end."

"You should have left her alone," Bakku said.

"I knew she would lead me to you," Brynn said.

"And your army would lead me to you," Bakku said, glaring at the mayor.

"What is that supposed to mean—" Brynn started, but Bakku laughed. He raised an arm off the trailer. Heavy chains tightened. It was no more than a tug and Bakku had snapped the first shackle.

Brynn backed away a step and ordered the gores to hold Bakku down. The beast flexed his other arm and broke free from that chain also, sending gores flying.

"She fed me well, Janus," Bakku said, kicking his legs free. "Chains can no longer hold me." He flicked off the gores that had climbed over his flesh. The few that returned he flung against the cave wall. Their gore husks fell lifeless to the floor. Bakku swung his legs around and jumped to the ground. The top of his head touched the high cave ceiling. Mayor Brynn pressed his back against the wall.

"Open the gate!" Brynn yelled to the gores, and the black creatures pulled away from the cart and rammed their bodies straight into the new iron doors. It was only barricaded from the outside and not yet sealed. The force of twenty gores pushed, but the gates resisted. Brynn ordered the gores again, and they pressed harder. The iron gates bowed and closed, bowed and closed, as those outside of Nerikan resisted. But soon the gores in their overpowering numbers won out and burst the door open.

Philippa snatched the torch away from Graeme and swung the fiery club at Reeve's temple, knocking him to the ground and sending orange shards around the cave. Then she ran. She ran past Brynn; she ran past giant Bakku, and she ran past the confused and agitated gores. And as Bakku closed in on Mayor Brynn, Philippa ran out through the Nerikan gates. Sunlight shined down all around her as she ran into the armed circle of Koertig's army.

****

Edwin crawled back into the black stone nook and placed a hand under Marko's shoulders. His head rolled lifelessly into Edwin's chest. He was nearly gone. "Water," Edwin offered, as Marko murmured. He held the leather to his lips, a feeble elixir for a mortal wound. Comfort is what he needed now as his body lay weakly in Edwin's arms. Edwin's seed was to blame for all of this, he thought. Had this Aurling curse never dragged him north of Ulm, he never would have met Marko, and the trickster merchant would still be plowing the highways of Eisen, selling his wine and saving up for whatever future truly awaited him.

Her, Edwin thought. *For the love of her*, was what Marko said had started him on his journey. One of his many lies. How was it possible to care so deeply for a person when all you truly knew of them were the falsehoods they had wanted you to believe? *Painting in the edges*, Marko had once said, but Edwin had not understood. Painting in the edges, to distract from the center. Not just lies, misdirection. *Funny thing is*, Marko had said, *people were more eager to trade with 'Marko' than they ever were with me!* And who is Marko Meloon, he had asked. *Marko Meloon is tolerable.*

They had accepted the character of Marko because *crazy* was something they understood, something allowable. Before he had become Marko, this kind man who laid dying in his arms had been anything but tolerable. He had been an abomination. Only then did Edwin truly understand the life of his friend, and the desire to drain the coffers of all who had abandoned him. Here, at the end, his friend would not be abandoned.

He cupped Marko's head in his palm and held the leather flask to his lips. "Drink, my friend. It's all I have." He poured the liquid into Marko's mouth, and it rolled down his cheeks. Edwin wiped it away. It clung thick and sticky to his fingers. "Oh heavens!" Edwin said as Marko gasped and coughed. "I'm sorry, dear Marko, I thought it was water." He pulled the flask away, but Marko reached out for more. He pulled it to his mouth and drank, and his muscles tightened. Marko took long deep breaths and then sipped again from the stolen flask. When he had his fill he placed his elbows on the ground and looked to Edwin. Even in the faint light, he could see Marko's eyes were wide and searching.

"Medicine?" Marko asked, handing he flask back to Edwin.

"I am not sure," he said, sniffing the nozzle. He jerked his head away. "Rancid, like the Illsbrook sewers!" He cautiously took a swig and vitality rushed through his veins. "What is this? I stole it from one of Mayor Brynn's men."

"Aurling magic, perhaps?" Marko offered, shifting his position, and drank again.

"Try not to move," Edwin said, holding the cloth in place over Marko's wound. Marko slid a hand down his side and felt. Then he grabbed Edwin's hand and moved it over his wound. A puffy scar covered his lesion. It was days, maybe weeks before a scab like that could form. "Aurling magic indeed. Can you walk?"

Bright white, Marko Meloon's teeth lit up the dark cave. "Edwin, my friend, I can run!" They wrestled over each other for pulls from the flask as they tore at Edwin's barricade. Each man with the strength, energy, and confidence to challenge anyone or anything they would encounter in the twisting maze that was Nerikan Prison.

***

Some of Olen's young sisters were bent over in pain. They grabbed at their stomachs, and coughed. One by one she released them from their cages, and one by one she marveled at the bones of the creatures they had been sitting on. The solid tusks, the elongated teeth, the thick and heavy skeletons. These were all creatures meant to intimidate and attack. Brynn was not merely trying to acquire seeds. Before he had stumbled upon Bakku, he had been creating a horrific army.

She got the last girl out of her cage. It was Marta. A quiet girl from the Ward. "Sister Olen?" she said softly. "I'm remembering things."

"You have been through a lot," she said.

"No, I mean I'm remembering things I never did," she said, her voice quavering. "Ever since I was put in the cage, I've been remembering someone else's things."

Inside Marta's cage lay a small pile of bones. The skeleton was child-like, with no obvious distortions. It was small. She thought it may have been a young boy or girl. A child. All of the sisters appeared dazed and unsure of themselves as they stood around her. Many held their stomachs, others shook cobwebs out of their heads. She cast out a far light across the vast room and saw all of the Aurling bones. Here were the seeds that would control the destiny of an entire world, and many of them had just chosen little orphaned girls to be their hosts.

"The sickness will pass," Olen told her sisters. "It did for me."

She wondered what magics, what powers her sisters had just absorbed. Bakku had said everything anyone could imagine, every force, every emotion, every strength and weakness, had a seed in the Ether—guarded by a creature of pure Aurling light. And now these seeds were active again.

Racing footsteps and laughing voices pulled her attention back to the moment. Olen doused her light and pulled her sisters in close. "Quiet," she whispered, huddling in the dark.

"You couldn't run faster than me if you shaved your beard!" a familiar voice called out.

"Pipe weed has clouded your mind, my friend. Remember, not only did I outrun the guards in Brennan, but I also beat both you and the girl out of the city!"

"Because you were frightened! Fear turns men into swift-footed boys!" he shot back.

They huffed and puffed as rapid footsteps pushed the two men along the dark halls. They were arguing, laughing, racing, and acting like little boys in a field.

"Well, I could climb better than you!" Edwin blurted.

"Only because you are part monkey!" Marko laughed out.

The voices entered the vast room. They were still running in the darkness, unaware of the crowd of orphans not far ahead in the dark, and unafraid of rousing gores. Olen clenched her fists and rose. A sunburst ballooned out from her body and lit the room. Edwin and Marko fell backwards as their hurried feet slid forward on the stone floor. They put their hands up over their faces, shielding themselves from the bright light.

"Don't hurt us," Edwin pleaded. "We are friends of Janus Brynn!"

"Yes, Janus Brynn," Marko continued, but a childish giggle escaped his character. "You would displease your master by hurting us!"

"I have no master," Olen said, dimming her light to a soft glow.

"Olen Marine!" Edwin said, leaping nimbly to his feet and sweeping up the girl in his arms. He was thinner, and his muscles were strong and tight. He hugged her and bounced her like a baby.

"Hey, hey!" she said. "It's good to see you, too. Put me down."

He set her down and she saw his face. His cheeks were thinner, with soft taut skin. His eyes were intelligent and bright, no more half-moons under his lids. And the hair over his ears—

"Edwin, you're a brunette!" she said, as his grey hair had turned a youthful brown and the wide patch of bare skin atop his head had dwindled to a cup-sized circle.

He tugged at his ring of new hair, spinning himself in circles, but he could not turn his head far enough to see. Then he held up a leather flask, "It must be this! Aurling magic. I pilfered it from Mayor Brynn."

Olen snatched the flask and plucked off the cap. She sniffed the liquid, wincing at the familiar scent. She capped it off and thrust it back into Edwin's hands.

"Bakku's blood," she said. "It's how Brynn has stayed alive all of these years, and it's why he kept Bakku locked up in this prison. Brynn needs his hostage alive so that he himself can live."

"Yes, I see," Edwin said and looked to Marko.

They had each gained over a decade of youth from one flask. Youth, life, time to live over the years that had flown by. For such a gift to be readily available in this world, it would surpass wealth, power, and fame as the greatest motivators of men; and not even Olen could blame those who yearned for it.

Edwin held out the flask at arm's length, but gripped it tightly.

"It is okay," Marko said. "It saved me once, only greed would have me ask for more." Edwin dangled the serum in front of himself, youth in a bottle. "It is the greatest con of them all, Edwin," Marko concluded, "That flask holds only suffering."

Edwin held the first drops of eternal life in his hand. He studied the flask, seemingly reliving his lost years in this brief moment, and seeing how better they could have been, how better they still can be. Olen had grown to like the man, though she had never truly known his soul. She watched him now as he stared at the flask, hoping he made the proper choice.

Edwin gave a severe nod and spoke. "What is a story without an ending?" he asked, speaking directly to Bakku's blood. "Just a series of events that lose their connections. Days far removed from their past. When life's arc flattens and the horizon becomes ever distant, life loses its preciousness." He hefted the sack, appearing to marvel at the lightness of the blood weighed against the measure of the gift it bestowed. "When one no longer has the need to savor the fleeting moments, the corporeal palate becomes bland. I am happy with the brief life I have been granted, the lands I have studied," he clasped Marko on the shoulder, "and the friendships I have made. It would be wrong for me to deny my life's story its finale, my ode its coda."

He let the flask drop to the ground.

"Thank you," Olen said. "You are a good and wise man, Edwin Ashdown."

He looked at all of the girls gathered around her and clapped his hands together. "So! Good news from the Ward then, I assume?"

"Yes," Olen replied. "They are all here except Philippa. I'll find her next."

Marko cut in, "We have found her! She is at the front gate with Brynn and his men!"

She asked them the impossible, to remember their path through the black halls. Bakku's blood had not only revived their bodies, but strengthened their minds also, because they agreed on every turn, and on exactly how many footsteps they had paced down every hall.

"Do you intend to lead your sisters into such a fray?" Edwin asked. "Mind you, gores abound in these mines."

"No, I am going alone," she said. "The girls are your wards now until I can return them to Philippa. They will lead you out the same way they came in. There is a hidden doorway in Millthrace. Take them away from the city. Take them anywhere. I will find you." She dug inside her shirt and pulled out a small sack of coins. "One silver and one gold manor. Take care of my sisters."

"I have my savings," Marko said. "Do not worry."

Edwin added, "The girls will be safe and fed."

"Take it," she insisted. "Consider it tuition. The girls deserve a good teacher."

Edwin smiled politely and reluctantly accepted the golden coin, but placed the silver back in her hand. "Even you must eat," he said, and she accepted.

She told her sisters they could trust these men. She told them quickly about how Edwin and Marko had helped her on the road, and how they would help them. She promised she would bring Philippa back, and they would all be together once again. She moved over to Edwin and pulled him close. She whispered to him.

"And when their gifts start to emerge, and magic things happen," she said, as he raised a curious eyebrow. "Try to react better than you did with me. Comfort them. Help them along."

"I shall," he said, and hugged her once again.

"Exciting!" Marko whispered, listening in.

The group of girls and men filed away from her light. Fireflies floated out of Maggie's belly and spine and curled around them all. Marko grasped at the vaporous lights as they walked away into the dimly lit halls. Olen turned away and felt something underfoot. The flask of Bakku's blood.

***

"Brace the gates!" Koertig demanded, as he hobbled over to the bulging Nerikan gates. They had just been closed, and the Brennan iron workers had rolled their mobile hearth up to the spire. Koertig slammed his shoulder against the door, pressing the ground with his one good leg. His men rushed in after him, forcing their weight against the doors. The ironworkers, hard and brawny men, stood stunned watching it unfold. "Push!" Koertig called, but the gates resisted them.

The soldiers pressed against iron, desperately trying to hold it in place, but what was inside was stronger. A mighty thrust burst the gates wide open and sent armored men flying into the bushes. Koertig fell to a knee but quickly struggled to his feet. He expected the monster, yet it was not Bakku that emerged. Instead, a flood of black gores spilled out of Nerikan, racing past the Lieutenant Colonel. "Slaughter them!" he cried out, as he reached for an axe. His men bared their weapons, but the gores were already beyond the clearing. They had not attacked. They had run. The pitiful black creatures had fled from battle and disappeared into the woods.

Then something else came running out of the gateway, something he could never have dreamed of. It was a woman, young and blonde, in the guise of a nurse. She ran out of Nerikan's halls, peering back over her shoulder, her head turned away. It couldn't be her, he thought, but the fantasy grew. Her form, her stride, her yellow hair so long. There was no magic strong enough to bring back the dead, so it must not be true. But this image, a woman he had held. Then she turned her head and he saw, his Philippa. She ran out of Nerikan as if running out of the grave. Not dead, not burned to dust like her Ward.

She called out his name and ran to his side. She wrapped an arm around him and pulled him towards the woods, begging him to come away.

A lesser man would have followed; a weaker man would have wept. A fool would have asked what magics had brought her back and accepted any feeble answer. But not Harner Koertig. He knew the truth when he saw her alive. She had tricked him, played him for the fool.

She had let him think she had died in those flames, and cruelest of all had let him believe it was he who had killed her. The night of the fire he had nearly prayed to invisible gods to bring her back. Now he condemned her for injuring his soul. He tore her hand off his waist and threw her to the ground.

Three men ran out of the caves next. Reeve, Graeme, and Janus Brynn, still in his mayoral robes, still living his Aurling lie. They tried to scatter like the gores had done, but Koertig's men had regained their feet and drawn their swords. It was Bakku next who exploded through, thrusting his arms out wide and casting the iron gates over everyone's heads, far into the woods. He lifted his arms high above and roared. The Brennan iron workers dropped their hammers and fled.

Bakku snatched away Reeve in his bestial paw. Yet even as Brynn's fellow conspirator was jerked into the air, a hazy bubble spread out around him, forcing open Bakku's wide palm. The monster cupped his thumbless other hand over Reeve and pounded his great fist into the dense forest floor. Reeve tossed about within Bakku's grip, surely shaken, but no worse for wear thanks to his demi magic. Bakku squeezed harder.

Philippa stood and again pulled at Koertig.

"You fed off me," Bakku said, pressing against the invisible defense. His arms and shoulders tensed. "You locked me away!" he growled.

Bakku thrust his two-handed fist into the ground and leaned his body weight into it. "How long can you hold it, Reeve? Two hundred years?" Then Bakku lifted up his fist and slammed it back down, pressing all of his strength and weight into his grip. The ground broke away leaving a deep impression.

"Please," Philippa begged, but Koertig held firm.

With one hand, Bakku lifted Reeve high overhead. Koertig knew what came next but did not turn away as Bakku's long arm swung down and slapped the stony ground, bursting Reeve's defense and shattering the hazy bubble. Bakku's hand flattened the exhausted man as a hundred bones shattered and a thousand veins burst.

Philippa recoiled and again turned to him. She grabbed at his chest plate. "Run away before it's too late," she cried, begging him to go with her. "Harner, choose a different life!"

Koertig cast aside his axe and his girl and pulled a spear out of the ground.

Bakku tossed the limp and formless mess of hair, limbs, and blood aside and turned to Graeme. The thin Demi wasted no time. Graeme repeated the motion Koertig had seen him perform in Millthrace. He reached up, and even in broad daylight he seemed to grab hold of a piece of the night sky. He gave an apologetic look to Brynn who was too far away to join his escape. Bakku pounced but before he could reach him Koertig launched his weapon, piercing Graeme in the heart. As the Demi-Aurling disappeared into to infinite darkness, he stared blankly at his fatal wound.

Janus Brynn should have been next, but the spear had drawn Bakku's gaze to Koertig. The creature pounded both fists into the ground and leapt across the clearing.

51

The Battle

Olen's light burned brightly as she ran down the cave corridors of Nerikan. Again she ran effortlessly for what had felt like minutes, but could have been hours. Constant energy with unending drive is what her magic gave her. She turned a corner and entered a larger hallway. The path led uphill. She ran forward. Large chunks of rock covered in freshly turned soil lay in the path ahead of her. It appeared to be blasted out of a side passage. Inside the smaller hall, more fresh stones lay about. Amongst the stones lay a large iron bar, rusted and bent at a great angle. She stepped forward.

The hallway led back downhill and widened into a room. Against the back wall of the room sat a large iron cage, the largest one yet. The front bars lay open, bent up and in from the floor. On the ground inside the cage sat torn chains. This was his home, she thought. For over two hundred years, this was where her Bakku sat, slept, and starved. She stepped through the bent bars and into the cage. Even a cage this large left almost no room for a man his size to move. The chains would have cut movement even more. She had had a whole city to move through, and even that had not been enough for this orphaned girl.

The cage's iron bars dug deep into the back wall. Black Nerikan rock. There were gouges. Shallow cuts in the stone. She rolled her light over the wall. Images, crude drawings etched with an iron shackle, a devilish paintbrush that left thick scars on the artist's wrists. He had drawn low mountains, the Caraways, and rough-edged clouds high above. A sky he had thought he'd never see again. Below that stood a woman. She was round, and her hair was long. Her line-drawn hand held the hand of a small boy beside her. Beside the woman was the crude figure of a man. Not a monster. Not a ten foot tall beast. But a normal, strong but thin man. On his shoulders and hugging his neck sat a tiny girl.

It would have been pure black night in this cave for as long as he sat here. This image would have been seen only by touch. She ran her fingers over the figures and felt the edges, polished smooth by the constant caress of a heartbroken man.

He had been special, even among the Aurlings. He must have always known he would outlive his family. He would have steeled himself against the painful rush of time as his wife, his children, and even his grandchildren seemingly raced ahead to old age and death. Their memories and their love would have sustained him for a thousand years, until finally he too felt the slow tug of time pull his body into the ground. For he was not immortal, he was certain of that; nothing is. But he was not even granted the pleasure of watching his family live. This must be the age, she thought, as she ran her finger over the lines of his children. This must be the age they were when he was taken away.

Janus Brynn had done this to him. Edwin said he had seen the mayor heading to the front gate. Bakku would not be able to resist his own rage. Olen knew she no longer had to save Bakku from prison. She had to save his soul. She turned and ran as fast as she could.

***

Philippa jumped back as Bakku barreled into Koertig, casting him aside with his wide forearm. Koertig flew back into a cart and dropped to the ground. With one arm he crawled underneath it and out the back. She would not let him waste his life on this one impossible fight. She had to get him to leave with her. The ogre advanced on Harner as he tried to pull himself to standing. If she could not convince Koertig the fight was over, maybe she could sway someone else.

"Stop!" she yelled to Bakku. He paused and looked her way. "He did not do this to you! He was just a pawn of Brynn's as you were! Let him live. Let yourself live. You are free again. Run away."

Perhaps he considered it, maybe he even accepted it, but she would never know for at that moment a barrage of spears soared over the oven and into Bakku's back. Martz called his men for another volley, and spikes flew at Bakku slicing deep into his hide. He roared and pulled at the spears as Koertig struggled to his feet. Harner then hobbled over and picked up the golden sword. He was a one-armed man, limping and mostly broken, but far from defeated. He stepped on the sheath and slid out the sword.

"Do you remember this?" he yelled at the creature through fractured breaths. "It took your thumb! It will take your head too!"

Bakku advanced onto him. Koertig stepped back with each step the creature took forward. Janus Brynn tried to flee into the woods but was held at spear's length by Martz. Other soldiers had hefted the axes and hatchets of the woodcutters and launched those at the creature. The hatchets dug deeper into the beast's flesh but hardly slowed him at all. Koertig stepped back again, taunting the fierce Bakku. Philippa pleaded for them to stop.

Koertig again stepped back, nearing the still burning stoves of the iron workers.

"Come!" he challenged the beast. "You took my arm! Let me take your head!"

Bakku pounded the ground with both fists, and when he did, Koertig dropped his sword and reached into the fire. He pulled out a red hot poker and thrust it into Bakku's great eye. The howl could have toppled the Rückraadt Mountains and flattened all of the trees of Ma'alabrad. Bakku reared back, the burning pole still deep in his socket.

"Go, go go!" Koertig cried out to his army, and the men flocked to the beast, stabbing and hacking away at his flesh. Koertig grasped again the golden sword and limped backwards, stumbling to one knee. Philippa rushed over and helped him up.

Bakku howled and grabbed the poker with both hands. As the

Millthrace soldiers attacked his body, he lifted his head and slid the hot iron out. He flipped the poker in his hands and thrust it straight into the ground, impaling a guardsman from skull to toe. He then swung an arm backhanded, sweeping away the attacking soldiers.

"Again!" Koertig cried to his men while pulling himself out of her grasp. He slipped behind her as Bakku quickly disposed of the army. When once again the monster stepped towards Philippa and Harner, Koertig swung his arm around her neck and held her throat with his elbow.

Bakku paused.

"To your cage!" he cried out as she fought for breath. "Back to your hole!"

She clawed at his arms and kicked backwards, stamping at his feet.

"Kill me, and you kill us both," Koertig said to Bakku.

"Three," Philippa strained to say. "We are three. I carry his child, our son."

"You carry nothing of mine!" Koertig yelled and pulled on her neck. "But even if you kill us, it will not stop! My men will find your girl. She will not so easily resist the blade!"

Bakku howled.

"Back to your cage now, and we will pursue the child no more! She will be safe and free!"

"It's not true!" Philippa cried. "He will never stop hunting you or her!" And only then did she know that to be true. Harner Koertig would spend the rest of his life pursuing those like Bakku, those like Olen, trying to eradicate their so-called impurity. He would never change because he did not want to change, and he never would. Then she said the words she knew were right, but even then, still felt wrong. "Kill him. Kill us both if you have to. It's the only way to stop this, and the only way to protect Olen."

Harner Koertig pulled his arm off her throat. Her temples throbbed as blood surged back into her head. Then she saw, more than felt, the golden blade poke through her chest, just above her belly. Yellow sunlight glinted off the blade, only to be blurred by a red flow of blood.

Then pressure on her lower back. A foot, a boot, her lover's boot in her back, kicking her away as his blade retreated. She stumbled forward, blood bubbling out of her stomach and soaking her whites. The sounds of the forest faded away and the treetops blurred. She staggered past the mountainous beast as the first black dots appeared before her eyes. The shouts and roars and muffled charges seeped through her clouded ears as war erupted behind her. Still she stumbled forward, one hand on her damp belly, one hand feeling the air ahead in the quickly onrushing night. The cave. The gates. She moved ahead into darkness as her knees buckled. Blood down her spine flowed onto her legs. She fell to her knees on the floor of the Nerikan mines. Her senses deadened and thoughts slowed. Darkness. Silence. And the flowing fountain of red, draining life from her and her child. Her vison fell; her fears waned.

And her life, her too brief life, played out in her mind. A tale of suffering and loss. She reached out, miming the action as she remembered the blonde girl of Illsbrook, crying screaming, as a carriage rolled away, carrying the oversized rough-cut pine box that held her father. She saw this child breaking free of the men that held her back, racing after the carriage, only to watch it pull away out of the city. She watched this child, little Philippa, fall to the ground desperately wailing as the gamblers, drunkards, even her own aunts and uncles stepped around her, bothered by the homely nuisance.

She saw a point of white light now, as if at the end of a tunnel, and remembered traveling under the suffocating Eisen sun as she and two other children, dark skinned and speaking not a word of her tongue, were hauled around the Iron Road looking for a home. Weeks later, she had been the last child in the carriage when they had reached the great geared city. Silent now and hardened, the blonde child had sat sunburned and withdrawn in the market square as the heavyset woman in red came upon her. She spoke no words, only sat beside her in the carriage, shoulders and thighs touching. Much later, after the sun had shifted and the marketplace had emptied, this woman placed a soft warm arm around Philippa and pulled her in. She let the child cry until the cool chill of night. Then she stood her up and walked her home.

Her suffering was over now. Her heartbeat slowed in her ears as the outside sounds subsided, and calmness took her. The tiny point of light grew, white and welcoming as the tunnel brightened. A doorway to another life, a life beyond this one. She would go. She would fight it no longer. Her duties here had ended; her struggles were over. Home. A new home. A home of her own. Just her, and her perfect child, in the blissful beyond.

At the very end she had a wandering irrational fear. She worried the light might not know of the child growing inside of her, and that the gates would only allow one soul to pass through. She held out a hand and greeted death with only one plea, her final sacrifice.

"My son," she said, as a glowing white angel came upon her. "Take my son."

The angel laid her onto the ground and sat her head in her lap, and she knew her child was saved.

"An eternity of this," Philippa pleaded, as the angel soothed her in pure white light. "An eternity of this."

The angel held her head in her hands and spoke but one soft word, "Drink."

***

Koertig's consequence was swift, for even as he slew Philippa, he knew he would stand unshielded before the beast. The creature leapt forward, swiping away a jab from the golden sword. The monster grabbed him, cracking, then crushing his hips. His insides shifted. Pressure, like an overfilled wine bladder, formed in his abdomen. Blood spilled into his gut, even as the monster squeezed. His feet left the ground. Then he was flying.

The beast whipped him into an ironwood. Ground and sky rushed past him as he flew. His neck, just above his shoulders, hit first. Another crack, loud behind his ears, and he felt no more. His limp body fell to the ground. His eyes faced to the battle. Bakku snapped the golden sword in half and tossed it aside. Koertig lay immobile; his arm and legs useless, like dead branches on a fallen tree. Even his breath he no longer commanded, as some involuntary will now worked the bellows in his chest, slowly, much too slowly against his aching desire for a deep gasping wind. Men swarmed the creature. The ogre plucked them off one by one. The beast crushed them, tore them apart, and tossed their lifeless bodies away. The battle turned. The beast was winning. Koertig could only stare.

"Harner," the voice said, as Koertig lay dying.

He had failed his father. He had failed his family. He had failed Philippa. A soldier collapsed under the creature's wide foot. When his men were all dead, the beast would come back and stomp out whatever life remained in him. His neck was broken, life slowly slipping from him. Measured breaths forced calm upon him. As war ravaged in Ma'alabrad Forest, his mind drifted to possibilities. He thought of a life where his father had never ridden away. A life where his mother had never taken the shameful walk to Illsbrook. Tears he could not wipe away rolled down his cheeks as for the first time he let himself ponder the life that could have awaited him if weeks ago, he and Philippa had simply slipped away to the Never-Ending Ridge, where snowbell stems push through the morning frost—

"Harner," the man's voice said again, pleading. "There is still a way." Janus Brynn slid his face into view. "You know we can end this," Brynn said, dashing glances between him and the war. "There is still a way. Burke—Bakku—was a mistake. An experiment," Brynn said, and ducked as a torn chest plate crashed next to him. "I can control it now. I can make you stronger."

He understood what the Aurling offered. His choice was death, or a life sustained by Aurling magic. Bakku raged at the army and tore apart the camp. He and Brynn lay out of view. This creature would run free forever, terrorizing his father's great land. A new Koertig, a scion-Koertig could stop him.

Brynn continued, "I knew your father well. It was for me he hunted Demi-Aurlings. It was for my cause he went to war. My only regret was that I was not there when he was defeated. I could have offered him the same salvation I offer you. And my friend, I promise you, he would have accepted. Son, finish your father's crusade!"

It was true, he thought. His father would have taken the offer. By firelight, in their cabin above Illsbrook, his father had relived the tales of his crusades to a young wide-eyed Harner and his worried mother. And as he spoke of the Demis he had destroyed and the powers they possessed, his words would trail off and his eyes would peer far beyond the walls of the cabin. Then his father would say, as if to himself, "If only these powers were laid upon an honorable man, we would need no wars."

An honorable man, he thought. A man who would do what was right. There was only one such man, and he lay here now, broken, defeated. The beast roared, and two more soldiers fell. An honorable man would give up his life for what he believed. Koertig would happily do the same, but the beast still lived. He could not retreat from battle and escape to death while the war raged on! Philippa was dead, and the last of the Koertig's along with her. His family line deserved one great victory before it ended!

"Koertig, help me stop this monster!" Brynn pleaded.

"Yes," he said, a nearly unheard whisper.

Bakku smashed the mobile hearth, sending fire-red brick about the camp. An open flame leapt into the sky.

"I need an offering," Brynn explained. "A sacrifice."

Scions. Beasts combined. He understood what he asked. Janus would make him strong. Stronger than Bakku, stronger than his entire army. But he needed an offering, a man whose essence he could claim as his own. A strong man to make Koertig stronger. A great man to make Koertig greater. There was one such man. He whispered a name Brynn could not understand. He leaned in closer to the Lieutenant Colonel.

"Martz," he whispered through a slow exhale. His only friend. It had to be Martz.

Brynn called Martz away from battle. He came reluctantly but fell to the ground when he saw his commander.

"Life is leaving him quickly," Brynn said. "He wanted to see his best soldier one last time."

"Sir, I'm afraid it is *one last time* for all of us. The creature is too strong."

Koertig whispered, and Brynn interpreted. "He says you have served him well."

"I would die for him, he knows that," Martz said, looking back on the battle.

"That you shall," Brynn said, and grabbed the officer by the throat. Martz seized as if caught in a lightning bolt. His eyes widened, and his mouth gaped open. His cheeks sunk deep into his face, and his skin darkened and thickened to a deep brown leather.

"Now, Martz," Brynn said, raising his eyes to the treetops. "Give me your life."

He threw the officer to the ground next to Koertig. Martz fell under Brynn's grasp, his entire frame rigid. Brynn leaned over the officers and laid hands on them both. Heat warmed Koertig's bones. Leaves and forest debris swelled up around the men as a great wind grew. The winds circled and darkened into a dusty cyclone. Brynn forced his hands deep into the flesh of the two men, his own hands blurring away while pressed into their chests. It was wind, and then light, and then a screaming gale as the Aurling labored. The sensation of life trickled back down Koertig's spine and down through his legs. His chest swelled and his muscles thickened. Koertig grew. Still Brynn worked, and still the bright glowing cyclone churned.

A shadow appeared behind Brynn. The mayor did not see it approach, but Koertig did. It was like a soldier, but much smaller. A wild thought entered Koertig's mind as his bones stretched and thickened. He thought perhaps Brynn had made him so enormous his own soldiers appeared as little children. The small soldier wore battle gear just like Koertig's. Exactly like Koertig's. Black braids dangled out of its helm.

"The girl!" Koertig called out into the storm, but Janus Brynn was lost in a trance.

Olen lifted her faceplate and hoisted a thick ironwood branch. She swung at Mayor Brynn and cracked the limb on the back of his skull. He fell unconscious into the unfinished fusion of Harner Koertig and

Terrel Martz. The cyclone exploded and sent a wide beam of light straight up above the forest. The light collapsed back down and sent a blast along the ground toppling trees, soldiers, and even the great Bakku.

52

The Ether

It was not complete darkness. There were stars. Points of light, flickering in the vast night. Sentient and wise they flared. Hundreds of them, thousands. Creatures of light floating against the dark forever. They sensed the being once known as Koertig, and he sensed them. They spun slowly away from the void they had been contemplating and observed the interloper. They considered him, assessed him. He floated amongst them, a pebble amongst diamonds. Their thoughts passed through his mind, questions, accusations. Then nothing, emptiness. Their appraisal had ended. Their conclusions final. Unimpressed, the lights turned back to the void.

Then he was falling, no not falling, fading, vanishing into the void. Fire passed over him, angry raging flame. A wide yellow and white blaze. It had form. It burned within itself. Its figure changed. A head. Now a torso. Now a flaming arm reaching out. "You are not allowed here," its thoughts burned inside his head. It was Brynn, an Aurling unbound. A creature of light in its natural form. Brynn's Aurling fire grew as Koertig faded. It was absorbing him.

But Koertig was stronger now.

Harner Koertig reached out into the darkness. Two thick arms reached into Brynn's flame. He grasped hold of the creature. It burned his hands, but Koertig was no stranger to pain. The flame raged and struggled to break free. Koertig pulled it close. Leave here, Aurling Brynn's thoughts called out, but Koertig pulled it in, fire burning up his arms.

Aurling Brynn's fire shifted and formed a face. It was the raging face of Janus, anger rippling over his brow. A flash of fire and the face changed again. Brynn thickened and powerful muscles bulged in his arms and chest. Flame, and the body morphed feral. The wide head and jutting tusks of a wolf-boar snapped at Koertig. Still he held. Brynn shifted. Now an eagle, screaming, talons tearing at a man who welcomed agony. Flash, now a beast goat-like, braying, with a thick horn curving back on its skull. Fire, now a woman, soft and small, pleading. "Leave here," she begged, as Koertig pulled her in. "Leave," it cried out, as it changed again.

The stars wheeled overhead, their interest in Koertig briefly revived. Faster now Brynn flashed through the beasts of Eisen, each a creature he had manipulated over the years. Men, beasts, foreign creatures of the unknown. Through it all Koertig held and grew stronger, as the Aurling known as Janus Brynn weakened. Brynn's light faded, and Koertig pulled him in, enveloping the Aurling. Koertig absorbed the Aurling Brynn completely and one tiny light in the Ether was no more.

Koertig triumphant floated amongst the Aurling lights, one with them now, perhaps even greater than. He approached them, fearlessly chased after them, their new master. Then he bashed against a hard nothingness. A wall, an invisible barrier in the sky held him back. A crystal veil in the starlit darkness refused him passage to the Ether. The distant fires again lazily turned away and dimmed to black night.

Koertig drifted alone just outside the Ether. Strong limbs now, and a vast mind to control them. Brynn and Martz, the essence of, lived within him, subservient to him. He was a powerful being now and he was fire, most raging. He beheld his new form as he fell back to life.

53

The Last Scion

The blast had knocked Olen into a thick brush pile. Blood dripped down from her forehead and into her eyes. Dirty Millthrace rags covered her small frame. Her ears rang from the explosion. She forced herself to her feet and peered out into the clearing. The last of the soldiers had fled into the wilderness, their leaders finally gone. A deep and wide crater smoldered where Koertig, Martz, and Brynn had lain. Bakku too had regained his footing and leaned against a large tree, sucking in deep breaths. What looked like rags, much like her own, hung from his legs and arms. But it was deep hunks of skin, hacked away and dangling from her exhausted friend. Impatient scars already spread across his wounds, halting the loss of his precious blood. His damaged eye was shut, sealed over by a scabrous lid that would never again part. He was injured and dazed, but he would live. It was his curse.

She crept out of her hiding spot.

"Bakku?" she said, but he did not hear her. She moved over to him. "Baboo?"

Bakku turned towards her, his face blank.

"They're gone," she said. "Brynn, Koertig, everybody."

He turned away and pressed his forehead into the tree. Bodies lay everywhere. Soldiers. Militia. A few brave iron workers. Crushed, stomped, and segmented. In the clearing the ground was stained with not just Bakku's blood, but the spilled blood of nearly forty. "I should have stayed in chains!" he cried.

"They should never have chained you!" she challenged back. She moved through the bodies and stepped over the crushed armor. She placed a hand on his leg. "It's over."

"It will never be over," he said. "As long as I live. Jealousy, hate, and fear rule them all. They will forever create wars to stop me, and many more will be killed. Stop me they will, but only until I again break my chains, and we start again."

"Then let me show them how good you are!" she demanded. "Let me tell the people you are not to be feared!"

"But I am to be feared, don't you see?"

"That's not true. I don't fear you," she said, "And your family didn't fear you either."

He swung his head and glared at her. He turned back away and pressed his forehead into the tree. "That was long ago, before I was a monster."

"Before they made you a monster!" she corrected. "You and me, we will go to away. We will go past the Melle and Calderra all the way to the frontier. We will live out our lives there alone."

"Your life," he said.

As if confirming his words, color poured back into his cheeks. His recovery continued, his body healed. She had no response, nothing she could counter. He was right. She would grow old and die, as mere seasons seemed to pass for Bakku. After she was gone, he would grow bored and lonely, and drift back into society, or perhaps society would come to him. Explorers, developers, tradesmen would open up the frontier and build cities just like in Eisen. They would hear tales of a monster living in the woods. They would fear him, and the wars would start all over again. Bakku would pray for death, while also submitting to that primal instinct to stay alive. It would never end.

"What do we do?" she asked.

"You know what I have to do," he said, and she knew he spoke of Calderra.

"There is another way," she said. "I can send you home. Brynn is gone, and I can control it now. I got my friends through the mountain, I can get you back to the Ether."

"You don't understand!" he cried out and smashed his fist into the ironwood. "You must never open that doorway! It was sealed for a reason. So many Aurlings wait beyond, desperate to escape into life. But you must see now, that can never be allowed. They know your seed has been found. They know it has a new master. They will be waiting. And when you open the doorway again, all will come, and your world will change forever."

"Hold them back!" she demanded. "You are strong, Bakku! Fight them! Push them back as you go home!"

"Stop!" he shouted at her. "Calderra is the only answer!"

A gust of wind blew the leaves in a circle around the crater were Koertig, Brynn, and Martz had lain. A small cyclone appeared and darkened as it sucked up dust and debris. A wide hole opened in its center, and a bright churning light burst out. A white beam like a lightning bolt crashed out of the sky and into the center of the storm. The cyclone broke apart, and the light flashed. The fog dispersed, and out of the crater rose a creature, proud and strong. On rising it studied its sleek and strong frame, as if seeing it for the first time. Taller it grew, as it rose to its full height, a head taller even than the great Bakku. Hands like bony tree branches squeezed the air, and long arms rippled with flexing muscle. Steel and bone, iron and skin, the creature had become one with its armor. On its shoulders and back, at haphazard angles, silvery thick plates jutted out of bone, and patchy steel mail grew like kiln-forged scabs on its flesh. The Scion-Koertig kept a face much like his own, but with sharper angles and deeper furrows etched into its eyes, cheeks, and brow. It was a face disgusted with all but its own glory. Scion-Koertig climbed out of the pit and felled an ironwood with its newly-formed right arm.

Bakku pushed Olen into the woods. "Go!" he said and flung himself at the beast.

***

Philippa lay among the stones inside the Nerikan gates, thumbing a wide pink scar that had grown just above her distended belly. She had seen Olen as an angel, perhaps she was right. The angel had offered her life, a foul liquid she had nearly spat out. But her son, she thought, as her palm slid below the wound, for her son she would endure. The mound was firm and warm. He was alive. Bakku's blood had saved them both. For two more seasons she would carry her child, but when his day finally came, she knew her child would be healthy and strong. Thanks to Bakku, thanks to Olen.

Lightning flashed, drawing her gaze out of the cave. She had seen the man she had loved flash away into the unknown with Martz and Brynn, and now she witnessed the birth of what Koertig had become. And as this new scion-Koertig engaged with Bakku, he looked no different than a god, a demon.

The behemoths rolled together, tearing at flesh and bone. Bakku landed a blow to Koertig's skull, and Koertig wrapped two hands around Bakku's wide neck. He thrust Bakku's head into the ground and dug his thumbs into his throat. Bakku kicked hard into Koertig's gut and rolled free. One of these creatures would win, Philippa thought. One would die or somehow be subdued, and the other would survive. If Koertig survived, then it would be a whole new world. This beast would not be content with a Millthrace commission.

This was Koertig unchained, she thought, his soul made flesh. Here he was released from the constructs of decency or shame and allowed to run free. This was not some arbitrary creature concocted by chance. This was the true form of the man he had always hoped to be. Strong, perfect, and unquestionably righteous. *This is the man*, she thought, *I tried to love.*

Bakku grasped Koertig's wrist with both hands and twisted. Koertig laughed and with a flick of his arm, knocked Bakku to the ground.

"I am stronger than you now!" Scion-Koertig roared, his voice a metallic clang. He leapt at the Aurling. Bakku caught Koertig in his arms and dug his teeth into his shoulder. His strong wide jaws tore away a large hunk of flesh. Koertig fell back howling and covered the gaping wound with his hand. White light burst from his palm and into the gash. When he pulled his hand away, a wide tube of flesh came with it. The tube hardened and bent at familiar angles. Koertig gazed at what he had created, as a third powerful arm now angled out of his shoulder.

"Wound me, and I become more powerful!" he bellowed at Bakku, and the two crashed together again. The new hand tugged at the back of Bakku's head, while his two other arms tore at his flesh.

So many days he had slept under her watchful eye, she thought. So many nights he had lain there vulnerable and unguarded. Many times over she could have stopped him, ended his life completely, and no one would have known. Such a wound he had taken that night in the forest, such a fight he had made to live. And she had helped him. Would she have been able to do it, she wondered. If she had known then what he would become, would she have stopped it before it ever started? Her cheeks dampened as she watched him fight, and she knew there were no possible timelines besides the one they shared.

Bakku ducked out of Scion-Koertig's grip and slid under his arms and behind him. He grasped the back of Koertig's head and smashed his face into a thick ironwood. Koertig stumbled, dazed for just a moment, as a hunk of meat hung off his forehead. He felt the wound and again an Aurling light burst from his hand. As he pulled away, a large black horn grew out of the wound.

Bakku plucked a spear off the ground. He jammed it into Koertig's chest, but the tiny spearhead snapped and the wood splintered on his armored flesh. The scion knocked him back against the Nerikan spire. Stones fell around Philippa as Bakku collapsed. He rose again, and wrenched free the massive black falchion that for hundreds of years had marked his prison. It fell to the ground with a thud. Even the great Bakku struggled to raise the enormous blade.

"I am the master of Brynn's seed," Koertig said. "I own his thoughts. He could only make scions, but I can do better. I absorbed him, and

I will do the same to you. Give me your life!" White flame blazed in Koertig's palms as he advanced.

As the two beasts closed in on each other, Philippa saw Olen approach the clearing, again glowing with a brilliant bright light.

* * *

Olen walked into the wooded battlefield. Bakku held the vast sword unsteadily, high above his head with both hands. Scion-Koertig advanced on him, Aurling fire burning in his palms. If Bakku refused to go back to the Ether, perhaps there was another way to end this war. She would open the pathway before Koertig. Send *him* back to the Ether, she thought. Let the Aurlings be sentinel over their own creation. Her light burned fiercely as she walked before the giants.

Koertig connected first, sending Bakku stumbling back. The heavy sword fell to his side, cutting a deep furrow in the ground. Olen called forth her powers and opened her gateway before Koertig, but the new scion had stepped back just in time. A ball of light appeared in the clearing between the three, and a confused Koertig stared into it as if it were a looking glass. A dry desert shone through as Bakku forced himself to his feet. Again he lifted the great sword above his head and staggered forward as the desert flashed and a winter vale emerged. Olen focused on the swirling image, and the lands passed by rapidly. A field, an ocean, a barren rock-strewn wasteland. Then darkness. Night. She pressed again, and for the third time in this land's history, an invisible crystal veil cracked, and two worlds joined.

* * *

Koertig would win, Philippa knew this now as she watched from the cave. The odds were against him, but he would survive. Olen would die; Bakku would suffer, but somehow Harner Koertig would endure. Three images stood before her. A small child holding open an enchanted doorway to a dark and frightful land, a colossal Aurling with a gigantic sword raised above its head, and her Harner, transformed into something he never should have become.

She rose to her feet. She hoped she was right about Koertig. Not about him winning, but that he loved her. She had loved him once, and she believed he had loved her too. If that were so, then with a word she could end this all. A test perhaps, a fatal one at that. Offering herself again, Philippa stepped out of the cave.

She walked up to the battle and stood opposite of Olen. Four of them stood now, points on a gear, surrounding a deep black void. The vast nothingness between them sucked in dust and leaves and battle debris. The flawless scion-Koertig had not noticed her, as he howled at Bakku and the glowing girl.

"Harner," Philippa called out, and drew her lover's eye.

Scion-Koertig's arms fell to his side, and he stared dumbfounded at what was once his Philippa. She still wore her uniform, but it was stained deeply red from the wound he had inflicted. From the torn cloth just above her belly, through her skirt and down both of her strong legs, Philippa was wet with blood. But she was not hurt. When she should have been dead, she stood before him, still alive, still fighting, just like him. This look was all she had wanted.

What were his thoughts, she wondered, in that brief moment before Bakku's sword came down on his neck? He stood transfixed, amazed that again this woman had survived. Even as he had turned his head to look at her, Bakku swung down with the giant blade. I survived, she said with her eyes and her stance. I survived you. This is the partner you could have chosen. This is the woman who would have loved you and supported you until your final days. Instead, Harner, this is the woman who ends you.

She stood, not defiant, but kindly and maternal before her lover. She hoped he saw the small rise in her belly and understood her child survived too. She needed him to know a new line of Koertig started today, a line stripped of the flaws that had tainted that name for so long. But she also wanted him to know, here at the end, that at least for a brief moment in his life, Harner Koertig was loved.

Bakku's sword sliced down and through. Aurling magic would not heal such a wound. The great soldier's eyes fell shut, last peering upon the image of Philippa Cree.

***

...and in that moment the flames were but glowing coals, gentle in his mind...and the wars that had raged were children throwing pebbles on to the streets...for there she stood, rising above it all...good Philippa who had loved him, when she never should...and he was not a god, not to her...and he never had been, not to her...and this life had been so hard with so little to cherish, except for—

***

The black void was no longer black as distant flames raced towards Olen's open gate. Burning Aurlings flew towards the opening seeking the corporeal life that others had achieved so long ago. Koertig's lifeless head and torso fell into the nightlike chasm, tumbling out of this world forever.

"Close it!" Bakku yelled, but the Aurlings' approach was swift. Already the fiery forms had crossed the void and neared the swirling orb. Only Bakku knew what horrible, what wonderful, what impossible powers this swarm of Aurlings carried with them. So few had traveled to this land with Bakku, and still their damage remained undone. Now armies of Aurlings raced to a worldly existence, to a physical life.

"I can't!" Olen cried back, trying to shake free. She had thought she could control it, but she could not. Something fought her.

"It is they!" Bakku said. The Aurlings held her gate open.

Bakku ran into the glasslike sphere as the first Aurling approached. His wide frame pushed back against the otherworldly fire, between worlds, neither there, neither here. More came, firelights crowding the orb, mere steps separating the two worlds.

"I'm sorry!" Olen cried, still trying to close the void.

Bakku struggled against the lights. They burned at him, fire melting his flesh. He stepped towards the Ether, pushing the mass back with him. Angry flames whipped at him, reaching beyond his great bulk. It was fire, but with sentient menacing flames. Another step toward the Ether, and a soft glow lit his frame. He spun and pushed backwards, his strong legs and arms pressing against the swirling walls and blocking the way. The Aurlings flashed and burned, and still Bakku pushed them back, protecting the world he had learned to love.

The farther he moved back, the harder he pressed, straining against a universe. He neared the back of the sphere and his heel touched the Ether. White fire burst all around him, and he looked to Olen, desperation in his eyes. She understood. If he gave up the fight, then all of the Ether would destroy her world, but if he kept pressing them back, he would leave this world. She could then close the portal behind him forever.

"Go," she said, and that was all it took. She did not want to say it, she did not want him to leave her, but she knew it was right. He had to go. He had to go home. With one word she released him from the burden of protecting her and this world. A thousand years of suffering melted away from his brow. With that word she released him from her.

He said a word that sounded like goodbye and took a final step back. Muscle and bone flashed away. Yellow beams burst out of the sphere, forcing Olen to turn away. An intense warmth washed over her and blew her back a step. When she turned back to the breeze, a new sun burned where Bakku once stood. The man he had been for hundreds of years, Bakku, Burke, Baboo, was gone, and the creature of light he truly was reappeared. He was Aurling once again, and he was glorious. His bright star, blinding yellow, thrust the Aurlings back into their void, scattering them. He wheeled in the great abyss, like a great rotating sun, brilliant yellow light illuminating the two worlds. Olen and Philippa, buffeted by warm Ether winds, stood enraptured as the great universal lantern slowly revolved just beyond the crystal veil. Frightened points of Aurling firelight scurried away from their returning kin. Then this new star flickered and sent a pulse back to this world.

Olen shivered, and a tremor traveled through her body. He had shaken her again and broken her free from the trance. The crystalline sphere that had joined two worlds collapsed and vanished. Leaves and dust fell to the ground, and the forest was once again quiet and empty. Olen's white clothes faded to rags.

He was gone.

"No," Olen said, searching where the orb once stood. "This isn't right. I changed my mind." She clenched her fists and called out, "Bakku!" But her glow had left her. "He can come back, now! Bakku!" Philippa put a hand on her shoulder. Olen pushed it away. "He beat them! He didn't think he could, but he did! Come back!" she yelled, but she could not make the doorway open. "Bakku!" she cried, focusing hard on the space in front in her trying to make the point of light appear again. She was too young, too weak.

"Olen," Philippa said, again touching her shoulder.

"Come back, Baboo!" she cried, and again, nothing. Philippa tried to pull her in but the young girl collapsed to the ground. "He's gone," she sobbed, as Philippa knelt beside her and stroked her back. "He told me not to open it, but I did, and now he's gone."

She cried for too long before realizing she was not the only one who had lost someone. She looked at Philippa who shed no tears.

"Koertig. You loved him," she asked, wiping her eyes. "Why?"

Philippa brushed Olen's hair out of her face and dabbed her apron at the girl's wet cheeks. "I would not have made this child had I not seen good in him," she said. "Yes, I loved him," she added. "And a sad, small, frightened part of him loved me also."

She looked up at Philippa.

"Call me a fool, but I know now it is true," Philippa said confidently. "In those moments when he stopped worrying about pride and duty and let emotions rule his mind, he loved me. And he hated himself for that. In the end it was a choice though. He chose not to love—me, my child, anything. He simply chose not to love at all."

"I loved Bakku, too," Olen said.

"I know," Philippa said. "But you must remember, your Bakku is not gone."

Dead soldiers with crushed helms lay about. Weapons sat scattered in the field. Overturned carts and felled trees littered the area, and a deep crater scarred the ground. A tall spire of rock reached high above it all, and two broken gates lay beside it on the ground. Among the desolation of men and monsters sat two orphan girls of the Ward. A hundred old accusations and complaints floated away like dry leaves in the wind as Olen let Philippa pull her into her warm arms. She smelled of lilacs and lye soap.

Evening was overdue in Ma'alabrad Forest as daylight fought off the night. Warm beams streamed over the spire as the sun fell slowly, still shining, still strong, so late in the day.

54

Ode to Bakku

The ox-drawn wagon slowed to a halt outside the city of Daegan. Olen leapt off the cart as a boy with the first hints of a mustache pulled out short steps for Philippa. The mound on her belly had started to show since their time in the forest. They had walked out of Ma'al-abrad and into the Ode. The last drops of Bakku's blood had kept them alive on the Merchant's Trail until travelers happened by. Each time Olen had drunk from the flask, she had looked to the stars, thanked Bakku, and had asked for his forgiveness. They rode with the travelers to Illsbrook and stayed with them all around the Iron Triangle, one silver honor, and the kindness of the traders sustaining them. At every stop they asked tradesmen and townspeople if they had heard or seen of two men caring for a large group of young girls. After three weeks on the road they were pointed to Daegan.

"Thank you," Olen said, offering the few coppers that remained.

"You owe us nothing," the migrant trader said, as he held up a water bucket for the ox. "You just tell Marko the highway misses him, and tell Chef we miss his cooking."

The girls thanked the family and walked into the city. Daegan was not a big city like Millthrace or Brennan. It was more like an oversized outpost in the northwest corner of their world. It was a seaport to the Olmere Ocean, but since there were few destinations in the frozen lands north of Daegan, it was hardly the bustling sea-trading center like Brennan. The ships that came in and out of Daegan were merely for cold-water fisherman and brave explorers. Edwin was here, with Marko and the girls.

A small group of traders sat around a tiny town square selling the wares they had not sold in Millthrace. A young boy of about six years sat on a jumbled pile of chiseled stones and stared at the girls.

"What's the wares?" Olen asked.

"Bricks from Bran's Wall," he said, and added a prepared hook, "Own a *piece of history*."

"Bran's wall?' she asked, playing dumb. "What's the wall for?"

"What are any walls for?" he asked.

"To keep something out, or something in, I suppose."

"Someone did not like that," he said. "So he busted it open, twice. They say it was a monster." He hefted a brick. "Two coppers for a *piece of history*."

"Sorry," Olen said, and shook her head. "I am looking for two men that may have come to town recently. They would have eleven girls with them."

"Yes, I know," he said. "One copper."

She dug into her pockets.

"Wait," Philippa said, and dug into a sack. She still had the small tin Olen had hid under Millthrace. "I believe this was yours?"

Olen opened the case. Buttons, metal clips, a key, pencil, and a few other things of unknown heritage. All of it had seemed so valuable to her at one time. She dumped it all into the boy's hands. "Keep the bricks," she said. "I only want information."

"Sure," he said, and smiled. "They're right here." He threw a thumb over his shoulder and pointed to a two story building down the alley. A crudely painted sign hung from a doorway and read, "Ashdown Academy." Below that in smaller letters and written in another hand was, "Proprietor, Marko Meloon."

She pulled Philippa down the alley and through the doors.

The sisters sat hunched over their benches, twirling their hair, staring at the floor, and altogether ignoring Edwin as he scribbled on a slate board. He taught the history of Daegan, and the building of Bran's Wall.

"When it was first built, the wall was truly impervious," he explained, and drew a line across a crude sketch of the Melle. "Nothing could get through."

"What about the passage through the Caraway Mountains," Olen asked.

The girls spun in their seats. Olen and Mistress Cree stood at the back door.

"There is no passage through—" Edwin said, then stopped cold. He turned around. "Olen Marine! You're here!" He fumbled for words and found two good ones: "Class dismissed!"

The girls rushed from their seats and tackled their two lost sisters. Marko stuck his head in from the kitchen and saw the commotion. Sonny the donkey peered in through the back door, lazily chewing green grasses. Marko threw his stirring spoons behind him and raced after Edwin. They piled onto the jumble of hugging arms and squirming legs.

Edwin dug through the mash of arms and legs and pulled out Olen. He hugged the child and held her out in the light. "Well, you're no worse for wear! And your friend, Bakku?"

She dropped her eyes and shook her head.

"Dead? Is it possible?" he asked.

She shook her head, "Back to the Ether."

"And the others?" he asked, wide-eyed. "News to Daegan travels painfully slow."

"All gone," she said. "It's over."

He seemed to understand, though as a true historian, he would have many questions later.

"Is it alright if we stay here for a while?" she asked.

"Alright?" Edwin said. "I insist!" He hugged her again, and passed her off to the waiting arms of Marko.

"I'm making dinner," Marko said. "Chef's recipe! Should be good!"

"I can't wait," she said.

Edwin pulled a swarm of girls off of Philippa and helped her to her feet. He gave her a hug also. "And you must be the Mistress Cree we have heard so much about! I am so glad you are here," he said. "I have never been one for discipline, but these girls are driving me insane. They do not listen, they will not study, and I caught one of them sneaking out at night. Mistress Cree, they need you," he pleaded.

"And I need them," she said. "You give them an education, and I will do the rest. I promise."

Olen addressed Marko, "I understand you're the proprietor of this place?"

"Fifty-one percent," he said, and smiled a wide toothy grin to Edwin. "Majority Owner!"

"He tricked me!" Edwin said, pulling away from Philippa just for a moment, wagging a finger at Marko. "It is still in dispute!"

"I would like to make a donation," she said to them both and unwrapped a sack. Edwin sidled over. She pulled out the broken golden sword. It had indeed been solid. "This should keep the girls fed for quite some time."

Edwin and Marko nearly drooled. Marko wrapped up the sword and tucked it under an arm. "By tomorrow it will be bullion," he said, nodding to her.

Then they all gathered around chairs and sat in a circle. There were so many stories to be told, so much to be worked out. Olen told the truth. She did not want to hide anything from these girls. They had to know how dangerous their powers could be. It was Philippa who spoke of Koertig and how power had deranged him. They all listened intently as the two girls spoke.

Soon night fell over Daegan, and a cool breeze came in off the sea. Marko ladled warm bisque into wooden bowls, and Edwin built a fire in the hearth. They all gathered around the warm flames. Philippa then spoke of the child in her belly, and how the sisters would soon have a brother. As her sisters asked questions, Olen moved to an open window and looked out over the slowly crashing waters of the Olmere Ocean.

There was a new star in the sky, sparkling and low, which all the travelers on the Iron Road had commented on. She had first seen it the night Bakku went home, and she had seen it every clear night since. A bright star, always there as she searched for home, following along, riding her shoulder and watching her.

Maybe someday, she thought, when she is older and stronger she will once again open the doorway between their worlds. He would be there waiting as he always had been, ready to carry her, protect her, and make her smile. He would greet her with his sideways grin and lift her to his shoulder. And together they would walk the world, father and daughter, running, laughing, and eating, always eating. Maybe someday, she thought, knowing she never would.

"Goodbye, Baboo," she whispered out the window. "And thank you."

A tiny ball of light danced past her face.

"Yes Maggie?" she snickered.

"Will you tell us more about Aurlings?"

"Of course," she said, taking her hand.

The new star pulsed and flickered in the night sky as Olen Marine turned away and joined her family at the fire.

—End

www.ingramcontent.com/pod-product-compliance
Lightning Source LLC
Chambersburg PA
CBHW031242310726
48971CB00004B/1132